UNDER THE SWORD

LUV LUBKER

HISTORIUM PRESS

THIS BOOK IS DEDICATED TO:

My Mom, Jaleen Lubker, who taught me my special research methods, and
asked strange questions I went searching to prove wrong,
only to find they were true.

My readers of my other books, whose kind praise has encouraged me.

My parents and friends, whose love and praise supports me on my journey.

Marta Grastye, for all her support of my research.

John Van Der Kiste, for the greatest compliment
I have received in my writing journey.

Ella McNish, for supporting me in the journey of writing this book.

The Emperor Frederick III, "Our Fritz",
who wished to make the world a better place.

THANKS TO:

My family and friends, for all your love and support.

My Mom, Jaleen Lubker, who taught me
how to find things I would never have thought.

My brother, Alex Lubker, for proofreading my book.

Ella McNish, for her feedback, support and inspiration.

Hans Rothfels, A R Allison, Otto Meisner and Winifried Baumgart for
their work in transcribing or translating Fritz's diary.

My publisher, Dee Marley, for all her wonderful work.

The other authors and researchers, who have written about so many
fascinating people, and spent so much time, effort, and money to publish
the wonderful collections of letters and diaries, which I know from
experience take years to transcribe.

To the Royals themselves, for living
such interesting lives and leaving us the legacy.

And particularly to The Empress Frederick, "Vicky",
for making the best of her life and writing her story.

NOTE ON THE GERMAN:

Much of the dialogue of this book is supposed to really be in German. I specifically mention when people speak English, outside of the English Royal family.

"chen" at the end of names or words is a diminutive in German, such as "Lenchen" as a nickname for "Helena".

I tried to use words which are more known or obvious from context, such as "danke," for "thank you", "Ich," for "I", "du," for "you", "ja" and "nein" for "yes and "no" and so on, or have the phrases repeated in English.

Pronunciation notes – the umlauts: ä is pronounced how English speakers say the letter "a", so "bäker" in German is pronounced similarly to "baker" in English, where as in German the "a" would be more of the "awe" sound. Ö and ü add a sort of soft "r" sound with them; it is difficult to describe. "ß" is an "s" sound, where as "s" is a "z" sound in German, and "z" is "tz".

CHARACTER CAST

In England: The Royal Family

Queen Victoria, Vicky's Mama

Uncle George, the Duke of Cambridge

Bertie, the Prince of Wales, future King Edward VII

Alix, Princess of Wales, nee Princess Alexandra of Denmark Bertie's wife

Eddy, Georgie, Louise, Victoria, Maud, the "Wales" children

Alice, Hereditary Grand Duchess of Hesse-Darmstadt

Affie, Alfred, Duke of Edinburgh

Lenchen, Helena

Louise

Arthur

Leopold

Beatrice

In Prussia – The Royal Family

Fritz's Papa, Helmkin, King Wilhelm I of Prussia

Fritz's Mama, Augusta, later Queen Augusta of Prussia

Vivi, Fritz's sister, Grand Duchess of Baden

Prince Charles, Onkel Karl, uncle to Fritz

Marie, Princess Charles of Prussia

Fritz Karl, son of Prince Charles, cousin to Fritz

Marianne, wife of Fritz Karl

Mariechen, Ebi, Louischen, daughters of Marianne

Fritz Leo, son of Marianne

Anna, Landgrafin of Hesse-Kassel, daughter of Prince Charles

Addy, daughter of Prince Albrecht

Wilmeck, Wilhelm of Mecklenburg-Schwerin, son of

Wilhelm "Willy", Charlotte "Ditta", Henry, Siggy, Little Vicky, Sophie,

Vicky and Fritz's children

Aunt Adina, Grand Duchess of Mecklenburg Schwerin, Prince Charles's
"best sister"
Leopold, Karl, Anton, and Fritz Hohenzollern-Sigmaringen, Catholic
branch of Prussian family and Karl is future King of Rumania

Other Royals

Louis of Hesse-Darmstadt, Alice's husband
Aunt Feodora, Queen Victoria's half-sister
Fritz Augustenburg, claimant to Schleswig Holstein
Ada, daughter of Aunt Feodora, wife of Fritz Augustenburg
Dona, Calma, Fritz Leo, children of the Augustenburgs
Bernhard and Elsa Meiningen, children of Fritz's favorite cousin Lotte,
step-children of Aunt Feodora's daughter Feo
Uncle Ernst, Duke of Coburg
Oscar, King of Sweden and close friend of Fritz
Alexander, Sascha, Tsar Alexander II of Russia, Fritz's cousin
Sasha, Tsarevich Alexander (later Alexander III)
Minny, Dagmar, wife of Sasha
Franz Joseph, Emperor of Austria
Victor Emanuel III, King of Italy
Prince kaMpande, Prince of Zululand

In Prussia: The Royal Household

Wally Paget, nee Hohenthal, formerly Vicky's lady-in-waiting, now in the
diplomatic corps in Denmark
Valerie Hohethal and Hedwig Brühl, Vicky's lady-in-waiting, Wally's
sister and cousin
Count Seckendorff, Vicky's former page
Emma Hobbs, Vicky's English nurse
Georgianna Hobbs, Vicky's English housekeeper
Rosa, Vicky's maid
Mademoiselle d'Arcourt, Charlotte's governess
Hinzpeter, Willy's tutor
Schrötter, Willy's first governor
o'Danne, Willy's second governor

POINT OF VIEW KEY

TABLE OF CONTENTS

UNDER THE SWORD

PROLOGUE

Potsdam, Brandenberg, October 21, 1864

The carriage drove on, almost silently, the padded wheels making soft noises in the grass and autumn leaves. There had not yet been any snow. Everything was black; every shining part of the harness was covered; the coachman was dressed in dull black. Four cloaked figures sat inside, a young woman dressed in deepest mourning, her face buried in her handkerchief, and, huddled next to her, were three little girls. A single small trunk sat behind them.

"Mama," the eldest girl said, "Where are we going?"

"I do not know yet, Mariechen. We must arrive in Anhalt if we can, and I shall decide further then."

"Is Charlotta in the trunk?" the youngest girl asked quietly, as if speaking to herself.

"What do you mean, Louischen, how would she be?"

"The little girl in the glass over my bed. I always kiss her goodnight. And I didn't... before we left." The little girl tried to control a sob.

"Oh," the other girl groaned, rubbing her eyes. She had fallen asleep between the other two. "Mama, can we not stop? I think I'm going to be sick," she murmured.

"No, Ebi, we must go on, as far as we can tonight. And I want you to be very careful when we do stop. Stay together, and don't call each other by your names – but do not use your titles either. We must think of some other names to use. We don't want anyone to recognize you."

"But, we will go home, won't we, Mama?" Louischen looked up at her, her big eyes filling with tears again. "Will we see Aunty Vicky and Uncle Fritz again before we go on? Why were they crying when they came here? Why were you crying, Mama?"

"*Ach, meine lieblings*[1], what can I tell them?" the woman sobbed to herself. She thought of the goodbye which had taken place a couple of hours before, when she had embraced her friends and cousins, the Crown Prince and Crown Princess, for what might have been the last time. "*Gott* be with you, *am wiedersehen*[2], Marianne," Fritz had said, with the kindly look he always had for her as he squeezed her hand, but there had been sorrow in his eyes at the same time. Vicky had thrown her arms around Marianne impulsively, and kissed the little girls goodbye, clinging particularly to Louischen.

Marianne looked down at her three daughters with a lump in her throat; three such small, pitifully helpless morsels of humanity. Ebi, thankfully, had not been sick. Marianne's heart twisted at the sight of her sweet little face as her head leaned on her sister's shoulder, her mouth dropping open as she drifted off again.

She sadly shook her head. *No*, she thought, *you will never see Aunty Vicky and Uncle Fritz again.* She covered her face with her hands. She could never bring her little girls back to Berlin as long as her husband and his father lived.

---

[1]   Oh, my darlings
[2]   Till we meet again

PART ONE:
A TREACHEROUS PEACE

CHAPTER ONE
SEVEN YEARS OF HAPPINESS

Kronprinzen Palais, Berlin, January 25, 1865

"Can it really be seven years since you were married? Sometimes it seems so much longer, sometimes – no time at all."

Fritz smiled at Vicky and Alice as they rose to say farewell to their dinner guests, Professors of Chemistry and Mathematics, musicians, artists, diplomats, and men and women of science.

"Seven years of happiness," he said quietly, taking Vicky's hand as the last man left the room. He turned to Alice. "Where is Louis?"

"Asleep. He was quite tired." Alice said.

"He doesn't enjoy these gatherings, besides the musicians, does he?" Vicky asked her sister.

Alice shook her head. "He doesn't care for the lessons – the knowledge that I crave. Vicky, it makes me long to be with you all the more. I feel so – intellectually stunted – in Darmstadt, though our life is very happy and peaceful and I wouldn't change my position for the world."

"Come," Fritz said, "let us see if the little ones are still awake."

There was a knock at the door, which opened, and a footman entered, clicking his heels and announcing *"Prinzess Friedrich Karl"*.

Vicky and Fritz turned in welcome and looked on in surprise as Marianne entered the room. Her face was thin, her dress seemed to hang from her, and it was of thin, poor-quality fabric.

"Marianne, what has happened? Why have you never come before? We knew you have been back since December! What has happened?"

October 22, 1864

Marianne looked up as the carriage stopped. *At last, we are at an inn*, she thought. The coachman jumped down and knocked at the door.

"I'll stop here to change the horses, *Ihre H – meine Dame*[3], and you had better speak to the master if you wish to stop here tonight."

"*Ja*[4], but, please, don't call me even 'my lady'. And be careful and call us by the names we agreed on," she said. The man nodded, and hurried toward the inn.

Marianne looked around. Could she leave her girls here, in the carriage, while she went inside to speak to someone? Fear seemed to clutch her throat. *No.* Surely someone would come out from the inn and she could ask where they could stay. She would wait for the coachman to come back.

She sat, waiting and watching, and at last the man came back, with another man from the inn.

The coachman began to unharness the horses as the other man came up.

"You would like a place to sleep, I suppose," he said. "Are there more in your party?"

"Yes, three children. And I would like to be lodged as the poorest people are, though I can pay for the horses' care and for food."

The man looked at her questioningly, but only nodded, motioning to a large door far to the right of the main door. "Your lodging's that way, then. Go through that door. It is only women and children there, and I lock the gate at night. Your carriage shall be in the coach-house, and shall remain as you leave it – locked. I can bring you your trunk if you wish."

Marianne nodded. "*Danke*[5] – so very much," she said, trying to keep the tears out of her voice. "Do we eat inside or in the lodging?"

"You can come and eat inside if you wish," he said. Marianne nodded, and turned to wake the girls.

---

[3] Your Highness – my lady

[4] yes

[5] Thank you

"Oh, I feel so sick," Ebi moaned, rubbing her eyes and holding her stomach.

"Where are we?" Mariechen asked, looking about.

"I like the man," Louischen said. She had already been awake when Marianne was talking to the man from the inn. "His voice is pink."

"Come girls, stay together and don't talk more than you have to. And remember our names."

When they went in, the man showed them to a room on the second floor. It was warm, bright and cheerful, and the food was good and plentiful.

"I can't eat," Ebi said, laying her head down on the table with an agonized expression.

"Hush, rest then," Marianne whispered, and motioned to the other girls to be quiet.

"I will light your way," the man said, as they came out again to go to their lodging. "Everyone else is gone to bed, so I will lock the gate behind you."

Marianne nodded gratefully to him as he closed the door.

Inside, the passageway went down a little, then up again, and then came out into several large – stalls, it looked like. Marianne gazed, and realized it was indeed an old sunken stable. There were only cloth "doors", and the upper part of the wall was open to the cold night. A woman looked out of one of the stalls.

"The master said there was a new family here for the night. The last is empty. Make yourself comfortable," she said, handing Marianne a roll of bread as she passed. "Feel free to ask if you need help with anything."

Marianne ushered the girls ahead of her, and they passed the cloth door, gazing at what was their bedroom for the night.

Berlin, January 1865

Alice and Louis of Hesse were in Berlin for the first time, for Vicky and Fritz's seventh anniversary. They had brought little Victoria, and the new baby, Ella, who was a plump, dark-haired creature, a great contrast to Victoria with her wildly curly red hair.

"Victoria's hair is just the same color as Beatrice's," Vicky had said when she saw the little girl.

"And Charlotte's," Fritz added.

"Baby is sleeping," Willy whispered to Vicky as she and Fritz and Alice came in. He knelt, leaning over one of the two cradles.

Vicky glanced down, surprised to see that it was Ella, and not her own baby, Sigismund, Willy was speaking of. She glanced about. "Where is your little brother?" she whispered, embracing him. Willy pointed across the room. "No, Willy, I mean Baby, not Henry."

"With Hobbsy," Willy answered, kneeling down again. His gaze was fixed on little Ella's peaceful, sleeping face.

Vicky went into the next room, finding Mrs. Hobbs with Siggy in her arms.

"How is he?"

Vicky turned to see Alice at the doorway. Mrs. Hobbs turned, placing the baby in her arms. Siggy bounced up and down, laughing.

"He is such a big, lively little fellow for four months," Alice said.

Vicky nodded, opening her mouth to speak, but paused, thinking over the last few months.

October 22, 1864

"Settle down, girls, and make yourselves comfortable," Marianne whispered, taking a seat in the corner of the stall on the pile of straw. She looked about. There were three walls and the cloth door, the sunlight coming in still from the open upper wall beyond. There were two large piles of straw, and several blankets – clean ones, she was glad to see. The man she had spoken to had brought their trunk, and Marianne had wrapped the roll of bread in a scarf and put it inside.

The girls sat down around her, nestling against her as she embraced them.

"I feel safe here, Mama," Mariechen said.

"My feet are warm," Louischen murmured.

"Mama," was all Ebi said, and they clung together, until Ebi sat up again, gazing at her mother with a distressed look in her eyes.

"Be quiet, girls, let me go and ask the woman something," Marianne whispered, and slipped out.

She tapped at the cloth door of the stall occupied by the woman who had given her the roll. "One of my girls is sick, where should she –" Marianne trailed off, feeling embarrassed.

"There is a bathroom at the other end," the woman nodded in the opposite direction from the stall the girls were in.

"Oh, but I don't never mind, thank you." Marianne turned away.

"What's the matter?" the woman asked. Marianne turned back.

"I don't wish to wake the other girls so often, but I don't wish to leave them alone," she murmured.

"I will watch them, if you like," the woman said with a kind smile.

Marianne hesitated, and then returned her smile. "*Danke.*" She held out her hand.

The woman stood, and went back into the stall. "You may call me Greta. I live here, me and my daughter; we have no other home," she said, as she came back carrying a small baby. "I can tell you aren't poor, but I understand things, and won't ask questions," she said, taking Marianne's hand and holding it next to her work-worn one.

"Yes, please, and don't let the girls talk. It is better for everyone we meet if they do not know who I am."

Greta nodded. "I've seen other such stories. But this is a safe place, and the master's a good man, and the gate is always safely locked at night. One wouldn't expect this place to be where the women lived, either," she said, as they came to the cloth door of Marianne's stall. "I work here, and it is a much better place than where I was before," she said, glancing at her baby as she went in and sat down, gathering her cloak around her.

The girls clung together, gazing at the stranger with wide eyes. "Girls," Marianne said, "she is a friend, and will stay with you while I take Ebi to –"

Ebi rose and took her hand before she finished her sentence. Marianne nodded to Louischen and gave her a small smile before she went out.

At the end of October, a few days after Fritz's birthday and Siggy's Christening, Vicky and Fritz had left on their trip to Switzerland. As they had been ordered, they left Willy, Charlotte and Henry behind, but Vicky kept Siggy with her. She brought a wet-nurse with her, as her father-in-law the King had commanded, but the woman wasn't given that position in reality.

On the way to Switzerland, they met Bertie and Alix in Hanover. The meeting was a bit awkward, Alix being rather stiff and reserved, and even Bertie was rather cold to Fritz, who realized uncomfortably that he was wearing one of the decorations he had received during the war against Denmark – Alix's home country.

In Switzerland, they enjoyed the Alpine beauty, and the company of many friends. Fritz's old tutor, Monsieur Godet lived here, with his eighty-seven-year-old mother, who had been Fritz's nurse. Vicky was glad to meet them and the whole large family, and was glad to see someone from Fritz's childhood who he had actually been close to.

In Switzerland, they met Fritz Augustenburg, the claimant to the Duchy of Schleswig-Holstein, which had been taken from Denmark in the late war. He had been Fritz's closest friend at college, and was married to Vicky's cousin, Ada, the daughter of Queen Victoria's half-sister Feodora.

Fritz and Ada also had their children with them. Vicky quickly became very attached to their baby, Ernst Gunther, who was very small for his age, and, as the nurses said, had "water on the brain". His head was strangely swollen, but he had such a sweet, bubbly personality, he won everyone's heart.

On the way back to Berlin, they had passed the third anniversary of Papa's death in Darmstadt, where Affie was also visiting Alice and Louis.

Dezember 1864

In Berlin, Fritz found the town still in great excitement over the victory of the late war. He could not understand it. Of course it was important that they had won the war, but the celebration of the defeat of a small enemy who never stood a chance was far too over-done.

Three days after their return to Berlin, Fritz was at one of the celebratory dinners. Toasting began, but Fritz sat unmoving. He would not toast Bismarck, the Minister-President, who was largely responsible for what now seemed most likely to take place: the annexation of Schleswig-Holstein.

Fritz refused to believe it, though he knew it was probably true. But this destroyed any good which the war had brought. He had led the men, and so many men had given their lives, for the cause of freeing Schleswig-Holstein from Denmark, where they considered themselves oppressed.

If they were absorbed into Prussia, instead of being set up as an independent state within the German Confederation with Fritz Augustenburg as their Duke, they would find themselves much more oppressed than ever. Bismarck hated the Augustenburgs. Fritz believed that they would soon find themselves exiles.

October 22, 1864

Marianne woke, shivering from the cold. She would have to scold her maid for leaving a window open.

She opened her eyes, and remembered what had happened. The girls lay between her and Greta, nestled together in the blankets. Marianne wore a cloak that Greta had given her, which was quite warm, and she hadn't felt the need of a blanket as well. They had settled down in the straw, and had really been quite comfortable.

"I work here," Greta had said the night before. Marianne reflected. She had planned to go to Anhalt, appeal to her father and brother, and bring a case against Prince Karl, and Fritz Karl, too. But she hadn't known what Fritz – the Crown Prince – had told her when they said goodbye. A woman had to have her husband's permission to be at a legal trial. Of course that was impossible in this case.

She was sure her father and brother would have received her and the girls kindly, but law was law. "My girls" were Prussian Princesses, and would be expected to grow up at the Prussian court. *No. No! I cannot take them back!* She bent over the girls, their faces still peaceful in sleep. She looked at Ebi's face, creased in the uncomfortable expression which was becoming habitual to her. She was seven years old, nearly eight now, but they had not been seven happy years. The poor girls ought to have a happy and innocent childhood. Yes, it would be better for them to grow up serving at the inn, making an honest living for themselves, than…

Marianne shuddered, and then smiled to herself. A verse of scripture Vicky had read aloud floated through her mind. Marianne had never read the Bible particularly thoroughly before Vicky had begun reading it with the girls, but she was coming to know it quite well.

"Better a dinner of herbs where love is, than a stalled ox and hatred therewith."

Marianne smiled again, and settled back down to rest. That was very true.

CHAPTER TWO
IN THE ENEMY'S DEN

Kronprinzen Palais, Berlin, January 25, 1865

"How did you know? How did you know I have been here?" Marianne spoke quietly as Vicky took her hand.

"We saw you arrive. We were on the river." Vicky glanced at Fritz, who nodded, and took Marianne's other hand, encouraging her to take a seat. She trembled and seemed exhausted.

***

Toward the end of December, about a week after their return to Berlin, Vicky and Fritz had gone out on the Havel for the last time. Everyone had moved to Berlin already, but it had been a mild winter so far, and they wanted to enjoy it.

Clouds of birds sailed overhead as they sat in the boat. Vicky raised her opera-glass to watch. Birds of many sizes flew on together, from songbirds to eagles. It was a very late migration.

"Fritz?" She caught Fritz's hand. They weren't far from the Marmor Palais, though they were in such a position as to be able to see towards the courtyard, and not only the front of the palace which faced the river.

There was a carriage, draped in black. "That is –"

"Marianne," Fritz said, taking the opera-glass. The carriage door opened and Fritz Karl stepped out.

"He's holding something," Vicky said, straining to see what it was.

"*Someone,*" Fritz said. "It is Louischen."

Vicky took the opera-glass. Marianne also appeared. There was a great bruise on her forehead, and her left sleeve was almost torn off. Vicky could hear her voice in spite of the distance, and Fritz Karl's too, though she couldn't understand what was said.

Marianne snatched Louischen from his arms and set her down as Mariechen and Ebi climbed from the carriage. The girls stumbled, Louischen almost falling. The elder girls were crying, looking about, rubbing their eyes, obviously making a great effort to walk straight. Fritz Karl picked Louischen up again, and hurried inside, the others following.

*****

January 25, 1865

"Yes," Marianne said. "He brought us back. I couldn't escape. I couldn't do anything to help my poor girls." Vicky put her arms around her as she shook with sobs.

Marianne had told about the inn, and about their return. "But how did he find you?" Fritz asked. "Did they not protect you, as they said they would?"

Marianne looked perplexed, beginning several times to nod, then to shake her head. "I must tell you everything," she said finally. She began to speak, her eyes fixed on the chandelier as they had been before, as she told her story.

November, 1864

"Mama!" Marianne woke. Mariechen was shaking her arm to wake her. "Mama, Papa is here."

Marianne felt fear grip her by the throat. She sat up, rubbing her eyes, moving cautiously to where she could look out through a gap in the wall, where the sun had melted the snow and cast a dim light into their refuge. "Hush, Marie, don't wake the others."

Greta stirred, yawning. Marianne touched her hand, and when she opened her eyes, Marianne put a finger to her lips, and pointed outward. Greta nodded.

Marianne returned to the gap in the wall. She could see nothing but snow, but she heard voices. Yes, that was him. Fritz Karl was brusquely asking the master if a young woman had stopped here, a young woman with three children.

"Yes, but they have –"

Fritz Karl cut him off loudly, demanding to see inside the inn.

"They stopped here for the night, and to change horses." Marianne smiled grimly. That was what she had told the master to tell anyone who inquired about her.

There was more conversation, but in a low tone she couldn't hear. Soon, however, it became clear that Fritz Karl insisted on being shown over the place.

Marianne jumped at a sound behind her. Greta sat up, rocking her baby, who had begun to whimper in her sleep. *Oh, don't let the baby cry!* Marianne prayed. *Don't let the baby cry, or Ebi wake and be sick!*

There was silence. The minutes dragged on to two hours. Marianne sat tensely, huddled behind the wall of straw, glad that she had the insight to request that the men build it so it went over them as well, with a wooden support, so that there was just enough air flow for them to breathe comfortably. It hid them well, with the passage blocked for the night. It was also very cozy and warm. It looked as if the last stall was simply full to the top with blocks of straw.

Marianne nervously snatched up handfuls of straw, stuffing them into the gap in the wall, throwing them into almost complete darkness. No one was likely to look there, but it made her feel more secure.

"And she has left my carriage behind!" Marianne froze as she heard Fritz Karl's voice. "She has not only absconded with it, but left it behind! And my horse, too, I see!"

"She told me it was her own horse, your Highness," the master said. "And she said she would send –"

"It is my property. She has no right to steal them and leave them behind at a rubbishy place like this!"

"She said she would send for the carriage when she could, for it to be taken back."

Marianne couldn't hear Fritz Karl's reply to this. The door to the stable creaked open. There were no other women living there at the time, and Marianne had asked that some of the horses be housed here, to throw people further off the trail if anyone should inquire after her.

Fritz Karl was getting very near now. She could hear the spurs of his boots – *clink, clink* – closer and closer at every step he took. He came to the end of the passageway, stopping just in front of the wall of straw.

"What is this?" he asked, striking the straw.

"Straw for the horses bedding," the master replied.

You are a cavalry officer, and yet you have rarely been inside a stable, and don't know how the horses are cared for, Marianne thought. She loved her horses and had always visited them regularly.

"Where are they? I know they are here. She wouldn't leave her horse behind altogether," Marianne heard him mutter. She froze, holding her breath, pressing her hands over Ebi and Louischen's ears, where they lay with one side of their head buried in the straw. Greta rocked her baby, pressing her to her, also covering her ears.

The straw shifted slightly, but the wooden support stood firm. Fritz Karl, it seemed, had climbed onto the straw, trying to look down and around it. He seemed to suspect it was a hiding place. But the men had built it well, taking this into consideration. There appeared to be no gaps from the outside. The straw shifted again. Marianne thought he must be just at the wall separating them from the next stall.

"Eeeeyaaah!" Marianne heard a scream, a wild snort and whinny from her horse, and a loud *thump* on the floor outside. There was a loud thump against the wall between them and her horse, but thankfully, it held firm.

She heard Fritz Karl's voice again. Now it came from the floor. He was swearing and cursing at her horse.

"Fetch me a cloak! I can't go out in this state!" he screamed at the master. Another man's footsteps sounded on the floor. "Give it here! The carriage shall come with me, but this horse ought to be shot! It's a monster, and always was. You may deal with her." Footsteps of three men sounded on the floor, and there was silence for a few minutes.

She heard his voice again, but she couldn't understand what was said. She heard the door of a carriage close, and the coachman's call to the horses. He was going away.

Marianne pulled the straw from the gap in the outer wall, letting more light in again. "That was a close call. I am so thankful the children did not wake," Marianne whispered to Greta. She looked down. Louischen's eyes were wide open.

"Papa – here?" she asked.

Marianne nodded. "Yes, *meine Liebling*, but he is gone away again now. It is safe to speak. You were a good girl to be so quiet."

Marianne heard the stable door close, but footsteps heading her way. "Hush," she whispered.

"*Meine Dame[6]?*" It was the master. He bent down, pulling a block of straw out from the bottom, and wriggled inside. Someone pushed it back into place.

"You will have heard what has gone on," he said, looking at Marianne. She nodded. "I am amazed the children remained silent," he went on.

"The baby didn't wake, and neither did Ebi. I was so thankful." She paused, looking at him again. "What happened? What made him scream?"

The man chuckled, shaking his head and covering his mouth. "Has he been cruel to your horse in the past?"

Marianne felt her face flush. "Yes. Why do you ask?"

"That horse of yours reared up while he was up on the wall, and tore out the seat of his trousers. He was lucky the floor outside was covered with straw, or it would have been a hard landing."

Marianne covered her face with her hands, stifling her laughter. "To return to serious matters, did you show him everything? And did he take the carriage?"

The master nodded. "Yes. I let him go through every room. He feels satisfied you aren't here, I believe."

"We thought we were safe," Marianne went on, meeting Vicky's eye again. "We felt quite safe. Things went quite peacefully for some time. Ebi – Ebi was a little less sick, and –" Her gaze fell, and she hid her face with her hands.

Vicky was about to speak when Marianne looked up again. "Mariechen seemed quite content, but Louischen missed home. She missed you – she even missed – 'dear Großpapa', as she called my father-in-law." Marianne's voice became harsh and sarcastic as she spoke the last words.

---

6   My lady

"Marianne," Vicky began, but Marianne shook her head.

"I must tell you everything in order. Otherwise – I can't go back to these things! It is over, and I don't wish to speak of it again!"

Vicky nodded silently, squeezing her hand.

"Later in December – I don't even remember what day it was – we were in the garden. There were a few plants still, which had been covered and survived the first snow. We were to help to bring in the last – I do not remember how to speak of it, it is all so new to me – when a carriage drove up. We were dressed in heavy winter coats, of coarse fabric, and, I hoped, were unrecognizable. Ebi was in our stall, asleep, but Mariechen and Louischen were with me.

"I whispered to the girls to go inside – casually, without drawing attention to themselves. It was Fritz Karl. I went on working, keeping my face down and covered, but he came near me – and – everything is a blur! I felt a burst of panic, and turned to run, hoping the master would help us. I ran towards the door, turning to look back. I did not run straight, and I felt the side of my face hit the wall. Everything went black, and I tasted blood."

Marianne's voice broke, and she hid her face as Fritz gently took her in his arms, soothing her like a child. She wept silently, trembling violently.

Vicky rose, then sat down again. She felt so terribly helpless. There must be something to do, but – there wasn't. Marianne sat up straight again, nodding gratefully to Fritz. "When I woke, I was in the carriage, Mariechen and Ebi with me, either asleep or unconscious. Fritz Karl sat in front, with Louischen in his arms."

Her face changed, taking on a fierce expression Vicky had never seen. "He wouldn't let me take her. He said–" Her voice caught in her throat, and she stared again at the chandelier, her gaze fixed. "When we arrived at the Marmor Palais, he got out, taking Louischen. The girls had finally woken, but they were–"

"Were – were they – drugged?" Vicky whispered the last word, hardly able to believe she was asking the question. She had never imagined she would be involved in such a thing. "We saw how disoriented the girls were."

Marianne shrugged. "I don't know. Mariechen told me what had happened. When I ran into the wall, Fritz Karl came behind me. He was in a terrible rage, and he was drunk as well. When the master came to help me after I had knocked myself out, Fritz Karl drew two pistols, one trained on him and the other on me, and declared he would fire if anyone attempted to help me.

"He said that they must give up the girls. The master had begun to speak, but Mariechen said she couldn't hear what he said. She could hear Fritz Karl all too well, and she brought Ebi and Louischen, helping them into his carriage herself. The girls gave themselves up to save me and the master." Marianne shuddered, her gaze still fixed. She trembled visibly as Fritz soothed her again.

Vicky shook her head. "What else could they do? No one else was armed, were they?"

Marianne shook her head, but still gazed fixedly at the chandelier. She was shivering now, Vicky realized, not only trembling with emotion.

"She's in shock," Vicky whispered to Fritz. "It's no wonder. Oh! How can we stand by and let such things happen?"

Fritz shrugged, his face very grave. He began to take Marianne's hand, but she turned suddenly, her hand flying up and catching a blow to his face. "Oh! I didn't –" She burst into tears as Vicky embraced her. "I haven't been able to come here," she began again. "They wouldn't let me at first – at least, they wouldn't let me take the girls. I wouldn't leave them. I was at the dinners which my Mama-in-law gave, but nothing else. But today, I felt I *must* see you! But – oh, no, I cannot speak of it! I – to say it would be to admit it was true!"

***

Berlin, February 10, 1865

"It is so pleasant to be here for so long, and I will miss you so much." Alice slipped her hand into Vicky's muff to squeeze her hand. They were all bundled together with Fritz in a Russian sleigh with three horses, a troika, as Louis had called it. Louis had gone to Schwerin to visit his sister, who was newly married to the Grand Duke. Vicky wondered how a shy girl like Anna of Hesse would manage as the daughter-in-law of Fritz's Aunt Adina.

"I'll miss you, and the children will miss their cousins." Vicky smiled, squeezing Alice's hand. "I'm so pleased they get on so well together. Willy is certainly in love with your Baby!" She and Alice both laughed. Ella was only three months old.

Vicky paused, looking at Alice again. "This would have been Mama and Papa's silver wedding anniversary," she murmured. "And she's so – look out!" Vicky called, sitting up straight as they came around a large, ice-covered bush. Another Russian sleigh headed towards them, but the driver turned the horses just in time, saluting in the same movement.

"Is it – surely it cannot be!" Fritz turned to watch the sleigh go by. Vicky turned to look. He shook his head. "It is my parents!"

"But they never go about together!" Vicky said, turning to look at him.

"They were at the costume ball two days ago. Didn't you see them?"

"I saw her, but she's often at such things," Vicky answered. "But I didn't see your Papa."

"He wore a domino, and flowers in his buttonhole," Fritz laughed. "I hardly knew him myself. But I believe you had never seen him out of uniform."

****

All through February and March, Vicky saw very little of Marianne or the girls. They remained at the Marmor Palais throughout the winter, instead of returning to Berlin as they usually did. Marianne occasionally appeared at balls and dinner parties.

Once, she brought Mariechen and Louischen with her. Little Louischen was quite ecstatic to meet Vicky and Fritz again, and Mariechen greeted them with her usual shy, serious smile.

Marianne still looked very thin, but she dressed as she normally did for the parties. Vicky tried to draw her into conversation, but she hardly seemed to hear her. Her face was set in a strange, tense expression, her eyes in a fixed gaze, and Vicky could see the traces of tears on her face. She avoided Vicky and Fritz particularly when they were together, only occasionally stopping to speak to one of them individually.

One day towards the end of March, on a drive through Potsdam, Fritz stopped the carriage outside the courtyard of the Marmor Palais. Vicky caught a glimpse of two small figures and an older woman. It was Mariechen and Ebi, and Mathilde, or Tilla as the girls called her, who was the new maid who looked after the girls. Frau Kampmann had been away all of September and October last year, and had left again since the girls' return.

Vicky turned to Fritz as they drove away. "Did you see Ebi?" she asked. Her voice would hardly come out above a whisper.

Fritz shrugged. "I saw them all, as well as I could."

"But did you see her figure?"

Fritz shook his head slowly, but didn't speak as he met Vicky's gaze.

***

April 13, 1865

Vicky slowly climbed the stairs in the Marmor Palais. She turned towards the corridors which led to Marianne's suite of rooms.

The early morning sun streamed through the windows over which no curtains were hung. Quietly, Vicky went upstairs to the nursery, where the girls slept. Marianne had given her a key to the rooms. She slipped inside, bending over the little beds.

Louischen slept peacefully, a small smile on her face, a little doll which Fritz had given her clutched in her arms, its velvet dress pressed against her cheek.

"Mama?"

"Mama is downstairs," Vicky said softly, turning towards Mariechen's bed. Between the two, the third bed stood empty.

"Aunt Vicky! Why are you here?" Mariechen asked.

"Your Mama wishes me to be with her. You know why, don't you?"

Mariechen nodded as Vicky sat on the bedside. "I hope Ebi is –" She met Vicky's eyes, squeezing her hand. "But don't speak of it to Louischen. Mama doesn't wish her to know, as she talks so much about everything. She hasn't seen Ebi since the beginning of February."

Vicky nodded. "I must go." She bent down to kiss Mariechen's forehead, and turned to look at the empty little bed. *Let it not be empty forever,* she thought, her eyes filling with tears as she turned away.

She locked the door carefully behind her, and went back downstairs, into Marianne's suite. In the room next to her boudoir, three doctors hurried in and out. Vicky glanced in. A small bed with a high canopy stood in the middle of the room, a tall dressing screen nearby, on the side of the room towards Marianne's boudoir. Vicky could see sticking out from the brown sheets which covered the bed, two small feet. Ebi was there already. A table stood by its side, with two of the brightest lamps Vicky had ever seen. On the table stood a small bottle, and several small objects she couldn't see well, but she didn't stop to look. She hurried into the next room, fighting a sick feeling which grew in her stomach.

"Marianne?" Vicky called, looking about. She wasn't there. Vicky tapped on the door of the bedroom.

"Is it time?" came in a whisper as the door opened slowly. There was Marianne. Her face looked thinner than ever, and the tears were still damp on her cheeks as Vicky embraced her.

"I wanted to be here for you," Vicky whispered, tears flooding her eyes. Marianne nodded. "Do you want me to stay, or should I go and talk with the girls more?"

The clock struck eight. "The doctors said it should be at half past two, as the light will be best then," Marianne said. "I wish to be alone." The look of pain on her face faded for a moment. "I am so grateful to you, Vicky, but – I must be alone." Her face tightened again, and she turned away, covering her face.

Vicky stood still. She wished to comfort Marianne in some way, but she had just said she wished to be alone. She turned away, passing through the room where the bed stood, again averting her eyes from the objects which lay on the table. She reached the door, and turned back again, taking a deep breath. She turned, and walked over to the table.

It was the surgical instruments she had imagined which sat there, in a glass case so clear she hadn't been able to see it. She turned to the bed.

"Aunty!"

"Ebi!" Vicky knelt down beside the bed, taking the little girl's hand. It was cold, in spite of the blanket spread over her, which did nothing to hide her figure. Tears came to Vicky's eyes. Whenever she had thought of the situation, she had felt numb at the horror of it, but now, seeing the preparations for the operation, her emotions overwhelmed her.

"Aunty, I haven't seen you in so long! I miss you."

Vicky nodded, trying to think of something to say. "I've missed you, too."

"Aunty, what is Mama so sad about? What is happening to me?" Her voice trembled. "Where – how – oh, Aunty, the doctors' talk scares me! And I want to – I want to see Louischen. I want to see Uncle Fritz, and I want to –. I'm afraid, Aunty. The doctors talk as if – as if – I might –"

"Shh. Do you have something you'd like me to say to Louischen? I'm going to see her."

"Oh, Aunty, must you go?"

"Tilla will be here," Vicky said, stroking the hair out of Ebi's face.

"No, oh, no!" Ebi shook her head, beginning to sit up. "Don't – I don't want *her*!" she cried. "Why isn't Amy here? I want Amy!" Amy was what the girls called Frau Kampmann.

"Shh, don't upset yourself," Vicky said. "I'll stay here a while. Would you like me to tell you a story?"

"Oh, yes," Ebi said, a smile creeping over her face. "I'd like to hear about your Papa. I have heard you speak of him to Mama. I wish I had seen him."

"You did see him. Mariechen remembers. My parents came to Babelsberg when you were a little thing, six months after I first came here.

"My Papa was everything to me. He was always so kind, and loving, and gentle, and he could teach me anything I wanted to know.

"When I was just about your age, Ebi, my Papa taught me to swim. I was so frightened of the water, but he was so gentle, and helped me to learn to swim very quickly. I was never frightened again."

"He wouldn't strike you if you were frightened and wouldn't do what he said?" Ebi asked timidly.

"No! Certainly not! That is no way to teach a child."

"Was he as kind as Uncle Fritz is?" Ebi's face softened, and the look of fear faded.

"Oh, yes."

"I wish –" Ebi murmured something to herself, turning her face away.

Vicky began to sing softly, watching Ebi's face. A few tears flowed, but soon her face was peaceful. Vicky rose, stepping away. Ebi didn't stir. She was asleep.

Vicky slipped away to the nursery again. She would read to Mariechen and Louischen until the time came.

***

Marmor Palais, 2:40, April 13, 1865

Vicky sat on the sofa in the boudoir. Marianne sat next to her, clutching her hand, her face tense and fearful. At first, Vicky had attempted to talk, but Marianne cut short every remark.

"Wah! Wah! Wah!"

Vicky jumped at the sound. Marianne sat perfectly still; it seemed as though she hardly breathed. Vicky, too, listened intensely. The sound of the baby's cry continued, and she could hear a low murmur of the doctor's voices.

The minutes crept by, seeming like hours. A step sounded outside the door, and Mathilde came in, carrying a tiny bundle.

"He must be kept warm, and be fed regularly," she said, speaking in smooth, strongly French-accented German. "The doctors said he seems likely to be able to nurse, in spite of being a seven months child."

Vicky rose and took the baby. Mathilde left the room. Vicky held the baby to her, rocking him gently. He was the tiniest baby she had ever seen, and seemed to weigh almost nothing. "Is there a wet-nurse arranged for?" she asked. "Marianne?"

Marianne finally shook herself, looking down and shaking her head. "Not unless they have arranged it," she said shortly. She didn't look up, and Vicky looked at her, realizing her eyes were fixed on the baby.

Vicky gently passed him to her. "I'll go and ask. And if there isn't, I'll nurse him myself when I'm here. I'm well able to, as I haven't weaned Siggi."

She hurried into the next room. A young man stood at the end of the dressing screen, facing away from the bed. "*Mein Herr[7]*," Vicky called. "Do you know if there is a wet-nurse? Has the baby been fed?"

"Yes, the baby has been fed. And he is a strong little fellow for the circumstances." The young man's eyes met hers for a moment. One of the other doctors walked past, but did not look at her, and hardly acknowledged her presence. "You know all about this?" the young man asked, motioning to the bed. "I don't. What is this place? This is an awfully fancy operating-room." He looked about at the marble columns and scuffed his shoe on the plush carpet. "They brought me here with a blindfold. Where am I? Shouldn't something be done about such a young girl –" He trailed off, looking confused.

"Please, don't speak of it. It will only cause trouble for the girl and her mother if you do," Vicky said quickly. "I assume he was fed from a bottle, and there is no wet-nurse?"

The doctor nodded again. Vicky shook her head. She would arrange for the wet-nurse she had for Siggi to come here. She wasn't necessary for

---

[7]   Sir

Siggi. And she, Vicky, would nurse the baby herself whenever she had a chance.

She returned to Marianne, who still sat perfectly still. The baby had gone to sleep on her lap. Vicky took him, sat down, and opened her mouth to speak, when she heard a weak voice call "Mama! Aunty?"

Friedenskirche, Potsdam, May 1865

Fritz stood at the entrance of the church, waiting for Addy. He smiled as she came up and took his arm, with the same little smile that Lotte had always had for him. He had always been fond of Lotte's little sister, his "baby cousin" as everyone called her – she being the youngest of the Royal cousins of his generation. Of course, there were her morganatic brothers, Onkel Albrecht's sons with his second wife, Countess Hohenau, who Fritz had only ever known as a lady-in-waiting to Addy's mother. But they lived in Saxony, and Willy and Fritz Hohenau were closer to being the next generation, being very close in age to Mariechen and Ebi.

"Fritz," Addy murmured, "I'm not going to the dinner at Glienicke this evening." She clutched his arm nervously. "You understand, don't you?"

"*Ja, natürlich*, of course you wish to avoid Onkel Karl's *plackerei*." His voice sounded hard, but he could not keep down the bitterness.

On the first of May, everyone had moved back to Potsdam from Berlin. Only Marianne and Fritz Karl and the girls had remained in Potsdam through the winter. Onkel Karl had also returned to Potsdam for the summer, his position as Governor of Mainz only requiring his presence in the winter.

"I am glad you wish to avoid him. I always wondered if you –" Fritz paused, helping Addy into his carriage. He glanced around, but the guards were turned away, and no one else stood nearby, and the coachman was in his place. It would not be helping Addy to let her be seen riding alone with him in a closed carriage. "People have always said it appeared you allowed him to seduce you," he murmured. He did not like saying such a thing. Addy was such a nice girl, but Fritz had witnessed stranger things.

"Oh, no, *no!* It is entirely different," Addy murmured, her face flushing deeply. "I *can't* do anything else! What am I to do?"

Fritz shook his head. "I do not blame you for doing what you must so that he will not harm you in other ways. And I am proud of you for resisting his attempts to put you under his spell. That is what Vicky did," he whispered, feeling his face flush now.

"Yes – I thought so," Addy whispered back. "But that is not why I do not wish to go to the dinner. I do not wish to go – because – Wilhelm of Mecklenburg-Schwerin is here – and – he wants to marry me."

"Wilmeck – marry – you –" Fritz whispered to himself, shaking his head.

"Oh, yes, and your Papa approves it! Or rather, Aunt Adina has made him approve it! She thinks it so good for her sons to have such nice girls as their wives! I wish it could have been the Grand Duke, if I had to marry one of them! And that is not ambition; you know I have no wish to be a Grand-Duchess. I simply despise Wilmeck! Prinz Schnapps, both his enemies and his friends call him!" Addy's voice grew high and shaky as she went on. "And I will be forced into the constant companionship of Fritz Karl! You know they are best friends! I would love to see more of Marianne, and her little girls, but oh, not to trade myself for that! And it means I will never leave here, besides our brief visits to Schwerin, as Wilmeck is in the army here!"

"You can say no, can you not?" Fritz asked gently, squeezing her hand.

"Oh, I don't think I can! They confused me so, when I was left alone with him, and he asked such questions as well; I never thought I said yes, but they all say I did! I don't remember what I said, I was so angry and ashamed!"

Addy had tears in her eyes now, and her hand trembled. "Do you –" Fritz sighed and looked down. He knew how difficult things were for Vicky to speak of, but she always said it was a relief now when she *did* speak of them. He wanted to give Addy an opportunity to speak, if she wished it. "Do you wish to say what you were angry and ashamed of?"

"Oh, no – oh, yes!" Addy shuddered and buried her face in her hands. "But no, I can't," she sobbed. "But I won't go to this dinner and let Onkel Karl gloat over the fact that I will not escape by marrying. You know what Vicky spoke to me about last year?"

"Yes, of course. She wished her brother Alfred or her Uncle George could marry you."

Addy nodded. "How I wish that could have been! I don't wish to feel that I'm a – I'm a –" She hung her head, her face turning crimson.

"I know," Fritz said, patting her hand again as the carriage reached the Potsdam Stadt-Schloss, where Addy lived in the summers. "I know what you mean. Vicky felt the same."

***

Düppel, August 10, 1865

Fritz looked up at the mill on top of the hill. It had been rebuilt since its destruction at Onkel Karl's command – and there was lush green grass growing everywhere. Everything looked so different after a year of peace. The farms were rebuilt and prospering.

"Over here – that hill. That is where we all were at the last storm," he said, pointing to the Spitzberge.

Vicky followed his gaze, and then looked up at him. "I can't imagine this place as you described it! It was snow and ice – and then mud and blood – and now it's so beautiful!" She turned, motioning to a field full of color.

Fritz flinched as he turned to follow her gaze. Over the mass graves danced the colorful faces of many flowers. Fritz had always heard it said that flowers grew beautifully where much blood had been shed. It had always been a grotesque thought when he was young, that flowers would flaunt themselves over the deaths of so many men, but now, he saw something else. Those men had fought for a purpose – they had given their lives for their country – and now the flowers bloomed over them, showing the beauty of the love behind the sacrifice those men had made.

Neues Palais, Potsdam, August 17, 1865

"Our little boys are doing very well," Vicky read in a letter from Bertie. She smiled. She was so glad to know that there were now two little boys in the next generation in England. The little one's birth had come on the third of June, just before Addy's engagement had been announced. It had been a day of mixed emotions for Vicky.

Vicky had returned to Potsdam. Fritz would be in Berlin for a day, and then continue his military tour, returning in a few days when they were to meet Mama and the *Geschwister*[8] in Coburg. It would be the first meeting of all the siblings in seven years! They hadn't been all together since Vicky's wedding.

"Ada and Fritz Holstein will be with us in Coburg, and Christian, too," Mama had written in her last letter. "I hope all may go well for Lenchen."

Fritz had been very good friends with Christian and Fritz Augustenburg since their college days, and Vicky had become fond of Christian, too. He was very fond of children, and spoke good English, and, as far as one could tell, would soon no longer have a home. It looked very likely for Schleswig and Holstein to be annexed by either Prussia and Austria or only Prussia herself.

Lenchen was to be introduced to Christian during this gathering in Coburg. If they took a liking to each other, it would be a very pleasant arrangement for everyone, as Mama did not wish Lenchen to leave her, and Lenchen herself had no wish to leave England.

Vicky picked up another letter, one with the King's seal. She hoped it would be a kind one this time. After Fritz's parents being so amiable and even affectionate to her and to each other in February, they had gone back to being very stiff and hard to get on with. She tore open the letter.

"I wish you to act as hostess at this dinner… this is the wish of your King." Vicky scanned the letter, then turned back to the first page to read it thoroughly.

Prince kaMpande, the heir of the Zulu people in South Africa, was making a tour of the European courts. He was to be in Potsdam in two days. His time was very tightly scheduled, and a dinner was to be given in his honor at Glienicke. Prince Charles would be the host, as the King was absent in Baden, and, as the Queen, Princess Charles and Marianne were all away, as well as the King's sister, the Grand Duchess of Mecklenburg-Schwerin, and the Dowager Queen no longer took such functions, Vicky was the only possible hostess for the dinner.

Glienicke. Vicky had gone to Glienicke last year. She had been with Fritz, of course, and Fritz wouldn't be there this time. He wasn't to return before they met Mama in Coburg. But the visit to Glienicke last year had been for a State dinner for the Russian Imperial family. She had felt quite comfortable, sitting between the Emperor Alexander – the visiting sovereign – and Fritz. She would ask Abbat to accompany her, as Fritz would be unable to.

---

[8]   The siblings

She would write to Mama about this. She had promised Mama she would tell her whenever she went to Glienicke, which from the very beginning Mama and Papa had always cautioned her against. She would write to Fritz, too, though she knew it probably wouldn't reach him before the dinner. Letters often took longer to arrive which were being sent within Germany than those all the way to England. But Mama was in Coburg, so hers might not arrive in time either.

She took a piece of paper and a pen. It would be quite safe, she was sure. Fritz had thought so last year. A state visit could not be the scene of a crime within the Royal family.

Glienicke, August 20, 1865

Vicky clutched nervously at Abbat's arm as they passed the Lion's gate and passed through the variously colored rooms. Reaching the door to the tan room, where the guests had waited on her previous visit here, she paused.

"Abbat, do you smell that heavy, sour smell?"

Abbat shook his head. "Others who don't come from here mention it, but it never seems to bother anyone."

Vicky shook her head. "It always makes my head ache." They went on.

Entering the tan room, Vicky looked about. There was Prince Charles, and a few people she recognized as gentlemen and ladies of his household stood about the room. Prince Charles rose, going to a side door.

As the door opened, Vicky looked up at the tallest man she had ever seen. She had heard that Prince kaMpande was very tall, but she hadn't expected him to be this tall. Several other men followed him. None of the others were so tall, nor so dark – many of the Zulu people being part Arab. The Prince and several of the others wore a large gold hoop around the top of their head. Vicky knew this to be their symbol of marriage. She remembered Mama laughing over the idea of people wearing their wedding rings on their heads.

The other men stood in a sort of formation behind the Prince, and suddenly all raised their right hand and knee, stamping the floor and calling out.

Vicky imagined thousands performing this salute, out of doors. It was an impressive sight, even as it was. Prince Charles came towards her, and she shrank back against Abbat.

"Prinz kaMpande," Prince Charles said, then, turning to the Prince, he gestured towards her, saying something in a foreign language, the only word of which she could understand was "Victoria". He turned, returning to the seat he had occupied when she and Abbat had entered.

Prince kaMpande turned to look down at her again, and raised his hand. He put a finger under her chin, making her look up at him. She tried not to flinch. She knew from official visits paid to England that people from other cultures had very different customs of greeting women, and tried to play along as she knew Mama always did. She didn't wish to be discourteous to a foreigner simply because of a different culture, and she knew many of the European Princesses were quite rude about this sort of thing.

He touched his forehead with his finger tips, and then laid his fingers on her forehead. She wondered if she should do the same – except it would be impossible for her to reach his. She touched her forehead, and raised her hand. He laughed, gazing down at her, an amused expression crossing his face.

She studied his face, and she realized she had seen him before. Her thoughts went back to a passing memory of her and Fritz's visit to Tunisia three years ago. When they were in the town of Tunis, she had seen a very tall – though he hadn't looked as tall as he actually was at a distance – black man watching her. She had noticed the gold hoop on his head. She had known that was the Zulu token of marriage, but she hadn't known he was the Prince. She had turned away, but continued to feel as if she was being watched. She had looked back, and their eyes had met. He had been with another man, whom she also recognized now as the man who seemed to be the second-in-command of the Prince's entourage. In Tunis, she had seen the Prince touch his forehead, and then gesture in her direction, with this same movement of his hand. The other man had laughed, shaking his head.

Now, Vicky saw a glance pass between the two men. The Prince nodded, raising his eyebrows and bending down to whisper something in the other man's ear.

He then turned back to Vicky, and held his hands out, palm up. She glanced around. Several of the other Zulu men did the same in greeting to both the ladies-in-waiting and the gentlemen, so this must be a general greeting. Prince Charles held his hands out, palms down, and gestured towards the household. All the ladies and gentlemen followed suit, holding their hands above the Zulu men's hands, not touching.

Vicky did the same in response to Prince kaMpande. His hands were huge, and appeared even more so in comparison with hers. He nodded. *How I wish there was an interpreter,* she thought. Prince kaMpande spoke no European language except a very few words in French – none which would help her in this situation. No one had said anything except Prince Charles. They hadn't even acknowledged Abbat's presence.

Finally, Abbat cleared his throat loudly, and clicked his heels. Prince Charles looked up from a paper he had been reading, glanced at Prince kaMpande, and rose.

"...الأميرة المتوجة" Vicky heard the Prince say something, and Prince Charles answered him.

"...سيكون قريبا"

Everyone followed through several rooms until they reached the red dining-room. The two doors on the other side of the room were closed.

Vicky was seated at the head of the table, between Prince kaMpande and Abbat, Prince Charles at the foot. She was glad he was so far away. She glanced at Abbat, and he gently squeezed her hand.

Vicky wondered how this dinner would proceed, when she and Abbat hadn't been assigned an interpreter.

Everyone else had begun to eat. For the Zulus, there was only milk and a plate of fresh fruit – apples, cherries, strawberries, peaches, oranges and figs. Her plate was set out similarly. The fruit looked tempting, but Fritz had warned her never to eat or drink at Glienicke.

She glanced at Abbat. He was picking at his food, moving it about, never taking a bite. "What should we do? I can't understand this. It is so strange. There seems no reason for this dinner, without our being able to understand each other."

Abbot nodded, leaning towards her to whisper. "What did Onkel Karl want a hostess for if he is not even going to provide her with an interpreter?"

Vicky shivered. Why did he want her to come here? There must be a reason. She was about to whisper something to Abbat again, when one of the doors opened. She looked up, and stared. It was the Grand Duchess of Mecklenberg-Schwerin.

Abbat watched, stunned. He had believed Aunt Adina to be in Russia. This was why Vicky had come here at all. The Queen, Aunt Marie and Marianne were all away. Aunt Adina was the only other possible hostess besides Vicky, as Aunt Elisa no longer held such a position as Dowager Queen.

He stared, not believing what he saw. He knew Aunt Adina was on very bad terms with Vicky and Fritz, and on good terms with Onkel Karl, but he hadn't thought she would lie so blatantly as this.

She came closer, sitting down in a vacant chair, which one of the footmen placed next to – or rather slightly behind – Vicky, on the same side Prince kaMpande sat. Behind her walked another man, very like Prince kaMpande in the face, only with a slight beard. But this man was as small as the Prince was tall. This man was small enough to walk comfortably under the table, which he proceeded to do at the same moment Aunt Adina sat down.

"Oh! Ouch!" Abbat had turned to try to look under the table to see what the little man was doing, when Vicky cried out. He felt her hand on his shoulder, and she leaned heavily against him, apparently having fainted.

Abbat caught her in his arms before she could fall from her chair. He rose, but suddenly felt dizzy, and had to sit down again. The other door opened, and he vaguely saw Fritz Karl enter the room, before he felt a burst of pain, and everything went black.

CHAPTER THREE
"WHERE AM I?"

Gotha, August 22, 1865

Fritz sat in the sunshine, waiting. Surely Vicky would come? One train had already come and gone. This was the day she had written that she would join him; this was the station which joined the railroad from Berlin. He had read for the first half-hour, but then the time seemed to grow long. The sunshine was quite hot now, and he would move his carriage. He had driven himself here, wishing to meet Vicky privately.

He got out to fetch a bucket of water from the station for the horses, when he heard a distant train whistle. Perhaps she was coming at last!!

He climbed back into the carriage and sat, watching as the train drew into the station with many shrieks and groans. There were not many passengers, and he waited impatiently when it seemed that everyone had gotten off.

Finally, the door of another car opened, and a man looked out. Fritz only got a glimpse of him before he disappeared again. The other passengers were gone; they had driven off in waiting carriages.

The man's head appeared again. Was it – yes, it was Abbat. Fritz was surprised. He had not expected anyone but Vicky.

The Rosenau, Coburg, August 20, 1865

"Affairs in Prussia are going on in a simply shameful manner," Ernst Stockmar said, "and the King and Bismarck's behavior is infamous. The

Crown Prince is certain now, as we all are, that Schleswig-Holstein is to be annexed. But the King – the King wishes to know if you will see him.”

The Queen listened, her thoughts on a conversation between Albert and the old Baron Stockmar during Vicky's engagement. “So we are sending her in to the enemies den,” she remembered saying.

“Aunt? Excuse me, but you said I could enter without knocking.”

“Yes, Ada,” the Queen said. “Excuse me,” she turned to the young Baron for a moment, and then back to Ada. “Who is it from?” she asked, when Ada held out a letter.

“Vicky. The messenger said it was urgent.”

The Queen nodded. “Return to me in half an hour,” she said to Ernst Stockmar as Ada kissed her cheek. They both left the room.

“Dearest Mama,

“You will have seen in the papers Prince kaMpande is making a tour of Europe. He is to come here – to Potsdam – and the King has sent his command that I am to be hostess. It is to be at Glienicke as the King is away; and, as my Mama-in-law, Princess Charles and Marianne are as well, I must be hostess. I don't like the idea of being there when Fritz is away, but you will remember we attended the dinner there for the Emperor Alexander last year, and I feel sure it will all be well...”

Gotha, August 22, 1865

Fritz watched anxiously as Abbat stepped off the train, half supporting, half lifting someone down the steps. Fritz jumped out of the carriage and hurried forward.

“One more step – and here is Fritz,” he heard Abbat murmur encouragingly to her, putting his arm around her as she stepped awkwardly down, nearly stumbling.

“Vicky!” Fritz cried, clutching her in his arms, almost snatching her from Abbat.

“Fr… Fritz?” Vicky murmured, her voice slurred almost as if she were drunk. He lifted her head, trying to meet her gaze. Her eyes were glazed, but there was a brief glimpse of recognition before she sank limply in his arms.

He lifted her carefully, carrying her to the carriage. He took his handkerchief, and hers, wetting both from a bottle of water he had in the carriage. He spread one over her hot forehead, and, with the other, let a few drops of water into her mouth. She stirred, her eyes fluttered, and she murmured, "Fritz?" She seemed only asleep now, not faint.

Fritz turned back to the train. Abbat still stood at the bottom of the steps, watching him.

"Abbat! What has happened?"

"I – tried to –" Abbat hung his head, and seemed unable to speak.

"Come here," Fritz said, putting his arm through his cousin's. "We are alone. You can tell me everything."

"But – oh! I don't know! I mean – neither of us know – exactly, though I know, and I mean –" Abbat went on, speaking confusedly.

"Stop," Fritz said. Abbat stopped and looked at him. He, too, had something of the glazed look in his eyes, but did not sound drunk as Vicky did. "Where were you? Why did you come with her?"

"You know, Fritz, the Prince of Zululand has been making a tour of the European courts?"

Fritz shrugged. He had seen something of this in the papers, but he never paid much attention to South African affairs. "What does this have to do with you?"

"You did not get Vicky's letter?" Abbat asked. Fritz shook his head. "He came here – to Potsdam I mean – and the King, your father – wrote to Vicky asking – no, not asking, *ordering* her to be the hostess. No other lady was available. But Aunt Adina was there! I went with Vicky – I tried to protect her! I failed you!"

Abbat's voice broke at the last words, and he shook his arm free of Fritz's, sinking down to his knees and covering his face. Fritz's thoughts went back to those same words – the words, "I failed you," which he had been unable to say to Vicky.

Tears filled his eyes as he took Abbat's hands. "Abbat, I do not blame you. Whatever happened, I do not blame you. Tell me what happened. Where was the dinner?"

"Glienicke." It was what Fritz expected. Abbat covered his face again, but remained standing. "But how can you ever trust me again?"

"It is not your fault!" Fritz said, making him face him. "Look at me, Abbat. It is not your fault! You should have heard what she said to me when I blamed myself after Charlotte's birth! You tried to protect her! You did not fail, you simply – what happened?" he asked, realizing he still did not know.

Vicky tried to sit up and look about, but she couldn't make her eyes stay open, and the same memory of that day – she thought it was the same day at least – kept repeating in her head, as if it were happening over and over.

She had felt as if she was struggling through an inky cloud of darkness as she forced her eyes to open.

"*Ach!* Oh!" she groaned. She tried to sit up, but her head swam, and she didn't seem to be able to move her arms. "Fritz, I've never had such a headache in my life," she muttered between groans. "Fritz?"

"Where am I?" a voice came from across the room, obviously also labored and painful.

"Fritz?" Vicky called again.

"Fritz isn't here," the voice said, and Vicky realized the voice was ever so slightly higher than Fritz's.

"Abbat?"

"*Ja*. But where are we?"

"I don't know. Can you open your eyes? It's – very – painful," Vicky gasped, as she forced her eyes open again.

She lay in a strange bed with no curtains, the walls around her a soft green. Abbat lay in another bed, a few feet from her.

"Glienicke – the dinner – Aunt Adina was there," Abbat said. "What can have happened? We never left, did we?"

Vicky tried to understand what he was saying, but her head spun maddeningly. At least there was none of that heavy, sour smell, which was the last thing she remembered. Abbat repeated himself several times, but she still struggled to understand him. She couldn't remember anything about the Grand Duchess of Mecklenburg-Schwerin. She vaguely remembered the meeting with the Zulu Prince, but nothing after the meeting. She shook her head and struggled to free her arms, realizing she was wrapped tightly in a blanket. At first, she wondered if it was tied round her, but it was not.

"Ah!" she almost screamed as she fell to the floor, still wrapped up. Luckily, the floor had a plush carpet, which was the same soft green as the walls. The color was soothing to her eyes.

She rolled over, then suddenly rolled back, clasping the blanket to her. "Abbat! I – I –" She couldn't finish her sentence.

She was completely naked.

She glanced around the room. Abbat had obviously realized her predicament at the same moment. He knelt by a table at the foot of her bed, on which her clothes lay. He picked them up, placed her dress on her bed and her underclothing on the floor by her side, and nodded awkwardly, his face flushing. He looked around the room, and opened a door, which revealed a small closet. Vicky heard him close the door.

She began the slow, painful operation of dressing herself. Frequently, she was compelled to lie down as her head pounded and swam, a sick feeling rising in her throat.

Gotha, August 22, 1865

"We were at the dinner. They did not give us an interpreter, and you know Onkel Karl speaks Arabic. Aunt Adina was there, and Fritz Karl, too – we thought both of them out of the country – they came in after the dinner was going on, and – I do not remember very much after that. It is a blur – and – we woke up, in a different room, and everyone was gone. I don't think Vicky saw Fritz Karl. But it was as if no one had been there – all the furniture covered, as if for a long absence – and – but, we woke up in a bedroom – and – she –" Abbat covered his face again.

Fritz sighed deeply. "Tell me," he said softly.

"She was – wrapped –" Abbat turned his face away, speaking very softly. "She was wrapped in a blanket – and – and –"

"Undressed?" Fritz asked quietly. Abbat nodded, not meeting his eye, his face flushing bright red. "And where were you – what was your condition?"

"I lay on another bed – dressed as I was."

Fritz nodded, sighing deeply. At least they had not put them in bed together.

"I had to come with her, she was so disoriented. I had – I have a headache, and I can't think straight, but I know where I am. She didn't and she tried to leave the train at the wrong station, and wander away when we were at the stations. And it hasn't gotten better."

"Has she had any water to drink?" Fritz asked. Abbat nodded. "Will you come with us?"

Abbat shook Fritz's arm away again, staring at him, his eyes expressing the deep pain which Fritz felt inside, but had not yet allowed himself to realize. "How can you ask that?! How could I go with you, and look her family in the face?" Tears started to Abbat's eyes. "How can you ask–"

"Abbat," Fritz said gently, taking his arm again, "it isn't like that. Think of how I felt, when we went to England before Charlotte's birth. I felt just as you do. I promised her parents I would protect her, as you promised me. I know – and I should not have made you promise in the words we did use, as I know it is impossible. But they would not blame you. They would be grateful for your coming with her, to see her safely with me. I am grateful. What do you think would have happened if I had been with her? Abbat, you are feeling this about Addy, too, are you not?"

Abbat nodded. "I am responsible for Addy. I have been for so long, and it –" His voice trailed off again.

"I know. I ask you again to come with us. You do not have to meet her family if you do not wish to, but I do not think you are fit to travel alone."

Abbat nodded, tears brimming in his eyes again, and he joined Fritz in the carriage.

"What happened – I mean – was she able to dress herself? How –?" Fritz murmured to Abbat as he gave Vicky a few more drops of water.

"Yes. I left the room while she dressed, and then we went out. It was so strange; Fritz, it was as if no one had been there."

Fritz waited for him to go on, but Abbat stared blankly, his eyes twitching. He murmured something, but seemed to be reliving the scene which he probably thought he was telling Fritz.

Glienicke, August 20, 1865

Abbat had knocked twice at the door of the closet. "Vicky, are you finished dressing?" He waited, but there was no answer.

Finally, he heard a weak voice call, "Abbat? You can come out."

He found Vicky sitting on the bed she had been in. He sat down beside her, gently rubbing her back. "Are you ready to go?"

Vicky turned her face to look at him, her eyes wide with a strange expression. Suddenly, she lurched forward, throwing her arms around him, attempting to kiss him, pressing her lips to his chin as he turned his head to avoid her.

"Vicky!" Abbat caught her shoulders, holding her back. "What are you doing?"

"I don't know," she said thickly, snatching at his hand and clasping it to her chest.

He stood, putting his hands behind him. "Vicky," he said, "Who am I?" He spoke a little higher than usual, emphasizing all the differences he could think of between his voice and Fritz's.

"Abbat," she said dully, rising and clinging to his arm as he went to the door and cautiously opened it. No one was there. "I have to go to the station, and go to Coburg, and meet Fritz," she muttered.

"I had better go with you. You are in no state to travel alone." Whatever had happened, he already felt quite clear-headed. Whatever had been given to them – and they had obviously been drugged – he had been given a much smaller dose, or perhaps something different altogether.

He led her forward. She struggled to keep her eyes open, her head lolling against his shoulder as he walked.

Soon, they were in the red hall, but all the furniture, all the decorations were covered over with dust cloths. All the doors Abbat tried were locked.

"How are we to get out of here?" Vicky murmured.

In the front hallway, Abbat noticed a stack of the large gold rings which the Zulu men wore on their head to denote their married state. He continued on, through several rooms, and finally, came to one which obviously smelled of fresh air. "Come, Vicky," he said, putting his arm around her supportively.

There was an open casement window. He helped her out carefully, and stepped out, closing it after him. He glanced around. There were no guards in sight. No creature met his eye except several cattle grazing in the distance. "Those are Zulu cattle, are they not?" he asked aloud, though he didn't expect Vicky to answer.

Glienicke, Potsdam, August 26, 1865

Louischen stood up on her bed, gazing at the little girl who stared back from the looking-glass over her bed. "I am so glad we came back, Charlotta. I missed you. I missed you almost as much as I missed Aunt Vicky and Uncle Fritz. I missed Willy and Charlotte and Henry, and – *not* Papa. I *never* miss Papa."

Papa had brought her and Mariechen and Mama here to Glienicke the night before. Louischen was glad, though Mama seemed very upset. Louischen preferred Glienicke infinitely to the Marmor Palais, although the Marmor was much prettier. Glienicke was all small, box-shaped rooms and bold colors, which confused her sometimes.

She had asked Mama where they were every day while they were away, but she wouldn't tell her. Louischen loved the orchards at Glienicke, and the wide, green fields, and the little ponds and forests. She had missed the pretty park here. The place where they had been was so confined, with only a little garden, and always "indoors" even when they were outside, sleeping in the stable.

She sat down on her bed, staring at her fingers. The old burn marks were almost gone. "I miss my gloves," she added. She began to lie down, but sat up again. Tilla hadn't come to help her undress. It was strange for there to be no one about, though it was still light outside, and it would be some time before Mariechen would come to bed. "I miss Ebi. Mama never lets me see her.

"I miss Amy," she whispered. She missed her old nurse terribly, but Amy – or Frau Kampmann, as Mama called her – had still not returned. Amy's Mama was not well, Mama had said, and she wished to stay with her for a while. But Louischen didn't like Tilla, Tilla with her cold, grey, stony voice. Amy's voice was always so warm and purple and comfortable.

Louischen longed to be out of these horrid, scratchy, uncomfortable clothes, though the nightgown she knew she would wear wasn't much better. "I miss my pretty clothes, and I missed *mein lieber Großpapa⁹*," she murmured to herself, glancing up at the glass. She stood up again. There was Charlotta looking back at her. "*Guten Abend¹⁰*," Louischen whispered, kissing her.

The yellow haze of her voice hovered around the glass, so it almost seemed as though it belonged to Charlotta. The little girl returned her kiss, but Louischen didn't feel it. All she felt was the cold touch of glass on her lips, and there was no color but that of her own voice.

"No! *Nein! Nein Nein!*" she heard a voice cry passionately. Was it – yes, it was Mama! But her voice was so entirely red Louischen could hardly recognize her. Her words were muddled, but she heard something about the Queen, something about men, and something about the nursery. Mama almost screamed the words, and now her voice turned blue.

The door opened. Mama stood in the doorway, obviously trying to block the way. Louischen heard Papa laugh unpleasantly, and he pushed Mama roughly aside. She darted towards Louischen's bed, standing there, blocking his way again.

The voices were so red and so harsh and so jumbled together she could hardly understand what was being said. Louischen watched over her shoulder, and then looked at Charlotta again, seeing the terror in her eyes. There was a movement from Papa; Louischen saw Mama crouch down out of the corner of her eye. Louischen felt frozen with fear, unable to move. She still gazed into the glass, Charlotta's face taking on an expression of anguish, then seeming to shiver and break apart.

Louischen tried not to scream with fear as the glass above her shattered all over the bed.

She didn't think he was close enough to have actually touched the glass, and she hadn't seen him throw anything, either, but that must have been what happened.

She stood perfectly still. She knew she couldn't move without having that awful pain, such as when he had ordered her to fetch him another glass after he had broken one, and her feet had been bare.

But she was screaming now, almost involuntarily. "Papa! You have killed Charlotta! How can you kill Charlotta?"

She couldn't turn to face him; she mustn't move her feet. Her face was wet with tears; her own voice now filled with blood as she almost always

---

⁹   My dear Grandpapa
¹⁰   Good evening

saw his. She was vaguely aware that Mama still knelt beside the bed, but she only saw this mist of blood. Papa stepped forward, snatching her up, and almost ran from the room.

"No!" Marianne cried, springing up and rushing to the door. But Fritz Karl slammed it shut, locking it from the outside, leaving the key in the keyhole. Marianne was a prisoner in her own nursery.

She sank down again, covering her face. What was he doing? Where was he taking her? Would she find her locked in some closet, as she had Ebi? And how would she find her? It was Louischen herself who had been able to find Ebi.

She rose slowly, her hands shaky with anger and her head almost swimming. She must do *something*, but what could she do? She would collect the shattered glass. She must keep busy, and not sit still and let her thoughts torment her any more than necessary.

"Mama? Mama, I am unhurt, I think!" Louischen cried as she stood outside the nursery door. Papa was unlocking the door, pushing it open and retreating back to a different room.

Louischen saw nothing but the green stars of happiness which covered Mama's face as she ran to her, falling to her knees to embrace her.

"Oh, Louischen, you are unharmed?" Mama sobbed, but her voice was still green, not blue.

Louischen clung to her, nodding. There was such a lump in her throat she couldn't speak around it, and she realized she was crying, too.

"What happened? Where did he take you?" Mama asked her, as she closed the door, and knelt down on the floor.

"I'm not sure," Louischen said. "Papa had his riding whip, did he not? That is how he broke –" Louischen felt herself choke, and she burst into sobs, hiding her face against her mother's shoulder. She mustn't speak of Charlotta. It was too painful.

"Yes. He didn't touch you with it, did he?" Mama asked, anxiously.

Louischen shook her head. "I wish Papa would go away and never come back! Why did *we* have to try to?" She paused, but Mama didn't say anything. "Papa took me to one of the green rooms," Louischen continued, "but I don't know which one. Where – where was I? I don't remember if Papa was there all the time. Großpapa was there, and he was very – *very* nice, and he gave me a kitten – such a lovely purry one. He is white, with streaks of brown, and when I pet him, I think of the white heather Aunt Vicky showed me. I can call him 'Lucky' – 'Glücklich' in English – as Aunty said the Scots always said white heather was for 'Good Luck' – 'viel Glück' in English. Großpapa also gave me this pretty dress."

She looked down, stroking her hand across the plum-colored velvet of her dress. It was almost exactly like Aunt Vicky's voice, in color and texture. She preferred it infinitely to the uncomfortable, tight, yellowish-grey dress Mama had her wear since they came back, when she didn't wear black. The yellow was very like her own voice, with the grey tint it had after Großpapa said certain words in her hearing. She knew they were words no one else ever said, but she couldn't quite remember what they were.

Her stockings and other underclothing were a bright, clean white, not the dirty tan which she had been wearing, perfectly soft and smooth against her skin, and her little plum-colored shoes fit to perfection. Her feet felt more comfortable than they had in a year. She only wished he had given her a nice, soft nightgown as well, so she wouldn't have to change from these soothing garments into the scratchy nightgown she knew was waiting for her.

A strange look went across Mama's face, but she nodded, and Louischen went on, "He wanted to see me in the pretty dress. I like it. It is so warm and soft and velvety, like Aunt Vicky's voice. Mama, why won't you let me wear the things I used to? I don't feel like me in the ugly, scratchy clothes we have worn since we went away."

Another strange look passed over Mama's face, and Louischen remembered, *Mama wanted us not to be us when we were away. She said so.*

"Did anything else happen while you were there?"

"I don't think so." Louischen felt suddenly as if her face was burning hot, with tears flooding her eyes. She curled up in Mama's lap, hiding her face. She couldn't remember exactly what had happened, and Mama wouldn't understand if she did tell her of the field of orange flowers she had seen, and the flood of brownish-orange everywhere, but with a bitter, pungent taste which almost choked her. She didn't understand it herself.

She vaguely remembered hands touching her, gently and caressingly, but that was Tilla, who had helped her change.

Großpapa had been in the room, and that was why she had felt the sticky net of the black cloud fall over her, covering her so that she could still feel it on her skin after she was dressed.

There had also been a strange pain, but she remembered it so vaguely it didn't really seem real. It must only have been part of the bad dream she had the night before.

"No." She looked up at Mama again. "Tilla helped me to change. I think that is all that happened."

Mama lifted her up so she stood before her, looking into her eyes. "Try to remember very well, Louischen. Did he touch you? Did he –" Her face twisted, and she clutched Louischen to her again. "I don't want anything to happen to you, Louischen. I don't want –" Her words became choked and barely understandable, but Louischen could tell she was saying something about Ebi. "Did he touch you?" she repeated, her hands clutching Louischen's arms tightly.

"Ah!" Louischen cried, trying to pry her fingers away. Louischen looked at Mama's face. She had already looked so unhappy, and now tears flooded her eyes as she realized she had hurt her. "Mama, it didn't hurt so much," she cried, pressing Mama's hand against her cheek. "Großpapa took my hand, and kissed my head, as he always does when he gives us things. He lifted me up and let me kiss his cheek." She made a face. "I don't like that. His beard is so short and prickly, not like Uncle Fritz's. His is so soft and curly." She paused. "Großpapa said he was sorry he wouldn't be here to give us treats at Christmas."

Louischen shook her head. As she spoke the word "*Leckereien*[11]", everything had gone strangely blurry, and Mama's voice was colorless as she began to speak.

"That's right. He will be away again." At the word "*Recht*", Mama's voice turned pink again, with another shower of green stars. "I am so thankful."

Mama rose and went out, coming back with a maid. Louischen sat on Mariechen's bed, watching the maid changing the blankets and carefully

---

[11]   "Treat" in the sense of food

gathering the shattered glass. Louischen tried to stifle a sob. Those bits of glass were all that was left of Charlotta.

Finally, Mariechen came, and Tilla with her. "Mama," Louischen called, "I don't want this!" Tilla was trying to help her into the scratchy, grayish nightgown.

"Hush, Louischen. It is better so," was all Mama said. "You will see Ebi tomorrow," she added, bending down to kiss Louischen and Mariechen several times in turn, her voice its usual warm, pink color, with a faint smell of roses.

The door closed, and Louischen shivered. She wished she could talk to Charlotta, but there was no Charlotta to speak to. Besides, she never spoke so when Mariechen was present. Mariechen didn't understand. She said she tried to, but she didn't really.

Thoughts played over and over in her mind, about Mama's questions. What had happened? What were the strange feelings she vaguely remembered?

The color Großpapa's voice had turned was nearly brown – burnt ocher, as Aunt Vicky had called it, when Louischen asked what it was when she saw it in her paints. It was so nearly brown that she wasn't sure if it was at all similar to the other orange.

She always saw orange in Aunt Vicky and Uncle Fritz's voices when they spoke to each other. But it was a lighter orange, and always tasted sweet and tangy and pleasant, like the actual orange Aunty had once let her taste. And she couldn't see the flowers then. That only came when she herself was touched by another person.

She vaguely remembered Tilla helping her change, but when Tilla helped her to change into her nightgown in the evening, and to change again in the morning, she always saw purple pansies, not these strange orange flowers.

She saw the flowers or trees whenever someone touched her, but that was part of how she saw *the person*, even though it was when they touched her. It was usually a tree for a man or a flower for a woman. But with Großpapa, she couldn't see the tree she expected to see when a man took her hand or embraced her. She couldn't see the color of his voice through the black cloud she saw around him, unless, it seemed, his feelings were very strong.

But she remembered his voice had become a flood of that dreadful, thick, choking orangey brown; then it had disappeared, but the field of flowers appeared then.

This field of flowers seemed to be part of how she had seen herself. She put her hands together, and then raised her hands to her cheeks. She never saw anything when she touched her own hand or face. It didn't make sense.

CHAPTER FOUR
IN SEVEN YEARS

Coburg, August 25, 1865

"Your Papa wrote imploring me to act as hostess as no one else is available. I consider the King's orders as you do, and shall obey. Of course I don't like the thought of going to Glienicke – and particularly without you – but I think of last year – the dinner there with the Emperor Alexander, and how safe everything feels at a state dinner with many people about from another court. It's so different from when it's only the family. Abbat, too, will go with me, so I feel quite secure…"

Fritz read over Vicky's letter again. If he had received it before the dinner, it would not have done any good. It was such short notice; there would not have been time to write or to go to Potsdam.

Vicky seemed much better today, though she was still not her usual lively self. She said she had a bad headache, often forgot what she was speaking of, and had difficulty judging distances, but her speech was no longer slurred.

This morning, at eight o'clock, Uncle Ernst and Affie had received them officially in Coburg. Affie was twenty-one now, and participated fully in the ceremonials as the heir to the Duchy of Saxe-Coburg-Gotha.

Bertie and Alix had also arrived, and soon, everyone met in the entrance hall of the Rosenau, the little castle where Prince Albert had been born. Tomorrow would have been his forty-seventh birthday, and a statue was to be unveiled in the presence of the Queen and all her children.

"Vicky," the Queen smiled as she embraced her daughter.

"Mama," Fritz said as he bent down to kiss the Queen's cheek. She looked as young as ever, and more cheerful than he had seen her since her husband's death.

"Where are the children?" the Queen asked.

"Oh!" Vicky shook her head, looking up at Fritz. "I wrote to the King to say we wished to visit you," she went on, speaking to her mother. "I wrote that I wished so much to go home after not doing so for two years. He never answered – for three weeks! And now he wrote to Fritz saying he didn't see why I wished to go to England. He said I could bring the children here, and you could see them."

"Yes, you wrote to me about that," the Queen said.

"No, it was only – but this is the twenty-fifth? I'm thinking it was only yesterday! But the King's letter *was* on the fourteenth."

"There was no question of you bringing the children, as things were," Fritz murmured, taking Vicky in his arms and kissing her forehead gently.

The Queen looked up at Fritz with a questioning look in her eyes. Fritz kissed Vicky's forehead again, and nodded seriously. "I must speak with you alone," he said to the Queen.

He kissed Vicky's forehead again, leaning down and putting his hand on her cheek to turn her gaze toward him. She was still so unsteady, but she met his eye. "Go to your *Geschwister*[12]." Fritz spoke gently, almost as he would to a child, and nodded towards a door which had opened, revealing Lenchen and Beatrice. Vicky turned toward them, and turned back again to wave at Fritz. His heart ached as he saw the strange, blank look in her face instead of her usual smile.

He turned to go to another room with the Queen.

"Abbat did not wish to come with us," he said, after explaining the situation. "He did not want to face you after what happened. But I felt – would anything have been different if I had been with her instead of him?"

The Queen nodded, taking Fritz's hand. "You were right in what you said to him. It isn't his fault any more than it was yours. I'll speak to him and reassure him of this."

Fritz had shown her Vicky's letter, and told her everything Abbat had told him, and what little Vicky had spoken of.

"Before we were here – when you met us," Vicky had said. "I was dreaming it again and again – but now – it's all a blur. I only remember arriving at Glienicke with Abbat – and – *ach!*" She covered her eyes, shaking her head. Trying to remember brought the headache and disorientation more than ever.

---

[12]   siblings

Coburg, August 26, 1865

Vicky gazed up at the monument as it was unveiled. Tears sprang to her eyes; the statue was so like Papa. She glanced around. Mama had her veil down; Alice and Lenchen were both in tears. She saw Fritz, Affie and Louis all putting their handkerchiefs away.

It was so good to see everyone, but so strange to see them all together again at last. How everyone had grown up! Little Beatrice was eight now.

Later, they all gathered outside the Rosenau for photographs to be taken, all the *Geschwister*[13] together and also with Fritz, Louis and Alix. Some were also taken with Uncle Ernst and Aunt Alexandrine. Vicky smiled as she watched everyone shuffling about to fit into the picture. Affie and Uncle Ernst looked so similar, and that similarity was emphasized by the fact that they were the only two in the group wearing top hats.

Arthur, Leopold and Beatrice – "the little ones" as they would always be to Vicky and Fritz, and Arthur was still shorter than Vicky – were gathered around Fritz. *If only I had brought the children!* Vicky thought. It would have been so special to have them in these pictures too. The whole family would not be together too often, as they all grew up.

Kranichstein, Hesse-Darmstadt, September 1, 1865

"I can't say how upset my Mama-in-law was when she heard you didn't plan to see the King," Vicky wrote to Mama.

Two years ago, Mama had come to Coburg, and had met both Vicky's father-in-law and the Emperor Franz Joseph of Austria there. Just about the same time, there had been a meeting of all the German reigning Princes, including the Emperor of Austria – at least it was supposed to be all of the Princes, but the King of Prussia hadn't been present.

Now, Mama was in Germany again, but had written that she would not invite Fritz's father. Fritz's mother was already upset by the fact that she

---

[13]   siblings

hadn't received an invitation to the unveiling of Papa's monument. Vicky knew Mama had sent an invitation, but it hadn't arrived in time.

"How can your mother think of not seeing the King when she is here? He must see someone who will give him wise advice!" Fritz's mother had said to Vicky.

Vicky nodded. "I'll write to Mama how you feel about it. I'm sure she will be willing to see him."

"It is not only a question of feelings! It is such a vital consideration. You never seem to see this–"

"Of course I do!" Vicky cried, and then took her mother-in-law's hand, trying to remain calm. "Mama," she began slowly, it still seeming strange to call Fritz's mother "Mama", "I know how vital it is. Of course I –"

"Everything is lost without someone to advise him!!" Fritz's mother rose, walking agitatedly through the room. "And he will not listen to me! I often feel that everything is lost. Schleswig-Holstein will be annexed by Prussia, and that is the end of our dreams of a peaceful Germany. There is nothing more to hope for, and –"

"Mama, you will –" Vicky tried to break in, but Fritz's mother only glared at her. Fritz had always said his mother was very stiff about being interrupted.

"But how could your mother not invite me? Does she think I do not care about your father's memory? Does she think it is nothing to me that he is no longer here? He was my – my greatest friend and ally; your parents were the only people I could ever speak to with absolute honesty. You wouldn't be here if it weren't for my friendship with him!" She paused, looking at Vicky, and went on, "but sometimes I begin to think you would prefer that." She turned away.

"Mama! Don't think that! I love Prussia! I have a mission here, dear Papa's mission, which we carry on in his and your names. I love Prussia as you do, and wish the best for her! I would never exchange my position for another, even if my marriage elsewhere would have been as happy as mine with Fritz is! Nothing can ever change that!"

"You think that," Fritz's mother said. "You think that nothing can change that. But – I know. I know!" Her voice trembled. "Something could. You are still childish enough to have illusions. I am glad and sorry for you at the same time, and pray that time will not teach you differently." She turned away, hurrying from the room. Vicky saw her raise her handkerchief to her eyes. She had never seen her cry before.

Neues Palais, Potsdam, September 11, 1865

"Mama writes that Lenchen likes Christian very much," Vicky said as Fritz came in. "They all like him quite well." Vicky had hoped everything would go well. Ada and Fritz Augustenburg had been in Coburg, and his brother with them. "I shall be glad to have another of your old friends in the family. I was only concerned how Bertie and particularly Alix would take this announcement, with how she felt about the Augustenburgs before. But now that the war is over, she told Mama that she much prefers the idea of Fritz Augustenburg reigning there than that of the Duchies being annexed by Prussia and Austria."

Fritz smiled. "I hoped your family would welcome him."

Vicky rose, throwing her arms around Fritz. "It's good to be home again, but it was nice to see Alice's home with Mama," she whispered, reaching up on tip-toe for a kiss. Fritz turned his face away, and only kissed her forehead. She slipped away, turning to whisper, "I have news for you," as she closed her dressing-room door.

"I have news for you, and to write to Mama," she whispered again as she lay down. Fritz put his arm around her, and she laid her head on his shoulder. "I – we – have hopes again."

Fritz seemed almost to jump at the sound of her words. "Are you certain of this?"

"Oh, yes. I weaned Siggi in June. I'm quite certain that I'm at the end of the second month."

Fritz nodded, and Vicky felt him sigh deeply. "Fritz, why are you so serious?" She sat up, looking at him, before rolling over to blow out the candle. "Why – why, you didn't seem at all pleased!" She leaned over him to kiss him again, but he pushed her away again, but then put his arm around her, drawing her to him and kissing *her forehead.*

"Vicky," he said, "do you not remember? Do you not remember *anything* of the dinner at Glienicke? I mean, after arriving, and before Abbat brought you to meet me?"

Vicky closed her eyes, struggling to remember. Everything was vague. She remembered greeting Prince kaMpande, and sitting down between him and Abbat. It was a little further than she had remembered when she told Fritz before. But after that, all was a blur.

"Do you remember what was served to you?"

"No."

"Abbat said it was fruit. Do you remember that?"

Vicky covered her eyes again, searching her memory. She remembered dreaming something again and again, just before she woke to find herself with Fritz, but now she couldn't remember that, either. When she tried to, her head swam again, and even the moonlight streaming in through the window seemed too bright.

"Do you remember waking and finding yourself in a strange room?"

She shook her head.

"Then you will not remember – that you woke – wrapped up in a blanket, and –" Fritz trailed off.

"Oh! I do remember that," Vicky cried, images flooding into her mind. "I can see the green walls. And – the Grand Duchess of Schwerin was there! I – yes, I remember it – and – oh!" She broke off. "I was *entirely* – undressed." She whispered the last word, and hid her face against Fritz's chest.

He gently raised her head so that she looked him in the eye. "You understand, do you not? Why I do not kiss you? And my relief when you said you were at the end of the second month? Of course, it is too soon to know, if it had been otherwise, but you understand why I was alarmed at the idea of your expecting a child?"

Vicky nodded silently, hiding her face again. "Yes, Fritz," she whispered. She felt as if she would cry, but no tears came. "I don't know – what happened."

Fritz nodded. "I know, but we can understand at least something of what must have occurred," he said seriously. "You were at Onkel Karl's house, and you were – in that condition." He paused. "You said you remember Aunt Adina. Do you remember the little man behind her? Abbat described him to me."

Vicky shook her head. "No, but – there is this," she whispered, sitting up and drawing up her nightgown. On her ankle was a large, angry looking swelling. Vicky had been puzzled by its presence, having no idea what it was. "I've been thinking it was some odd insect bite. I remember I felt a great pain in my ankle. It's just the same spot! And it hasn't gone away, for over three weeks now."

Glienicke, Potsdam, September 14, 1865

Louischen sat on the broken branch of a tree which leaned over a little stream, gazing down into the water at the round face and big eyes of the little girl who seemed to look back up at her. Her face, too, was streaked with tears.

"Oh, Charlotta, I'm so glad I found you here," she whispered. "You are Charlotta, but I must call you Charlotta the second, as Charlotta – the first – is gone forever. Papa – Papa killed her. I never thought he would do such a thing, but I saw her shatter into pieces with such a look of anguish! Oh, I can tell you everything, Charlotta." She looked away and sighed. "Only, I can't see you indoors. I can only see you here. Charlotta – the first – was with me so often. She was in the little glass over my bed. And – oh, Charlotta, I was so afraid. I couldn't move, because there were bits of glass all over my bed, and I was afraid. But he can't smash you. The wind can blow you away, into little bits, but you will still be there," she whispered, as the wind blew and the face in the water rippled away for a moment.

Her little yellow voice seemed to float around Charlotta's face, instead of hers. At first there had been waves of blue around the sides, but now, shimmering stars of deep, piney green fell over it. She sighed happily.

"I feel so peaceful here. But I wouldn't dare to go to sleep here – the wind might blow me down and I wouldn't want to sleep in your bed. No – I would rather sleep in the orchard, if I slept outside – in, or under, the cherry trees. It would be so nice to be buried in their petals, I think. But you will never know that, unless –" Louischen took a cherry pit out of her pocket, and looked at it. "Unless I planted one here, but the gardener says it would take years before it could rain down its pretty petals. But perhaps…" Louischen slipped carefully down from the branch, dug a little spot in the ground, next to the water, and covered it over. She bent down and kissed the spot. "Make a blanket for Charlotta, please," she whispered.

She turned round and threw her arms around the pine tree, kissing it. "I have something for you, too," she whispered. She took a bunch of pressed cherry blossoms from her pocket, and tucked it under the pine needles. "You belong together," she whispered, turning her head on its side to look at the flowers peeking up, and smiled at them.

"Goodbye," she whispered, and ran across the little island, carefully stepping across the fallen tree.

***

Oktober 18, 1865

Louischen ran out the back door. It was to be the last day at Glienicke this year.

Großpapa was going away; she would not see him until May or June. That was so very far away! He would not be there to give her the nice presents for Christmas, but he had already given her things – another pretty dress, the same lovely pale pink color as how she saw Mama's voice, and a nice, soft, white nightgown to go with the stockings and things. She felt so comfortable.

She wondered why Mama disliked Großpapa so much. He was always so nice. Now, she would have to be at the Schloss in Berlin, or at the Marmor Palais, with Papa.

She wondered what made Papa so nasty. There were a few times she remembered, when he was very gentle and kind. At those times, his voice was purple. This was so strange. It was women's voices which were usually purple, not men's. But most of the time, she couldn't see his color. He usually wasn't even gray, like so many of the household and servants. She simply saw the emotions he experienced. It was as if there was no "personality" beneath them – he was all feeling.

But Großpapa was always so nice, and he said he liked her company, as she was one of the few who could understand him. He understood her, too. They could talk about the colors endlessly. It was so nice to be understood. Mama and Mariechen always said they tried to understand her, but then said things which made her feel they really did not. Aunt Vicky and Uncle Fritz always asked her questions, and did try to understand, but they, too, could not. Only Großpapa could.

He would ask her how she saw different things. Some things were different for him. The strange, bitter orange which Louischen sometimes saw and tasted meant anger to him. She mentioned seeing it, and he said he knew what it was for her, but he couldn't tell her now. She wouldn't understand.

When she first came to him, she would feel nervous as she entered the black cloud which surrounded him. She didn't like the feeling it gave her, as if she were covered by a sticky net.

But he would change his tone; he would say certain words, which she couldn't remember, and then her voice would turn greyish instead of the strong yellow, and the black cloud would turn to pink.

She always trusted a pink voice. She felt she could talk about anything to someone whose voice was so pink. Mama's voice was pink, and Großmama's was too, when they were with Louischen and her sisters. It was so comforting. Großpapa had told her that to him, a voice like that, which made you feel absolutely comfortable and as if you could tell someone anything, was a soft, creamy haze.

She asked him how he made it change. He didn't answer at first, but watched her.

"Would you like to learn how to do such things?" he had asked her once.

"Oh, yes, Großpapa!" she had answered. He nodded, and told her he would teach her, but only if she was loyal to him.

"Loyal to me." His voice became soft and droning, as he repeated the words. She felt as if something should make her uneasy, but it didn't. His voice was too pink to be untrustworthy.

But Uncle Fritz and Aunt Vicky disliked him. She wasn't sure why; their voices always showed a complex mixture of feelings when they were around him or spoke of him, and they used words she wasn't sure what meant. She felt as if promising to be loyal to Großpapa would be promising to be disloyal to them and to Mama, so she only nodded and said again that she would like to learn.

"Loyal to me," he repeated, as he lifted her up to sit on his knee. She didn't like the scratchy feeling of his short, bristly beard when he kissed her face. It wasn't so soft and curly like Uncle Fritz's. Then everything would go blank, and all she could remember was the strange field of orange flowers again.

But now, it was time to say goodbye. She must also see Charlotta again, to say goodbye before she left for so many months.

She had found Charlotta again on Mama's birthday. Now, it was Uncle Fritz's birthday, and she wanted to put more flowers under the pine needles, even if they couldn't be the cherry blossoms which belonged there.

She ran towards the little island, smiling to herself. She looked up, looking for the fallen tree.

"No!" she cried. The gardener was there with several other men; they were cutting down the trees and shoveling dirt into the creek.

"No!" Louischen screamed again. One of the men looked up, and grunted when he saw her.

"What's the matter with her?" he muttered. His voice was a smooth, cold gray which made Louischen shiver.

"Oh, why, why are you doing this?" she sobbed, running to the gardener and grabbing his hand.

"Your Papa has ordered it. This place is to be made into an extension of…"

A single thistle was the only flower in sight. *A thistle.* That meant Papa. She tore it up and threw it away, where it would be buried by the men, smiling grimly in spite of the sting.

She didn't hear any more of what the men said. She was blinded by tears and choked with sobs as she ran back towards the Schloss. He had killed Charlotta again. And her cherry tree – her hope of a cherry tree to come, to give Charlotta a beautiful blanket. *Oh, why must he do so?* She stumbled into the orchard and threw herself down at the foot of one of the trees. The ground was bare, the petals having been blown away long ago. "Oh, Aunty, why? Why must everything beautiful always be taken away?" she sobbed, imagining she was speaking to Aunt Vicky. When Aunt Vicky held her, when she embraced her, she always saw the branches of the cherry trees at their most beautiful stage, full of blossom, and sweetness, and hope.

On board the Osborne, October 28, 1865

"Are we really here at last?" Vicky groaned as Fritz woke her. It had been such a relief to fall asleep. The crossing to England had been horrible with a rolling sea and the wind against the ship.

They had gone to Brussels, to see Uncle Leopold. He was looking old and frail, and admitted himself that he felt frail and shaky. This was a great sorrow and surprise to Vicky, as in the past, he would never admit when he was ill. But his mind was as clear as ever. He was indignant over the state of affairs in Prussia. His advice was so clear, and so like Papa's. Vicky felt terribly sad to see him in bed, and so unwell.

She had brought Willy to Uncle Leopold's bedside. He was very fond of "our boy", but Vicky wished so much that her children could have gotten to know him, as they had never known Papa.

"Shall we lose him, too, before long?" she murmured to Fritz. She wiped her eyes, and thought of Mama. Papa was gone, Stockmar was gone, and now Uncle Leopold was… She didn't want to finish that thought.

Her thoughts were still in Brussels as she leaned against Fritz as they went ashore. She looked about, and looked up at Fritz. He, too, was scanning the waiting carriages.

"No Equerry, no brother, nobody!" he murmured. "There is no one here!"

"The ship was late, so they did not expect us, perhaps?"

Fritz shrugged. He looked more upset than she would have expected about something like this.

They drove to the Embassy, but again, no one expected them. The Bernstorffs seemed quite startled at their appearance.

"We didn't receive any message about your coming," Frau Bernstorff said to Vicky. "The Queen has said nothing."

"But we sent the little ones to Mama. They are with her, aren't they?" She felt anxiety grip her, until Frau Bernstorff nodded. They had sent the little ones ahead, only having Willy with them in Brussels. It would be the first time Mama would see little Siggi. Vicky missed him intensely, as she had almost always had him with her at night until the last week. "Our letters must have not arrived, and we didn't send telegrams." Vicky sighed. "Where's my brother? The Prince of Wales?"

"He is away, hunting. The Princess is in London, but engaged already, so she can't come. You may stay here, as I do believe there are no rooms ready for occupation at Buckingham."

Vicky turned to Fritz, who seemed about to leave. "Shall we remain here? I'm so tired, I must sleep more. I don't feel settled yet after the rocking ship."

Fritz nodded. "I will go and see Alix, so that they will know we are here."

Sandringham, November 8

"Hurrah!" Fritz heard cheering and the clink of the billiard balls, but felt like covering his ears. He sat at the far end of the room to get as far away as he could from the strong odor of cigar smoke. He stayed for Bertie's sake.

Tomorrow was Bertie's birthday. He would speak to Bertie seriously. This gambling over games of billiards was not a good way to spend one's birthday. Fritz knew how unpopular the Queen's uncle, George the fourth, had been, in a great measure because of his gambling debts. Fritz did not want to see Bertie go down the same path.

CHAPTER FIVE
A NEW BROTHER

Marmor Palais, Potsdam, November 9, 1865

Louischen sat in a little room near the nursery. It was her favorite room here, with its high, colorful window which sent magical streams of color over the walls, with its flowering vines climbing up the walls, reaching for the window.

This was the most beautiful place here. She liked to sit here; it was far more satisfying than going out into the dull, square courtyard with the poor little orange trees in pots. There was no beauty outside here, like at Glienicke, with its forests, orchards, islands and fields. She didn't like to look out the windows here on the other side, where the palace was on the edge of a great, great stretch of water. She often felt as if the whole place would fall in, if people weren't careful. And Papa certainly *wasn't* careful.

But she didn't want to think about Papa. "This is where the Fairy Queen ought to have her throne-room," she whispered, cuddling her kitten, Lucky, closer to her. He began to purr as she stroked his neck. The image of the white heather Aunt Vicky had showed her flooded her mind.

"Amy told me all about the Fairy Queen," she went on. "She had a whole book about her, and this room is just the place for her." Louischen smiled, pressing her cheek against Lucky's soft, warm fur.

It was so nice to have Amy back, and Tilla nowhere to be seen. She loved Amy quite as much as she did Aunt Vicky, or Mama, in some ways, even more than either of them. Until this year, Amy had always been there to kiss her and tuck her into bed, whether Mama or Aunty were there or not. Since her departure, Louischen had felt lost.

It was also very nice to have Ebi back again. She seemed quite normal, only more easily tired than ever. But she would always let Louischen talk about how she saw things, and not call her strange as Mama and

Mariechen did. She didn't understand like Großpapa did, or try to, like Aunty Vicky and Uncle Fritz, but it was nice to have someone to talk about it to now that she couldn't talk to Charlotta.

It was so odd that Mama didn't understand, when she liked to draw pictures of things which were, in a way, similar to how Louischen saw things. But Mama's drawings combined things in a way Louischen didn't understand, either.

Mama had moved back to the Schloss at Berlin at the beginning of November. For a while before this, Mama hardly ever came to see Louischen. Mariechen and Ebi were sometimes taken to see her, but Louischen hadn't seen her in a long time. How people talked about her was confusing. In some ways, it was how they had talked about Ebi, but no one seemed dreadfully upset as they had about Ebi. Louischen wondered what it was really about.

Today, Amy had told her, was Aunt Vicky's brother's birthday. Aunty and Uncle Fritz were also gone. They were gone to "England", Aunty's mysterious home of the past, which Louischen often heard her speak of. Louischen vaguely remembered being taken somewhere, somewhere people called "Anhalt", which was where everyone said Mama came from. Louischen almost always slept when they took her on the trains, so she wasn't sure how long it took to get to each place.

One time, she had stayed awake, going from Marmor to Glienicke, so she knew it wasn't so very far. She had also heard Papa and Uncle Fritz say it was possible even to ride a horse from one to the other in one day.

Louischen remembered that long carriage journey, when Mama had taken her and Mariechen and Ebi away. It had gone on and on for the whole night. Mama had said they would go to Anhalt, and they hadn't come anywhere near it then. Trains went faster than carriages, and went all night, so Anhalt must be even farther away.

Aunty had told her that England was even farther than that. They had to go on a train for two days, and then on a boat – and it was a far bigger stretch of water than outside here. Louischen thought that sounded frightening, but Aunty didn't seem to think so. Then there was another day on the train, before Aunt was home.

"Why did you go so far away, Aunty?" Louischen had asked her. Aunty had smiled, and said something about Uncle Fritz. They loved each other, she said, but Louischen already knew that. But what Aunty had said next had surprised her.

"We will be King and Queen of Prussia, some day. I must live here, and not in England."

Louischen had been startled by that. From what she understood, from what Großpapa spoke of, she had thought that Papa would be the next King, not Uncle Fritz. Aunty had explained that Uncle was called the "Crown Prince" because he was the next person who would wear the crown.

"But what if Papa wore the crown?" Louischen had asked, "and no one knew? Would that make him King?" Aunt Vicky had laughed, and explained that she hadn't meant someone had to literally wear the crown. She simply meant Uncle Fritz was the next person who would be King.

"I'm glad, Aunty," Louischen had said. "I don't want Papa to be King. I want him to go away!"

Right now, more than anything, Louischen wanted to go back to Glienicke. It was so beautiful there, and it was so nice to be understood as Großpapa understood her. It would be so long, so long, before the time came to go back.

Lucky began to struggle, and Louischen reluctantly let him go. She sat watching him, and then rose to follow him as he left the room. Everyone had told her not to let him roam about here, that Papa wouldn't like it. She must catch him and take him to the nursery.

But Lucky was running; he was fast. "Lucky!" Louischen ran after him, thinking of nothing but catching him. "Puss! Pussy!" she cried, but he only ran faster. She had heard Mrs. Hobbs, the nurse for Aunt Vicky's children, call the cats "pussies," and that word was also in the English story books Aunty had showed her.

He turned, running down the stairs. Louischen followed him, but he kept running.

Finally, he stopped when he came to the end of a passage. There were three doors ahead, but all of them were closed. Louischen stopped, looking about, realizing she had come into a part of the palace she didn't know. She turned and looked back, but there were two ways back, and also two staircases. Which way had she come? She had never gone downstairs alone before. She had always simply followed Mama or Amy or whoever she was with, if she wasn't carried.

One of the doors was slightly open, and Lucky was squeezing through. "Pussy! Don't go! Lucky! Come back!" she cried, pushing the door open. She wasn't sure where this led to, but she wanted Lucky back.

She froze as she heard laughter and the clink of glasses. Colors and shapes flooded her mind as she heard voices. Papa and the Duke of Brunswick.

Fear crept down her spine, a rainbow of different shades of blue and red filled her vision, and she felt as if she couldn't move as Papa rose and turned towards the door. A strong breeze blew through the room from a large window, which stood wide open.

Louischen bent down to grab Lucky and run away, but he darted forward just as Papa stepped towards her. There was a shriek, and Louischen couldn't help covering her eyes. Then came a crash, then a splash.

"How dare you bring this creature into my room?" Papa shouted. His voice was so filled with blood, it was too overwhelming to listen to. She couldn't understand all the words, and she knew she didn't want to. Papa lay on the floor, having obviously tripped and fell. His boot was no longer the usual pure, shining black. Long scratches covered it.

But where was Lucky? Louischen still stood frozen with fear, not knowing what to do. Papa rose, and bent down over her. "How dare you –" She tried not to listen to his tirade as he took hold of her shoulders, shaking her. His fingers gripped her dress, her lovely, plum-colored velvet one which made her think of Aunt Vicky's voice. "…miezling! You dare to come here and you will –" She heard the fabric of her dress tear, and she shuddered as she felt his hand on her neck. In her mind, she saw a purple thistle, and felt the sting as if she had plucked it up and held it to her neck.

"Here, now, Fritz, don't do this!" It was the Duke of Brunswick. She had barely been aware of him, though she knew he had sat still and watched what happened until now. He had spoken once, but his voice had been a dull grey. Now, it was a deep, rich green, the color of the ferns in Großmama's rooms. "She is only a little girl."

"This is my house; you will not come between me and my –" Papa rose suddenly, his hand still gripping her dress, causing the fabric to tear further. He brought his other hand up, and Louischen thought he would strike the other man, who had come close to him. But the Duke caught his arm, holding it fast, and looked into his eyes. He whispered something Louischen couldn't hear.

Papa didn't finish his sentence. As the Duke whispered, Papa's voice turned grey, and his gaze fell to the floor. He let go of Louischen's dress. The Duke bent and picked her up, stepped out of the room, and closed the door.

"Hush, now, *Kleines*[14], you shouldn't come downstairs alone." He mostly spoke English to her, with only the occasional German word, though he had spoken to Papa in German. "This is no place for little girls to go wandering about alone." He walked swiftly, and before long, they were at the nursery door.

"But where is Lucky? Where is my pussy-cat?" Louischen asked. She felt rather dazed at everything that had happened.

The Duke knelt down, looking her in the eyes. His eyes looked very sad as he sighed, and his voice was blue. He shook his head. "There is no hope for your poor little pet. He – he –"

Louischen suddenly realized what must have happened, before he could speak further. "He kicked him out the window, didn't he? Into the lake!" She covered her eyes and sobbed. "Lucky! Poor Lucky!"

The Duke nodded slowly. "Your Großpapa gave you that kitten?" he asked. Louischen nodded. "You ought to keep your kittens at Glienicke, not here."

"But everyone is away; he'd starve," she sobbed.

The Duke shook his head. "There are people there to look after the place. Why do you think the grass is so short when you come, and nice to walk in? You don't think it stops growing when everyone leaves, do you? There would be people to look after your kittens there."

Louischen tried to smile, but another burst of sobs overwhelmed her. FW"I'll ask Großpapa for a – a – another kitten. And another dress." She reached up to feel where Papa had torn her dress.

The Duke nodded, patting her head. "Now you should go back in here, with your sisters. It's safest there for you."

Louischen looked up at him. "But my sisters aren't here; they're in the school-room," she said, sniffing as she reached up and struggled to open the nursery door.

"Never mind. You will be with them soon. And you will have another little creature to occupy you soon – one even better than a cat," she heard the Duke say as he closed the door.

---

[14]   Little one

Windsor Castle, November 14, 1865

"I agree with Mama that it's best for Lenchen to stay here," Vicky said to Fritz, as they walked arm in arm down the Long Walk. "She'll be happy, and I know Mama often doesn't agree with Louise, so things will go more smoothly if Lenchen stays."

Fritz nodded. They had taken a long walk with Mama the day before, discussing the question of Lenchen's engagement thoroughly. Lenchen had repeatedly spoken of Christian since their meeting in Coburg; soon, he was to come to England.

"I shall be very happy to have him as a brother," Vicky said. She thought Fritz was about to answer, when a movement caught his eye.

One of the messengers ran towards them. "From Berlin," he said, holding up a telegram for Fritz to see.

"Hmm." Fritz didn't speak, but went on walking, nodding to the messenger, who continued on his way to the castle.

"What is it?" Vicky asked, clutching at Fritz's arm. His face looked very serious. "Is there bad news?"

"The telegram says Fritz Karl has a son," Fritz answered. "So –"

"So Marianne has had her baby!" Vicky looked up at Fritz.

Fritz nodded. "Did she have a son, or have they finally succeeded?"

Berlin Schloss, November 14, 1865

"And here is the Fairy-Queen again," Amy pointed to the picture on the last page of the book. Louischen smiled.

"Amy, why do you only let me have picture-books?" Louischen asked, looking up at her nurse. "I can read as well as Mariechen can."

It was Louischen's first day in the schoolroom. Everyone said she was too young, but she had begged with the others.

"I get so lonely in the nursery, and you said you didn't want me to go wandering about here as I did at Marmor."

They had moved back to the Schloss at Berlin. It was such a huge place, Louischen always felt intimidated by its size, and felt as if she would never want to go out into the corridors alone. But she had convinced Amy and the governess to let her join Mariechen and Ebi, "and," Amy had said, "you can share your lessons sometimes with your cousin Charlotte, when the Crown Prince and Princess come back."

"Oh, can I? That will be lovely!" Louischen had cried. She liked the idea very well, but more than anything, she liked the idea of going to be with Uncle Fritz and Aunt Vicky. She felt so safe with them, and so secure in knowing Papa wouldn't storm in at any moment.

But she still hadn't seen Mama. She had expected to, when they moved back to the Schloss. "It will not be long," Amy assured her.

"Aunt Vicky's children already read, and Charlotte is only a day older than I am," she said. "I could already read before Willy could."

Amy shook her head, and said something about her having memorized her favorite stories. Louischen knew she could read. She had always been able to read. She always remembered seeing the words spell themselves out in her mind when she spoke.

"I wish they would call Charlotte 'Charlotta'. It looks so much nicer. And Uncle Fritz does call her that. He always has such a nice, remembering smile when he says it. Not like Aunty. She – I don't know why she doesn't like Charlotte. But she doesn't."

"Don't say things like that! Of course she likes her own daughter," Amy scolded.

"But she doesn't like her! I can see it!" Louischen had looked at Amy, who shook her head again.

"Here, Louischen, read this if you can." Amy handed her a book she had never seen before. Louischen opened it, beginning to read aloud. "You see, I can read," she said, looking up and meeting Amy's wondering smile.

Boom! Boom! Boom!

They both jumped, and Ebi jumped up from her seat in alarm, running to Amy and throwing her arms around her neck.

"What is that?" Louischen asked, looking up at Amy.

She smiled and looked at Mariechen. "Very good. Count how many it is."

Mariechen continued to count. "Thirty-three, thirty-four, thirty-five, thirty-six, – oh, Amy, it is over thirty-six!"

Amy smiled. "I hoped it would be. It will be time for you to see your Mama very soon," she whispered as she hugged Louischen and Ebi to her, waiting.

Louischen looked up when the door opened, feeling tense all over as Papa looked in.

"*Fraulein*," he said, nodding to Mariechen and Ebi's governess and to Amy, "bring the girls."

Louischen shook herself in relief. His voice had been grey, which was usually not reassuring about someone, but it was so much better than when his voice was colorless except for his extreme emotions. He hadn't stormed in to snatch one of them away, as he often did. Usually, what he took them to do wasn't so very frightening after all, but his manner of doing so was terrible.

Amy took her hand, and Fraulein and the other girls went ahead, following Papa and a page, who stood outside. After a while, Amy lifted Louischen in her arms. The Schloss was far too big to go wandering in. Louischen's legs ached from having to walk so far here.

"Wah! Wah!" Louischen heard something ahead. Her vision was filled with yellow at the sound of the cry. Doors were opened as they passed through, and finally, they came to a room with the windows covered, a shaded lamp on the table, and a big canopied bed.

"*Meine Lieblings*[15]," Mama said in a quiet voice, as they came up to the bed. She reached out to stroke their heads, and lifted a little bundle which lay by her side.

"This is your little brother," Papa said. He met Mama's eyes. Louischen studied both their faces, but it was as if an unspoken conversation was going on. Finally, both nodded.

Louischen reached up. "Can I hold him?"

Mama shook her head. "Not today. Tomorrow you shall have him," she whispered, and Amy lifted her up again, taking her from the room.

"Is this the little creature the Duke of Brunswick mentioned?" she asked.

"Yes. We hoped it would be a boy this time, and it was. God has answered Papa's prayers."

"No, no!" Louischen cried, squirming to look up at Amy. "You know Papa never prays, and he does what Aunt Vicky read to me that you should

---

[15]   My darlings

never do." Louischen squinted her eyes, trying to remember the words. "Not to be vain about the name," she murmured in English, "no, that isn't right."

"Never to take the Lord's name in vain," Amy said, sighing. "You are too clever to let anything go by."

"I am too clever? But, isn't being clever a good thing?"

December 1, Windsor Castle, 1865

Vicky's birthday had passed happily. The Queen had her band play in honor of one of the Royal birthdays for the first time since Prince Albert's death. She had also declared that she would be present at the Opening of Parliament for the first time again.

Fritz knew Vicky had been anxious about her mother's seclusion and the rumors which sprouted from it, and she had seemed much relieved.

But they were to leave England tomorrow, leave this peaceful, loving atmosphere and return to the "cage", as Fritz often called Berlin.

But before their return, they were to welcome a new member into the English Royal family. Fritz felt inexpressibly happy over this new marriage. Christian had been one of his best friends since his college days; it would be another way of showing his support for the Augustenburg family. Bismarck would certainly be furious over it.

Fritz joined Vicky. Aunt Feodora – the Queen's half-sister and Fritz Augustenburg's mother-in-law – had talked with Christian for a long time, while Lenchen was with her mother. Now, the Queen appeared, without Lenchen.

Everyone stood about awkwardly. "Vicky, what is happening?" Fritz turned at the sound of Beatrice's voice.

"Hush, Beatrice. You're to meet your new brother soon," Vicky whispered.

"Brother? But he's too old to be my brother! He looks older than Mama!"

"Don't be rude, Beatrice," Vicky whispered. "Lenchen is to be engaged."

"Na engaged?" Beatrice whispered. She had always called Helena "Na" when she was small, and hadn't given it up.

The door had opened, and Christian and Lenchen appeared, hand in hand. Beatrice ran to Lenchen, whispering something in her ear. Fritz and Vicky stepped forward to embrace Lenchen and Christian.

"*Willkommen, mein Bruder*[16]," Fritz whispered. Christian nodded, but had tears in his eyes, and seemed too moved to speak.

Berlin Schloss, December 5, 1865

"My sister is quite happy," Vicky said as she embraced Marianne. "Do you know Carl Ruland?" Vicky asked as Marianne went to the door and looked out, and carefully locked it. She then led Vicky into the next room, again locking the door. "He's the Grand-Duke of Weimar's private secretary."

Marianne nodded. "Yes. I know he is a spy for Prussia," she said bitterly, as they sat down.

Vicky nodded. "That's what Mama said, too." She shook her head. "Papa trusted him. We all did. He was the boys' art tutor, and helped Papa with his Raphael collection. And you will keep this to yourself, of course. I know you are good at that," Vicky smiled, and squeezed Marianne's hand. Marianne said nothing, and stared at the chandelier. "Lenchen had fallen in love with him, but of course such a thing couldn't be allowed."

"So she marries a Prince, as I did," Marianne said rather absently. "May she remain happy."

"Oh, yes, I'm quite sure she will. Christian is a very kind fellow, and you know he's been our friend for years. But enough of *my* news; I'm here to see *your* baby!"

"You are too late!" Marianne cried, rising and walking through the room.

"He's alive, isn't he?" Vicky asked, alarmed.

"Oh, yes, *he* is alive, but they have taken *her* from me!" Marianne said. "It was a girl, Vicky. I have never had a son. There was no one here to be with me, this time, to be a witness, as you were with my Annchen."

------

[16]   Welcome, brother

"So, you had a girl, and they have declared – Ebi's baby?" Vicky broke off, not sure what to say as a look of pain crossed Marianne's face.

"Ebi's baby! You say it so calmly," Marianne cried, sitting down again. "I am too young to be a grandmother," she sobbed. "But yes, they have taken him. And, oh, Vicky, he is such a sweet little thing. He is so tiny, they will pass him off as the baby at the Christening. They will have him wrapped up, as they do the little babies here, which you were so indignant at with my little Annchen." Marianne smiled faintly, and then began to cry again. "But I miss my baby so much!"

"What happened to her?"

"Mathilde – the new nurse my father-in-law appointed last year – took her with her. She left to visit her family and she took her with her. I don't know where! I don't know where my baby is!" Marianne rose and began to pace again. She turned to look at Vicky again. "So you have a new brother just as my girls do," she went on, making an obvious effort not to speak sarcastically. "I don't mean to ignore your news. And I am certainly glad you feel that your sister is in good hands. May God bless her!"

CHAPTER SIX
A WEDDING AND A FUNERAL

Charlottenburg Schloss, December 6, 1865

"Addy is a good girl, and has no absurd romantic expectations. No girl ought to expect anything more from her marriage than I did. That is only a good way to be disappointed and miserable all through one's life. I am so pleased that both my sons have chosen good German brides who will bring no *unglücklichen* foreign ideas with them."

Vicky saw the Grand Duchess of Mecklenburg-Schwerin glance her way as she spoke the last words.

Vicky had just entered the room at the Charlottenburg Schloss, where Aunt Elisa, the Grand Duchess and Princess Louise of the Netherlands were gathered with their ladies-in-waiting.

"Our Crown Princess has not been disappointed in her 'romantic expectations', I think," Aunt Elisa said, obviously oblivious to Vicky's presence.

"Humph," the Grand Duchess snorted. "I wouldn't call such scenes as I saw in August very romantic, and neither would her poor deluded husband if he had been there. But where was he? In Hesse-Kassel, visiting his cousin," she went on knowingly.

"Fritz was nowhere near Hesse-Kassel; he was in Silesia, and then waiting to meet me in Gotha, while you helped and planned and –" Vicky broke off. She would not speak of what had happened in Glienicke before the others. It would only give the Grand Duchess more food for scandal. The Grand Duchess knew more exactly what had happened than Vicky did, and she would only twist her words to say she was hiding something if she said she didn't remember.

"I do not wish to speak to you if you will continue to delight in accusatory half-sentences," the Grand Duchess said, and swept out of the room.

"Poor Addy, I do wish she had a better chance," Princess Louise said.

The Dowager Queen sighed. "She has given her word, and she told me the other day she will not go back on it. She talked with me a long time, and seemed quite content."

Vicky shook her head. She quickly greeted Aunt Elisa and Princess Louise, and left the room.

Poor Addy. Everyone thought she was content, but she hadn't really confided in anyone but Vicky, Fritz, and Marianne. Vicky remembered her manner and expression when she talked with her.

"How I wish your Mama had taken your suggestion more seriously," she had whispered to Vicky at one of the dinner parties. "Your suggestion that I should marry in England. I'm afraid of Wilmeck, Vicky. Afraid of him! Can you imagine marrying someone you are afraid of?"

Vicky had listened, feeling helpless. Addy went on in this way, but at the same time insisted that she couldn't break the engagement. Now, the wedding was only four days away.

Kronprinz Palais, Berlin, December 9, 1865

"Vicky?" Fritz called as he went back to the bedroom. "Vicky?"

"What is it?" Vicky appeared at the door of her dressing-room, already wearing the skirt of the dress she would wear to the wedding, but only her corset and other underclothing which Fritz could not remember the names of.

Alix had shown Vicky her dresses which she wore while they were in England, which were separate skirts and tops, rather than a whole dress. Vicky had been delighted at the idea, it being much easier to refit when she was expecting a child.

"Uncle Leopold is not at all well," Fritz said, putting his arm around Vicky. She looked up at him, alarm clear in her eyes. "He is not well," Fritz repeated. He was not sure what to say next. "This looks very nice," he said, as she put on her top. Her skirt was pink with gold and silver ruffles, her top shimmering gold.

Vicky hurried with Fritz to the chapel connected to the White Hall in the Schloss, where most of the Royal weddings took place in Berlin. Everything was ready, and many had already arrived. Vicky went in to place a few flowers around the altar, and then went to find Addy.

"I am ready," she heard Addy call when she knocked at her dressing-room door. Vicky entered. Addy wore a heavy silver brocade dress, and her hair looked beautiful. Vicky went to the dressing table, and picked up the bridal crown. It was a special crown which all the Prussian brides wore. Addy sat down for her to pin it on, and then a wreath of myrtle in front of it.

"Here you are, and you look lovely," Vicky said encouragingly. She attached a bracelet around Addy's wrist. It held tiny miniature portraits of Vicky, Fritz and the children.

"*Danke*[17]!" Addy cried, throwing her arms around her.

Vicky took her arm, and led her to the door, where Fritz and Abbat were waiting when they went out. The King waited further on. Vicky curtseyed to her father-in-law as he took Addy's arm.

"Papa won't be here; the King will give me away," Addy had told Vicky. "I would have liked Abbat to, but he will walk with me too."

Vicky hurried with Fritz to take her place in the group near the altar, and the ceremony soon began.

Wilhelm of Mecklenburg-Schwerin, or Wilmeck, as they all called him, stood at the altar, flanked by his brother, the Grand Duke Fritz, and Fritz Karl, who was best man.

Just as Addy appeared, walking between the King and Abbat, someone moved behind Vicky and Fritz. There was a messenger. Fritz stepped aside for a moment.

Vicky's gaze was fixed on Addy's face. She looked so nice in her silver gown, though not at all bridal to Vicky's idea. As she approached the altar, her face changed, and tears came to her eyes.

"More bad news about Uncle Leopold," Fritz murmured, taking Vicky's arm again. Vicky's heart ached. If only they had been able to stay

---

[17]   Thank you!

with Mama longer, to support her in this new grief. But Vicky didn't want to abandon Addy either.

"Do you wish to take this woman as your wife?" Vicky heard the question, and Wilmeck's brief answer, "*Ja.*"

"Do you consent to be this man's wife?" Silence fell. Vicky waited tensely for Addy's answer.

"*Ja.*" Her voice was very quiet, as she obviously swallowed several sobs.

Everything was so sad, Vicky couldn't help crying herself. The news about Uncle Leopold weighed on her heart. A long speech – one could hardly call it a sermon – followed, and its ending seemed so completely out of place in this melancholy wedding.

"May your Royal Highnesses long live together in the greatest happiness," Heym, the clergyman went on. Vicky's heart twisted at the look on Addy's face.

The ceremony was over. Addy still stood at the altar with her new husband, who bent down and kissed her. Addy seemed to shrink into herself as the Grand Duchess, Fritz Karl, and many others came up. Finally, the circle broke. Vicky saw the Grand Duke Fritz put his hand on Addy's shoulder and whisper something in her ear. Addy's face suddenly seemed to glow with gratitude, but another flood of tears followed as he bent to kiss her cheek. Vicky and Fritz followed, embracing her, and finally, the King took her hand, and everyone followed into the *Weise Saal*.

A solemn march was struck up by the band, and the *Fackeltanz*, or torch dance, began. Vicky smiled, and glanced across the room at Abbat. The music was his composition.

Addy and the King, followed by Wilmeck and his mother, as Fritz's mother was absent, circled the room arm in arm, followed by pages bearing torches. At the end of the circle, the King sat down, and Addy took her husband's arm. Vicky and Fritz followed them, more and more couples joining the procession, changing partners at every round.

***

December 10, 1865

Uncle Leopold was dead. Gone was the man who had been like a father to Mama; gone was the man who had been one of Papa's advisors; gone was the man who in different circumstances would himself have been Prince

Consort of England. Gone was the last of the three loving advisors, Papa, Stockmar and Uncle Leopold.

Almost exactly four years. Four days less than four years since Papa's death, but it seemed so fresh. With this new blow, it seemed as if they had never gotten over Papa's death at all.

Fritz would go to the funeral and be at the Oath of Allegiance to the new King, Leopold II. But he would not leave until December 14, the saddest day on the calendar for their family.

Brussels, December 17, 1865

"It was a great shock to see Leopold and Marie and Philippe receive me as Uncle did six weeks ago," Fritz wrote to Vicky. "The funeral was finally settled, in spite of the absence of the will."

Uncle Leopold's funeral had been made awkward by the fact that the directions for his burial had not been changed since he still lived in England. Other parts of the will were obviously made quite recently, while the burial instructions still read, "I wish to be laid to rest by the side of my beloved wife, Princess Charlotte." Princess Charlotte had been the heir to England's throne. It was impossible for the King of the Belgians to be buried in England. But the funeral was still awkward, as the burial of a Protestant King of a Catholic country.

"I saw him at the last lying in state," Fritz wrote, "looking quite like himself, with his wig, his features peaceful. I remained at the door as the others came in, and last of all, a young woman, not so many years older than you, and two young boys – the Countess of Eppinghoven and her sons, George and Arthur. These boys, as you know, are your Mama's young cousins, and the same age nearly as Arthur and Leopold."

Berlin Schloss, December 21, 1865

Louischen stood with Mariechen's arm around her, gazing about the room. Everyone was finally here again, except that Aunt Vicky wasn't at this particular event. But there was Mama, there was Uncle Fritz near her, Amy stood behind Mariechen, Ebi by her side, and Großpapa stood closer to the altar. Großpapa would be here for Christmas, after all!

Louischen could hardly restrain herself from jumping up and down, though Amy had told her to be quiet and still. Usually, when they were brought in at dessert and to other events, Louischen felt and saw Mariechen and Ebi's nervousness so much it overwhelmed her. Now, she was too excited and happy to let it.

She broke away from Mariechen's grasp, and ran to Großpapa, reaching up to take his hand. He looked down, and lifted her up, so she could see the King holding the little bundle which she knew was her brother.

She hadn't seen much of the baby so far, being now out of the nursery, but she felt sure what the Duke of Brunswick had said would be true. But she still wanted another cat as well as a little brother.

"You'll give me another kitten, won't you?" she whispered in Großpapa's ear. "I'll keep him at Glienicke."

"You can keep *her* at Glienicke. But you haven't told me what happened to Lucky."

Louischen shivered, and shook her head. "I don't want to think about that. I feel so happy everyone is here again, and I want to be happy." She glanced around the room, and saw Mama whispering something in Uncle Fritz's ear. He nodded and looked at Großpapa, a look on his face Louischen had never seen before.

Louischen couldn't understand what was said, but she could see sadness and anger in their voices. She watched them still. Mama's face looked painful, and Uncle Fritz's somehow almost frightening.

Fritz stood next to Marianne, watching Onkel Karl as he took Louischen up in his arms. "I must be able to do something!" Marianne whispered in Fritz's ear. They had been discussing the girls' situation before they arrived for the Christening.

It was the first time Fritz had seen Onkel Karl since Sigismund's Christening last October, before his appointment as Governor of Mainz.

He had been away, and then Fritz himself had been so much away in the summer and autumn.

The sound of Heym's voice distracted Fritz for a moment. The King handed the baby to the clergyman, and the ceremony went on.

The baby. This child whose mother was literally only a child herself. Fritz glanced over to where Mariechen and Ebi stood with Frau Kampmann. Ebi's gaze was fixed on the bundle in Heym's arms.

Fritz had not felt such burning anger since the day when he and Onkel Karl had first met again in November six years ago. He had known of the girl's situation for so long now, and mostly, the thought of it had only caused a dull, numb ache. Now, standing in the room with them all, and seeing Louischen in Onkel Karl's arms, brought a surge of anger. It still had not really seemed real before.

Vicky had not attended the Christening. She was not a sponsor, and Fritz was, but this was not the reason for her absence. Fritz did not wish her to be anywhere near Onkel Karl.

Another wave of anger swept over him as he thought of what had happened in August.

Fritz was glad Vicky had almost no memory of the first day in Coburg. It would be such an embarrassment for her. Abbat had told him that she had attempted to kiss him when they were leaving Glienicke. She had also tried to kiss Onkel Ernst.

Fritz had asked her certain questions about what had happened, but he did not want to risk reawakening most of these memories. He remembered her feelings in '59 all too well. The greatest pain for her had been the feeling that, even if it had been forced and coerced, she had participated in intimacy with another man, without, in the moment, fighting against it. It had made her feel as if she had been unfaithful to Fritz, even if it was unwillingly. She had said that she felt that "her body had betrayed her… and him."

Vicky seemed well, but that in itself was a great trouble. This very fact that there were no memories which stood between her and Fritz, as there had been in '59 and '60, could result in a disaster.

As Vicky herself had said, she had been his ward during that time, not his wife. He had treated her as he would a daughter. It had been quite natural. Now, there was none of that. She had none of the nervous little mannerisms which had torn at his heart, replacing the child-like innocence which had always characterized her; none of the nightmares; none of the trembling horror of even a kiss.

But this very discomfort and horror had saved them from a disaster. The sight of Anna's poor, blind little boy came to Fritz's mind. Charlotte, too, had the rash and deformed fingers. They had been so lucky that the illness which had affected Vicky at that time did not remain contagious for any length of time, and the fact that if the child was a girl, it did not affect the woman's other children.

But now, Fritz felt uneasy. He could feel that something was not right.

Two years ago, in 1863 and 64, Onkel Karl had been seriously ill several times, and the doctors had made no secret of what sort of illness he was being treated for. They had made it plain also, that the treatment would most likely only conceal the symptoms, but not remove the illness, or the possibility of contagion.

It had astonished Fritz then how easily it could become natural to treat Vicky as he would a daughter or sister, but it had. Now, though, it seemed impossible. Married life was natural, and everything about her which had always captivated him seemed to draw him more than ever now, when he wished to resist it.

Fritz had slept on the lounge at the foot of the bed all these months since August. They must not take any risks.

"Put me down," Louischen whispered again. Großpapa still held her, but she struggled in his arms. "Please," she called, her voice almost a cry. Großpapa set her down, and she saw Mama say something. "Mama isn't happy when you hold me," she whispered to Großpapa, and then turned toward Uncle Fritz.

Uncle's face still wore the strange, frightening expression. Was he angry with Mama? Louischen had meant to go to him, but she felt shy now, and she had never felt shy about going to him before. Mama whispered in his ear again, and a shimmer of relief covered her voice, and his face had relaxed when she looked up at him again. She ran to him and he picked her up. She reached up to stroke his beard, laughing as he bent so it tickled her face.

She looked up, and froze. Papa was staring at her. She had hardly noticed him before, but of course he was here. It was his son after all.

But that seemed so strange. She had been asking Amy a good many questions about babies. Amy had said something about married people loving each other in a special way, but Louischen didn't understand. Amy had said she expected that, and that she shouldn't understand until she was older. But none of this made sense in connection with Mama and Papa. They certainly didn't love each other. And what did all of this have to do with babies, anyway?

She thought of Aunt Vicky and Uncle Fritz. *They* certainly loved each other, and in a very special way. The colors of their voices when they spoke to each other, or even when they looked at each other while speaking to someone else, were more beautiful than any Louischen had ever seen. As well as the plum purple and pine green of their voices, there were the green and pink stars of happiness and love, as well as that mysterious streak of orange, which tasted so sweet and tangy, and more pleasant even than the real orange Louischen had once tasted.

This streak of orange became stronger at certain times. It was more obvious when they held hands, and almost overtook all the other color in their voices when they spoke after kissing each other. They kissed in that strange way, which she had thought no one else ever did, kissing each other's mouths. She thought it looked uncomfortable, and it gave her a strange, ugly shiver, but they obviously enjoyed it. Was this orange, and this kissing, part of this "special love" Amy had mentioned?

But if it was, it wasn't only married people who loved each other that way. Last year, Louischen remembered, a man had been here in Berlin, who Mama seemed very fond of. When they spoke to each other, their voices turned orange, and the slightest touch of his hand on Mama's brought it as powerfully as it did with Aunt Vicky and Uncle Fritz when they kissed. Once, she had seen them kiss each other's mouths like Aunt Vicky and Uncle Fritz did. It was the first time she had ever seen anyone else do it. Louischen had noticed this, and tried to ask Amy about it, but Amy had said little girls shouldn't ask such questions.

Louischen was frustrated when people said such things. There were so many things she wished to know about, but no one would tell "a little girl".

CHAPTER SEVEN
CHILDREN… AND THE DELIGHT OF HAVING THEM

Kronprinz Palais, Berlin, January 1866

"Wally, Wally, oh, how welcome a sight you are," Vicky cried, running to throw her arms around her friend.

"Yes, I am so happy to be here again," Wally said, sighing as she looked around Vicky's sitting-room.

"And how is Mr. Paget? He hasn't been drowned again has he? I heard you had been out sailing several times lately."

Wally smiled and shook her head. "He has practiced swimming with his boots on," she said. "His legs get very strong. Everyone jokes that it is more dangerous to be kicked by him than by his horse."

Vicky laughed. "You mean *you* say that." Wally was always full of fun and jokes, but pretended that the jokes originated elsewhere. "Georgiana, tell Emma to bring the children," Vicky called as her housekeeper hurried by.

"I am sorry Fritz isn't able to see you," Vicky said, turning back to Wally. "He isn't well, and has had a bad sore throat and fever and headache, though he is much better today than he was yesterday."

"Do you remember Vic?" Vicky asked Willy when Mrs. Hobbs had brought the children, and Wally's children had come in with their nurse, Mrs. Adams.

"Vic?" Willy looked up at Vicky, and then at the other little boy. He shook his head. "You remember Wally?" Willy nodded and ran to Wally.

Wally had visited a couple of times since her marriage, but it had been some time, and the children had grown a good deal. Wally's eldest was a little boy whom she had named Victor Frederick William Augustus. Her daughter's name was Alberta.

Charlotte and Henry stepped forward, smiling at Vic and Alberta. Vicky was glad. Charlotte, and Henry too, were usually so shy with strangers, but the children were soon playing happily together.

"How do you feel about Charlotte now?" Wally whispered, retreating to the opposite end of the room.

Vicky stared at her for a moment. "Oh, you were still here when she was born, so you remember all my feelings at that time," she said. "I was puzzled for a moment."

Wally nodded. "Do you still wish you could have Marianne's little girl instead?"

Vicky looked down. "Louischen is a sweet little thing, but I am glad we kept Charlotte. She is sweet in her own way, and I *can* say that now," she said, meeting Wally's eye as she finished. It had been over two years now since Vicky had to push Charlotte away in revulsion. She still steadily avoided meeting her eye, but she felt she treated her quite the same as she did the others now.

"Did I ever tell you of the day," Wally began, "when Marie and I lived at that little house, when I came home, and found your father-in-law – the King – the Prince Regent, as I still think of him – sitting and reading my letters?"

Vicky nodded seriously. "Yes. But, Wally, he told me of it too, and why he was there. Prince Charles had come there, and was waiting for you to come home."

Wally's face turned pale, and she didn't speak.

Vicky nodded. "My Papa-in-law saw him go in, and went there and made him leave. He told me after – Charlotte."

Wally nodded. "While I was still with you?"

"Yes. But I never told you. It was all so terrible a subject to me at the time, I couldn't bear to speak of it."

Wally nodded, her lips pressed together in an expression Vicky didn't quite understand. "Vicky," she began, almost in a whisper, "do you remember that Marie went away in the autumn of '58, before Willy was born?"

Vicky nodded. "She was unwell, her family said."

Wally looked at her. "You understand, don't you?"

"Was it *him*?"

Wally nodded. "We didn't wish to worry you."

Vicky shook her head. "We all should have told each other what was going on, and told Mama, too. We could have helped to protect each other."

Wally laughed. "I remember my perplexity at your Mama ordering us to write everything to her, and your saying 'don't tell Mama!' about so many things. We didn't know whose orders to follow, the foreign Queen, or her daughter whose ladies we were."

Vicky smiled. "You should have disobeyed me," she whispered, and they both laughed as the children suddenly rushed across the room and crowded around them.

"Bring the babies," Vicky called to Mrs. Hobbs and Mrs. Adams. They soon returned.

Vicky took Siggy in her arms. He bounced up and down, squealing with laughter as he often did.

"Oh, he's such a lively, pretty little fellow," Wally crooned, taking him and letting Vicky take her little boy, Ralph.

Vicky felt her face glow. Everyone always praised Siggy so much. But, she always felt, why wouldn't they? He was such a sweet, happy baby. "He's my little darling. I love him as I love no other creature in the world." Vicky smiled to herself. She couldn't describe how she felt about him.

"How is Augustus's brother, and his family?" Vicky asked. Wally's husband's brother had six children, and they had been dependent on him for several years. Things hadn't been easy in Wally's household during the early years of her marriage, but Vicky had asked Mama to help the brother to gain a diplomatic position as well, which eased their situation a good deal.

"They are very well, and we are too," Wally said. "We wouldn't have had Ralph if things hadn't changed. We could hardly afford Vic and Alberta's care, and I didn't have anyone to help me with the children the first two years. Mrs. Adams joined us the year after you helped us so kindly."

She looked from Vicky's figure to the crowd of little people behind her to the babies. "We have both been occupied in augmenting our families, I see," she laughed. This was an old joke between them, originating from the memory of a pretentious speech made by an English clergyman to Wally about the births of Vicky's children.

Vicky smiled, and then sighed. She wouldn't tell Wally of the serious subject of the conversation she had with Fritz the night before. It may or may not be true, and she couldn't be sure until the birth. She didn't want Wally to worry about her.

But there was that old habit. She had just told Wally that they should have told each other, and Mama, what happened to them. But Wally wasn't part of her household anymore, so it wasn't the same. Still, Vicky needed to catch herself when she did that. She must tell Fritz whenever something felt uncomfortable, and not let herself go into such dangerous situations as she had.

She sat down on the floor, beckoning Wally to join her. She set Siggy down on his feet. He walked a few steps before he fell, rolling over and giggling.

"Bay – Bay!" he cried, reaching out towards Wally's little boy.

"That's his way of saying 'Baby'," Vicky said. She sighed, picking up her little boy and hugging him to her. He didn't walk and talk as he should. He seemed to be developing in that way quite as slowly as Willy had, or perhaps even slower, and he didn't have the impediment Willy did in his arm.

"That child's not well," Mrs. Adams said. "I'd say e's got water on the brain," she went on. "May I see 'im?"

Vicky let the woman take Siggy. A shiver of fear went over her. Surely nothing was seriously wrong with Siggy? It couldn't be, he was too precious.

"Wally," she began, trying to rid her mind of the idea, "did you nurse your little ones yourself? You said you had no one to help you."

"Yes," Wally smiled. "You did Siggy?"

Vicky nodded. "How did you know?"

"The look in your eyes when you look at him tells the story," Wally answered. "I remember how frustrated you were at neither your Mama nor your Mama-in-law supporting such things."

"They still don't," Vicky said, taking Siggy again, and looking up at Mrs. Adams.

" 'e certainly 'as water on the brain," Mrs. Adams said again.

"Is there – is there anything to be done?" Vicky felt a chill pass over her again.

The nurse shrugged. "Not that I know of. Some survive it, some don't. I don't mean to be 'eartless, but 'tis the truth. The hold Hemperor of Haustria 'ad it. 'e lived a long life."

***

January 27, 1866

"Come, Willy, we have something else to show you," Vicky said, taking her son's hand and leading him away from the table full of presents.

It was Willy's seventh birthday. This meant it would soon be time for him to leave the nursery, and be under the care of a tutor and governor, rather than nurses and governesses. "Can you believe our little son is a 'big boy' now?" Vicky had asked Fritz that morning.

They entered another room. There were two desks, side by side, with three chairs; a slightly inclined board with a very thin layer of padding over it; and a large metal contraption, consisting of a frame with two arms which held a horizontal bar. These were connected with springs and other machinery; in front of it was a small metal frame, adjusted to be just the same height as Willy. There was also the machine for electrotherapy, a large, low book case, a cot in the corner, and two large, comfortable green armchairs. On the walls were stretched large maps; one of Prussian territory, one, all of Germany, and several of Europe and other countries.

"Wilhelm," Fritz said, "*Kommst du[18].*" Fritz sat at the desk on the right, patting the seat beside him. Willy sat down, Vicky taking the seat on Willy's left side, taking his left hand, and gently stretching out each finger individually, rotating his wrist, and helping him to raise his arm as high as it could go. The thumb and first finger had some independent movement, and had grown faster than the other fingers, which still remained curled together, unless specifically manipulated.

"You will have your exercises with Dresky," Fritz said, putting his arm around his son. Dresky was a young officer whom Vicky and Fritz trusted. He came to the palace every day, guiding Willy through various easy gymnastic exercises, and encouraging him to use his left arm as much as possible. "And soon you will have a Governor and a tutor. You are a big boy now, and you will have your own room."

"Which you'll share with Henry and your tutor," Vicky said.

"*Nein.*" Fritz's voice was sharp, and Vicky and Willy both jumped. He sighed deeply, and then went on, "You shall share your room with Heinrich, but your tutor will have his quarters elsewhere."

Vicky tried to meet Fritz's eye, but he kept his eyes averted.

---

[18]   Come here

"*Kommst du*[19]," Fritz said, and Willy followed him to the metal frame, stepping backwards into it.

"No," Vicky said. "Take off your coat and shirt," she said, and helped Willy to do so. "This will be cold, but you can put them back on in a moment."

Vicky flinched in sympathy as she saw Willy flinch at the touch of the cold metal against his skin, but she must be able to see how his shoulder joint and shoulder-blade responded to the brace and exercise, so she would know if it worked properly.

Fritz gently closed a latch across Willy's waist, and another across his chest, under his arms. Fritz lifted Willy's left arm, placing his hand on the bar supported by springs. "Grip the bar," he said, and Willy took it with the other hand as well.

"Make a circle," Vicky encouraged, joining them.

Willy raised his arms, making a circle. The bars and springs moved smoothly. Vicky stood behind him, watching his back. The brace helped him to stand straight, so that certain muscles could be isolated and exercised which were not developing properly. When they simply raised his left arm, the muscles in the chest struggled to make up for the weakness in his shoulder. His left shoulder-blade was barely visible, and many of bones on the left side were considerably smaller than those on the right.

Fritz flipped a switch on the side of the frame. The resistance could be adjusted, making it so that he bore more weight with his left arm, without the risk of his dropping something heavy and seriously injuring his already weak hand and arm.

Vicky met Fritz's eye. They both nodded in satisfaction.

"Papa, will you take me riding? Can I come to the riding-school with you?"

Fritz smiled, and ruffled his son's hair. "Not yet. Only when Mama brings you, until three more years."

Willy nodded. "Three more years and I'll be a soldier, like you and Großpapa!" His face beamed with pleasure at the idea. "I'll ride as much as I can. Mama always said I'll have to become a great horseman!"

"He'll need to be more concerned about keeping up in the infantry training than the cavalry, I think," Vicky whispered to Fritz. "It'll be impossible for him to march with the long-legged fellows."

---

[19]   Come here

Vicky had worried when Willy was very little that he would never be able to ride well. How would he have the balance to, with his arm as it was?

This had proved to be much less of a problem than she had expected. When he was a year and a half old, Mama had given them a tiny pony named Tommy, on whose back Beatrice had also learned to ride. At first, Willy was strapped into a little seat on the pony's back, but by the time he was walking steadily, he also had his balance on his little pony, and loved to be led about. Vicky also had him sit in front of her when she rode.

He had often ridden with the rest of the family during their stay at Balmoral two years ago, and at Windsor, when he had stayed a few weeks with "Grandmama" after the war.

Vicky sat down at the desk, and took up a paper she had drafted, reading over it again. It was instructions for the new military governor, Captain Gustav von Schrötter. Schrötter was a scholar, not a typical guards-officer, and someone they felt they could trust.

Willy was to have free access to drawing and painting materials, with basic illustrations to copy, to occupy him while he was read to. He was to have lessons in spelling in French and English with Mademoiselle Octavia d'Arcourt, Charlotte's new governess.

Willy had always taken an hour's nap in the middle of the day, but this time was now to be used, still lying down and resting, but in memorization, mental arithmetic, or being read to.

All his free time was still to be spent in the nursery with his siblings; the children should remain as close to each other as possible. Vicky vividly remembered what Fritz had told her at the Exhibition, of how he had never really gotten to know his little sister until she was seven years old and out of the nursery herself.

At the end of the document, Vicky added a note, stating that any difficulties or questions about Willy's education could be discussed either with Fritz or with her. "Our wishes are completely identical," she wrote.

She signed the paper, and turned as Fritz re-entered the room, having helped Willy to dress again and led him back to enjoy his presents.

"Fritz," Vicky called, and he came to her side, sitting beside her and putting his arm around her waist. He glanced over the note, a smile passing over his face. He signed the paper as well, and then leaned his head down on his desk.

"Fritz, what's wrong?" Vicky asked. She saw a tear drop on the table as he raised his head and looked away. "You're well, aren't you?" He had seemed better from his illness these last two weeks.

"Everything is wrong," he murmured, and then turned towards her, sighing deeply. "That is not true, I know. These matters with the children go very well. I have heard again from Hinzpeter, and that Willert has another position." These men were some of those being considered as Willy's tutor. "But – everything else. *Ich bin so müde*[20]," he murmured.

"Come," Vicky said, and they went to their sitting-room. She sat down at the end of the sofa. He lay down, laying his head in her lap. "You've been so quiet of late, I've been concerned. But you've been away so much, and we never talk at night like –" Her throat tightened, and tears came to her eyes, "– like we used to." Sleeping as they had been, she in the bed and he on the lounge at its foot felt so strange and lonely.

Fritz's expression hardened and he looked away. She took his hand, releasing his fingers from the fist they were balled into. She bent down to kiss his forehead and smoothed his brow.

"Tell me everything," she whispered.

He sighed. "Things are not going well at all in Schleswig-Holstein," he began.

Vicky nodded. "Ada writes me regularly. She's very anxious. She's expecting another baby, and if things go as it looks like they will –"

Fritz nodded. "You know they had settled it that Austria should be in charge of Holstein, and we Schleswig, with our having access to the military roads through Holstein. It isn't right, and they ought to be under their rightful sovereign, Fritz Augustenburg. Papa refuses to acknowledge this. Bismarck has him under his thumb, as usual. I have tried to help Fritz, suggesting letters he should write, as you do for me, but they have done no good. I do not believe Papa even sees them.

"In August, Bismarck arranged all of this without my knowing. I have seen a letter now, which obviously states that he does not want it seen in Coblenz, England, Weimar, etc. The partition with Austria was settled on the 17th, the day we parted before –" Fritz started up, striking his hand against his forehead. She put her arms around him, trying to make him lay down again.

"I should never have encouraged you to go to Glienicke when Alexander was here!" he cried. "I should never have allowed you to go!

---

[20]   I am so tired

Alexander would not have been offended, and it would not have made you feel it was safe to go for a State visit!" He sat up, rising before Vicky could catch his hand, and walking swiftly through the room.

"Fritz, come back!" Vicky called.

He returned, sitting down at her side, but hiding his face. He sighed again, shaking his head. "Why can I never see it? Why cannot we see through their vile plans?" He turned to Vicky, gathering her in his arms and kissing her hair. "And now there is disagreement with Austria. Bismarck is attempting to obtain an alliance with Italy, too, and everything looks as if he wishes to go to war. You know Italy wished to buy Venetia from Austria?"

"Oh, yes, the papers were full of that," Vicky said. "Venice ought to be part of Italy. They speak Italian, and it seems full of the very spirit of Italian beauty."

Fritz nodded. "The Emperor Franz Joseph refused. But if we have a war, Austria's army will be divided on two fronts. Italy will most likely take what she wants."

Vicky nodded. "But the Austrians – the Southern states will be on their side, wouldn't they?"

Fritz struck his forehead again. "That is the worst! Imagine what it will be – and it is not only the Southern states – Hanover, Hesse, Coburg – all of these, everyone says, will fight against us! It will simply be mutilating Germany," he said, making a snipping gesture with his fingers. "All for the sake of taking Schleswig-Holstein for ourselves – as I know they will never let Fritz have it now – and the struggle for power with Austria. Prussia and Austria will not both remain in the German Confederation any longer, I feel sure."

"Alice and Uncle Ernst, and King George," Vicky murmured, her mind still on the thought of being at war on the opposite side.

"And this war – this war – it would be fratricide, and literally, as so many younger sons of the Southern states are in our army! And I! I will have to leave you again!" Fritz's voice broke.

Vicky threw her arms around him, pressing her cheek against his. "Hush," she whispered, taking his hand and rubbing his fingers again. "We must take what God sends. But don't borrow trouble. You don't know there will be war. Think of after Willy's birth, when I was so afraid you would have to go. There are many willing to be mediators. I'll write to Mama about it again."

Fritz nodded, wiping his eyes. "I must speak to Wilhelm about all of this. He must understand what goes on. But not on his birthday. I do not wish to burden the day of celebration with political troubles. That will come soon enough for him."

***

Kronprinz Palais, Berlin, February 2, 1866

"Vicky?" Vicky looked up at the sudden, sharp tone in Fritz's voice. She lay in bed. He had sat up on the lounge at its foot. "Were there none of your ladies or gentlemen at the dinner at Glienicke?"

"N-no," she answered slowly. "I didn't think it would be right to take Valerie or Hedwig to Glienicke – you remember how he behaved towards Wally and Marie – so I left them behind. I didn't think of gentlemen – and Count Seckendorff wasn't well, and he's who I would have asked to accompany me. I guess Abbat didn't think of it. It's strange, I suppose, and just what they wished. They caught me so completely off my guard in so many ways."

Fritz had continued to ask her many questions – some prompting her memory from things he knew from Abbat, some spontaneous like this one.

Her memory had returned somewhat. She remembered clearly now, the whole dinner up to the moment when the Grand Duchess of Schwerin appeared, and afterwards, the moment of waking and finding herself wrapped in a blanket – naked. The memory was there, too, of Abbat taking her to meet Fritz, and her nearly wandering away at the stations, but the first day of the visit at Coburg was still a blur.

Fritz didn't say anything, and Vicky supposed he was asleep. She shivered. It was cold, alone in the bed without Fritz. She had taken to sleeping in her dressing-gown as well as her night-gown again, as she had when she was expecting Charlotte, but this time, it was for warmth, not because she felt uncomfortable being so nearly undressed. She smiled to herself, closing her eyes, and began to sing softly, a beloved old lullaby she remembered Papa singing. She felt the baby moving very strongly tonight.

She jumped at a touch on her shoulder. "Fritz?"

He stood by the bedside. "I cannot sleep," he murmured. She sat up, reaching up to embrace him.

"*Meine* Vicky," he murmured, cradling her face in his hands, then kneeling down so he looked up at her. "It is today eight years," he said in English. He paused, looking her in the eye and then away. "Eight years," he went on in German, "since you left England to come here." He rose, kissed her forehead, and stood straight again, turning away, but only to light the lamp on the bedside table. "Do you ever regret it?"

Vicky stared at him and shook her head. "Oh, Fritz, how I long for you to come to bed, if only to talk as we *used* to do." Tears sprang to her eyes. It was so strange to sleep in separate beds, never to wake up in his arms, never to lay her head on his shoulder while they talked. It had been so long since she rested in his arms, her head nestled where she could hear his heartbeat. "It's no wonder you feel so unsettled. I do too."

Fritz sighed deeply, and sat down by her side, putting his arm around her. She leaned her head on his shoulder, and took his hand, placing it on her abdomen.

"Baby is lively tonight," she whispered, glancing up at him. He nodded, looking away. "Fritz," she said, "why don't you like to speak of the baby? I know I was already expecting before – before I went to Glienicke! It *is* our baby! And it would be even if –" She sighed, and turned away, lying down, but still holding his hand. "Even if it is Prince Charles's," she whispered.

Fritz looked away again. "Yes, Vicky, it is our baby, but I cannot help feeling – something is not right. Something is not what we expect. I cannot explain it." He paused, looking away. "Did your Mama answer Papa's letter?" he asked, standing again.

"Mama wrote much upset by your Papa's letter," Vicky said, "the one refusing Lenchen and Christian the use of Gravenstein castle. She calls it an insult that the King should forbid a Prince from using a castle which has always belonged to his family."

Fritz laughed, and sat down again. "If your sister knew what that place was like, she would feel that being taken there for her honeymoon was an insult. Unless it is much changed since I saw it during the war, I must say it is a blessing for Lenchen." Gravenstein was the castle which had been used as the army barracks headquarters in the war two years before.

"I'm glad to hear you laugh," Vicky whispered, looking him in the eye again. "Fritz, you will love this child, won't you? You'll treat her as you do Charlotte?"

Fritz met her eye, smiling, but the look in his eye did not match his smile. "Of course," he said, leaning down to kiss her on the forehead and stroke her hair. "I only hope it *is* a girl. What makes you say 'her'?"

"I don't know. I suppose we both have premonitions about this little one," Vicky laughed. "It seems so odd, it's so opposite to – Charlotte. You are full of apprehensions, and I –"

Fritz smiled again, stroking a strand of hair off her forehead. He stroked her cheek, his thumb brushing her lips. Vicky sighed, closing her eyes and relaxing under his caress. "Fritz," she whispered, feeling a light touch of his fingers on her neck, then her collar-bone. "Oh, Fritz," she whispered again, her heart beating wildly as he leaned down over her. His lips touched her throat, and she threw her arms around him, clutching his hand to her heart.

He froze, trying to sit up. She held on to him, pulling him down again. He didn't move. His forehead rested against hers. Vicky felt his long, slow, controlled breath against her cheek.

"Fritz, please! It has been far longer than the three months," she whispered. "I don't see how you did it, and a whole year!"

At her words, he struggled to sit up again, releasing himself from her arms. "No, Vicky, we must not." He sighed. "I told you what the doctor said – Onkel Karl's doctor, when I spoke to him. You remember the illness which affected Charlotte – the man has *no* symptoms." Fritz looked her in the eye again. "You know what this means, don't you?"

"It's a different illness," she said. "Yes, I know. But I spoke to him too. He said that the symptoms come out almost immediately, and if one has none, one isn't contagious."

"And you have not had any – symptoms." The expression on Fritz's face every time he said the word "symptoms" made Vicky want to laugh, in spite of the serious subject. It was as if he had spoken a far more distasteful word.

"No," she murmured, "I haven't, and it's been long enough for the other." She caught his hand, pressing her cheek against his palm. "When you – a few minutes ago," she began, trying to retain her train of thought as his fingers began to retrace their path of a few minutes ago. She closed her eyes, savoring his touch. "It's been so long, *so long*, Fritz, since we even kissed," she murmured. She opened her eyes, meeting his gaze, raising her hand to touch his cheek.

Their lips met as he lay down, drawing her into his embrace.

Fritz held Vicky in his arms, pressing his lips against her hair. Her embrace grew more relaxed, her breathing gradually growing slower and more regular, and soon, she was asleep.

Fritz sighed as he watched her face. She was so peaceful, so unperturbed. He could not help thinking back to the nights when he had held her and comforted her through the restless nights when she was expecting Charlotte.

Things were so different than they had been then, as she said. It was *he* who was full of apprehensions this time.

All through the months when Vicky was expecting Charlotte, he had done all he could to let her know and feel that he loved her and her baby, that nothing could ever change that. Now, of course, he felt the same way. He always would. Her children were his, and he felt he ought to be delighted that they would have another little one, but many problematic possibilities flitted through his mind as she tried to bring him to speak of the baby.

Fritz had said that he felt something "was not what we expect". He had also told Vicky that he "could not explain it". But this was not the precise truth.

Vicky's memory of the incident at Glienicke in August was extremely vague. Every time they had discussed this child, she only thought of the possibilities of the child being his, or its being Prince Charles's. Marianne had told Fritz the truth of the matter – or at least what she knew from Fritz Karl's drunken revelations – and he understood that this was not the only possibility.

Fritz shuddered at the thought of what Marianne had told him. What if this child was a mulatto? Vicky's speaking of the baby's size made him all the more suspicious.

What would Papa and Mama's reaction be? Would they be allowed to keep the child?

Fritz clutched Vicky closer to him, kissing her hair. She smiled in her sleep, murmuring his name.

He was tremendously thankful for her sake that she had no memory –
at least no conscious memory – of the incident, especially since – but he
did not wish to think of that. But he did not wish to do anything which
might awaken whatever memory was there.

Should he tell Vicky his suspicions, and what he knew from Marianne?
He dreaded disturbing her tranquility; he dreaded placing anything
between her and her love for her child; he dreaded a repetition of the
relationship she had with Charlotte.

But was it right to keep things from her? They never kept serious
secrets from each other.

But that was untrue as well. Fritz still had a secret, a deep secret he had
never shared with anyone, not with Vicky, not with her parents. His mother
suspected it, but he had never confided in her. This secret was in the far
past, from when he was only a boy. Its existence made it easy for him to
understand Vicky's – and everyone's – feelings about Prince Charles.

Should he speak of that? Would he ever be able to tell her? Vicky's
saying that the boys would share their room with their tutor, and Fritz's
abrupt contradiction, had been the closest he had ever come to speaking of
it, besides one time shortly after Charlotte's birth.

He remembered the questioning look on Vicky's face on his birthday
five years ago, that other night when, like tonight – and yet so differently –
they had re-begun their married life. That night there had been no hour of
passion, but a time of love of a very different kind – of self-control and
self-sacrifice for them both – *"a time to tear and a time to mend"*. He was
very thankful there was none of that pain now.

But on that night five years ago, there had also been a question. "You
always say you know how I feel when you startle me," Vicky had said.
"What do you mean?" she had asked. But he had not been able to tell her
more.

*"There is not a secret which shall not be revealed, nothing hidden
which shall not be made known."*

Was it time to tell these secrets? The secret Marianne had told about
Vicky herself, and the secret of his boyhood, which, dreadful as it had been
at the time, helped him to feel for and help Vicky, to help his mother, to
help Addy, Maroussy, Marianne's girls, and so many others, who, if he had
not experienced the same sort of fear and dread himself, he would not have
understood.

He stared at Vicky's peaceful face, sighing deeply.

"Gott," he murmured, *"Du hälst die Wacht – am Mitternacht."*

It was a prayer which he had prayed many, many times, which comforted him whenever he pondered the intricacies of his life, whether personal or political. It was actually a line from a poem by Friedrich Rückert, a favorite poet of his and Vicky's, in whose words Vicky had expressed her love for him so beautifully a few years ago on their *Verlobungstag*[21].

Rückert, he remembered, was also a favorite poet of Vicky's father.

Tears sprang to Fritz's eyes as he remembered his father-in-law repeating the lines during the most difficult conversation they had ever had – when he had to tell Vicky's father that Prince Charles had committed an outrage against her, and that he – Fritz – had been unable to protect her.

"At Midnight

"I have I awakened,

"and gazed up to heaven.

"No star in the entire mass

"had cheer for me

"at Midnight."

"At Midnight

"I projected my thoughts

"beyond the dark barriers.

"No thought of light

"could comfort me

"at Midnight."

"At Midnight

"I communed

"with the beating of my heart.

"A single pulse of agony

"flared up

"at Midnight."

---

[21]   Engagement anniversary

"At Midnight
"I fought the battle,
"O mankind, of your suffering;
"I could not decide it
"with my own strength
"at Midnight."

"At midnight
"I surrendered my strength
"into your hands!
"Oh, Lord over life and death,
"*You* keep watch
"at Midnight."

Gott's *Will be done*. It was all he could pray. He did not feel the strength to tell Vicky the truth, but he knew all things would be told at the right time, as there was *"a time to keep silence and a time to speak"*.

CHAPTER EIGHT
"DELIVERED FROM A DAUGHTER"

Kronprinz Palais, February 3, 1866

Vicky woke in Fritz's arms, listening to his heartbeat, her cheek nestled against his chest. She smiled. It was so good to be there again, in his arms, where she felt more secure and happy than anywhere else. She pressed her lips to his chest, and then turned, gently releasing herself from his embrace.

She rose, careful not to wake him, and went to the window, moving the curtain just enough to look out the edge. The sun was just beginning to rise, throwing a slim shaft of light over the city.

She yawned, turning back to the bed. She was still tired, and she half wished she hadn't gotten up. Now she would probably wake Fritz when she got back into bed.

Her foot touched something besides the carpet, and she looked down. It was her dressing-gown. She picked it up, shaking it out, and hung it up. She stood, looking at it for a moment. Something seemed odd, but she wasn't sure what.

Her night-gown lay tossed aside on the bed. That was what it was. It hadn't been neatly laid out at the foot of the bed as it always was when she didn't wear it. Fritz had always done this. It wasn't like him to leave them lying about haphazardly.

She laid out her nightgown, and eased the blankets away, trying to slip back into bed without waking Fritz.

"Guten Morgen[22]," she heard him whisper, and he yawned and stretched.

"Fritz," she whispered. "You left my clothes lying about. It's so unlike you. You −" She tried to speak in a serious tone, but laughter bubbled up

---

[22]   Good morning

and prevented her from giving the mock-scolding she had intended. "It's *so* good to have you here again, I don't want to get up," she whispered as he drew her into his embrace.

The clock struck seven. Vicky sighed. Fritz would have to be at the council again by ten, she knew. She finally rose to dress for breakfast.

When she came out of her dressing-room, Fritz patted the bed beside where he sat. "Vicky," he said quietly, "I want to tell you something. Lie down, please."

She did so, looking up at him as he gently placed his hand on her abdomen. He leaned down, resting his head gently against her. "I will – I *do* love this little one," he said, looking Vicky in the eye. "I never meant to make you feel uncertain about that. It is *ours*, no matter what."

Vicky felt tears spring to her eyes as he helped her sit up, gathering her in his arms and kissing her. He rose, looking down at her.

"This looks very nice, but not quite – you," Fritz said. Her dress was one of cornflower blue, with a border of cornflowers – Fritz's favorite flower. But it was tight, and somewhat lower-cut than she generally wore.

"It looks very well with this," Vicky said, taking a black lace cloak and draping it about her shoulders. "But speaking of clothes, I've had to get more new dresses, in spite of the things Alix showed me. None of my dresses fit me at all. It wasn't like this any other time. Mama had my trousseau dresses made so that they could be let out and I could still wear them after Willy was born. This little one is *not* so very little. And it is only seven months still. Fancy what I shall be in two months! Even my night-gowns and dressing-gowns are getting tight."

"Your dressing-gown," Fritz said, again sitting down and taking her hand. "Never mind about breakfast," he said, when she motioned to the little clock in the room. "I am not hungry, and would rather talk, here," he said, drawing her closer. "Your dressing-gown – last night, I would never have –" He paused, turning uneasily. "Your wearing your dressing-gown to bed has always meant you were feeling –" He paused, searching for an appropriate word. "Inaccessible," he said in English. He met her eye. "Do you agree? Is that the word I am trying to think of?" he went on in German.

"Oh!" Vicky looked down. "I hadn't even thought of that! It's been so long since I've had to wear it – so long since I have felt *that* way. I always said 'uncomfortable', but 'inaccessible' is very descriptive. I certainly did feel that way when I used to wear it. But I was simply wearing it for warmth! I longed for you so much, Fritz! And it was so cold without you there. I never thought of my dressing-gown being a signal to you."

***

February 13, 1866

"How I do wish your Mama would mediate – her letters of late have not been helpful," Fritz said as he came into Vicky's sitting room.

She was painting, and Willy sat nearby, reading aloud. "Grandmama said she'd mediate!" Willy cried, looking up. "Did she, Mama?" he asked, looking at her.

"Yes, Willy, but I think Papa wishes to speak to me alone," Vicky said, and rose slowly, turning to Fritz. "What has Mama written?" she asked.

"I had written to her, cautioning her about certain things she had written in a letter to me, which I was to pass on to Papa. Her reply simply stated that if her remarks offended the King, she could only say that his had offended her." Fritz shook his head. "This must not go on. I cannot quarrel with her as I did over the last war," he said, his face reddening. "Write to her and explain things."

Vicky nodded. "Are you to go anywhere this evening?" she asked. Fritz shook his head. "Then come to the dinner. It's only our people and Marianne's – the ones we trust – so it will be a pleasant change." Vicky took his hand and kissed it. "Come."

***

March 16, 1866

"Dearest Mama,

"I have been so anxious these last days, and have spent so much time in tears. War seemed indeed galloping up to overtake us like a hideous monster, but today we feel hopeful.

"Fritz writes to you by his father's desire that we accept your offer to mediate. You may be a peacemaker as you have been many times!

"I fancy Bismarck knows nothing of any of this, as he is bent on war.

"Fritz expects your answer soon, and we hope and pray all may end peacefully!"

***

March 1866

"Bismarck speaks hatefully of me to the ambassadors," Vicky read. "He attempts to give them the impression I am the greatest idiot in the world." Fritz had left to go to the council again, and had left a note continuing their conversation. "For the last week, he strangely calls me the Prince Regent instead of the Crown Prince. But to continue on the previous vein, he insists that I do not understand politics, I have never read the books I mention, and I talk about things I cannot possibly understand.

"All of this is nonsense, of course. Those books you recommended last year have all been read at last.

"But to go on to the real purpose of this note – I hope you have not sent your letter to your Mama. Papa's acceptance of England's mediation is false – he has never said it – it is all a trap I hope we have not fallen into."

Vicky shook her head. She had sent her letter, and the messenger had already gone. What could she do?

It was a trap to make it seem as if Fritz was attempting to interfere in political affairs he was forbidden to touch. But it was so ridiculous for him to be forbidden! He wasn't the Regent, but he was the Crown Prince, and as such, ought to have a position in the government.

Mama had written that she felt sure Austria had done nothing to break the treaties which existed, and yet Bismarck marched on towards war.

Vicky sighed deeply, trying to calm herself. She must not upset herself. Things were difficult enough with the war looming over them. She only hoped and prayed Fritz would not have to go before the baby was born.

She was avoiding the family dinners at the Schloss, or anywhere else. Even with Prince Charles away in Mainz, these were far too stressful. Fritz had told her that there had been several scenes with Fritz Karl, and several arguments between him and the King.

"Papa asked Fritz Karl to host one of the dinners," Fritz had told her. "He refused, and there was a violent scene between them – violent in words, not in action, though it could have become so."

Maroussy was in Berlin again. Fritz had been at the dinner the evening after her arrival, at which she sat between Prince Charles and Prince Albrecht, Prince Charles being back in Berlin for a week.

"Poor Maroussy," Vicky said to Fritz. "I remember how incredibly difficult that situation is!" At her second dinner in Berlin, Vicky had been in this same situation. "I hope you helped her?"

Fritz smiled and made a little gesture as if dropping something. Vicky laughed at the memory of her first state dinner, when Fritz had broken a dish on purpose to distract Prince Charles.

***

Midnight, Kronprinz Palais, Berlin, April 12, 1866

"Fritz?" Vicky shook Fritz's arm as a pain clutched her back. "Fritz?"

"What is it?" Fritz yawned.

"I think the baby is coming," she said. "And we are still here." Vicky had wished to be in Potsdam, at the Neues Palais, for the birth, not in Berlin. "I think we have time to go if we go now."

Fritz nodded, yawning enormously as he disappeared into his dressing-room.

She leaned against him as they hurried to their carriage. The children would all be asleep. They could be sent for tomorrow.

"Oh," she groaned, as the carriage went over another bump.

"Here we are," Fritz said, helping her down from the carriage and into the night train. It was half past twelve in the morning.

On the train, half past four in the morning.

Fritz lay down on the sofa in the sleeping car, unable to keep his eyes open. They had both rested for a couple of hours. He, at least, had gotten some sleep. He was not sure if Vicky had. When he had woken again, she was up, pacing slowly up and down the train car. She sat down beside him, leaning against him.

"Oh," she groaned. "I wish we were at home."

"Do you wish we had stayed in Berlin?" Fritz asked.

"No. I do not wish to be in Berlin for this birth any more than you do. It is another of your presentiments, I suppose. But I feel it is very important." She groaned again as the train lurched. "Oh, Fritz, I do wish we were home. I think the time is drawing nearer!"

***

"*Meine* Vicky," Fritz murmured, trying to sooth her. "We are nearly there." She sat next to him in the carriage. The Neues Palais was in sight.

"I don't think – I can – wait!" she cried. "I mean I don't think I can walk all the way in!"

Fritz nodded. The carriage came to a stop at the entrance. Fritz hurried out, returning quickly, followed by footmen carrying a stretcher. "To the nearest bedroom; that will have to do," Fritz ordered, gently lifting her onto the stretcher.

***

Neues Palais, April 12, 1866

"Wah! Wah!"

They had made it to the nearest bedroom, Vicky's maids being hurriedly sent for. The baby was born ten minutes after their arrival. The birth had passed quite easily, despite the baby's size. Wegner had been in the room, as well as the midwife, Fraulein Stahl, but neither had much to do.

Nothing being prepared, the baby had been wrapped in one of Vicky's old petticoats.

"Miss Victoria," Vicky murmured, clasping the baby to her heart. She looked up at Fritz. "Mama wished the next girl to be called Victoria," she whispered.

Fritz sat by her side, taking the baby in his arms to study her face. Her skin was a light brown, very different from what the others had been. She was an enormous child, weighing nearly ten pounds – nearly three pounds more than any of the others. Her little fingers grasped his with a strength he had not thought possible in a newborn. When she lay on her stomach on the bed, she lifted her head to look around.

"She's a little warrioress," Vicky murmured, letting her grasp her finger as she took her back.

"What shall we call her?" Fritz asked. "I mean, what other names shall she have?"

"I should like her to have Frederica Wilhelmina," Vicky said. "There ought to be no question of your claiming her as your own." She paused. "We should talk the name over with your Papa, when he comes to see her."

"And what shall we call her? Not Vicky –" Fritz said, lying down on the bed and looking into the baby's blue eyes. "*Meine kleines*[23] *Möhrchen*", he whispered, stroking the baby's blond hair.

Neues Palais, April 13, 1866

"Fritz, is this really what you sent to Mama?" Vicky called, waving a piece of paper as he closed the bedroom door.

Fritz looked at her. "*Ja*. Of course. What is the matter with it?"

"You wrote 'delivered from a daughter', not 'delivered of a daughter'." Vicky laughed heartily, and the baby squealed. "I don't mean to laugh at your English," she said, looking up and taking his hand. "You speak it and write it so well now, and even to make jokes. But you know Mama and I – and all of us – find it very hard not to laugh. But you laugh just as much about people who don't speak German fluently."

Fritz nodded, squeezing her hand. He sat down by her side, laying the baby in her arms.

"What did everyone say? Who was there?" Vicky asked eagerly.

"Papa was very kind, but hardly even looked at her. I must say I was rather glad. He approved the names we had chosen, and would like Amalia to be added, too."

Vicky nodded. "Who else saw her?"

Fritz turned uneasily, leaning his head on his hand, covering his eyes. "Fritz Karl," he almost whispered.

Vicky rolled her eyes. "What did he say?"

Vicky flinched as Fritz's hand clenched. He closed his eyes, and shook his head. "Nothing you need to hear, and nothing I am going to repeat," he said firmly. Vicky nodded. "George – Papa's cousin – was there, too, but

---

[23]   My little

he was quite uninterested and only wished to speak of the war, and of Bismarck's illness, which he has great sympathy for."

***

Neues Palais, April 14, 1866

"Oh, she is beautiful," Marianne murmured, taking the baby in her arms. "Victoria, you call her? You name her well. She is worthy of your name, and your Mama's, and she is a little warrior, and would certainly be victorious, she is so strong." Marianne smiled as the baby clung to her fingers. "Have the children seen her?"

"No, we came here in such a hurry, nothing was ready. The children shall be here tomorrow. They're still in Berlin." Vicky paused, watching the baby's face as Marianne stroked her hair. "I would like to call her little Vicky, but of course that would cause confusion for Fritz and for Mama and my *Geschwichter*, so she'll probably have more than one pet name." Vicky looked away. "Fritz calls her Möhrchen." Vicky wasn't sure what to say. She hadn't told Marianne about what had happened.

"Vicky, I know – I know – everything about what happened to you last August. I know – far more than I, or you – wish to know." She met Vicky's eye, her face flushing.

Vicky looked at her, willing her to go on. She didn't want to ask questions, but she felt as if she knew what Marianne would say next.

"Fritz Karl," Marianne went on, leaning her head down on the pillow and half hiding her face, "Fritz Karl – when he was very drunk, he told me – all about it." Marianne shuddered. "He let everything out. And, oh, Vicky, he spoke of it in front of the girls!" Marianne's hand shook, and a look of intense pain crossed her face. "Mariechen and Ebi. Louischen wasn't there." Marianne quickly kissed Vicky's cheek, and turned away, hurrying to the door. She turned back. "Your little girl is lovely," she said, forcing herself to smile, and hurried away.

Vicky felt sleepy, but there was another knock at the door. It opened, and Fritz appeared, Abbat following him. Abbat knelt down at the bedside, taking the baby carefully in his arms. There was a look Vicky had never seen in his eyes as he looked down at the little face. "*Kleine* Vicky," he whispered, and laid her back in Vicky's arms. He met Vicky's eye, bent to kiss her cheek, and turned to embrace Fritz.

"Abbat," Vicky called, as he went to the door. He turned back. She beckoned to him, and took his hand when he knelt down again. "*Danke,*" she said. "Thank you for going with me. You did everything you could. May God's Will be done." She smiled up at Fritz as Abbat turned to go again. "God gave us a daughter," she whispered, squeezing Fritz's hand.

PART TWO:
VICTORY AND LOSS

CHAPTER NINE
COUNCILS AND CHRISTENINGS

Neues Palais, April 16, 1866

"Come see your new sister," Vicky encouraged. The children gathered around her.

"Why does the baby look so strange?" Willy asked. "I always thought they were pale, like Siggy was."

"She's not pretty," Charlotte cried, putting her arms behind her when Vicky tried to place the baby in her arms.

"Won't kiss *that*!" Henry said, shaking his head.

Vicky sighed and shook her head. Mrs. Hobbs put Siggy on the bed. He crawled toward the baby, staring at her face. The baby opened her eyes, staring up at him. Their eyes were locked for several seconds.

Siggy's arm buckled, and he rolled over towards Vicky, giggling and smiling up at her. "Ma-ma, ah, Bay Bay pitty," he said in his usual slow way, taking an obvious breath between almost every syllable.

Vicky sighed, and nodded to Mrs. Hobbs, who took the older children away. Vicky hugged her babies to her. They were such a comfort during a time like this.

Vicky did not feel strong after the birth. When she tried to rise, or even to sit up for very long, a strange dizziness and rushing noise in her head overtook her. She couldn't bear the excitement of the long, important political conversations she knew were so urgent just now.

Fritz was away so much, but this was understandable.

War seemed drawing closer and closer. No efforts at mediation seemed to help. The Government continued to view Austria as having broken their treaties of the year before, although it was clear to others that they had done no such thing. Both Mama and the Tsar Alexander had attempted to point this out to Fritz's father, but to no avail.

Besides all of this, Sophie Dobeneck, one of the nursery attendants for the children, was getting married. She was very happy, and Vicky was glad for her, but having any of her people leave at a time like this was terrible. She knew if the war came, she would be quite alone, with very few friends. It was terrible, indeed to think of Alice and Louis being on the opposite side of the war.

Mama wrote often about Lenchen, Christian being in England for a visit, and also about the engagement of Mary, Mama's cousin, who was only about eight years Vicky's senior but was only now getting engaged. The letters were a comfort and distraction, but couldn't take Vicky's anxiety away.

***

May 7, 1866

"There was an attempt on Bismarck," Fritz told Vicky as he came in. "Papa was extremely upset. Bismarck is perfectly fine."

Vicky looked up at him, unable to speak. She didn't wish to say the thoughts which flashed through her mind.

"Papa's windows were broken by stones when I was with him. It was very strange. Everything seemed perfectly quiet and peaceful outside, as if no one was there, and the few people in the streets did not seem to notice anything. It reminds me of the beginning of the Revolution in '48."

Fritz's face was tense as he bent over Vicky to kiss her and the baby. "There is no more hope against the war," he said, taking Vicky's hand and kissing it as he sat beside her. "There is no more hope," he repeated, shaking his head.

"You sound like your mother," Vicky whispered. "*She* said *that*, when she came to see me before going to see Vivi before the war begins. But where shall Vivi be during the war? Baden will be on the other side, too." Vicky closed her eyes. She was too tired to think about all of this, but it was impossible for her not to. "What would Papa say to all of this? How I wish we could ask his advice," she whispered, sniffing as tears came to her eyes.

"Now you sound like *your* mother," Fritz said, smiling but serious. "Louis comes here tomorrow. Do you wish to see him?"

Vicky covered her eyes, struggling not to burst into tears. "Of course! But it seems – it is too dreadful, to be on the other side from them," she sobbed.

***

May 9, 1866

Italy, Prussia and Austria had all called for the troops to be mobilized.

For Vicky it was hard to do anything but cry. She was feeling better and stronger physically, but the anxiety at the thought of Fritz's going was overwhelming. He would be in the war in a different way this time. He would be one of the army commanders this time, instead of being in the Headquarters entourage.

Baby was doing well, and growing amazingly. Her christening would be on May 24th, Mama's birthday. Vicky smiled. *Miss Victoria*. Mama had so much wanted her first granddaughter to be named Victoria, but Vicky hadn't been able to bear the thought of calling Charlotte Victoria. Alice's little girl was the first Victoria in this generation.

Vicky had written to Mama about the Godparents, or sponsors, as they said in Prussia. Mama would, naturally, be one, and Vicky had asked Arthur to be. Mama had written that Louise was much upset by this, as Arthur was younger than her. Bertie had been Willy's Godfather. Alice was Charlotte's Godmother. Affie and Lenchen both were for Henry, and Alix and Louis for Siggy. It did appear as if she had overlooked Louise, but Vicky felt she knew Louise so little. Louise rarely wrote to her, and never confided in her when Vicky was in England. Vicky often felt that Louise overlooked her. She knew Louise kept up a regular correspondence with Alice, and with Bertie, Affie and Arthur when they were away.

On the Prussian side, Fritz's parents and Aunt Elisa, Vivi and Fritz of Baden were to be sponsors. It was the first time they had only those whom she and Fritz really wished for. With Willy, Charlotte and Henry they had been expected to have more or less the whole Prussian Royal family as sponsors. That made it so impersonal, but, with many, Vicky wouldn't have wanted a more personal relationship for her children.

She had also asked Uncle Ernst and some of the other Coburg relations, and Maroussy.

***

Neues Palais, Potsdam, May 23, 1866

"Vicky, it's good to see you." Vicky felt a shiver go down her spine, and tried to hold back the tears which sprang to her eyes. Uncle Ernst's voice was so like Papa's.

"And you, Uncle," Vicky said, going to him and holding up her cheek to be kissed.

As she embraced him, and felt his mustache tickle her cheek, a strange sensation came over her. Her head swam. There was a vague image in her mind, but she couldn't quite make it out – she saw several people but only as if they were shadows; all men, she thought, but one. She heard a jabber of words which must be in a foreign language, and saw a strange blur of red. Then she saw the woman's dress again, and something covered her face.

She drew away from Uncle Ernst, raising her hand to her face. She looked up, and saw him watching her with a serious expression.

She jumped as Fritz took her arm. "Onkel," he said, looking at Uncle Ernst. "You are here as our ally, I have heard?"

Vicky's head still swam as she followed Fritz, trying to listen to his conversation with Uncle Ernst. She knew it had suddenly been announced that Coburg would be fighting on the Prussian side. Everyone had expected it to be otherwise.

The strange sensation overwhelmed her again, and she had a sudden urge to wash her face. They had come to her sitting-room, and she hurried to her basin in her dressing-room. She shook her head. She would go back and try to listen to the conversation. She didn't want to concentrate on – and possibly awaken – the memories which were trying to force themselves upon her.

"Fritz," Fritz heard Vicky whisper, as she lay down by his side. She had left the baby in her cradle for the first time tonight.

Fritz turned to face her, reaching out to draw her closer, but he realized she was wearing her dressing-gown as well as her nightgown.

"Are you cold?" he asked, kissing her forehead.

"No," she whispered, moving closer, and laying her head on his shoulder. "I'm – oh, something is trying to – I can't remember," she said, groaning as she covered her eyes. She shuddered, wiping her hands across her face. "Since I met Uncle Ernst this morning, I haven't felt well, something –" She shuddered again.

Fritz sighed, wondering what he should say. He put his arm around Vicky, kissing her forehead again. "Do you wish to know?" he asked seriously. He tried to meet her eye, but there was the strange, blank expression he had seen so often before and after Charlotte's birth. His heart ached.

"Yes," she said suddenly. "I wish to know. It is better than – this."

"In Coburg, after you were at Glienicke," Fritz began slowly, gently rubbing her back, "do you remember the first day?"

"I remember arriving at Coburg and first seeing Mama, I think," Vicky said, covering her eyes again. "I hardly remember anything else until the unveiling, and our photographs being taken."

Fritz nodded. "You do not remember greeting Onkel Ernst?"

She shook her head, and then froze. "Did – I try to – to –" Fritz felt her shudder. "Kiss him," she whispered, almost inaudibly.

Fritz nodded. She hid her face against his chest. "You were not yourself," he murmured. "You were not responsible for your actions."

"I know. But I haven't told you what Marianne said when she was here a few days ago," she whispered. "But – it is such a different feeling – than – about – Charlotte."

"What did Marianne say?" Fritz asked, holding Vicky in his arms and rubbing her back as she began to speak.

"Vicky," Marianne had whispered as she sat down beside Vicky on the sofa, "I wish to speak to you, and without the little ones. They must not – I cannot speak of it with them here."

Vicky rose, and went into the bedroom. "Come. The little ones will be fine here for a few minutes. Siggy is so good with her, and it brings him to life. Did you see how he watches her, and tries to make sure everything is safe for her? He never wants to be away from her. And he walks with a purpose now. He only fell twice yesterday, and he speaks better, too." She smiled. "Being a big brother is what he needed, I guess. It brings out a streak of determination in him which was never there before."

Marianne nodded, smiling. "It is so sweet to see Louischen with the boy." She could speak calmly of "the boy" now, Vicky noticed. "But it is very different, of course, as she has always been so fluent and able, from so early. But I must –" Her face suddenly grew tense, and she rose, walked the length of the room, and returned. "I must tell you." She shook her head. "I know I shouldn't; I spoke to your Fritz about it. He doesn't wish to awaken your memories of – but I feel it is important you should know. I don't know why, but I feel I must tell you!"

"What Fritz Karl told you? You said he told you – *everything*," Vicky shuddered.

Marianne nodded. "I will *not* tell you *everything*. But – you were not – unconscious," she said, obviously searching for the appropriate words. "They gave you something else."

Vicky nodded. "Fritz seemed to suspect such a thing. I don't wish to think about it." She looked at Marianne. "How much did the girls hear?"

"Mariechen and Ebi were there when he began," Marianne said, wringing her hands, her expression growing painful again. "I told them not to listen, and Mariechen covered her ears, as she always does when I say that. I got them away. They didn't hear very much."

Fritz jumped awake. Vicky shuddered in his arms, writhing in her sleep, attempting to struggle away from his embrace. "Ugh," she groaned, wiping her face with her hands. She clutched the blanket to her, curling into a ball. She began to shiver.

Fritz sat up, rubbing her back gently. "Vicky?" He shook her gently awake.

"*Ach*, ugh, hands," she murmured. "Fritz?"

"I did not wish you to continue the dream," he murmured. "Vicky, take my hands." He did not want to touch her unexpectedly, as he guessed what her dream was. "You are awake?"

"Fritz? I'm awake." Vicky yawned, and turned towards him, putting her hands in his.

"*Gut.*" He sighed as she pulled his arms around her and settled down. Soon, she was sleeping peacefully.

***

Berlin, May 26, 1866

"Serve *Gott* and serve your King! I have firm faith in my army, my cavalry, and my artillery. I know I can expect the best because of who is in the lead!"

Fritz stood, holding his horse's bridal at the head of his regiment, listening to his father's speech. The King stepped forward. Fritz did so too, holding out his hand.

He watched in confusion as his father turned the other way, walked across the field, and shook hands with Onkel Karl. He returned to his place, and went on with his next speech, addressing Fritz Karl's regiment.

At the end, the King again crossed the field, shook hands with Onkel Karl, and returned to his place.

Fritz shook his head. The King looked about, probably expecting the troops to cheer, but everything remained silent. Fritz stepped forwards. "Papa," he murmured. "You've not spoken to me."

His father stared at him for a moment, took his hand, shook it, and turned away.

Fritz returned to his place, and began his own speech to his regiment. He couldn't let the review end in this awkward manner.

The Christening had gone well. It had been a smaller gathering, compared to the other Christenings. Willy and Charlotte were still ignoring the baby, but Henry had begun to take an interest in his little sister.

There had been a "Council of War" the next day, with all the highest Generals, and all of Fritz's and Fritz Karl's staff. Onkel Ernst had also been present. He had spoken firmly, standing up for the southern states in many subtle ways even though he had "changed colors," as Vicky said her mother had written.

But today, there had been another council, and Onkel Ernst had spoken quietly, and asked for Bismarck's advice in many matters. His manner had changed; he seemed more subdued and more boisterous at the same time.

Fritz thought of his father-in-law. The two brothers had always been very different; Prince Albert always had a quieter, more reserved manner, even in moments of excitement. But this exaggerated manner Onkel Ernst showed was not a good sign. It reminded Fritz of his mother's strange moods, and of Fritz Karl.

***

Neues Palais, Potsdam, June 8, 1866

Fritz crouched down in the midst of the children, kissing Wilhelm and Charlotte. Heinrich still clung to his leg, sobbing.

"Pa-pa go bye?" Siggy toddled towards him, reaching up his hands. Fritz rose, lifting him up, kissing the sweet, smiling face. "Siggy love Pa-pa." Fritz sat down on the bed next to Vicky. "Love Ma-ma," Siggy said, reaching towards Vicky. "Bay Bay."

Fritz lay down, looking at the Baby, who lay on her stomach, crawling across the bed. She was already so big, although she was only two months old, and so strong. She lifted her head to look at him.

He turned, taking Vicky's arm. He bent to kiss Wilhelm and Charlotte again, feeling tears fill his eyes.

Four days earlier, he had gone with his father to Schloss Fürstenstein, in Silesia, in Prussian-Poland. This was to be his headquarters. He was back in Berlin the next day.

But now, it was time for the real goodbye. Vicky had cried so much in the last month, she had told him, on his departure on the fourth, she felt she could cry no more.

"Fritz," Vicky whispered, throwing her arms around his neck and kissing him. She looked up at him, and tears filled her eyes. Neither of them could speak. He bent down and kissed her, turned, and left the room.

"Mein Schatz[24],

"I can hardly believe I am writing to you, knowing again that you will not return – for who knows how long. I still feel the same horrible numbness as when you first left for headquarters.

"I dreamed last night – not the nightmare you woke me from, but another – and a worse one, in a way. I dreamed of a battlefield covered with arms and legs. I woke quickly – I never have difficulty waking from that kind of nightmare – and thought – thank God it was a dream!

"The children are all quite well, only Siggy has a bit of a fever and discomfort with his teeth. Not even Baby can cheer him."

---

[24]   My darling

CHAPTER TEN
THE GREATEST PAIN

Neues Palais, June 10, 1866

Vicky hovered over Siggy's little bed. He lay, burning hot, and, for the most part, perfectly still. She had stayed up all night watching him. He had rarely slept, and occasionally gave a short, extremely high-pitched cry, stretching his little arms up to her.

She had lifted him up, cradling him in her arms. Finally, he went to sleep. Vicky changed her clothes and washed thoroughly. She must not risk spreading any illness to the baby. She couldn't let Siggy be with the baby now, although talking about her was the only thing which would bring out his familiar smiles. Vicky's heart ached at the pained look on the little boy's face, even in his sleep.

She felt exhausted, but she could hardly sleep with worry. Baby was strong and vigorous, but needed frequent feeding. Vicky was insistent again that she would nurse her as she had Siggy, but with this worry about Siggy, Fritz being gone to the war, and her simply not being quite recovered from the birth, it felt rather draining.

She lay in bed, cradling the baby in her arms, watching her face, pressing her to her heart. She sighed. Nursing was so calming and soothing in itself. She thought of Fritz. He would be in Silesia now. He had written that they did not expect a battle for at least a few days.

Schloss Fürstenstein, Silesia, June 14, 1866
"*Meine* Vicky,

"Things are going well here. I had a long conversation with Fritz Karl the day before my departure, of which I had not the time to tell you.

"He spoke quite peaceably, and concerned about the formation of the army. He is in the lead of the First Army, and, as you know, I am in command of the Second. He is concerned that his army is not large enough to take on the Austrian troops.

"I hope to be able to reassure him. I hope to remain on good terms with him during this time, but of course, that can never be counted on.

"I feel quite secure in our troops, and *Gott* will be with us. His Will be done.

"I hope Siggy is no longer feverish. Give *die Kinder*[25] Papa's best love, and even more to your own dear self."

Fritz sat in the room which was his combined study and bedroom. Schloss Fürstenstein was large and comfortable, with plenty of room. Leopold Sigmaringen was his aide-de-camp and companion this time, Karl having been elected as the Prince and possible future King of Rumania.

He yawned. He had written to Vicky before going to bed, as he always did when he was away. He yawned again, rising from his seat, when there was a knock at the door.

"*Herein*[26]," he called, and the door opened. A messenger set something on the table by the door. "It is urgent," he said, and closed the door.

Fritz read the message, and leaned his head on the table, murmuring a prayer. Siggy was extremely, seriously ill.

There was a battle expected in the next two days, and Fritz felt there was no one who could take his place. Prussia's fate hung in the balance in this war. Defeat might mean the end of their existence as a state and dynasty.

He lay down, praying for Siggy and for Vicky. She was so alone, and he could not return to her.

---

[25]   The children
[26]   Come in

Neues Palais, June 16, 1866

Vicky knelt on the floor, watching Siggy. He lay with his neck and head held stiffly back, his eyes fixed looking downwards, his arms and legs twitching and jerking uncontrollably. The high-pitched cry was very frequent now.

Vicky felt helpless, watching her little boy suffer. What could she do? All of the court physicians had left with the army; the doctor she had been able to obtain a visit from knew little about childhood illnesses.

There was a knock at the door. Vicky hurried to open it. "He is no better," Vicky said dully. She had wept so much in the last months, she had felt she couldn't cry any more, but another flood of tears had come last night.

The night time, with Baby in her arms, was the only peaceful time. Mrs. Hobbs stayed with Siggy, promising to wake her if she was needed.

Fritz's mother had also come and sat with her. Vicky had never seen her so kind and tender. Vicky knew she loved the children, but her tenderness was usually directed solely towards them, not towards her. Now, her kindness broke Vicky down again, and she had wept in her arms.

"Oh, I would give anyth – no, no!" Vicky sobbed. She had been going to say "I would give anything to have him better", but she couldn't say that – she couldn't think that – when Fritz was in the war. That thought was too intolerably horrible, and sent her off into another flood of tears.

Vicky received Fritz's letters, but they were all full of military details she couldn't read right now. She was glad for his sake that he had the distraction of other things to think about. He would, by this time, have received her first telegram about Siggy's illness.

"In you, the soldier's duty takes first place," she wrote. "It must be, at a time like this." She read over the lines. Ought she to write in this way? She read them over again. It sounded bitter and hard. But she could write so little, her heart was so heavy.

Schloss Neisse, Saxony, June 17, 1866
"*Meine* Vicky,

"We have Civil war in Germany before war with Austria. We have declared war on and invaded Hanover, Electorate Hesse and Saxony. I hear that the King of Hanover has fled to England, and Hanover is in the hands of the Prussians. We have moved our headquarters to Neisse, and shall soon be on the move.

"My heart is very heavy when I think of our little boy, and my thoughts and prayers go out to you. May Gott keep you and the other children safe and well! The thought of you, alone and so sorely tried, weighs deeply on my heart, but I must keep to my post, and not give way."

Neues Palais, June 18, 1866

Vicky lay still on the sofa. She felt as if she couldn't move. Nothing would ever be the same again.

Siggy lay still in her arms, his neck still stiff and his poor little hands reaching out pleadingly. She clung to the warm little body, barely aware of what was around her.

"Vicky, let me take him, you can do no more now," Fritz's mother said in a tone which pierced through her grief. Vicky looked up, seeing her mother-in-law kneeling by her side with tears in her own eyes. "You must rest now, and stay well for your little ones."

Vicky felt arms go around her, and vaguely heard Mrs. Hobbs saying something in a choked voice. She lay still, blinded by tears as she felt them take Siggy from her arms. He was beginning to grow cold.

All day she lay there, hardly aware of what went on around her. Someone lifted her head and helped her to drink a bit of water. Towards night, she rose, going mechanically to change her dress and wash. She must be able to care for Baby.

The sight of Siggy's dreadful convulsions hung in her mind and would not go away.

Finally, Mrs. Hobbs brought Baby to her. Vicky lifted her in her arms, clutching her close to her. "My precious baby," she whispered, hungry for the touch of a warm, loving little one. She lay awake, watching Baby's face, feeling a glow of love for her she hadn't felt before.

Baby was a precious little thing, but there had been something, something very slight, hanging between her and the love she had been able to give Siggy. She nursed little Vicky as she had Siggy, but still, the passion of affection she had given him hadn't come. Now, it overwhelmed her as she pressed her cheek to the soft golden hair on Baby's head.

Headquarters, Neisse, June 1866

Fritz knelt next to his bed, leaning his head on his hands on the bed. He could not bear to face anyone tonight. He had asked Leopold Sigmaringen to leave the room.

He must be alone, alone with his grief, alone, as he had left Vicky. That fact tore at his heart as he read the telegram again.

How could he have done this, how could he have abandoned his wife and his child at this most critical time?

He thought of the last sight of little Siggy, his dear little smile and the last words he had heard him speak. "Siggy love Pa-pa… love Ma-ma; Bay Bay." He would never see him again.

There was a knock at the door. Fritz struggled to control himself, but deep sobs tore through him which he could not control. A pain clutched him as he tried to breathe normally, and he felt almost nauseated as he finally stood. He went to the door.

"*Eure Hoheit*[27]." General Blumenthal, his Chief of Staff, stood there. "Your Highness, I know what it is. I lost my boy a few years ago, when I was away and my wife was quite alone. You bear it much better than I did," Blumenthal went on, his eyes filled with tears. Usually, Blumenthal was gruff, unexpressive of any deeper emotion. Fritz knelt down by the bed again. He opened his mouth to speak, but the tightness in his chest was almost painful. He looked up at Blumenthal, nodded quickly, and motioned to the door. Blumenthal nodded. "I know what it is, but I wanted you to know you have sympathy." He opened the door. "I had very little, when I went through it."

Fritz rose slowly, and locked the door. He must be alone. Even such true sympathy, born out of common experience, was too painful to bear.

---

[27]   Your Highness

***

June 19, 1866

Fritz struggled out of bed at dawn. He must be up and ready for whatever came. They were expecting a battle very soon.

His head ached from crying, and he felt more exhausted than when he had gone to bed. He ate mechanically, speaking to no one.

At noon, he heard a train. This was, of course, not uncommon. The troops were still being organized, but he should go out to see who it was.

He couldn't make himself go out. Not yet. He could not face so many eyes on him, whether in sympathy or not. He did not wish to break down in front of the men.

There was a knock at his door, and he went to open it.

"Fritz." It was his mother.

Neues Palais, June 1866

Vicky still lay in bed. Mrs. Hobbs had brought her food, but she had been unable to take anything but a little water. Her head ached as if she had spent the night in tears, but no more tears would come.

After Mrs. Hobbs had taken Baby for her bath, Vicky rose, putting her hand to her head. The dizziness went away, and she went to the next room, where Siggy's little bed was. She gathered the rattle which lay on the floor, tossed away by his little hand, and his little clothes he had worn before his illness. She clutched the bundle to her, returning to bed. She must have something to hug.

Siggy's life had been so short, but it had been happy. Nothing had been spared which gave him joy or comfort. It was so painfully sad to think how well he had been progressing those last few weeks since Baby's birth. He had begun to speak more clearly, had walked without falling. Vicky had so much hope for him. But it was all over.

She wrote to Mama – a brief letter. She couldn't bear to write any details, but longed to be in her mother's arms, and to hear her voice.

She had written to Fritz, but she felt as if she didn't know how to write to him anymore. His letters were so absorbed in military matters, she felt detached and abandoned, but she must write something.

Fritz's mother had left for Headquarters to see Fritz. She had been certain he would come back with her for the funeral. Vicky felt a dull ache at the thought. The meeting with Fritz would be so overpoweringly sad, she felt she couldn't bear it, even though she longed for it more than anything else.

Headquarters, Neisse, June 20, 1866

Fritz sat on his bed, his head in his hands. Mama had been so kind. Her tenderness had touched him deeply – the look on her face, the tears brimming in her eyes as she told him of Siggy's last hours.

She had expected him to return with her, to be at the funeral and support Vicky. Papa, too, had given him leave to do so.

But how could he do so? War had been declared on Austria now, and the troops had been ordered to march to Bohemia. He could not abandon his post.

Neues Palais, June 1866

"Where's Fritz?" Vicky demanded.

"He could not leave his post," Fritz's mother said, putting her arms around Vicky.

"He couldn't leave his post? But he must come! I can't live like this!" Vicky cried, tearing herself away from the embrace and throwing herself on the bed again. "The funeral is all ready, but he must be here!"

Her mother-in-law sat on the edge of the bed, stroking her head. "Vicky, listen to me." Vicky looked up at her, but realized her voice was gentle, with none of her usual tone of command. "Fritz was bowed down with grief, as well as worry over you and the baby. But he must serve our country. He cannot leave his post. It is of utmost importance to our existence."

Vicky couldn't speak. She had gone through all the arrangements for the funeral alone, without help – only guided by what she remembered of Grandmama's funeral. Mrs. Hobbs had never been at a deathbed before.

Now, she would have to go alone. But no, she would take Willy with her.

***

The bells rang mournfully as Vicky's carriage drove towards the Friedenskirche. Her eyes were dry, her face set. She simply couldn't cry any more. Willy sat across from her, his face tear-stained.

Normally, Vicky would have been annoyed at the footmen giving Willy the position in the carriage facing the horses. This was the place always given in processions to the highest-ranking person in the carriage. The servants were always trying to flatter Willy, making a fuss of him, making a show of helping him before her and giving him rank over his mother when he was only a child. Vicky had always made a point of his getting into the carriage last, not wishing to pamper the vanity they were trying to instill, but this time, she didn't care. Willy didn't either, she could see.

The ceremony was a blur. The fact that her little boy was being buried, never to return, still seemed unbelievable.

At home, Vicky still lay in bed, barely eating. That night, she heard whispers and saw the light of a lantern.

She turned away. She didn't want to speak to anyone. She clutched Baby closer to her, but Baby began to cry and struggle.

Mrs. Hobbs appeared at the door, hovering uncertainly. "Yer 'Ighness, the children har so worried habout you. Can they come to see you?"

Vicky didn't move.

"Yer 'Ighness, if you don't heat or drink, you won't be hable to feed yer liddle 'un," she said quietly, stepping closer to Vicky's bedside. "She's been cryin' with 'unger hall the day".

Vicky turned. "Yes, Mrs. Hobbs. Please, bring me some soup."

Mrs. Hobbs nodded. "Can the children come?"

"Yes. And light a lamp, please."

Mrs. Hobbs did so, and then left the room. Vicky sat up, leaning back on the pillows, fastening her nightgown. She heard footsteps, and looked up. Willy, Charlotte, and Henry appeared at the door, and ran to her.

"Mama," Willy cried, "you seemed so unwell today, I couldn't help asking Mrs. Hobbs if you were going to die, like Siggy," he sobbed.

"Is Mama sick?" Henry asked, scrambling up onto the bed.

"You aren't going to die, are you?" Charlotte cried, throwing her arms around her mother's neck.

Vicky hugged them to her. "No, I am not sick. I am only sad and lonely. Papa didn't come home, and I miss him so much, as well as Siggy." She took Charlotte's hand, drawing her closer. "Wouldn't you like to see your little sister?" Vicky lifted Baby, holding her up.

"She is looking nicer," Charlotte said slowly, but didn't hold out her arms. Vicky saw her glance at Willy.

"Charlotte," Vicky said, a little sharply, "does Mrs. Hobbs – or anyone – tell you anything strange about Baby?" She spoke formally in her haste, saying "Charlotte" and "Mrs. Hobbs" rather than "Ditta" and "Hobby" or "Hobbsy".

"Why, no, of course not," Charlotte said uncertainly, her eyes wide.

"She says that she's not – well, she is our sister, but –" Willy began, trailing off, a blush on his cheeks.

Vicky looked at the children. What should she tell them? They were so young, but they must know someday. If they were old enough to ask such questions…

Vicky and Fritz had always made it plain to the children that they wished to have nothing to do with Prince Charles. They were not too young to understand at least somewhat. She would only speak generally, and answer whatever questions came as best she could, without frightening them.

"Come here," Vicky said, moving into the middle of the bed and beckoning to the children. "I must tell you something," she said slowly, looking at Charlotte.

CHAPTER ELEVEN
BROTHER AGAINST BROTHER

Neues Palais, June 1866

"Willy, do you remember when Henry was born? We had you and Ditta with us."

Willy looked at her, his face very serious. He shook his head.

"You understand where babies come from, don't you?" Vicky asked gently, putting her arms around Willy and Charlotte. Henry sat in front of her, with Baby in his arms.

"We have seen the birth of a little lamb at the farm," Charlotte said quietly.

"And of a litter of puppies," Willy said. "And I watched an egg hatch."

Vicky nodded. "You understand the process of the birth. But were you ever there when they brought the ram and ewe together for breeding?"

Charlotte's cheeks reddened, and she hid her face. "Y-yes, Mama," she whispered.

"It – it looked – so painful," Willy said, shuddering.

"But for a man and woman," Vicky began, "It's different. God created a man and a woman. They were to come together in love. I don't mean the kind of love we have for each other – siblings to siblings or parents to children – but a very different thing. Many people call this physical intimacy love, but it in itself is not love. It's when the couple both love each other and care for each other that it's a beautiful thing."

She paused. "Charlotte, you've been reading so many of my old books about animals. You know, some animals have many mates, and some only have one. Do either of you know what this is called?"

"Mon – mongom – mongomy," Charlotte struggled to say the word.

"Monogamy," Vicky said, nodding. "But for people, we call it 'faithfulness' or 'fidelity'. God created some animals with this instinct, and some have many mates."

"What is 'stinct?" Henry asked.

"Natural behaviors which God created creatures to have. The animals *must* behave according to their instincts. They don't think like people do. When they come into contact with something which stimulates a certain behavior, they must act on it. If animals didn't do this, there wouldn't be any more of them.

"But for people, it's different. We can make conscious choices," she went on. She looked up. Henry had slumped forward, falling asleep. He had looked tired when the children first came in. Baby, too, slept peacefully. "We, too, have instincts, but we have to make choices, and learn to avoid temptations, and –" She trailed off, not sure what to say next.

"When one is somewhere around twice your age," she nodded at Charlotte, "perhaps a bit later – one's body begins to change. You know the differences between my body and yours, Charlotte. But there are internal changes, too, as one's body becomes mature. One begins to change, and it becomes possible for all of this to happen, and for a baby to grow inside of the mother." *Sometimes it is possible earlier,* Vicky thought, her thoughts going to Ebi.

Willy looked up at her. "Only married people do this, don't they?"

Vicky felt herself blush. "We believe that only married people – and by that I mean people married *to each other – ought* to do so. That is monogamy, or fidelity, or faithfulness." She paused. "Willy, do you remember when you saw Papa accidentally kiss Aunt Anna, thinking it was me?" Willy nodded. "Kissing – *that* kind of kissing – is part of all of this, and that's what I meant. I said people have to resist temptations. Papa would never have done so if he realized it wasn't me, but she often tries to kiss him."

There was a knock at the door. "Mrs. Hobbs?" Vicky called. The door opened, and Mrs. Hobbs appeared with a tray and a bowl of soup. Vicky took it. It was good to eat again, after eating so little.

"But, isn't it painful? Like for the animals?" Willy asked as the door closed. "I watched the chickens, and I felt so sorry for the poor little hen. The cock is so mean, grabbing her neck and –" He broke off, shuddering.

Vicky nodded. "That's what I must speak of," she said, sighing deeply. "It shouldn't be. I said, when a couple loves each other, and is married, it's a beautiful thing. You will understand this when you're older."

"But, what about –" Charlotte began, and then buried her face against Vicky's shoulder again.

Vicky sighed heavily. "What about Baby?" she asked gently. Charlotte nodded, not looking up.

"Hobby said Baby isn't Papa's child," Willy said.

Vicky nodded. "You said you felt sorry for the little hen," she said. "Is that because the cock forced her to do what he wanted?" Willy nodded. "People do that sometimes, too." She shuddered. "It's a terrible, terrible thing. I said that some people call the physical act 'love', but it's *not* love in itself. One must be loving for it to be love." She paused. She must have the courage to tell the children this. It was important that they understood, since they had asked the questions which led to this conversation.

"Ditta," she said, stroking Charlotte's hair and kissing her cheek, "do you remember how I would push you away, and couldn't let you kiss me?" she almost whispered.

Charlotte and Willy both nodded, looking at her with a nervous, almost frightened look in their eyes.

"You know we have always tried to keep you away from Prince Charles – Onkel Karl, as Papa calls him?"

The children nodded again, snuggling closer to her.

"He –" Vicky whispered, fixing her gaze on a lamp on the table at the other end of the room, "he did that to me – only –" She stumbled over her words.

Willy looked up, his face flushed with indignation. "He treated you like the cock treats the poor little hen? How could he?"

Vicky shuddered. "Not exactly," she said. "He –" She broke off, wondering how much to tell them. "Think of if there was something very, very special, and very private, which you did only with a certain person."

Willy nodded. Charlotte didn't look up.

"He – he made me –" Vicky began. "Sometimes, it can be worse to be gentle than to be violent," she went on. "To force someone to betray something, when they would never wish to do so." Tears sprang to her eyes. "He did – very bad things – and – it hurt me – I don't mean physically hurt. I mean, it makes me – not sad, but very uncomfortable – to think of it. I don't want to speak of this anymore." Vicky struggled to keep the sobs from her voice. "But, Charlotte, look at me."

Charlotte looked up. "Prince Charles," Vicky began again, "his eyes – his eyes are green, but their shape is just like yours. That is why I always try not to look you in the eye – because it makes me feel like I see him, and what happened. But Papa loves you, so, so much, as he does Willy," she said. "And I love you." She looked down. She felt Charlotte tremble, and kissed her cheek, stroking her hair as she hid her face again. "It was hard to love you at first, because of how your eyes reminded me of what had happened. But I do love you." She kissed Charlotte's cheek. "I do love you, and you are my little girl – that is what Papa always called you when you were tiny. My little girl, *meine kleines Mädchen.*"

"But why did you do it?" Willy asked.

"Because he threatened to – to hurt me," Vicky said, shuddering. "But there's another very important reason, too.

"We have often told you not to take things from people in the household," Vicky began again. Willy nodded. "Or from Großpapa and Großmama, or your little playmates." She felt Charlotte squirm and she hid her face against Vicky's shoulder again. "Charlotte," Vicky said. "Look at me."

Charlotte looked up for a moment, and then buried her face again. "Do you know the word hypnotism?" Vicky asked.

Charlotte didn't answer. Willy looked at Vicky. "Does it mean – to control someone else's mind?"

Vicky nodded. "Very good. How do you know?"

"Aunt Marianne talked to us about it."

Vicky sighed. "Good. Her children had to know and understand when they were very, very young, because Prince Charles is her father-in-law. Prince Charles is the master of a sort of hypnotism. You understand it all?"

"Not to take things, not to take them while in the same room, not to look them in the eye," Willy said, as he would something he had memorized to recite.

"Yes. But that is what Prince Charles was really trying to make me do. He wishes to have control of Papa and me, as he has over Großpapa and Großmama.

"Prince Charles wished to be King instead of his brother. Willy, has Herr Schrötter shown you our family tree?"

Willy shook his head.

"The eldest son in a family is the heir," Vicky began.

Willy nodded, but looked puzzled. "Why isn't Uncle Fritz Karl the heir, then? He's older than Papa, isn't he?"

"Yes, he is, but it goes down each branch of the family. That's why it's called a family tree. Großpapa is Prince Charles's elder brother. Papa is the heir because he is his Großpapa's son, and you are our heir, and Henry comes after you, and Siggy would have been next," Vicky wiped a tear away. "And any more little brothers you might have shall come before Prince Charles in the line of succession. He comes after you and your brothers, and then his son, and little Fritz Leopold. Then Prince Albrecht comes next, and Uncle Abbat after him, as his son."

Willy nodded. "But you said Prince Charles wanted to be King, Mama?"

"Yes," Vicky nodded. "He wanted to be. When he and Großpapa were boys, they were very, very close, like you and Henry are. But things happened – and Prince Charles took a bad path in life. He learned this – hypnotism, and he and Großpapa didn't agree anymore, and Großpapa married Großmama, so that his son – Papa – would be the heir, and Prince Charles wouldn't be King."

"But what does all of this have to do with Baby?" Charlotte asked very quietly. It was the first time she had spoken again.

Vicky sighed. What should she tell them? "That's Prince Charles's doing, too. But I don't remember what happened." She paused. "I must speak of babies more," she said, turning to Willy. "After a baby is born, the Mama must have time to recover. You have seen the animals. You have seen the blood which comes with the baby.

"You, Willy, were backwards when you were born. A little baby is supposed to be born head first. You were backwards, and that is part of what happened to your arm," she said, gently squeezing his left hand. "You were in a position which made it impossible for you to be born naturally, and the doctors had to put me to sleep, and help you – to be born." Willy's eyes were very wide. "I can show you the diagrams of a birth, and what should be. You ought to understand this."

"What do you mean, the doctors put you to sleep?" Charlotte asked.

"There are things called 'drugs'," Vicky said. "They are substances which affect a person's brain when one eats them, drinks them, sometimes, even smells them. They can be very dangerous, and are things which one should never, never play with." She paused. "These have to be used sometimes, like at Willy's birth, but also, some people are very foolish, and do wrong things. I don't remember what happened before Baby's birth, because Prince Charles – or one of his friends – gave me something like this. But it is a blessing, in a way. I don't have a bad, scary memory associated, and so I don't have the trouble I had with you." Vicky kissed Charlotte's cheek again.

Willy yawned.

"I'll tell you more later, when you are older," Vicky said. "This is enough for tonight, but you may ask me questions later. Ask *me*, or Papa when he is home, not Hobby or anyone else. I wish you to have your first lessons on this subject from us. Do you understand?"

Charlotte nodded.

"Are you satisfied for now? Do you understand about Baby?"

Charlotte nodded again, yawning.

"I would like it if you would all stay here," Vicky said. "Go to sleep. I must finish eating, and feed Baby, but I don't want to be alone."

***

June 30, 1866

Vicky finished folding the little clothes, stopping to wipe her eyes. She had packed away everything she had made with such love for Siggy. Most of the little clothes were too small already for Baby.

Tomorrow she would leave the Neues Palais with the children. She couldn't bear to be here, alone, without Fritz, and with the memories of Siggy's illness haunting her.

She had finally been able to read over more of Fritz's letters about the war, though still with a strange detachment she had never felt before. They were so far apart, not only in a physical sense, but in occupations. She had never felt this distance before, but her grief seemed to have built a wall between her and political thoughts.

At the same time, worry nagged at her. Mama had written about what she had heard from Alice and Louis. Alice was about to have a baby, and was quite alone. Louis was just about to leave for the war. Many of the armies suffered from want of food and water. This was a serious problem also for Fritz, as he was always sick at the very smell of the alcoholic beverages the troops would be forced by necessity to drink.

Tomorrow was Alice's anniversary; on the 5th was Lenchen's wedding day. Alice's little girls would be there. Alice had sent them to England for safety. Vicky sighed. If only she and Alice could be together. It would make things easier for both of them, but of course it was impossible with Hesse on the Austrian side of the war.

One of Louis' brothers was in the Prussian Army, but his regiment had been mobilized. Mama wrote that Alice said she did not know if he had received the King's message granting him leave not to fight against his own State in the civil war. Things like this brought home the true nature of "a war of brothers", as Fritz had called it.

***

Heringsdorf, July 2, 1866

Vicky sat on the beach, Baby in her arms, as the other children played in the sand.

She read Fritz's last letter over again. She felt her face glow as she read the last words.

He had taken to writing short, affectionate notes. Without her saying anything, he had realized her difficulty in following the military accounts at a time like this.

He sent her these, too, every day. Vicky followed the papers, reading superficially about the battles he was in, but she couldn't bear to read the full account now, when her heart ached, and the worry about Fritz was constant.

The one account of a battle she had read repeated itself in her mind. Fritz had written at length.

"We came out of the forest to the sounds of the guns. Immediately we were caught in the middle of a retreat. The terrain in the forest was treacherous, and the horses had to be led round a different path.

"And so I came out of the woods on foot. A platoon of Dragoons tore over the hilltop in a wild confusion, hurrying out of the action. Horses without riders ran as well, but were met by the wall of stone, impassible for horses.

"There were several cannons, still on their carts, standing about nearby. The road was quite blocked by the retreat, and though I called commands, no one heard me, and the loose horses nearly crushed me between the wheels of the cannon carts."

But Fritz was well; he was safe. That was what she needed to hear. She would read his full account after he was home again. But she felt a satisfaction and pride in the fact that the victories had been won by his part of the army, although the newspapers only mentioned Fritz Karl.

Besides, she knew there would be many friends and acquaintances lost in this war. She couldn't bear further grief, without Fritz here to comfort her. This gave her a twinge of pain. She knew Fritz had to bear all of these griefs alone as well.

She rose, laying Baby down on her plaid, and walked down to the shore, gazing out to sea. This place was much better for her than home, where Siggy's last cries echoed in her mind. Here, the soft wash of the sea and cries of the sea-gulls overhead spoke to her aching heart, soothing it.

Baby was doing wonderfully well, and was already trying to sit up without support, though she wasn't even three months old. Vicky marveled at her strength.

The children played happily at the beach, building sand-fortresses, Willy attempting to bring something of war into the games, at which the other children objected.

Willy asked Vicky frequent questions about his Papa and about the war. He was doing well, and none of the children were weighed down with grief. Time was kind to the children.

Charlotte had been extremely quiet since Vicky's long explanation to the children. Vicky wondered what she was thinking, but she never asked questions like Willy did.

"*July 4,*

"*Meine* Vicky,

"We all feel that yesterday was the decisive battle, and it came close to being lost.

"All of my army and Fritz Karl's had finally made their way through the Giant Mountains. These splendid mountains are a wonder of beauty, but it is not an enjoyable task to take an army through them. Fritz Karl was convinced it was impossible, and in every historical battle in this vicinity they were always avoided. However, I saw that it was the fastest way through, and we have done it.

"It rained steadily through the previous night, which was a great relief. I and many of the other men collected water in our helmets, which we poured into our canteens. It is a great relief, as I said, to know that other beverages are not necessary.

"This rain, however, made the marching extremely difficult. We were still on the edge of the steep slopes, many trails were obliterated, and the terrain extremely treacherous for the horses, even more for the men. We soon began to hear cannon-shots, then other gunfire, but it seemed as if it was coming towards us. This could mean one of two things. The enemy was approaching, or our army was retreating, fleeing from the enemy.

"In the distance, as we came to the top of another slope, we could see an enormous and solitary tree. The enemy was gathered there in such masses, the color of their uniforms seemed to form one great mass.

"Fritz Karl's army fought valiantly, but they were severely outnumbered. Even more alarming was the fact that this battle was directed jointly by Fritz Karl and by Papa himself. The prospect of the battle being lost which was directed by the King was a terrible one to all of us.

"The rain and the unevenness of the ground made the distance deceptive. I believed we were half an hour's march from the big tree, but it took an hour and half to reach it.

"Many were speaking of how badly it was going for Fritz Karl's army. The retreat went on, and the enemy came closer.

" 'Things aren't going well for my cousin, and the King is there too,' I called to those about me. 'We have two choices: we can join him straight on, but I believe it will be too late, or we can go straight ahead and take the Austrians on the right side. Sing, shout, fire away, let Papa and Fritz Karl know we are coming!'

"I had to hurry away and give orders to other parts of the army. With me, altogether, were one hundred thousand men. This would certainly overpower the Austrian army, but only if they could get there in time.

"I rode on, and soon, three parts of my army approached – a portion of the Austrians were encircled – and our First army was freed from their predicament. The enemy was soon fleeing in disarray, and victory stood before me.

"Victory, in the shape of the bloody, muddy, shell-torn valley; victory in the shape of men weeping, kneeling by the side of wounded and dying comrades; but also, victory in the shape of the meeting with Papa after such a victory.

"The sky began to clear, the sun pouring down. The news of the loss of several of our officers and several of my friends in the Potsdam regiments were brought to me. The feeling of grief began to overwhelm me, when I heard cheering. I looked about to find Papa, but it was Fritz Karl.

"We waved our caps to each other at a distance, then, in the midst of the cheering, weeping troops, he embraced me. 'Thank you,' he cried. 'You have saved our Army! If you hadn't come we would have lost! You were my savior!'. He wept in front of the whole battlefield, showing no shame or embarrassment in having to be rescued.

"My thoughts then flew to you and *die liebe Kinder*[28], to Mama, to Vivi. I seemed to see little Siggy before me. Then the faces of those friends I knew we had lost. Victory is not compensation for the loss of loved ones. Grief makes itself more powerfully felt than ever amid such surroundings.

"The wounded were being gathered, stray weapons gathered in a heap to be claimed. The wounded who could still walk struggled up the hill, using their weapons as crutches if they were not supported by a group of comrades.

"I looked about again for Papa, but the Grand Headquarters had withdrawn from the field. As I rode along, everyone I met who had been in Fritz Karl's army spoke to me the same way. 'The King said you would come today, but all hope seemed lost at the battle. We were going to be surrounded, till all at once the noise began in the distance and everyone cried "He is coming! The Crown Prince is coming!" Everything went well then, and everyone had the courage to go on, knowing you were on your way.'

"Soon, in my search for Papa, I came across Onkel Karl and Wilmeck. Both were slightly wounded in the form of slashes across the forehead. These had not been cleaned, and I was forced to turn away at the sight of the blood running down their faces.

"Finally, I found Papa. He embraced me, and neither of us could speak. He was the first to find his voice, and told me he rejoiced to think that I was the victor of this great battle. He said that I had won again the

---

[28]   The dear children

Order of Merit, which he had already intended to bestow on me for other victories my army had won.

"At this, tears started to my eyes. I had not received the message. It is the first decoration I feel I have won, and shall not be ashamed to wear, as a trophy undeserved, as I felt about those decorations I received in the Danish campaign.

"This battle shall be known as the battle of Königgrätz.

"Last night was my first entire night spent in bivouac. We settled ourselves down as best we could. There was no time to return all the way to Headquarters, and besides, Headquarters was moving ahead of us. After fifteen hours within the twenty-four being spent on horseback, rest in any place was very welcome. There was nothing to eat but a small bit of dry bread.

"In my dreams, I saw you vividly, you and little Siggy, and Willy by your side. Give *die liebe Kinder*[29] my love. My heart has had so many new impressions, but at every free moment, my thoughts fly to you."

***

Schloss Eisgrub, July 19, 1866

"*Meine* Vicky," Fritz began writing, "The army has marched on and on. With the advent of Papa's joining the army, a few days before the battle of Königgrätz, my independence has been put to an end. Grand Headquarters orders overrule other orders, of course.

"My army has marched on and on. We are on our way towards Vienna, where Papa wishes to take the city and annex Austria. I cannot say how much against this I am. We must not be a harsh victor. The exclusion of Austria from German affairs is enough.

"This place, Eisgrub, is a lovely castle, reminding me an English castle and church in one much more than what we know as a Schloss. The architecture draws one's constant attention. I have come here ahead of my men, to join the First Army once more.

"I had hoped to have a long, sensible conversation with Fritz Karl, as I have had many during this war, but I am afraid that is not to be. Up until our last meeting, he has been gentle and cautious as he was through much

---

[29]   The dear children

of the Danish campaign, but on our last meeting, he brusquely refused to speak to me, and there was a look in his eye which does not bode well.

"He and Wilmeck are here. I shall be careful, and take no risks. Do not be anxious about me. I shall write again as soon as I can."

Fritz jumped at the sound of a loud crash. As he turned to lock the door, he heard a shout. The words which were clear were "It's the wine cellar!" It was Fritz Karl.

Fritz looked about the room. There was a table with a large armchair, a sofa, and a small closet, besides the tall bookcases. He would finish writing to Vicky, and then read until he fell asleep. It would be very good to rest.

He locked the door, pulled the sofa away from the wall, and pushed it in front of the door. Many of the men would be drunk; they had guns and swords; it would not do to trust Fritz Karl when he was in this state. He had promised Vicky he would not take unnecessary risks.

CHAPTER TWELVE
IN THE LIBRARY

Schloss Eisgrub, July 20, 1866

Fritz blinked; the sun was shining on his face. He looked about, remembering where he was. He was thirsty, and he realized that he had no food or water.

He would not open the door to go and find some. He had still heard the men, shouting and singing, obviously drunk. During the night he had been awakened by shots, obviously from inside the house.

"Catch them!" he heard one of the men shout. The men's voices sounded slightly farther away. He wondered if he should open the door and go out. He knelt on the sofa, listening at the door.

"Please, *mein Herren*[30], let me go!" he heard a woman's voice say in a strong Danish accent.

"Mama, Mama, what –?" It was the voice of a young girl, but her voice had stopped suddenly.

The tramp of the men's boots sounded on the floor again.

"Please, spare my daughter! Take me if you must, but spare my daughter!" The woman's voice sounded frantic now.

Fritz looked through the keyhole. The library was positioned so that he could see straight through to the front door. It stood open. On the road stood a small cart. In the entrance-hall, the men stood in a staggered circle. Fritz Karl stood in the middle, his arm round a young girl, her mouth gagged. His hand gripped her wrist, so she could not struggle away; his other hand held his pistol against her chest.

The girl's mother stood in the midst of the group, slowly taking off her bonnet, then her scarf. She began to unfasten her dress.

---

[30]   gentlemen

"*Schneller!* Faster!" Fritz Karl shouted.

Fritz covered his eyes. He couldn't sit there and watch this scene! He couldn't sit and listen to the screams he knew would soon pierce his ears. He knew that Fritz Karl would not spare the girl, no matter what they might have told the poor woman. He glanced round the room, wondering what he could do to save them.

His eyes fell on his pistol. He caught it up, a plan forming in his mind. He ran to the farthest window, threw it open, and fired. He shut it quickly, ran to another window, and fired twice more. He waited a moment, hearing alarmed shouts from the men. He shut the window again, and pulled the curtains closed. He ran back to the sofa, and looked through the keyhole.

There was no one in sight. The woman's bonnet, scarf, and jacket lay on the floor; but the men had all gone, no doubt to see who had fired the shots at the back of the house. He heard the door of the room next to the library bang shut, and the latch secured. He heard the girl sobbing.

"Hush, Lina," he heard her mother say, but she was sobbing herself. Fritz hoped they would be quiet, so the men would not know where they had gone. The door had already been shut, so it would not seem any different.

Herringsdorf, July 20, 1866

Vicky sat in the little library, her book closed, her handkerchief spread on the table as she leaned her head down. She had never been unable to read before. Even after Papa's death, she had kept up her reading – indeed, she had felt a compulsion to read, to continue to learn, study and grow as he would have wished her to. Here, she had brought a few of her own books as well as those belonging to the children. The children's education must not lag behind because of the absence of their little brother.

Siggy had never learned to read, would never learn. Her heart ached when she thought of this. He had always been so happy, so cheerful, so easy to teach little things.

Vicky took Fritz's last letter. It was hard even to read these right now, though not so much as it had been during the first two weeks since Siggy's death.

"Siggy, Papa is here." Fritz woke, realizing he had been dreaming. He had seen Vicky standing in the doorway of their bedroom at the Neue Palais, welcoming him home, holding little Siggy in her arms. But this would never happen, he remembered. Siggy was dead. He rose and went to the window. It was a bright, moonlit night. He went to the door, bending to look through the keyhole. He could not see anything, but he could not hear anything either. He unlocked the door, cautiously opened it and looked out. Fritz Karl lay on the floor in the passageway, snoring loudly. Several of the other men also lay about, some holding bottles of wine. Even the men who were obviously on sentry duty had gone to sleep.

Fritz closed the door softly behind him, locking it again from the outside. He stepped carefully over two of the sleeping men, making his way to the large front door, which had carelessly been left open. He stepped quietly to the woman's cart. There were apples, bread – fresh bread, compared to the rations the men had – and water. He picked up one of the flasks and drank deeply. It was cool and sweet. The breeze blew, and he glanced around. No one stirred. He took a cloth bag from the cart, put several of the apples, another flask of water, and a loaf of bread in, went inside and cautiously closed the front door. Someone coughed, but no one woke.

He went to the door of the room next to the library, softly tapping at the door.

"I won't open to you, you filthy scoundrel!" he heard the woman's voice hiss at the keyhole. "And don't you dare be staring at us through the keyhole! Leave us be, please!" Her voice broke and he heard the girl whisper something.

Open to me. Fritz cringed as the sort of jokes Onkel Karl would make about something like that flooded into his mind. He shuddered. He hated it when things like that invaded his mind, as if they were his own thoughts. He did not think that way.

"Please, be calm," he called softly through the keyhole. "I am the Crown Prince,"

"The Crown Prince," he heard the woman say. "The Crown Prince of Prussia?"

"*Ja,*" Fritz answered. "I will bring you some of your food if you will open the door."

He heard whispering, and then the door slowly opened, the woman standing with a large piece of wood in her hand, the girl half hidden behind a sofa.

Fritz entered and shut the door. "Please, you have nothing to fear. It was I who fired those shots which allowed you to escape. I was watching through the keyhole of the next room, wondering how to save you."

The woman looked at him suspiciously, but slowly stepped closer. Fritz went to the door and locked it. "This is the master key, you see. But, Fritz Karl – Prince Friedrich Karl, the man who took you captive – is a locksmith, so we must be on our guard. That latch would not hold very long if they attempted to force the door. But please, eat something, and I will make it my business to see that you are paid for the food. It appears that you were on your way to the market?"

"Yes, *mein Herr,* but you see," she began, speaking slowly in her strong Danish accent, "my family. We were not poor," she said, beckoning to her daughter and hungrily biting into an apple. Fritz took one also. "We were quite well off, as far as farmers go, but my son – my only son - was killed in the war two years ago. I believe it was in a fight where the enemy was commanded by that man." She motioned towards the door with a shudder.

"My cousin, Prince Friedrich Karl?"

"*Ja.* My husband was in the war also, though he was not well, and this blow came very hard on him. He was taken prisoner, and taken to Germany. We – we did not know what to do, but decided to set out to see him, but news came of his death after we arrived in Hanover. We had left our home because it was in the war-torn territory at that time, and now we had no home to go back to. After that war, I heard from a friend that our farm was gone, torn to pieces by shells, and so we were now very poor, and homeless, and Lina was all I had left. She *is* all I have left."

Her voice shook with emotion. She looked up at Fritz, her face streaked with tears. "I have worked hard on a farm which belonged to a man who was kind to me, but now he is in this war, and I do not know what shall happen. I didn't realize the market was within the war territory, or I would certainly never have brought Lina. I have worked so hard to bring a little money in to give her a home, and so that neither of us would – would have to become – a woman of the streets." Her voice broke, and she raised her hand to wipe her tears. "And now, yesterday, when that man took her, and – they would have – she is *all* I have." Her voice faded and her words were broken by sobs.

Fritz realized his eyes were full of tears. He looked up as the girl slipped her hand into his. "*Danke*," she said, looking up at him. The gentle touch of her hand and the sweet, trusting expression in her eyes brought to his mind the image of Vicky as she was at the Great Exhibition, when she had sat at his side with her hand in his. The feeling that he must protect this innocent little girl and her mother swept over him even more strongly than before; the girl was no older than Vicky had been then.

He met the woman's eye, and leaned forward, gently kissing the little girl's forehead. "I know what it is to lose someone very dear," he said, speaking slowly. "I lost my father-in-law a few years ago, and just last month – my youngest son. My wife is at home, alone with the children, and we have gone through this dreadful time separately." He met the woman's eye again. She reached out, also taking his hand, a look of sympathy melting her previous somewhat hardened expression. "I would like to do something for you," he said, looking at the girl. "Do you like little children?"

"Oh, yes," the girl said, looking up at her mother. "I had a little sister, but she died just before my father did."

"Would you be willing to come to work at the Palace?" He looked at the woman now, and she slowly nodded. "And your daughter can be one of the nursery maids for my little Viktoria. My wife's name is Victoria, you know, don't you?"

"*Ja*. We know you well, it seems, from the papers. I always hoped you were as kind as they said. We have found it to be true, just as true as is the cruelty of your cousin which they describe just as frequently."

Fritz nodded. "My father – the King – will be here soon, and Fritz Karl will soon go on. I will be sure you are given safe passage to Heringsdorf, and you can take a message from me to my wife." He bent down and kissed the little girl's forehead again. Her eyes had grown very wide when he mentioned the King and the prospect of her working in the Palace, but she said nothing as her mother curtseyed and kissed his hand. "You will be like an elder daughter to me – to us," he whispered.

CHAPTER THIRTEEN
OUR BROKEN HOME

"Eisgrub, July 27, 1866

"Meine Vicky,

"I find myself today in great agreement with Count Bismarck. I must admit that he is acting very correctly and I am giving him my support. What a flip-flop this is from the usual conditions.

"For several days he and Papa have been in severe disagreement – Papa has said such things to him that he actually cried the last evening. I was called for, as usual, to be the voice of reason.

"I met Moltke on my way to Schloss Nikolsburg. He greeted me by telling me that Papa and Bismarck had locked themselves each in their respective rooms and refused to speak to each other.

"It is all on the matter of peace, and that matter I mentioned before of Papa's wishing to annex Austria. The Emperor Franz Joseph has offered peace with the mediation of the Emperor Napoleon, and Papa has attempted to refuse. Everyone else says that the peace should be accepted.

"Bismarck, no doubt, will consider me his ally after this, but I shall not be led astray. Peace is on its way, and everyone speaks of Papa returning to Berlin by the fourth. If it is so, I shall accompany him, and we shall soon be in each other's arms.

"We shall have great changes with the break-up of the German Confederation and the probable formation of a new North German Confederation. The annexation of Hesse-Kassel, Hanover, Schleswig-Holstein, and several other states is in progress. This is not welcome news, of course, but after the course of events which have passed, I can hardly say I would wish the sovereignty of Schleswig-Holstein on Fritz Augustenburg. It would be a less pleasant position than ours is, and quite an empty title.

"Speaking of empty titles, Saxony, too, becomes powerless, though the family is not to be exiled or stripped of titles. Hesse, too, which is most troubling personally to us, is split, where Upper Hesse is part of our North Confederation, while Lower Hesse, where Alice and Louis are, is not. This will cause great complications for them.

"I hope that Charlotte's birthday has passed pleasantly, and often wonder if you have heard from Marianne. How does Wilhelm go on, and does he have his lessons at Heringsdorf? Has he the maps to follow our progress?

"You shall have visitors soon, if they are not with you already. I hope you will be as fond of them as I already am."

***

Berlin, August 4, 1866

Fritz saluted and waved. The carriage he and his father rode in was quite full of flowers by this time. The return journey had been filled with congratulations.

There was the Schloss. The carriage drove up, and they stepped out. There was a hand on his shoulder. He turned.

"Mama!" Fritz cried, feeling as if the ground shook under his feet. He recalled their last meeting – after Siggy's death – and felt the tears flood his eyes.

There was a crowd pressing around him; many hands shook his; a wreath of flowers was hung round his neck – but he could not speak. He could barely see through his tears. He followed his parents into the Schloss, where they went out onto the balcony to be greeted by the roaring crowds, but Fritz's thoughts were far away.

He stepped into his carriage again, at last, and drove across the square to the Kronprinz Palais.

"*Eure Hoheit*[31]*!*" Valerie Hohenthal met him at the door. "Vicky sent me here to meet you," she said.

Fritz nodded. "I am going at once. You can come," he said briefly. Everywhere inside it was dark, as he went to his suite to collect a few things before leaving for Heringsdorf. The darkness was far more in

---

[31]   Your Highness

harmony with his feelings than the cheering crowd he would have to face again outside.

No victory could bring back lost loved ones.

In the woods near Heringsdorf, August 6, 1866

Vicky walked up and down the forest path. The children followed her, looking about. The woods were thick here, little sunlight penetrating the place. Vicky stopped to listen.

"Shh, be still," she murmured, taking Willy's hand. She had heard the train arrive and depart, and yet no one came. But yes – there was a step; a twig snapped.

"Fritz!" she cried, running to him and throwing her arms around his neck. He held her tightly, then leaned down to kiss her. Tears ran down his face, and Vicky realized she was crying too.

"God has given you back to me," she whispered.

Fritz nodded. "But he will not give Siggy back," they both whispered at the same time.

Fritz looked well, but thinner, and a good deal older. There were a few strands of grey in his long beard.

"Papa!" Willy cried, clutching at Fritz's hand. Fritz knelt down, gathering the children around him. The tears still flowed down his cheeks as he kissed each of them. He rose, and they turned towards Vicky's carriage.

"Here's Baby," Vicky said, as they entered the door of the White Castle.

"Lina," Fritz said, wiping his eyes and smiling to the girl who stood in the entrance way. He took the little one from her arms, looking into her face.

Baby looked back at him, and screamed. "*Meine kleines Möhrchen*," he murmured, kissing her forehead. She struggled in his arms, and Vicky took her from him.

"Of course she doesn't know you," she said. Baby had only been two months old when he left. Now, she was four months old, but she appeared as if she was a good deal older. She was so big and strong.

"Papa, Papa, let me show you something!" Wilhelm cried, and took his hand. Fritz let his son lead him through the rooms of the little Schloss. "Here is where you won the victory for us," Wilhelm said, pointing to a point on a map marked "Königgrätz".

"No, Wilhelm, that is not exactly where it was. It was closer to here," Fritz said, pointing to another spot. "Papa wished it to be called 'the Battle of Königgrätz', though it was a few miles away from Königgrätz."

"But why would it not be called by where it was?"

"The King has say of what it is called," Fritz answered. He looked around. The little schoolroom looked very nice. "Wilhelm, how do you get on with Herr Schrötter?"

"Very well," Wilhelm answered. "He shows me such interesting things, and showed me our line of succession – Mama spoke of that, but the family tree is so interesting. And, Papa, Mama told us about –"

Fritz knelt down and embraced his son. "I must go to Mama now, Wilhelm," he said, and turned to leave the room.

"Vicky?" Fritz called. She was not there when he came out into the main hall again. Valerie motioned towards another door.

Vicky lay in bed, clasping Baby in her arms. She heard the bedroom door open and close, but she didn't look up.

"*Meine* Vicky," Fritz murmured, sitting by her side and stroking her cheek.

"Fritz." She looked up at him through her tears, reaching up to touch his cheek. She couldn't speak further. He stroked her cheek, and she closed her eyes, relaxing under his caress. "Fritz," she whispered again, as he bent down to kiss her. "Why? Why didn't you come home for Siggy's funeral," she sobbed.

"I could not leave those thousands of other women's sons to go out without their leader." He looked into her eyes. "Vicky, you wrote that I was entirely absorbed in the war, in military matters, in politics," he began, lying down beside her and gathering her in his arms. "I had to be. My duty demanded it. And I could not let my mind go into my usual occupations. You remember, in the Danish campaign, Mama was concerned at my only writing about military affairs. It is so hard –" He paused, swallowing to calm a little quiver in his voice. "It was so hard to leave you, to know that you were alone in this trial. But I have had to bear it alone as well."

He paused, laying his cheek against hers, and she felt him tremble all over. "I thought I disliked war after that campaign. I did not know what war was, really." He sat up, looking her in the eye. "To be at headquarters, in the Supreme Command, as I was two years ago, is an entirely different thing than being one of the field commanders, marching or riding for fifteen hours a day on nothing but a bit of bread, sleeping under the stars no matter what the weather.

"But the physical hardships are nothing compared to the internal," he said, tapping his forehead and putting his hand over his heart. "To keep a straight head to give commands; to take in all that goes on in a battlefield stretching three miles, with nearly half a million men, and all the while one's heart is aching as mine was!"

Fritz lay still, with tears in his eyes. Vicky watched his face, the realization of how exhausted he must be sweeping over her. But she had felt so detached, and so alone for so long, she was still wrapped inside her own grief.

She sat up, lifting Baby and placing her in Fritz's arms. She kept her facing her, looking into her face. She didn't scream now when Fritz took her and kissed her.

"Vicky," Fritz said, stroking Baby's golden curls, "you watched our little one suffer and die – "

"Fritz, how can you say it so calmly?" Vicky sobbed, burying her face in the pillows.

"I do *not* speak calmly," he said, laying his hand on her arm. It trembled violently, as did his voice as he went on. "I watched many men die – promising young men, whose mothers are mourning as you are. I saw the bodies of men missing their – oh!" he cried, not finishing his sentence. "Even the horses would turn away from such sights!"

"You know, Vicky," he said as she turned to face him again, "we knew that all was not right with Siggy. He may have suffered far more if he had lived longer."

Vicky nodded. "I know, Fritz. I'm just so selfish in my grief, I can't see anyone else's suffering," she sobbed.

He shook his head. "It is not selfishness. So many mothers and sisters and wives and daughters are feeling just as you do now. It is not wrong to grieve." He sighed. "I have to learn how now, after pushing my grief aside for so long."

***

Schloss Erdmannsdorf, Giant Mountains, Bohemia, September, 1866

"My name is Alberto," the young man said in broken English. Vicky took his hand gently in hers. The bandages had only just been taken off, the stumps of the two smallest fingers showing plainly. The third finger was curled, immobile, perhaps permanently paralyzed. Only the thumb and first finger returned the squeeze.

"Your name is my father's name," she said slowly in Italian. "Here is your macaroni," handing him a steaming bowl. The young man's eyes seemed to glow with gratitude.

Vicky had begun to learn Italian four years ago, during the tour of the Mediterranean, but hadn't found much time to continue her studies. But most of the so-called Austrian soldiers were Italian, Rumanian, Hungarian, Polish or Bohemian, the Austrian Empire being of such diverse population. Hardly any of those Vicky had met spoke German or French.

Vicky had often visited the hospitals since arriving here. With the change of scene, and having Fritz back with her, she felt better and lighter. She felt different, too, in contact with the suffering Fritz had spoken of. She had visited many of the wounded – the fine, promising young men Fritz had spoken of – and striven to understand their language, to help to care for them. She had their favorite dishes cooked in her kitchen – polenta and macaroni for the Italians. She had tasted many foods she had never tried before.

Fritz was often silent now, and she woke sometimes, finding his face wet with tears, and she could realize now how he must be feeling after having pushed his feelings aside for so long.

Occasionally, on the days they didn't visit the hospitals, they took excursions into the mountains. Vicky stopped frequently to take in the breathtaking view. She felt Fritz's hand tremble at the sight of certain places, and turned away. The troops had spent difficult days passing through the mountain tracks.

She found herself able to smile again at the sight of Fritz climbing the steep slope with Charlotte clinging to his neck, Willy struggling to keep up on the rocky incline.

***

Neues Palais, Potsdam, September 21, 1866

Vicky had watched the men march through the Brandenburg Gate, Fritz riding at their head. He saluted as he passed the King, and the men cheered as they came to a halt.

The entry of the troops was always a great event, but Vicky's heart felt heavy. Today was their first return to the Neues Palais. The return to the scene of Siggy's illness and death.

The King had made a wonderful speech, and had greeted Fritz with extreme kindness, such as Vicky hadn't seen in years.

Now, she sat, hand in hand with Fritz, in their carriage, looking up at the Neues Palais. That dear home, where they had spent so many happy hours, now held dread for her.

Fritz opened the door, and helped her out. He looked her in the eye, bending down to kiss her.

Vicky felt her throat go dry as they went through the rooms, and her vision blurred as they entered her sitting-room. "Here," she heard herself say. "Our home – my heart!" She struggled to speak clearly.

Fritz put his arm around her, and led her away. She looked up at him, tears blurring her eyes. "Our little circle is broken, but we are together now," he murmured, taking her in his arms. "*Gott* was with us. His Will be done."

PART THREE:
A PERSONAL ATTACK

CHAPTER FOURTEEN
MADNESS AND MARRIAGE

Kronprinz Palais, Berlin, October 15, 1866

"Vicky."

Vicky looked up from her book at the sound of Fritz's voice. She sat opening and reading letters. "Yes?"

"I have been invited to the Tsarevich's wedding," Fritz began. "It is to be on Bertie's birthday, and he is going as well."

"Oh, you must go. It'll be good for you and Bertie to meet again. So many have tried to stir him up against us, and I hope he'll come here, too."

"But will you go?" Fritz asked, meeting her eye.

Vicky looked down, shaking her head. "I'm not ready for such festivities," she said slowly. "I would be so interested to go to Russia, but not yet."

Fritz nodded. "I did not expect so. But I am pleased Bertie goes. The poor girl will have little support, with Alix unable to go, and the parents too, as they are still paying their war indemnity to us." Alix was expecting a baby, and not feeling well. "At least she will have her brother and her brother-in-law. *My* presence will certainly not give her pleasure."

Vicky shook her head, rising and leaning over the back of Fritz's chair to kiss him. "Your presence will be more welcome than any other Prussian representative, and Prussia must be represented."

Fritz nodded. "I was only thinking of how cold Alix was when we met after the Danish war. And Bertie was, too."

Berlin Schloss, October 18, 1866

"It ought to be *you*," Fritz heard Aunt Adina say to Onkel Karl. "Mouffy always asked *you* to come to all of *her* events. You were at her wedding, her coronation, Nikoshka's funeral, and many others. But I suppose one must acknowledge the younger generation some time, and Fritzch was at the coronation, too. And to think that Fritzch should deign to travel with Vicky's little reprobate brother! I must say I didn't believe the rumors about him at first. One wouldn't think any of Prince Albert's sons capable of proving himself a man…" She whispered something, and then went on audibly again, "But what can one say now? He is the talk of Europe, and one would think Fritzch would think himself far too good to associate with someone like *him*."

Fritz sighed, and looked at Vicky. She did not seem to have heard the conversation.

Fritz smiled to himself. He knew Vicky and her mother were anxious for Bertie to travel with him to such a decadent court as that of St. Petersburg, for the very reason Aunt Adina thought he would not wish to associate with Bertie. Bertie always looked up to him, and strove to behave well when Fritz was there. Fritz was glad to be a role-model for Vicky's brothers, and particularly for Bertie, who had always rebelled against certain of the values Prince Albert had held up for his children.

"I cannot help thinking it a great joke that Prince Albert thought it possible to change the English family – or rather I should say the Hanoverian family," Aunt Adina went on. "The Guelfs never change! Try as he might to change their image – to 'raise their reputation', as he would have said – it all ends in the way it always will. One can see that plainly enough, with all that goes on with the Prince of Wales, not to mention the Duke of Edinburgh, and of course the Queen herself! Have you seen the latest reports? I hear that Vicky's little sisters themselves call *Herr Braun*[32] 'Mama's lover.' "

Fritz jumped as Vicky took his arm. "I am so pleased you will go with Bertie," she whispered. "He will behave himself with you, as he would not in any other company."

---

[32]   Mr. Brown

"I am glad Onkel Karl leaves for Mainz before our departure," Fritz said, squeezing her hand. Today was Fritz's birthday – his thirty-fifth. Onkel Karl was to leave soon after, as his appointment as Military Governor of Mainz had first been announced on Fritz's birthday two years ago.

But this was his last term there. He would be back in Berlin during the season again after this.

*****

Kronprinz Palais, Berlin, Oktober 23, 1866

"Fritz?" Vicky called as he closed the bedroom door. "I've heard the most disturbing news," she went on, taking his arm. "Have you heard that poor Charlotte is out of her mind?"

"Charlotte – who?" Fritz asked, looking down at her.

"Cousin Charlotte of Belgium – of Mexico," she said.

Charlotte of Belgium was Vicky's cousin – really her parents' first cousin, as the daughter of Uncle Leopold, but only a few months Vicky's senior. She had married Max, the brother of Emperor Franz Joseph of Austria, who had been present at Beatrice's Christening. He had been the Austrian Viceroy of Venetia – but now, after the war, Venice and its surroundings were to become part of Italy, so there would be no position there for him to return to.

"Things have gone terribly wrong in Mexico," Vicky went on. "And the French have withdrawn their support entirely. That isn't right," she cried. "It's their doing which sent Max and Charlotte there in the first place!"

The Mexican Empire had been set up as a satellite state to France. The Emperor Napoleon had supported the idea of a Monarchial Empire in North America. But the United States of America supported the Mexican Republic, and the Civil Wars – in Germany and America respectively – had proved disastrous to the Mexican campaign.

The end of America's Civil War had freed troops which were now sent to Mexico, while France had withdrawn troops from Mexico, wishing to consolidate their army in the case of a wider European conflict growing out of the Prussian-Austrian war.

"She's afraid of being poisoned; she went unannounced to visit the Pope and ate out of his dishes, seeing him eating safely. She hadn't eaten in days, the Ambassador writes. She returned to her old home, Miramar, but they've treated her as if she were insane! Leopold and Marie have sent for her, but – oh, it's so dreadful!"

Fritz sat down on the bed, lying down and taking Vicky in his arms. He met her eye, and was about to speak, when she went on.

"Mama says it's all true – and all the Ambassadors write of her as well, so I must believe it, but it's too dreadful!" Fritz felt Vicky shiver. "I first heard of it several days ago, but I didn't like to speak of it until I knew if it were true! And of course I thought you would have seen things in the papers." She paused, looking Fritz in the eye.

"I have not seen anything about it, but I have been very occupied," he said. "But – Max! Is it true he is taken prisoner? I did see that report."

"I don't know. I know Charlotte came to Europe to try to gain support for him. But – oh, it would be better to be – *dead*, I think – than to live without one's reason! And she was always so clever, and so calm, and quiet – so smooth a disposition, so quiet an imagination. I think of her compared to myself, Fritz. You know how easily agitated I am! I often wonder that *my* mind hasn't turned, with all that's happened to me, and to us! What must she have gone through, to drive her to such a condition?"

Fritz felt her shudder again. He hardly knew what to say. The circumstances his mind placed before him were frightful – but he must not speak of that to Vicky. She was agitated enough, without his adding fuel to her imagination.

"Vicky," Fritz said again, "when you first said something was the matter with 'Charlotte', my first thoughts went to our Charlotte."

Vicky stared at him. "But she's done nothing to make you think she's out of her mind, has she?"

Fritz shook his head. "She has been so quiet of late, and several times, when I went to see the children, she has asked me if I really loved her. What – what has put that question into her mind?"

Vicky looked down. "The children have been asking questions, and Mrs. Hobbs doesn't answer them in the way we could wish. About Baby. I had to tell them, and of course, that meant telling them about Charlotte."

Fritz nodded. "You told them about Onkel Karl, and –"

Vicky nodded. "I told them very carefully, and answered their own questions as best I could, without frightening them too much. I always dreaded the thought of having to speak to them about it, but I think it much better that they should know now, than that it should come later, when they're in society."

"*Ja*," Fritz sighed heavily. "I understand. And I understand Charlotte's questions."

Kronprinz Palais, November 4, 1866

"It's very good to see you!" Vicky cried, throwing her arms around her brother. "It has been nearly a whole year since I've seen any of you."

"Yes, indeed, and it's good to see you *well*," Bertie said, kissing Vicky's cheek. "You still didn't seem so when I saw you last, though you were better than in Coburg." Vicky felt her cheeks flush. "I felt so much for you when I heard of little Siggy," he said gently, squeezing her hand. "I cried when I read –"

Vicky nodded, struggling to hold back tears. Fritz entered the room, and Vicky hurried away.

The Winter Palace, Petersburg, November 9, 1866

"*Meine* Vicky,

"The wedding has gone very well, and Bertie's birthday festivities as well. Watching the Orthodox ceremony of course brought many memories of my first visits to Russia, and of Aunt Charlotte's Coronation particularly.

"I find the bride and bridegroom a much more affectionate couple than one could have expected, and they do not at all give the idea of an arranged marriage.

"The sparkling tunics, caftans, coats, and stars, and the priests with their golden mantels and long flowing hair and beards make a wonderful scene. The ladies' dresses are equally impressive, with their trains, tiaras, and other finery, of which I am afraid I still am too ignorant to remember the names. Writing this last line reminds me vividly of a certain moment I shall not mention in writing – I will only say that I miss *meine liebe Frauchen* very much indeed, and am very glad I shall be home in time for your birthday to be spent pleasantly.

"Min – Dagmar has grown up; she is as pretty as ever, though grown taller. My appearance at the wedding was obviously no pleasure to her in the first days. I heard her speak bitterly of the Prussians as the cause of the fact that her parents were unable to attend their own daughter's wedding – as of course Denmark is still paying her war indemnity to us – but on the second day, after a private dinner with only the family and visiting Royalties, I had a little talk with her.

"She looked very uncomfortable at my approach – her dark eyes darted about in every direction, as if eager to escape, but Bertie, knowing my intention, purposely stood with several of the others in the path of her possible retreat.

" 'I am very sorry that your parents could not attend your wedding,' I began. She drew herself up and looked at me in a way which made her seem to double in stature, and then away, looking very splendid in her wounded pride. 'I nearly had the misfortune of not having my father attend my own wedding,' I went on.

" 'I can imagine that it is not pleasant for you to meet me after the occurrences of two years ago. But I humbly beg you simply to look on me as a cousin, who, in his own name and his wife's, wishes you every happiness. May you be as happy as we are.' I held out my hand. Her face melted into a charming smile, and she thanked me cordially, in a way which much reminded me of Alix at her respective wedding.

"Sascha – Alexander, as I have always called him until now – is full of attentions and kindnesses. He asks much after you and your family, and sends his deep sympathy for our sorrow. As to my calling him Sascha – though the Tsar is my first cousin, he is so much my senior I never felt it quite respectful to call him 'Sascha' – you know well that I did not grow up accustomed to familiarity based in true affection.

"In writing, everyone in the family here calls the Tsar 'Sascha', and the son and heir and bridegroom 'Sasha'. Of course, in speech this makes no difference to anyone but those who grew up with a Russian ear. But I must say the bridegroom seems relieved that no one but his mother has called him 'Saschi' in his bride's hearing. It does seem rather an embarrassing name for such a big fellow.

"You will be pleased to hear that Bertie stays with me a great deal and proves the rumor-mongers wrong, Aunt Adina in particular. He takes an interest in all I tell him, has never spoken violently against Prussia, and, above all, keeps early and respectable hours. I must admit I was rather anxious at having the responsibility (in your Mama's eyes) of keeping an eye on him, as you know this court is considered less respectable even than that in Berlin. The first days he tried to slip away, but I have succeeded in keeping his interest, and I have even stayed up so late that I kept him talking in my room till he was unsteady on his feet from sleepiness."

Kronprinz Palais, Berlin, November 14, 1866
"Mein Schatz[33]*,*

"What you say about the bride and bridegroom is cheering. Everything I had heard had led me to believe that he had no wish to marry her.

"I would miss you indeed, *mein Schatz*, if you were compelled to spend my birthday far away – it has never been so. *That* moment is vivid in my mind as well, and I long for your return.

"I am very pleased that you appeased Dagmar's pride, and I see you are now on familiar enough terms with her to call her by her name – as I know well from Alix's letters that 'Minnie' is what she is called. (Please, *mein Schatz*, do not take this seriously or think that I do.)

"I am so thankful all goes so well with Bertie, and that he does not attempt to run away from you. It is just what Mama and I hoped.

"The Schwerins are still here, and the Grand Duchess's company is as charming as ever. But I must say, it is very, very pleasant indeed to see Addy, and to see that she does not seem unhappy. She seems quite content, and is unchanged.

"Your Papa is extremely kind. He is never fractious or bad-tempered, but as kind and tender as he was to me after Willy's and Charlotte's births. He has not behaved so in for years; it is such a comfort while you are away. He comes to have dinner with me nearly every evening, and he is very kind to your Mama, too, and writes to her a great deal.

---

[33]   My darling

"Of course, it would not be so if Bertram and Robert[34] were not away. (Did I show you Mama's letters speaking of the play of *Robert le Diable*? If I did not, I must leave you to interpret whom I speak of, which ought to be easy enough.)

"Willy asks with much curiosity about the great court of Russia, and wonders if you have seen any bears or wolves, and remembers his Godfather the Emperor Alexander very well.

"I have heard no more about poor Cousin Charlotte, but to say that she is in good care and kind hands now.

"Henry is to go to Grandmama, to be out of Berlin this winter. I hope it does him much good.

"Marianne and I have had a long talk, and think of something – for the future, of course, but which we both like very much. It is the idea of Mariechen perhaps someday being Mrs. Arthur? She is such a nice little girl and already quite a mother to the little ones; she would make a splendid wife for him someday! Of course, to Marianne, this would give a reason for them all to be much in England and under Mama's kind protection.

"It only comes to the meeting and seeing if they fancy each other when the time comes. I can't help laughing to myself as I think of Mama's words about Marianne's little girls when she and Papa were here – oh, how long ago that seems! 'Perhaps one of them might be Arthur's wife, some day?'"

***

Kronprinz Palais, Berlin, February 14, 1867

"All's going so well," Vicky sighed as she sat down next to Fritz at the little table in their bedroom. "The children get on so nicely. I would be so glad and happy and proud if – and I am. But seeing them all, and seeing Baby getting on so nicely, makes my heart ache for Siggy."

Fritz took her hand, and she looked up at him, finding his eyes were full of tears. He nodded. "I do not see how it can ever grow easier," he said softly.

"Seeing Alice with her little ones was very nice," Vicky said, squeezing his hand. "Alice and I had several nice little talks. And she

---

[34]   Meaning Prince Charles and Bismarck, referencing character similarities
       from a play

contributed some of her drawings – and Louis' – to be sold at the bazaar. Mama has sent me some things too – photos of herself and the *Geschwister*[35]. We've raised over ten thousand thallers already! It'll do great good for the poor widows and orphans."

Fritz nodded, smiling. He had begun an organization, calling it the "Viktoria" *Stiftung*, to raise money to support the widows, orphans, and wounded from the war.

"Alice and I also had a talk about governesses and tutors, which is quite necessary, with our little flocks growing so quickly," Vicky went on. "Hinzpeter does very well, and I wish to be as pleased with Mademoiselle d'Arcourt as I am with him. But I wish we had an English Head-Governess, not French."

Fritz laid a letter on the table. "Karl Sigmaringen had written that he hoped to come to Germany this year, but he fears he will not be able to now. But he feels it is time that he looked for a bride."

"You will be very pleased to see him, when he does come here."

Fritz nodded, and then covered his eyes. "It is just as you said," he murmured, wiping his eyes. "Such little things bring Siggy to mind. Karl was his sponsor." Fritz swallowed, blinking. "Umberto is engaged again."

Umberto, the Crown Prince of Italy, was another good friend. He had been engaged the previous year, but his bride had died horribly, after accidentally setting her dress on fire, attempting to hide from her governess the fact that she was smoking a cigarette.

Vicky shuddered. "That horrible story only gives one a further horror of smoking! How can anyone find pleasure in it?"

She felt Fritz's hand tremble as he took hers. "I cannot help thinking of what might have happened to you when we were engaged," he said in a choked voice. Vicky had caught her sleeve on fire on a candle when sealing a letter.

"You mentioned the Sigmaringens – or rather Karl," Vicky said, glad to change the subject. "Marie's wedding will be in April. I know the family hoped Karl would come then. It'll already be so sad without Anton." Anton Sigmaringen had died of injuries he had received in the war.

***

---

[35]   siblings

Anhalter Bahnhof, Berlin, April 25, 1867

"May you be as happy as we are," Vicky smiled, reaching up to kiss her cousin's cheek one more time as the train groaned to a stop.

Philippe smiled, squeezing her hand. Philippe was Uncle Leopold's second son, and had just been married to Marie Sigmaringen. Vicky smiled at a memory which floated through her mind, of a children's ball long, long ago, when she was a little girl of six years. She and Philippe had danced together – he was three years her senior – but someone had bumped into her, knocking her down. Philippe had lifted her up in his arms, kissing her as he did so.

Fritz kissed the bride's cheek, and shook hands with Philippe. "It is quite certain we shall be able to attend the Exhibition," he said as he helped Vicky back into their carriage.

There had been political difficulties with France, and this next Great Exhibition was to be in Paris, so that their attendance had been uncertain.

Vicky was weaning Baby, in anticipation of going to Paris. Paris! It had been eleven years since Vicky's first visit to Paris, as a girl of fourteen, before she was even engaged. She remembered that visit so well. It would be a great pleasure to be the guest of the Empress Eugenie again.

But what could she wear? She smiled again at the memory of the Empress Eugenie giving her "doll's clothes" – supposedly to fit a life-sized doll, but really for her to wear. Those dresses had been the most elegant Vicky had ever owned, and in a pleasant, modest style she was comfortable with, in spite of being Parisian.

But all the new clothes Vicky had bought or made were now too large. Since Baby's birth her other dresses fit well again. She must wear some of these, as she could not afford another new wardrobe, when she had just gotten one two years ago, and twice again while she was expecting. There were still so many improvements to be made in the Neues Palais and the Kronprinz Palais, she would much rather the money go to these than to new dresses. Fritz's income had still never been raised to that appropriate for the household of the Crown Prince.

***

Berlin Schloss, May 8, 1867

Vicky stood near Fritz, talking quietly with Abbat, whose birthday it was. In the evening the King of Greece, Alix's younger brother, had arrived. Vicky hadn't seen him since Bertie and Alix's wedding.

The dinner in honor of the birthday and the visiting King was about to begin, but no one had formed the procession to the dining room yet. Vicky wondered what was going on.

Finally, the King rose. So did everyone else, only to sit down at a motion from him. He went out, and everyone waited. There were footsteps at last, and the door opened again, the footmen clicking their heels and announcing, *"Seiner Majestät der König, und Prinz Karl[36]!"*

Vicky clutched at Fritz's arm as they both turned toward the door. So Prince Charles's appointment in Mainz was at an end. His absence from Berlin for most of the season for three years had been very pleasant.

Vicky looked across the room, and then stared. She glanced about. Everyone else stared too.

Prince Charles entered the room at his brother's side. His right arm hung in a sling, an obvious splint on his wrist. His left eye bore obvious traces of serious bruising, and a long, painful-looking cut ran from above his left eye to his right temple.

---

[36]   His Majesty the King, and Prince Karl!

CHAPTER FIFTEEN
A SCHOOLBOY ON HOLIDAY

Neues Palais, May 21, 1867

"I would like to speak to Wilhelm before our departure," Fritz said. They were to leave that evening for Paris. "I have not had an opportunity of reviewing his understanding of the political horizon."

"Let's have all the children there," Vicky said. "It will be good for them to hear his explanation." She opened the nursery door. Fritz lifted Charlotte up in his arms, talking softly to her as they went to the schoolroom. Lina followed with Baby in her arms.

Vicky took Henry's hand, leading him along the corridor. She looked up at the sound of a laugh, just before Fritz opened the schoolroom door. It was Charlotte. Vicky realized she had hardly heard Charlotte laugh in all these months since she had told her and Willy about her being Prince Charles's child. She glanced at Fritz. Charlotte's face was beaming as he kissed her and tickled her face with his beard.

"*Fünfzehn*[37], thirty, sixty, *einhundertzwanzig*[38], two hundred forty," Willy's voice came. He lay on the inclined board, obviously in the midst of mental arithmetic. Hinzpeter and Herr Schrötter sat across the room.

Vicky heard Hinzpeter say something she couldn't quite make out, and then Willy's answer came, "Großpapa *ist unser*[39] seventh King; Papa will be – Papa! Mama!" Willy leapt up, then looked confused, turned to Schrötter and saluted him, then ran to Vicky's side, kissed her hand, then turned to his father, saluting and clicking his heels.

"What's this, Willy?" Vicky said, embracing him. The children, as they left the nursery and entered the schoolroom, were trained to kiss their

---

[37]   Fifteen

[38]   One hundred twenty

[39]   Grandpapa is our

parents' hands in greeting, in view of future participation in court events. But Vicky and Fritz had attempted to keep everything as informal as possible between Willy and themselves, and had certainly never encouraged military discipline within their household.

Fritz said something to Hinzpeter and Schrötter, then set Charlotte down, crossing the room to the map of central Europe. "Wilhelm," he called, "can you show me where Luxembourg is, please?"

"Here," Willy said, running to the map and pointing.

Fritz nodded. "Can you explain what has been going on? We are going to Paris, but for a time it was uncertain if we were. Can you explain why?"

"France promised to be neutral during the war," Willy said, pointing to France on the map. "Luxembourg has been the property of the Netherlands since 1815, like Schleswig-Holstein belonged to the Danish King before we took it. But Luxembourg was also a member of the German Confederation, as Holstein was. We had a fort there, with *thousands* of soldiers."

Willy gave a little hop as he mentioned the soldiers, and paused to catch his breath.

"If France had joined Austria during the war, they think they would have beaten us. But they couldn't because the Emperor Napoleon wants to be friends with Italy. And Italy was on our side." He paused, tracing several paths on the map with his finger.

"France wanted to buy Luxembourg, like Italy wanted to buy Venetia," he went on. "But Italy has got Venetia through the war, and we have got Schleswig-Holstein through a war. Will France want to get Luxembourg through a war? Will there be another war?" Willy looked up at Fritz.

"I hope not. Peace seems quite certain now," Fritz said, looking Willy in the eye. "But go on."

"*Jawohl!*" Willy clicked his heels again, saluting Fritz, and began to speak again. "Bismarck objected to France's buying Luxembourg, because that takes away one of the borders between us and France. But he challenged France. You did think there would be war, didn't you, Papa?"

Fritz nodded.

"There has been a conference in England. But I don't understand all of that yet," Willy said. "Will Grandmama make everyone behave?"

Fritz turned his head, covering his face, pretending to cough. Vicky met his eye. He turned back to Willy.

"That was an excellent explanation, Wilhelm, and you have learned it very quickly, seeing that all of this is still going on. Do you have any questions?"

"Hinzpeter said that the King of the Netherlands would have sold Luxembourg, and that he wanted the money. What did he want it for? What did he want to buy? Hinzpeter wouldn't tell me, and Schrötter wouldn't either." Willy looked up at Fritz, and then at Vicky.

Vicky saw Fritz blush. He had showed her his diary, which she hadn't seen in a while, and she remembered well what he had written there – "The King wants money for his mistress's household."

"He needs to pay someone for something – private," Vicky said.

"Our soldiers had to leave Luxembourg, didn't they?" Willy asked.

Vicky nodded. "So as not to continue the perceived challenge to France, we had to disarm the fort."

"I would have kept them there!" Willy cried. He looked up, met Fritz's gaze, and hung his head.

"We must preserve peace," Fritz said. "Two wars is enough." He was silent for a moment. "Wilhelm, is everything ready for your tour in the Black Forest?"

"Yes. Hinzpeter says I will be with Cousin Fritz of Baden."

"Yes, this is a holiday for you boys, but you must do as Hinzpeter says. You understand that?" Willy nodded. "And I trust you will treat your cousin courteously as the higher ranking Prince that he is," Fritz said seriously.

"But Baden is only a Grand Duchy, and we are a Kingdom!" Willy said.

"He is first in line to his country's throne, while you are second," Fritz said. He knelt down so he looked straight into Wilhelm's eyes, and whispered something Vicky couldn't hear. "We will be home before you are, most likely," he said, as he stood again. "Now go and get ready, as Mama and I must also."

"*Jawohl!*" Willy clicked his heels again, saluting Fritz.

"Now, Willy, we place Hinzpeter in higher rank than Herr Schrötter for this very reason," Vicky began. "I don't want military discipline in my household."

"But Mama," Willy cried, staring up at her, "Papa is a hero, and he ought to be celebrated as such!" He clicked his heels again, but this time it seemed more like a defiant stamp of his foot.

"Of course, and I am very proud of him, but – Willy, family love is more important than all the military glory in the world." She looked up at Fritz, who nodded seriously.

Willy looked unsure, but nodded and kissed Fritz's hand.

"Lina, take the children back to the nursery." She paused, smiling at Charlotte as she passed her. "We will come to say goodbye before we actually leave."

"He certainly has your spirit," Fritz whispered to Vicky, smiling as they returned to their suite. "I could just see you in my mind's eye, when you wished to go to the opera with us when we were at the Exhibition."

Vicky felt herself blush, but she nodded. "Every time Mama sees him, she says every little mannerism of his reminds her of me when I was his age."

"Military discipline in the household certainly breeds more obedience," Fritz said, looking out the window. "I would never have imagined speaking to my parents in that manner when I was his age."

"But – of course, Fritz, I don't mean it about you personally – it is simply what I have observed everywhere here – it breeds unthinking obedience. I would far rather have my children speak their minds and ask questions than submissively do exactly as they are told – and half the time only be obedient to our face."

Fritz nodded, his face very serious. "Yes. That is exactly what I wish to avoid with our children."

***

Paris, May 25, 1867

"Look!" Vicky pointed at a building which looked very familiar. It was a smaller model of the Palace in Tunisia, just inside the grounds of the Exhibition.

They had arrived at the Prussian Embassy in Paris the day before, on Mama's birthday, but it had been too late to visit the Exhibition. In the morning they had been received by the officials of the Prussian exhibitors and led all round the building, which was oval shaped, having ten rounds surrounding an inner garden. Each round, or aisle, was dedicated to a different class: Works of Art; Apparatus of Liberal Arts; Furniture; Clothing and Fabrics; Industrial Products, Mining, Forestry; Food and the Preservation of the same; Livestock and Agriculture; Live Produce and Horticulture; the Improvement of Living Conditions and Society; and Weaponry. Within these categories were divisions for the many countries. Anything too large for the aisles was outside in the fairgrounds.

"Vicky!" a voice called as they entered the English art display, and Affie soon appeared.

Vicky embraced her brother. "I'm so glad see you," she whispered, finding her eyes filled with tears. Besides Bertie's visit at the end of the last year and an occasional glimpse of Alice, she had seen none of her family for a year and a half now.

At two o'clock there was to be a dinner at the Tuileries, and they were to meet their hosts, the Emperor Napoleon the third and the Empress Eugenie

***

"Your Majesty," Vicky said in French, curtseying to the Empress Eugenie.

"You are looking very well, and this is very pretty," the Empress gestured to Vicky's dress before kissing her on both cheeks.

Vicky looked up at her, wondering at the compliment on her dress. She had noticed many people seeming to stare at her, and she wondered what the fuss was about.

***

Paris, May 30, 1867

"What do you think of Paris this time?" Fritz asked Vicky as they entered their suite at the Embassy.

Vicky sat down and shook her head. "I think of it more as you do, I think." She looked up at him. "I was still a child when I came here with Mama and Papa, and of course I saw nothing of –" She trailed off, looking up at Fritz, grimacing. "I didn't know where to look during the whole performance! And to think it was a command performance! It's just what Mama and Papa would refuse to attend."

174

Fritz nodded. They had just returned from the theater. Throughout the whole play, they had talked together, avoiding watching the so-called "entertainment".

"Bertie would probably like this sort of play," Vicky whispered, feeling herself blush.

Fritz looked down at her. "That is what I kept him away from in Russia. I saw Alice and Louis were seated not far from us, and Arthur and Affie too."

"Alice and Louis looked as embarrassed as we were! And I'm glad to say Arthur did too, but I'm afraid Affie isn't so shy and blushing as he was formerly. I saw him watching the dancers with his opera glass."

Fritz looked away. "As Onkel Karl always does," he said. He looked Vicky in the eye. "He has been –"

"I don't wish to speak of this anymore," Vicky interrupted. "I'd like to enjoy this visit as much as I can. I'm *so* glad *he* isn't here." She paused. "I hope to see Alice and Louis sometime – I mean, to talk. We've *seen* them several times, but they always go in opposite directions from us. Alice is looking very pretty, but I thought she looked – not well, at the same time. Something – something – I long to have a long talk with her."

"Where would you like to go tomorrow?" Fritz asked. "You know the Agricultural aisle is the most likely place for us to find Louis, and Alice has gone about with Arthur."

"I'd like to rest a little tomorrow, and go out of town. It's too much for me."

***

June 6, 1867

Vicky stared up at the huge new cannons of the Prussian armaments, the new French systems for water sanitation, the bomb- and bullet-proof carriages provided by the Emperor Napoleon himself. They had stood in line to be on the new lifts, or "elevators", as everyone called them.

The Tsar Alexander with three of his sons, Alexander, Vladimir and Alexei, had arrived a few days before. Vicky was glad to meet the Tsar again, and to see the Tsarevich, but was disappointed not to see the Tsarevna. Minnie and Sasha, as Fritz called them, had the misfortune of losing their first child, and she hadn't come to the Exhibition.

The younger Russian Grand Dukes stared rudely at Vicky when they were introduced to her, and soon turned away to mutter to each other in Russian. Vicky felt their whole manner was extremely impolite, even to the Emperor and Empress, and they refused to admire anything at the Exhibition.

Yesterday Fritz's father had arrived. He had greeted Fritz and Vicky very cheerfully, and seemed to enjoy himself far more than Vicky had expected.

***

"Fritz, look, what has happened!?" Vicky cried, pointing.

Fritz looked up. Ahead of them one of the horses staggered; a stream of blood was pouring from its back. Fritz clutched Vicky's hand. "Thank *Gott* we are in these carriages!" he whispered. All the Royal guests had been provided with the bullet-proof carriages during their stay in Paris.

They were in a procession – seven Kings and Emperors were all on horseback – those of France, Prussia, Russia, Belgium, Austria, Sweden, and Turkey – she and Fritz, Alice and Louis, and many others following in carriages.

"You don't think it was an attempt, do you?" Vicky looked up at Fritz. "I didn't hear anything."

Fritz shrugged. "We will hear soon enough."

There was a commotion when the procession was over and they had reached the Tuileries. There had indeed been an attempt – on the Tsar, it was thought. The man hadn't been caught.

Vicky shivered. She remembered the rumors before the Great Exhibition of '51 – Papa's Exhibition – which the old King of Hanover had spread, rumors that revolutionaries would plot together to kill the Royal families who came to attend the Exhibition. This had been the reason why Fritz's family had been the only Royal family attending besides the Coburg relatives.

***

"How are the children?" Alice whispered as she sat by Vicky's side. Vicky had finally found an opportunity to speak with her, as they had both declined to attend that night's entertainment. Alice's manner was constrained, as Vicky had observed before.

"Willy's gone on a walking tour with his cousin Fritz of Baden and Hinzpeter, and the other children are quite well at home. They're quite safe with Nastya," Vicky laughed.

"Who is Nastya?"

Vicky smiled. "One of the Vassiltschikova sisters. Nastya and her sister are my new attendants – or rather Nastya is the children's attendant, and Alga is mine. But you should see them! Alga is six feet tall! And strong enough to lift a man." Vicky laughed. "I'm very glad to have them!"

"Oh, Vicky, how I wish I could have had one of them with me," Alice said, suddenly hiding her face against Vicky's shoulder. "I know! I know how *you* felt! *He* is back in Berlin, isn't he?"

"Oh, Alice, you – you don't mean –" Vicky trailed off, unable to speak further as a horrible idea entered her mind.

Alice nodded, embracing Vicky and continuing to hide her face.

"I *know* what *you* went through, Vicky. I understand how you feel about *Charlotte*. I always tried – to speak about her with you, but I never could. I didn't want to say anything which might hurt you! I understand it *all* now!"

Vicky shook her head. She felt as if she ought to cry, but she couldn't. She didn't know what to say. She embraced Alice, feeling her relax, and she knew Alice felt her sympathy without her having to speak a word. The pain she had seen on Alice's face was all too familiar – and yet she hadn't been able to recognize it.

"Was it – was it – did Louis – ?" Vicky paused. "Prince Charles arrived in Berlin with a broken arm and a gashed face. Was it him?"

Alice looked down, and nodded very slightly.

Glienicke, Potsdam, June 8, 1867

"Charlotta," Louischen whispered, "you will *not* disappear here. Papa can't smash you, and he can't bury you. The spring which makes this little island is so lovely, and Großpapa has cultivated it – he encourages it. It is part of his beautiful gardens." Louischen smiled at her reflection as she bent down to lift a blossom from the water. "What is this?" she wondered aloud. She wasn't sure what kind of flower it was, but she was near the hothouses, where many wonderful things grew.

She bent down, watching her reflection in the water again. A twig snapped. She froze, wondering who was there. She shrank closer to the tree. She heard someone alternately humming a tune and groaning with pain.

She listened more carefully. The voice had brought no color to her mind. But she felt sure it wasn't Papa. She relaxed, and leaned over the pool again. Now, there were obvious footsteps on the other side of the thicket.

"Ah, so I have surprised the dryad admiring herself in the water," a voice said. It was Großpapa. She hadn't been able to recognize him. He hadn't been well, so the black cloud wasn't as noticeable as usual.

"Are you feeling better, Großpapa?" she asked, running to him and taking his hand.

"Yes, and I shall be all the better for a pleasant walk and some fresh fruit." He turned towards the cherry orchard.

"Oh, wait, let me say goodbye," she called, and ran back to the island. She was so happy she had found another island, and this was one which Großpapa had made specially, so she was sure it wouldn't be destroyed. "Goodbye," she whispered, leaning down towards the face which looked up at her from the water. She turned, throwing her arms around the pine tree and kissing it.

She joined Großpapa again. He was smiling. "What is funny?"

"I had all sorts of fancies when I was your age. I talked to my reflection."

"But were the trees like friends to you?" Louischen asked. He nodded. "The pine tree is like Uncle Fritz," she said, smiling and glancing back at it, "and the cherry blossoms are like Aunt Vicky." She looked up at Großpapa again. "Großpapa, do you see the trees or flowers when someone touches your hand? Or any touch of a person or animal?" He shook his head. He walked more slowly than usual, and seemed tired. "Does your arm still pain you so much?" she asked anxiously, slowing to meet his pace.

"*Nein,* and I shall be rid of this sling soon," he said. She looked up, shaking her head. She could hear and see the pain in his voice. "I must get well enough not to miss my Paris holiday." He was talking to himself now.

"Helmkin goes, and Fritzch, and I am stuck here with this –" He broke off, obviously realizing she was listening.

He shrugged, and reached up and plucked a cherry from the tree above them, placing it in a small pail he had suspended from his belt. He was dressed casually, not in uniform, as he always was in Berlin.

"Großpapa, I was going to ask you what kind of flower it was I found floating in the spring, but you startled me, and I dropped it."

"Never mind," he said, "We shall go to the hothouses, and you may ask all the questions you like about the flowers." He paused. "The cherries –" he murmured, and stood still, watching her. He plucked another, holding it out. She took it from him, looking at it carefully before she ate it. She had gotten one with something wriggly in it before, and was more careful than she used to be.

"Louise," he said, with a small smile, "what do you see – what color is your feeling for me? What is that care, that affection, for those you truly care for?"

"Pink," she answered. When he spoke the name "Louisa" with the "a" sound at the end, as it was always said in German, his voice did turn very pink. When he called her "Louise" as it was said in English, or Louischen, his voice was different. Simply "Louise" brought no particular color to his voice, and when he called her "Louischen", she saw a flash of pink which immediately turned to harsh, bloody, dripping red.

"That feeling is soft, warm, velvety pale pink, with the smell of roses," she said softly, feeling the velvety sensation on her cheek. "I think it so beautiful. What is it to you, Großpapa?" She paused, reaching up to pluck a cherry from a particularly low branch.

"It is a creamy haze – not like milk, but like fog," he said. "And what is happiness? You told me before, but – refresh me." He bent down and took the cherry she held up with his lips, closing his eyes and sighing as he chewed and swallowed. "That is very refreshing, but refresh my memory."

"Green stars around the edges of the person's voice. But a green voice itself is a man's voice."

"And a woman is purple?" he asked. She nodded.

"Come, Louisa," he said, and turned back again. Soon, they came to the hothouses and the orangery. Louischen had never been inside, though she had often gazed with fascinated eyes through the glass at the beauties inside. "Have you ever tasted a peach?" he asked. She shook her head. "A pineapple?"

"No."

"An orange?"

"Only a tiny piece, and it wasn't a very good one, Aunty said, but I liked it very much."

"Would you like to taste each of these?"

"Oh, yes!"

He took a key from his pocket, and she followed him into the hothouse. She waited at the entrance while he talked with one of the gardeners. The man nodded, then shook his head, speaking too low for her to understand. She saw him take several fruits from a basin and slice them up before disappearing through a small door.

Großpapa soon returned to her. "The pineapples are not ripe, and if they are not, they are very painful to eat."

"Because of their spines?" she asked. She had seen a pineapple, but she didn't see how to eat it.

"No, the soft fruit inside has something about it – it is as if it burns the tongue, when it is not ripe."

Louischen shuddered. "Have you ever burnt your tongue, Großpapa – I don't mean with hot food, but how do you not, when you smoke your cigars?" He had no cigar today, she noticed.

He laughed, and took a piece of fruit from the bowl. "The outer end of the cigar is the burning end, of course."

Louischen was about to ask why he had no cigar today, when he said, "I have none because I wished to enjoy the fresh air and the fresh fruit." It was as if he had read her mind.

"Besides, when one only has one arm –" he said, his voice growing harsh, with a tinge of the blood of anger. He took a piece of cloth from his pocket. "Tie this around your eyes, and give me your hand."

Louischen did as he told her, stepping carefully as he led her forward. "Come now, smell this, and taste it. Tell me what you think of it." He placed something in her hand.

It was moist, but part of it was fuzzy, and she guessed it was a slice of peach. She had felt them before. She smelled the fruit, then took a bite. A burst of flavor she couldn't describe overwhelmed her.

"Oh, it is wonderful," she finally said. "But I feel the fuzzy feeling all over when I swallow it. I often feel that way when a food has a strange texture."

"And this?"

Louischen took what he handed her. It was a soft, oblong piece of fruit. It felt strangely dry to her hands. She took a bite, chewing slowly, riding the wave of sensation which swept over her.

Her vision, in the first moment, was filled with orange – the same shade of orange as she saw in Uncle Fritz and Aunt Vicky's voices when they spoke to each other – then, as she chewed and swallowed, a shiver went over her, and yet it wasn't exactly a shiver. It was a strange, inward sensation, which seemed vaguely familiar, but she couldn't understand why.

"Großpapa?" she cried, starting away. She swept the cloth off her head. He stood at a distance. She shook her head. She was sure she had felt someone touch her, but there was no one else. The gardener hadn't returned. Großpapa was obviously watching her closely, an amused, interested, and – some feeling she couldn't identify – look on his face.

She began to chew a second bite, closing her eyes again. The sweetness and tang of the juice were both so strong. The previous sensation returned, growing stronger, and she felt her heart beat wildly. Her vision was suddenly filled with that mysterious field of orange flowers. The flowers appeared to blow in a wind, opening slowly, and releasing a sweet smell.

The flowers faded, and nothing was left but the green plants, which quickly turned into a shower of green stars. This had never happened before. The other times she had seen those orange flowers, they had remained perfectly still, then disappeared, as had her memory of what had happened at the time she had seen them.

"You have fed me oranges before? Those times when I don't remember?" She looked up questioningly, meeting Großpapa's eye. "But it must have only been the juice. I don't remember eating it, and I remember textures," she went on, stroking her hand over the back of his coat, feeling the texture and seeing the streak of blue which shot across her vision. "But you must have given me orange juice. Why wouldn't you tell me? Why did you say I wouldn't understand, if it is so simple? And why didn't I see this, and feel this way, when I tasted the orange Aunt Vicky gave me?"

Großpapa looked down. "This only happens with very *perfect* fruits," he murmured. "You said that one you tasted wasn't very good." His face was slightly flushed as he looked up again, gazing into her eyes. She felt as if she couldn't move.

"You don't need to describe it," he whispered. "That is what the cherries are for me," he said, letting her go.

"Großpapa," she whispered, as they began to walk again. He had led her to the hothouse now. She suddenly felt very shy. "I want to ask you – about a flower."

He nodded. "I said you could ask all the questions you want."

"But – I don't mean one of your hothouse flowers," she whispered, hiding her face in her hands. "You showed me what those strange orange flowers mean. It is something like that – something I see." She peeped up at him through her fingers. He looked at her questioningly. "It – it is a very common flower," she went on, her voice catching in her throat. She took his hand, playing nervously with his fingers, keeping her eyes fixed on his hand.

"What is it?"

"A – a thistle." She looked up at him. "A purple thistle. It is what I see – what I feel – when Papa touches me. Why – why is it a purple flower? A man is always a green tree."

Großpapa's face had flushed bright red the moment she mentioned Papa. His expression changed, his face looking almost ugly. He opened his mouth, but didn't speak, only sighing deeply, but she still saw a flash of blood-red anger.

He shook his head, sighing deeply again. "That is the only flower I do not wish to speak of, and you may *not* ask *any* questions about it." He spoke crisply, his words more and more abrupt as he went on. He strode forward towards a potting table, not facing her. *Bang!* He brought his fist down on the table.

Louischen stood still, wondering if she should slip away and leave him alone. She watched him, wondering what had upset him so badly.

Finally, he turned, looking at her with a smile again. He stepped forward, picking a pale pink flower and placing it gently in Louischen's hair. He bent to kiss her forehead, and she ran forward to search for the flower she had found in the water.

Paris, June 7, 1867

Fritz watched as the carriage drove away, and then turned back. Vicky had decided to leave Paris early. With the anniversary of Siggy's loss approaching, she had said she could not bear to remain in the midst of the festivities and frivolities of Paris.

Fritz understood how she felt, but he had not wished her to leave. The Emperor and Empress had been kind and understanding, but he could see that they were disappointed. There was to be a great ball and dinner tomorrow.

Fritz yawned. He was glad there was no command performance tonight, as he was quite tired, and he knew tomorrow would be a late night.

When he reached the Embassy, one of the footmen hurried towards him. "Your Highness, your things have been moved to the Mars Pavilion in the Tuileries, as the Embassy is far too loud tonight," he said quickly in French.

Fritz nodded. There was a great deal of hammering and other loud preparations going on for the event of the next day. He turned to go.

"You have a visitor," the footman went on. "As she said she was part of your family, I showed her to your suite. She will be waiting for you. Here is the key. She's in there, but doesn't have one, so she can't be gone."

Fritz nodded, and hurried back to his carriage. It must be Alice. His heart ached at the thought of what Vicky had told him of her conversation with Alice the night before. He remembered Vicky's words when she first heard of Onkel Karl's appointment to Mainz. "But it means he is to be near Alice. Mainz isn't far from Darmstadt." He felt a hot wave of anger rush over him.

His thoughts had often gone to the sight of Onkel Karl with his arm in a sling and the long gash across his face. He had wondered what had happened, but this possibility had not entered his mind.

Fritz hurried into the Pavilion, asking the way to his suite. All the rooms were lavishly decorated with thick, plush red carpets and brocade curtains. A faint floral scent wafted through the rooms. Finally, he closed the door. The door of the next room was open, and there were lights in the inner rooms, but not the one he would enter first. "Alice?" he called, then paused. He heard a voice in the next room, and hurried forward. "Alice?" He heard the rustle of a woman's dress. "Alice." His voice broke. He vaguely saw someone rise from a sofa and come towards him. He paused, not turning to face her. How could he look her in the eye? "Alice, Vicky told me everything." He could not go on.

She stepped towards him, throwing her arms around him. "Fritz."

It was Anna

"Vivi, it's nice to see you," Vicky said, kissing her sister-in-law's cheek.

Vivi nodded briefly, not answering, but took Vicky's arm.

Vicky wished Vivi was easier to talk to. She was her other sister in Germany besides Alice. They had been good friends before Vicky's marriage, but since then, she had always been very stiff and quiet. Vicky supposed Vivi was simply on her guard, as everyone from the Berlin court must be.

Vicky had stopped in Baden on the way home. She was still undecided whether she wanted to be at home on the anniversary of Siggy's death or not. She must decide, and write to Fritz. He had promised to be with her on the day.

She picked up a paper to read. It was one of the Bismarckian papers – not the Kreuzzeitung itself – one which she would normally never read, but she was curious to see what the papers had to say about the Exhibition, and about the crowd of Royalties present. The Kings and Emperors of France, Prussia, Russia, Austria, Sweden, Belgium and Turkey were all at the Exhibition, and there were more Royal visitors going soon. Bertie, she knew, would soon attend. As well as Fritz and Bertie, the heirs to the thrones of Italy, France, Turkey, Saxony and Japan would all soon be present. It was an unheard of gathering.

She glanced over the part of the paper mentioning the Royal visitors to the Exhibition, and the accounts of the entertainments and command performances set before Napoleon's guests. This paper was from a few days ago, and mentioned her and Fritz.

"The Crown Princess of Prussia... has so little sense of what is proper as to appear everywhere in old gowns of two seasons past... as a purposeful insult to the Empress Eugenie."

Vicky rolled her eyes and shook her head. She had chosen her dresses so carefully, and they seemed to her to match those of the present style quite well, with her usual adjustments which she would have made in any case, even if she had bought an entirely new wardrobe – those of a higher neckline and not quite such full skirts, which made it impossible to fit easily through doorways or to walk in crowds, both of which would be necessary for the visit to the Exhibition.

The Empress Eugenie had frequently complimented her on her gowns, and had appeared sincere. She was so often so diffident about her own position, not having been trained in Royal duties, having been a Spanish countess before she married the Emperor. Vicky could not believe she would not have spoken to her honestly if she hadn't truly admired Vicky's gowns.

It was absurd to say that she had worn these gowns as an insult. Anyone who knew anything about Vicky knew of her admiration of the Empress Eugenie. It had been written of in the papers at the long-ago visit to Paris when she was fourteen.

The gown Vicky had worn at the particular time the paper spoke of was one Fritz had greatly praised on the two occasions she had worn it before, even writing in his diary that she had looked *"vorzüglich"*. This, she decided, was all the praise that mattered. Praise from her husband and praise from the woman whom she had always admired most in the matter of dress and style were worth far more than the empty praise of one who could write such a false accusation for the amusement of Vicky's declared enemies.

"Anna!" Fritz cried, pushing her away and taking hold of her arms so she could not attempt to embrace him again.

"I had to see you," she cried. "I had to see you, even though you –" She broke off, snatching her arms from his grasp and dashing towards the door.

Fritz breathed a sigh of relief. But she turned, coming towards him. Now she was blocking the path to the door. Her full skirts would make it difficult to go around her if she stood in the way. She was not leaving.

"Even though you betrayed me!" she cried. "My husband and I arrived last week, but I chose to come privately and not be received. I couldn't bear to see you, knowing how you have betrayed me!" Her voice trembled, as did her hands as she tried to take his. He stepped back, putting his hands behind him.

"How have I betrayed you, Anna?" he asked calmly, stepping farther back. He was nearly in the next room now, and the light shone on her face. The color of her lips and cheeks were strongly emphasized as usual, but her face was streaked with tears.

"How have you betrayed me? You fought against my country!" She clasped her hands together.

Fritz shook his head. "I was in the Bohemian army, not even in Germany," he said. "And you know me, Anna. You know I never wanted war." He stepped back, then tried to step forward again, but was too late. *No!* He shook his head. She had closed the door behind her as she came through it.

"But I had to see you," she went on, ignoring his words. "I couldn't come here, and see you at a distance, and not – not see you like this, *mein Schatz!*"

Fritz stumbled, falling back onto a sofa. He struggled to rise, but his feet were entangled by her skirts, and before he could rise, she had knelt by his side and leaned over him, pressing her lips to his face. He turned his head so she didn't touch his lips, and pushed her away. But she, too, rose quickly, and was at the door before him.

Fritz shook his head again. What could he do? He had vowed to himself long ago that he would never use any kind of violence against a woman. But she blocked his way, and her full skirts made it easy for her to block his way. He wouldn't risk tripping again.

"Anna, come here," he said, offering his arm. He put his other hand in his pocket, feeling the key the footman had given him. It was a key which would work for all the locks in this suite.

She stepped forward, taking his hand in both of hers rather than taking his arm. She looked at him, her face beaming. He watched her face for a moment. She turned towards him, blushing deeply, but he turned away, carefully avoiding her gaze.

"Come," he murmured, and walked through the open door towards the inner rooms of the suite. He felt himself blush. *What would Vicky say if she saw me?* he thought as he entered the bedroom.

He went forward, sitting down on the edge of the bed. Anna sat beside him, putting her arms around him, trying to press him down onto the bed. He turned his head again as she tried to kiss him. He raised his arm to push her away, but she snatched at his hand, clasping it to her chest. "Go." He motioned to the door of a large dressing-room. "Prepare for bed," he said, feeling his face flush hotly.

Anna blushed deeply, and disappeared into the dressing-room. She hadn't closed the door, but he couldn't see her. He rose as quietly as he could, and rushed to the door, closing and locking it behind him.

CHAPTER SIXTEEN
ONE YEAR AND TEN YEARS

Neues Palais, June 16, 1867

Fritz softly opened the bedroom door. Vicky was asleep. It was just after seven in the morning, but he had only just arrived. He slipped quietly into his dressing-room to change and go to bed. He yawned. There had been trouble on the way home, as there had been an accident on the same railroad his train was on.

"Fritz!" Vicky murmured, rubbing her eyes. "I'm so glad you are home," she said, as he lay down at her side. "I was afraid – that you wouldn't –" Her voice trembled, and she didn't finish her sentence.

"You did not believe I would not keep my promise, did you?" he asked, turning to look her in the eye.

"Of course not. But there were the storms, and I heard there were several train accidents – so I was anxious as well as uncertain."

"I would have come by carriage and on horseback if I had to," Fritz said, taking her in his arms. "I would not leave you alone again on that day unless it was simply impossible to come soon enough."

Vicky turned to look at Fritz, snuggling closer and pressing her cheek against his shoulder.

"Vicky," he whispered, "that day – one year ago now, in two days – that day was the most painful in my life except one." He spoke seriously, stroking her hair. "You know what I mean?"

Vicky nodded, hiding her face. She felt as if she couldn't speak.

"My birthday, eight years ago," Fritz said very softly. Vicky nodded again. "That pain has healed for you?"

Vicky glanced at him, and hid her face again. "Yes," she said slowly, "but the memory of it will never go away. And I wouldn't want it to. It taught me many lessons. And to see you, Fritz – how tender and patient you were. I learned to love you in a different way than I had before. I told Mama, when we were in England in '61, that I had a more mature love for you."

She paused, looking him in the eye. Fritz stroked her cheek, kissing her.

"With – 'married love' – as I called it before we were married – taken away for one whole year, I learned how I really loved you. I never knew before. The infatuation – as Mama called it – was uppermost before that. I'm *not* saying that there's no infatuation in my feelings *now*," she smiled, "but – it was uppermost at first, so much that I didn't realize and appreciate many things."

Fritz smiled. "Vicky, I asked the children what you told them – I mean about Charlotte, and about babies in general." Vicky nodded, watching his face. "You told them that – physical intimacy – which many people refer to as 'love' – is not love in itself, but that it has to be loving, to be love."

She nodded. "They remembered my words very well. Which – was it Willy or Charlotte who told you?"

"Both, and separately. What you said made a deep impression, and the one we could wish, I think."

"Yes. And you were always so tender – when we first – on your next birthday –" She shook her head, tears coming to her eyes. "You've always been so tender and patient."

Fritz smiled, looking at her. "Love is patient, love is gentle," he began, stroking her hair. "Love does not insist in having its own way. Love bears up under anything and everything that comes, and never fades in any circumstances." He cradled her face in his hands. "What else could I do? I said I loved you, and I meant it."

"Yes, that passage always moves me," Vicky whispered with tears in her eyes. "I remember reading over it with Papa, the first time I read it after Mama had Miss Hildyard give me the full Bible. Of course I had read that passage before, but it never made such an impression on me previously. But it also says that 'love is never envious nor boils over with jealously'. When I talked with Mama a few years ago – that same time I mentioned – I had realized that – I had loved you, and respected you, but – I didn't always believe – I allowed myself to be jealous of Anna, even though I knew she is your sister, and that you would never –"

Fritz sighed heavily. "Speaking of Anna," he said, putting his hand over his eyes. "She was in Paris."

Vicky looked at him, but she couldn't think of anything to say. She would let him speak.

"The evening you left, there were loud preparations for events at the Embassy, and they moved my things to the Mars Pavilion. I went there, and the footman told me I had a 'family visitor' waiting for me. I expected it to be Alice, as you had just told me what had happened to her. I went in expecting her, ready to comfort her, and it was Anna! I did not even know she was in Paris."

Vicky nodded. "We saw Fritz Hessen arrive alone. I had no suspicions. What happened? Was she actually in your suite?"

"Yes, and she wouldn't let me leave. She was between me and the door. She has some strange idea that I have betrayed her in fighting in the war last year."

"*You* betrayed her? It's her Papa who betrayed her!"

Fritz nodded. "She would not leave. I had to trick her into going to the bedroom" – he paused, blushing but meeting Vicky's eye – "and lock her in for the night. I actually told her to 'prepare for bed', and she went into the dressing-room." Fritz looked away blushing again.

"You locked her in? Why didn't you simply leave?"

"She would not let me pass her – and you know how full her skirts always are – I tripped and fell once, and you can imagine how she took advantage of that situation," he said, a disgusted tone entering his voice. "I would not use force – even that of taking her by the arm and pushing her out the door. But that was impossible, anyway, as I said. I slept on the sofa in the entrance to my suite, and unlocked the bedroom door in the morning, when I left. I had heard her hammering at the door several times in the night, crying that I was the cruelest man in the world, asking how I could call myself a gentleman when I took advantage of helpless women, locking them up, and so on." Fritz's lips twitched, and he rolled his eyes. "She had food and water and a comfortable bed. It is not my fault if she did not take advantage of them. I had no qualms. It was she who wished to take advantage of me. I asked the footman not to allow anyone into my suite again, without my approval."

"But, you said –" Vicky sat up suddenly. "You said she was in your suite for some time before you arrived?" Fritz nodded. "And did you find all your things as they should be?" He nodded again. "Did you find my note?"

Fritz shrugged, and then sighed and covered his eyes. "Where was it?"

"In the outside pocket of your valise," Vicky said.

Fritz nodded seriously. "It was not there. I looked there, as I know your habits." He smiled, squeezing her hand.

"But –that means *she* got my note to you," Vicky cried. "And there will be –"

"It does not necessarily mean that," Fritz said. "It could have blown away when they moved my things from the Embassy. That has happened to notes I have left in that pocket. It is not a secure location for paper when one is out in the wind."

Vicky nodded, and lay down again. "I hope that's what happened," she whispered, laying her head on Fritz's chest where she could hear his heartbeat. "I hope it blew away, and will either remain unread or be found by someone who won't know my handwriting and my words. But I dread –" She pulled the blanket up around her face.

"You dread the idea of it falling into Onkel Karl's hands," Fritz said, realizing what she anticipated.

***

Kronprinz Palais, July 3, 1867

It was one year since the Battle of Königgrätz. Since then, Fritz had been hailed everywhere as a hero and the savior of the Prussian state. If the battle had gone otherwise, Prussia might have been annexed as Austrian territory.

Fritz opened the door of his study and stared. On every table, desk, or little shelf stood bouquets of flowers; draped over the chairs and on the walls were festoons and wreaths of laurels and more flowers. He stepped inside.

"Papa!" Vicky and the children stood there. Fritz had wondered where they were, as Vicky had not been in bed when he rose, and her dressing-room, boudoir, and the nursery and schoolroom, too, had been empty except for Baby asleep in Mrs. Hobbs' arms.

Wilhelm stepped forward with a slight click of his heels, saluted, and began to recite a little poem about the war.

Fritz smiled, feeling tears come to his eyes as Vicky stepped forward to take his arm. Charlotte and Heinrich clung to his hands.

"Willy can come to hear the speeches today, can't he?" Vicky asked. "He wishes to so much."

Fritz looked at Wilhelm, who stood there, beaming at him. He looked at Vicky. "Only if he remains with you the whole time, and does not attempt to –" Fritz paused, wondering what to say. He put his hand on Wilhelm's shoulder. "If you stay in the carriage with Mama you may attend."

Wilhelm nodded, kissed Fritz's hand and saluted again.

"I thank my glorious army for their bravery, endurance and devotion… The First Army fought bravely, but it is to the Second Army and the Crown Prince we owe our victory!"

Vicky sat in the carriage holding Willy's hand as the King spoke. Fritz was on the King's right, on his horse Cairngorm, whom he had ridden in the battle of Königgrätz. Nearby, to the King's left, was Fritz Karl.

There were many speeches, and finally Vicky thought Willy looked tired. "You will be with them someday," she whispered as he yawned. "You must learn not to be fatigued. Look at you, yawning away! Think of Papa, last year, on horseback for fifteen hours in a day!"

Willy sat up, opening his eyes wide. "I'm not tired, Mama."

Finally, Fritz dismounted and came to the small dais where the speakers had stood. He looked out at the crowd, then straight at Vicky, and smiled.

"You all know that I am not for war," he began, "and that the man who has never seen war little knows what war is. Everyone speaks of glory, but who speaks of the horrors? I can think of no sight worse than that of a battlefield the day after a battle, and I shall never forget it."

He shook his head, covering his eyes, and even at a distance, Vicky thought she could see a shudder pass over him.

He took an obvious deep breath, and began again. "Many, many of our countrymen and our enemies are now mourning the loss of sons, brothers, fathers, husbands and friends, as a result of this war. I, too, grieve the loss of many a kind friend, and many a promising young comrade whom I had seen grow up and take his place in the ranks by my side.

"I have no brother," he said, looking towards a group of young cadets, from whom a sob or two had been heard after the mention of the loss of friends, brothers and fathers. "And I have no son old enough to go to war. But I, too" – he paused, his voice shaking with emotion – "I, too, mourn the loss of a son. A little boy, not old enough to remember me if it had been he who had lived and I who had passed away."

Vicky wiped her eyes, and glanced at Willy. His face was buried in his handkerchief, and he shook with sobs. Vicky put her arm around him, and burst into tears herself.

"My Royal father, the King, granted me his kind permission to go home to my grieving wife and children, to see my child one last time, though it be in his coffin. I declined this favor, as I felt it impossible to leave my post at such a vital time for our country. The protection and guidance of my army had been placed in my hands. I could not abandon it.

"In this time of the greatest grief and pain, I had to lay aside my own cares, and care for my country. I had to push aside my grief and take command, in what has become the largest battle in history. This seems unimaginable to me now, looking back at the state of grief I was in.

"I can only say that God was with us, and has helped us. My guiding thought, as I fought against my grief, and made my sacrifice for our country, was this: 'Whatever your hand finds to do, do it with all your might.'"

He nodded, and stepped down from the dais.

Fritz stood in the crowd who swarmed around him. Many old friends and old enemies came up to murmur thanks for his speech, turning away still wiping tears from their eyes.

He jumped at the touch of a hand on his shoulder, and tried not to start away when he glanced back to see that it was Onkel Karl.

"Fritz."

Fritz blinked. It was the second time Onkel Karl had ever called him "Fritz" and not "Fritzch". He looked at him. Onkel Karl's right arm no longer hung in a sling, but there was no longer a cast on his arm. He shuffled his feet, glanced down and back up.

"Fritz, I lost a son, too, in the war. A fine, promising young man, as you said. He was only" – he paused, quickly counting on his fingers – "*vier-und-zwanzig*[40]. It is the first grown up son I know of – the death of." His voice became very quiet, choked with emotion. Fritz had never seen or heard such pain in his face and voice. "He was the son of the dearest woman to me in the world." He nodded, his gaze on the ground, and turned away, and Fritz could see that he was wiping his eyes. He turned back. "Your speech – moved me." He walked quickly away, disappearing in the crowd.

Finally, the crowd began to disperse, and Vicky's carriage came forward. Fritz hurried towards her.

Vicky reached up to squeeze his hand. Wilhelm's face was buried in his handkerchief.

As she drove on, back to the palace, Fritz remounted his horse, and turned towards the riding school. Just as he was about to leave the square, he paused, hearing Fritz Karl's voice.

"The King and Crown Prince imagine that the Second Army came to my aid," he said bitterly, "but there was no need for such a thing! I needed no support!"

Fritz shook his head as he rode away, remembering Fritz Karl's words on the battlefield. "*Thank you. You have saved our Army! If you hadn't come, we would have lost! You were my savior!*"

---

[40]   Four and twenty

Berlin Schloss, July 1867

Vicky held Willy and Charlotte's hands firmly as they entered the dining-room, Fritz leading Henry and carrying Baby. They had arrived somewhat early, but everyone but the King was already there. Fritz's mother was in Koblenz, and would soon be in England, where Alice also was.

"Mama, why does Prince Charles not use his arm?" Willy whispered, gazing across the room to the table, where Prince Charles sat, waiting as the page cut up his food. Prince Charles's arm no longer hung in a sling, but he still could not use it much, never raising it above the table. He ate awkwardly with his left hand.

"Hush, Willy, and sit here," Vicky said. "Read or talk quietly, and I mean *quietly.*" She gestured to the small sofa where the little children always sat during the family dinners.

"Charlotte, do you know what this is?" Louischen called. Vicky glanced quickly at the book Louischen held. It was a colorful book of flowers, but was mostly pictures. Charlotte often read Vicky's books about plants and animals and knew the Latin names almost as well as Vicky herself.

Ebi sat in the corner of the sofa, working away with her knitting needles. Mariechen sat by her side, a book open in front of her on the table, leaned against another stack of thicker books, so she could read without holding the book. Little Fritz Leo sat in her arms, and she occasionally paused to say something or to turn him around so he looked either at her or at the book.

Fritz Leo, or Fritzi as Marianne and the girls called him, was just the same size as Baby now – the same height, the same weight – though he was one full year older than she. He was so tiny, and she so big and strong, they appeared to be the same age.

Vicky and Fritz turned away to the grand table, but she turned back to watch the children. Willy knelt at a little table of books near the children's sofa, selecting two books she recognized well even from across the room. One was entitled "German Treasures of the Holy Roman Empire". It was a book he always loved, which Fritz sometimes spent hours crouched over, pointing out and explaining the history of various items in its collection. The other, in French, was called "The Bottom of the Sea". Both were large, heavy books full of paintings and other illustrations. The first, Vicky feared, was too heavy for him to lift by himself.

"Fritz," Vicky murmured, glancing up to catch his eye. "I was thinking–"

She broke off as there was a loud *thump.*

"Aus meinem Weg[41]!"

"But Mama says I should –"

"Nein!"

Thump.

Vicky stared at Fritz for a moment, seeing the look of alarm in his eyes at the sound of the commotion before they both rose and hurried to the children's table.

"Here is our boy," she heard in Fritz Karl's voice. She rolled her eyes. Fritz Leo was, as she had written to Mama, the principle attraction with most of the family. Willy was never noticed, but she was very glad of this fact.

"Mama," Willy cried, lying on the floor with the heavy book of "German Treasures" beside him. There was a bruise quickly appearing on his forehead, but he looked more angry than hurt.

"He pushed past me just when I was trying to take the book! I had it standing up, so I could slide it off and get my fingers under it," Willy said. "But he knocked it aside, when I was still sitting, and it struck my head."

Vicky heard the cry of a little child, and looked around. No one here at the sofa was crying. Henry and Baby were asleep, and Ebi still sat working away. Charlotte and Louischen sat with their arms around each other, whispering over a book.

"Does your head pain you?" Vicky asked as Willy sat up. She kissed the bruise on his forehead. He shook his head. "You know you shouldn't try to lift that book. It is heavy even for me. Papa always lays it on the floor when he shows you things."

Vicky returned to the table. Fritz Karl sat between his father and the Grand Duchess of Schwerin. On the little boy's head was a military cap – one so large for him it easily covered his eyes. The cry she had heard came from him, every time the cap fell over his eyes. At this, they all laughed.

Mariechen stood behind Fritz Karl's chair, watching the little one. Vicky saw that Marianne had also risen from her seat. She walked up and

---

[41]   Out of my way!

down the room, wringing her hands. Vicky hurried to her and tried to take her arm, but she shook her head, and turned away.

Vicky jumped at a touch on her shoulder, but it was Fritz. "What?" she asked. He had whispered something as he came up, but she hadn't understood.

"Fritz Karl –" he said slightly louder, and paused. Vicky saw Fritz Karl look up. Fritz had spoken loud enough for him to hear.

"How dare you," he muttered in a low, tense voice, staring at Fritz. "How dare you and the King call me a coward!" He pushed away from the table with a loud *screech* of his chair, beginning to rise.

Vicky started up in alarm. He had obviously forgotten Fritz Leo the moment Fritz had spoken.

Mariechen darted forward, catching the little boy in her arms and hurrying out of Fritz Karl's way. He didn't even seem to notice her.

"How dare you call me a coward, in front of the army?" Fritz Karl stepped up to Fritz, glaring up at him.

"I never mentioned you in my speech," Fritz said calmly. "Papa said that you and your army fought bravely."

"He said that it was necessary for the First Army to be rescued." Fritz Karl's voice grew harsher as he spoke. "I needed no aid, no assistance, no – no – *rescuing*!" Fritz Karl said. "My army are all brave soldiers, and I –"

"We never said you were not. Papa said you were very brave." Fritz said, nodding and walking away.

Fritz Karl stood glaring after him, and then returned to his seat. "Where is the child?" he cried.

Prince Charles looked around. Mariechen still stood holding the little boy.

"Bring him here," he said. Vicky saw Mariechen look at him and turn away.

"He said bring him here, you –" Fritz Karl burst out, but his father whispered something in his ear, and he dropped his gaze, not speaking.

"Bring him," Prince Charles said again, and Mariechen reluctantly stepped closer, placing the little one in his lap.

Vicky couldn't hear what was said, as Mariechen slipped away, back to the children's sofa. Fritz Karl looked up again, laughing as he bent down to pick up the military cap, placing it on the boy's head again.

"She's as fierce as a broody hen," he said. "How did you get her to give him up so easily?"

Prince Charles shook his head. Fritz Karl laughed again. "Speaking of broody hens, I think we have another one here, too." He took something from his pocket, showing it to his father. He glanced over it, and laughed.

Fritz Karl took a long drink of champagne, and glanced over whatever he held again. "*Deine kleines Hähnchen*[42]," he smirked as he read it. "And she misses the cock very much at night, particularly as she won't have the chick to share her room instead."

Vicky shook her head, feeling her face burn. It was her note she had left for Fritz when she left Paris.

"Fritz," Vicky whispered, taking his arm again, "please, we should go." She felt herself blush deeply as she heard Fritz Karl read more in a mock-whisper which carried very well. She looked about. Others were hurrying to leave as well. Marianne had sent for Frau Kampmann to take the girls, though Vicky knew Marianne would stay as long as they kept Fritz Leo there.

She hurried to the children's sofa. Fritz took Baby and Henry in his arms, and Charlotte walked by his side.

"Willy, are you sure you're feeling well?"

Willy lay on the floor beside the two books, but with his hand on his head. He glanced up. "I was only falling asleep, Mama," he said, struggling to stand. "But we are taking the book, aren't we? We aren't leaving it here?"

"Bächmann can carry it," Vicky said, nodding to one of the footmen who hurried after her. She paused, taking Willy's hand as he paused to watch the man lift the heavy book.

"Not even strong enough to carry a book... A one-armed man shouldn't be King!" She winced as she heard Fritz Karl's voice.

Willy's hand trembled as she tightened her grip. "Come, Willy, and ignore him. You must learn to ignore his taunts."

"But – but – how dare he say things like that!" Willy's voice trembled with indignation. "Why does he seem to think his little boy is the heir?"

Vicky shook her head. "He is *his* heir. But he's not the heir to the throne. But you know they all wish he was. Willy, you must ignore his taunts. Papa has learned to." Willy finally nodded. Vicky smiled. Saying

---

[42]   Your little hen

that Fritz did something or wished something was usually enough to get Willy to try to imitate him.

Vicky glanced back again, her eye falling on Bächmann carrying the book. He was quite grown up now, and a very handsome young man. Vicky always thought of him as the boy who had sat on the back of her carriage during the parade on Fritz's birthday eight years ago – the last person she had spoken with before she had gone alone, into the laundry.

***

Neues Palais, Potsdam

"She *did* get the note!"

Vicky nodded as Fritz turned to look her in the eye. "Yes. It's the note I left for you in Paris. And we had only thought of the possibility of Prince Charles getting his hands on it! I never thought Fritz Karl might, and that he would read it aloud!" She cringed.

"And that they should laugh over it, and about your use of that word," Fritz said. Vicky looked up at him, surprised to see him blushing.

"What – which – word?" she asked. Then she realized what he meant. "Was there another word – which I used – that has – a different meaning?"

Fritz sighed. "*Ja.*" He shook his head, and strode across the room. "I hate – I do not wish –" He clutched the back of the chair which stood at the window, where Vicky often sat to write her letters. "I do not wish to ruin your –" He paused, frowning, and muttered, "Innocence is not the right word anymore, but it is that, in a way." He turned to look at Vicky, a look of pain in his eyes. "They have done so much towards that!" He sighed, shaking his head again. "You remember, Vicky, our conversation on our wedding night? About endearments?"

"Of course," Vicky whispered, taking his arm and leaning her head against him. He looked out the window.

"I said I did not wish to use words which felt unclean to me – because of associations I had. But I loved – I *love* your endearments. But there are so many words – words with more than one meaning – which they take and contort to the meaning their vile imaginations give them – when you use it so innocently. I always love your innocence – and it is more precious than ever now – when you have gone through so much!"

Vicky embraced him, reaching up for a kiss. "I understand what you mean, Fritz, and if you don't wish to tell me what their meaning is, I won't ask. And I *will* be careful about using those words in letters." She paused, and he bent down to kiss her again. "You've done so well, so many, many times, in not allowing Fritz Karl to provoke you."

Fritz looked at her. "Do you remember what you said, on my first birthday after our marriage, when I was so angry at him?"

"To ignore his taunts? Yes, of course."

"But I have realized there is more to that. It is so important that I ignore his taunts, because it is part of his – part of how he acts when he is hypnotized. You know how when I ignore him, he stops, at least with whatever line of thought he is on at the moment. It is important, too, that I do not accept the honors which place me above him. That is part of why I refused to take a higher command towards the end of the Danish campaign. It is not just that it would offend him."

Vicky nodded. "And he was so offended at the idea of your having to rescue him."

"Yes. You noticed how I kept repeating that Papa praised his bravery? Though –" Fritz paused, looking down. Vicky saw his face was flushed as he turned to the light again. "He certainly did require rescuing. They would have been taken prisoner. And he acknowledged that at the time. He wept in front of the whole battlefield."

"Fritz," Vicky said, "Willy needs to understand things about Fritz Karl. And I think it would be better from you than from me. You understand it all, and have seen him at different times. But he begins to taunt Willy as he always did you. It began long ago, when he called Willy 'ugly monkey'. But what he said when we were leaving – it's just what pricks Willy's pride the most."

She paused, embracing Fritz again. "I must say again how well you've done in not taking their bait. I'm no better at it than ever. Sometimes I can act as if I don't know what they mean, but now, when I realize how many things there are I don't understand, I'm so embarrassed that they think I do."

***

September 1867

"I have spoken with Willy as you wished, and with o'Danne," Fritz told Vicky. "There has been no more trouble, and Papa signed the papers I

200

wished very quickly. We shall have o'Danne as Willy's governor for at least one year."

O'Danne was Willy's new military governor. Schrötter had left after the first year.

Schrötter was a well educated man, fond of literature and of poetry, and not at all a typical guards-officer. Vicky had been very pleased about this, but he had expressed worry over disagreements with Hinzpeter. He had felt that Hinzpeter was given fuller authority over the boy than he, which, he said, would make his position very difficult.

Hinzpeter was given power over rewards and reprimands in a way which Schrötter was not. This was opposite to the usual custom in the Prussian Court, where the military governor usually held full sway, the civil tutor being ranked far below him.

Other disagreements had followed, and Schrötter had resigned. He had declared that he did not wish his pupil to suffer from "incongruity and divergence between two differing points of view." In Vicky's original instructions to Schrötter she had emphasized how there was no need to discuss things with both herself and Fritz, as "our wishes are completely identical". She felt that in resigning over disagreements, Schrötter had shown great respect to her and Fritz's wish for the children to be brought up in a peaceful and harmonious household.

Fritz had met o'Danne two years earlier. When Vicky first met him, his manners strongly reminded her of Schrötter. He shared the same interests in literature. Everything they knew about him made them feel sure he would be a good choice. He had also attended the same military school as Fritz himself, which was a very important point. That school was not under the influence of Prince Charles.

August o'Danne had requested a private audience with Fritz, saying that he was unable to make ends meet with his officer's income, and he had many daughters to provide for.

Tresckow, the Head of the King's Military Cabinet, had tried to intervene and appoint an "experienced soldier" as the military governor. Vicky had dreaded this possibility. All of the men Tresckow might suggest, she knew to be tools of the Kreuzzeitung party.

Besides, Vicky wished for no harshness in the governor's temperament. Hinzpeter himself was strict enough; Schrötter's manner had provided a pleasant balance.

***

Kronprinz Palais, Berlin, January 25, 1868

"Ten years!" Vicky wrote to her mother. "Ten years of great blessings, great happiness, and great thankfulness to you and Papa and Fritz's mother. I think so much of that dear day, and of everyone with us then – dear Papa, and Uncle Leopold, and Grandmama. How little we thought dear Papa would hardly see my children, and that they should never know them.

"These years have brought great happiness, and great sorrow as well. There is still many a day I weep for Siggy. Though my earlier trials have, for a good part, been overcome, to look about here and see the trials of others with whom I can so fully sympathize but which they must carry alone – this makes me feel how great my blessings are.

"I am so glad you liked Willy's last picture. I am sorry to say his arm gets stiffer in the elbow, though he can use his hand more and grasp things more than ever. He has begun Latin and also has more serious drawing lessons, which he takes delight in.

"I must say there is something about Charlotte which makes me uneasy. It is nothing of my old discomfort about her – it is that she very suddenly has no remnant of her former shyness. She coaxes and wheedles whatever she wants out of everyone, and if she were a bit older I would call her a coquette.

"I often wonder how my children will turn out, and tremble at the thought of their growing up at such a court, but Willy always shows a great wish to imitate Fritz in everything, which delights me. I only wish he would imitate his father rather more than his mother in the matter of modesty in his achievements.

"Henry begins to have his lessons with Willy, but is dreadfully slow in reading and writing. Baby grows splendidly and is my delight."

Vicky looked up as Fritz opened the bedroom door. He bent over her, glancing over her letter.

"Tell your Mama I have read through her book," he said. "And do say that I must admit I had never finished the family edition until now."

Vicky smiled. Mama had selected passages from her diary detailing her travels in Scotland, up to the last before Papa's death. Two years ago, she had these printed, only for family members to read. Now, the Queen was a published author. She had added accounts of some of her earlier travels, and removed some of the more personal descriptions.

"What did you think of what she put in about our engagement, compared to what she showed us in her actual diary?" Mama had showed them various things in her diary during their last stay in England. She was going through her letters and diaries, working towards beginning a biography of Papa. But the one Vicky had read over the most times was the account of her engagement.

She sighed, smiling as she leaned forward to add the last lines to her letter. "I must finish this letter, before the light goes out." The candle was flickering. She had been about to go to bed, but felt she must write to Mama on this day.

"Must you?" Fritz whispered, bending over her and kissing the back of her neck. He had been out all day. Vicky had barely seen him in the morning.

The candle flickered out. Vicky rose, throwing her arms around him. "I'll finish it tomorrow. Fritz, do you remember what Mama showed us in her diary? She even wrote that you told her we shook hands," she whispered, laughing.

Fritz laughed. "I remember that. I felt at the time I did not dare tell that I had kissed you. I –" He looked down, and then met Vicky's eye. "I did not know what it was to trust and be trusted," he whispered. "I had never imagined being able to confide in one's parents about – intimate matters. And there were many things I would never have told, all through our engagement."

Vicky looked up at him. The moonlight shone on his face, and she could see his face redden even in the faint light.

"I would never have told your parents what happened when your Papa fell asleep."

Vicky lay down, trying to think of what to say. She had always felt the urge to tell her parents any little naughtiness she had committed as a child. During their engagement, it had been hard for her to understand Fritz's reserve, as much as he had been astonished at her frankness.

"But I have learned that trust is a beautiful thing," Fritz murmured, lying down by her side and drawing her into his embrace. "It is one of the most beautiful gifts I have been given, in all these ten years."

CHAPTER SEVENTEEN
THE 'OPES OF 'ESSE

Kronprinz Palais, Berlin, February 10, 1868

Fritz hurriedly took the telegram from the table at the door. "Boy," it read. He opened the door and nodded to the footman who waited outside.

He rose, pacing the room. He wished the telegram had said something more.

Boom! Boom! Boom! The gun-salute began, and the crowds began to gather. Fritz watched, and stepped out on the balcony after the thirty-sixth. The crowds cheered. This meant another son for the Crown Prince.

He turned back, going into the bedroom and sitting down. He wished Vicky had sent something more than simply the word, "Boy," but they must be discreet, as everyone believed Vicky to be in Berlin.

Neues Palais, Hesse-Darmstadt, February 10, 1868

"Look at him; he is quite obviously Louis' son," Vicky encouraged, putting her arm around Alice.

"Wah! Wah!" the baby in her arms cried loudly.

Alice shook her head. "No. Vicky, you know what it is, don't you?" She didn't open her eyes. She hardly had all through the night.

"I don't know." Vicky bent over Alice, kissing her forehead and stroking a strand of hair off her face. Her heart ached at seeing Alice so exhausted with pain, and with other suffering as well, which she understood all too well. "I always thought it might not have been so bad, if she hadn't had – *his* eyes, and if there had been the possibility of it being Fritz's, but – I don't know." She squeezed Alice's hand. "I sent the telegram to Fritz, as you wished."

Kronprinz Palais, Berlin, February 13, 1868

"Alice had a very hard time," Vicky told Fritz. "She was so exhausted by the pain, she looked as if she felt as I remember feeling after Willy's birth. And she has had the fainting, like I had. But look at him. He is obviously Louis' child." Vicky held up the baby.

Fritz continued writing in his diary. He had left the page of his diary blank, and wrote an account of the birth from Vicky's description as if it was about Vicky. Their own baby had actually been born a couple of months before, in Hesse-Cassel, and would be raised in England, in the Queen's household.

Fritz took the little one in his arms, gazing into the baby's eyes. "He is our son now," he murmured, putting his arm around Vicky. "We had better let the children see their new little brother. They have been so full of questions about him, and can't understand their not being allowed to see him."

March 7, 1868

"Fritz wishes the name Joachim, but I insisted that our little one not go by it," Vicky wrote to Mama. "Waldemar is what he is to go by; 'Friedrich Joachim Ernst Waldemar' is to be his full name. But as he was born on the tenth I wished to add the name Victor or Albert." The tenth of February was the anniversary of Mama's wedding. The baby had actually been born in the last hours of the ninth, but as the gun-salute had been given after the receipt of the telegram, they kept the tenth as his birthday.

"Waldemar Fritz Ernst," Vicky laughed to herself. In the novel *Ivanhoe*, by Sir Walter Scott, there was a character called "Waldemar Fitzurst", whose daughter's name was Alicia.

***

Reinhardtsbrunn, Gotha, April 20, 1868
Vicky sat next to Alice, reading Fritz's letter aloud.

"Munich, April 17, 1868

"Meine Vicky,

"All is well here, and I have been very kindly received. The Bavarians make no show of their anti-Prussian feelings to me. I had a long talk with my old playmate Queen Merrichen. How well I remember her wedding, when Mama had me begin my diary. And how well I remember my astonishment and fascination with a certain couple – the bride's elder sister and her husband – Louis' parents – and the fact that they were always together. I had never seen such a thing – never seen a truly loving Royal couple. That impression was very deep indeed.

"The King here is like a schoolboy – though he is twenty-three – I do not see how he goes on, though I know he actually has a regent, though not in name, just as my Mama's father had.

"I had a long talk with several of the Princes here and they seem neither satisfied nor contented, but not disgruntled, with the convention with Prussia. They have been given special treatment, and are grateful for it.

"I shall write next from Italy – what used to be Austrian territory. You will now be with Alice, who I hope is better. Give her and *die liebe Kinder* my love."

Fritz was on his way to the wedding of Crown Prince Umberto of Italy and Princess Margarita of Genoa. Vicky wasn't going, as Fritz had always avoided a possible meeting of her and the King of Italy. She had met him once, long ago, in England, but in those days he wasn't under the spell.

"Bavaria has been given special treatment indeed," Alice said. "We certainly have not."

Bismarck had been hard at work to convince the Southern German states to join the North German Confederation, rather than form their own Southern Confederation. Bavaria had been the most resistant, and Prussia had finally made an agreement with them which left their army independent, where all the other states which had joined were compelled to enter into military conventions which placed their armies under Prussian command in case of war.

"It is very difficult work for Louis," Alice said. "You know Prussia took Oberhessen. But it is still considered part of our territory as well. Louis has been put in charge of working to reorganize our army, with part completely taken over by Prussia and part under a convention. That – that is why he was to be away." She dropped her voice at the last sentence and looked away.

Vicky squeezed her hand. "I am so glad to be with you," she whispered, kissing her sister's cheek, "for your birthday."

A strange, painful look crossed Alice's face, but she didn't say anything.

Vicky put her arm around her. "Come, let us see Ada and Feo, and see how the children are occupying themselves."

Ada and Feo, Aunt Feodora's daughters, were also in Gotha, as well as Ada's husband, Fritz Augustenburg. They had brought their children with them, the eldest of whom hardly fit into being some of 'the children' anymore. Feo's step-children, Bernhard and Elsa Meiningen, the son and daughter of Fritz's cousin Lotte, were now sixteen and fourteen years old. Her own children were closer in age to Vicky's.

Vicky was very fond of Ada's children, Dona, Calma, Ernst Gunther and baby Louischen, who was just four days older than little Vicky. Dona's name was actually Augusta Victoria Frederica, Vicky, Fritz, and Fritz's mother having stood sponsor to her.

"Mama, Willy says we have to listen while he reads," Alice's daughter Victoria cried, running to her. "We wanted to go out, but he says we mustn't, and he says we must obey him, as he is the eldest and the highest ranking!"

"All you want to do is climb trees, and Willy can't, and the little ones are too small, and you'll only spoil our dresses!" Dona cried.

"Wilhelm's not the eldest," Ernie of Meiningen said. "Even if you exclude Bernhard and Elsa, as not being 'children' –" He glanced at his elder sister, who scowled at him. Elsa much preferred the children's romping to young ladies' accomplishments. "Dona is older than Wilhelm."

"He's the eldest grandson of the Queen of England," Vicky heard his mother say.

"I not want to go, I want Willy read!" Ella said.

"I shall read, and then we shall go out, and I *shall* climb a tree," Willy said.

"Victoria, come here," Alice called. She sat down on the floor, and Vicky sat next to her, beckoning to the children.

Vicky smiled at Alice as the little ones gathered to sit around them. Irene scrambled into Vicky's lap, tripping and falling over Henry, who lay stretched in front of Vicky. All the little ones giggled.

Willy began to read from the Bible. It was the story of Joseph and the coat of many colors.

"I want to go out," Victoria cried again, struggling away from Alice's grasp. "He just read that yesterday."

"Hush, Victoria, come here. Let Willy read," Alice said. "You can go out as soon as he finishes the chapter."

Elsa and Ernie Meiningen, Willy and Victoria all made a rush to the door as soon as Willy had finished the chapter.

"Now, what would you like to do?" Vicky asked, turning to the others.

"I want all the cu – cuddles to stay… and read," Ella said, reaching for a little basket of flowers which sat nearby.

"Cousins, not cuddles," Charlotte said, laughing. She sat at a little table, setting up a game of chess. Across from her sat Bernhard, who looked quite content to join "the children" in their games. Vicky watched them for a moment, her thoughts going back to a previous visit to Gotha and Coburg, when Bernhard had told Charlotte about the birds in a picture book when she was two years old. Every time they met, he always showed her the same gentle, serious attention.

"I would like to go out into the fresh air with the children," Alice said, "if we can trust you to watch the little ones," she went on, looking at Dona and Calma.

"You chose the right ones. They are the most motherly of all this brood," Vicky whispered, taking Alice's hand.

"I think we can hardly judge that. I know Elsa and Charlotte are not, at least not yet, but none of the other girls are old enough to be. Oh, look!"

Alice pointed to a tree ahead of them, one with many low-hanging branches. Victoria sat on a limb, swinging her legs. On a branch quite low to the ground sat Willy. He stood, leaning against the trunk, grasping the next higher branch with his right arm. He clambered about for a moment, his legs kicking wildly. Vicky felt her heart jump into her throat. He was going to fall, she was sure.

"Hurrah!" Willy cried, finally scrambling up to sit on the branch. Vicky waved, and he waved his hat back at her.

"April 24, 1868

"*Meine* Vicky,

"The reception as I crossed the Italian border was enthusiastic to the extreme. All the Royal Court is equally enthusiastic. King Victor Emmanuel met me in the throne room, and said very loudly how pleased he was to welcome me.

"He asked me if Papa was well, as the papers here in Italy insist that he has been having strokes such as our late King had.

"He is extremely grateful to Prussia's 'heroism' in the war two years ago, as Italy was not well prepared and would certainly not have won Venetia if the war had not already been decided in Bohemia.

"I wished to speak of the wedding and of peace, but he would go on about the war continually, speaking of a new long-range cannon they have which is light enough to be pulled by only two horses, the armaments in peacetime, and so on.

"I mentioned how I felt about war since two years ago, and indeed, have always felt, and that any order given towards war would only bring the death of so many men.

"He went on in a strange manner, saying that he had seen almost all the companions of his youth fall at his side, including one who lost his head – I could not listen any more, as his words brought a memory which was the worst I have ever seen. I think it will never fade from my vision – but he went on, saying that 'we are all brave soldiers, and I would go to war as often as need be – no, as often as possible, until I die. We are all of this kind.' His manner and certain phrases reminded me very much of Fritz Karl. He then took me to see his collection of armor and weapons, most of which are riddled with bullet-holes and other proofs of having been well used. It is no glittering show as Onkel Karl's collection is.

"The wedding has gone off brilliantly. The bride is a lovely girl, full of character and an intellect rare in a girl of her age – reminding me strongly of you.

"The King is comical in his distaste for court events. He certainly prefers the battlefield to the ballroom. He constantly asked my advice, as the head of his household has died a few days ago and there was no one to direct, to make sure everyone was where they ought to be at the moment they ought to be.

"All goes well, and I only wish you were here, only I wish, as ever, that you should never meet this King again. He speaks of you, of his memory of your 'charming appearance' as a young girl in '54. I have no wish for this impression to be made stronger."

Reinhardtsbrunn, Gotha, April 25, 1868

"Vicky," Alice said, turning to help Vicky brush her hair, "you mentioned you were glad to be with me for my birthday."

"Yes, of course, Alice. It has been eleven years since we spent it together."

"Yes, my birthday eleven years ago, when I was a little girl, an innocent, innocent little girl. But…" Alice paused, dropping the hairbrush and leaning down, hiding her face. "Vicky," she whispered, reaching out to clutch at Vicky's hand, "it was my birthday – last year – that… Prince Charles…"

Vicky couldn't speak as she turned to put her arms around her sister. "Alice, you know…" She paused. "You said Papa told you about… what happened to me. You know what day it was?"

"Fritz's birthday. Yes, I know, and I can understand. I remember, when you first brought your little ones to England, I couldn't understand how you could not adore Charlotte, even though Papa had told me. But now – oh! I can understand it so well. The feeling that the little one would be – *his* – and what you said when you were with me, Vicky. You said you thought if there had been the possibility of your child being Fritz's, you might have been able to –" Alice suddenly burst into tears, not finishing her sentence.

Vicky gently rubbed her back, kissing her cheek.

"Now, I can hold Waldie, and can look at him, but I am still glad you took him. I couldn't – love the little one, immediately, even though I know he is obviously Louis'." She paused, looking at Vicky. "But you haven't told me about your Victoria."

Vicky smiled. "It is so different. I love her so much, as I had no – no memory, even though we knew something had happened. Fritz felt that something would not be as we expected, and she certainly was unexpected. I knew – we – were expecting, already, but I had a suspicion about Prince Charles. I never guessed … anything else."

Alice shuddered. "I do not wish to think of that!" Vicky felt her hand tremble as she squeezed her hand.

***

Bornstedt, Potsdam, May 9, 1868

"That you have two little ones whom I have never seen seems impossible. How I hope to see you all in the autumn, but particularly my own dear firstborn…"

Vicky read her mother's letter, blinking back tears. It had been *so* long since she had seen Mama and heard her voice, which would have been such a comfort in all the events of the last two and a half years. They hadn't gone to England since December '65.

She rubbed her face. Her eyes felt strange, and not as they usually did from crying.

"Mama, why is your face so red?" Henry pulled her skirt. She sat outside the house at the farm which she and Fritz owned at Bornstedt, just outside of Potsdam. The children played nearby. Fritz had set up a tent for them, and they had their little ponies.

"I was only crying a little, Henry, over my Mama's letter, because I miss her so much."

Henry looked up at her, studying her face. He looked puzzled. "Your face doesn't usually look like that." He turned and ran back to join the others.

Vicky hurried inside. She smiled as she passed through the rooms of the little farmhouse. She had it refurnished and made very pretty as a surprise for Fritz.

Finally, she reached a room with a looking-glass.

"What?" She stepped forward, studying her face. She had felt rather uncomfortable, but she hadn't expected to look like this.

Her face was swollen, a deep red, her eyes swelling more as she stared.

It must be from those plants, she thought. She had fallen in a patch of slightly prickly plants which she couldn't identify that morning.

***

May 12

The itching and swelling continued, and Vicky's face grew so swollen she could hardly open her eyes. But it went away completely during the night.

Vicky was relieved. But at one o'clock the next day, she felt the same, strange, swelling, itching sensation. It lasted all day until about midnight, and then wore off.

"What can it be?" she wrote to Fritz. "And I realize it can't be from the plants, as I already had a slight bit of it when I was in Gotha with Alice. I did not eat all day two days ago, but nothing changed. I stayed in, or stayed in the sunlight all day long, and nothing changed. I don't understand it.

"But I can't show myself to anyone in this state. At its worst, it is as if I have no face, but rather a fire-red shapeless mound of redness. My nose and eyes and even my ears become so swollen, I must breath through my mouth, and I can't look up or down unless I move my whole head."

***

May 23, 1868

Vicky's face had returned to normal after about two weeks. The day of Fritz's arrival had been the last the rash had appeared.

He had entered the bedroom, where Vicky lay in bed. It was about six o'clock in the evening.

"Fritz," she had murmured, "please, don't look at me. I don't want you to think you have a red balloon for a wife."

He had taken her in his arms, kissing her forehead gently. "I love you no matter how you look," he murmured, stroking her hair.

"But you can't say you think I am attractive." Vicky sat up, so she could see in the glass on her dressing-room door. Her face was so red and swollen she looked as if she had hardly any mouth or eyes. "I don't have a face. I only have this – this…" Fritz embraced her, kissing her eyes and lips. "Don't! It itches so bad!" She lay down again. "I don't know how I

212

can go anywhere this season. Your Mama will expect me to, but – I can't show myself like this!"

***

Neues Palais, May 24, 1868

Vicky took Fritz's arm. They had just finished receiving the diplomatic corps, and a meeting with members of Parliament over the entrance of Bavaria and other Southern states into the *Zollverein*, the North German Confederation's Customs Union. Everyone had left.

"I am so glad my face did not swell today." Vicky smiled, squeezing his hand as they walked back through the Jasper Hall. It was one of the rooms Fritz had had redecorated a few years before – removing the paintings of nudes which had graced the walls during the occupancy of previous inhabitants.

"You did choose these with very good taste," Vicky whispered, pointing to the landscapes and biblical scenes.

"No, it is all your taste," Fritz replied, squeezing her hand. "I would not have known what to choose and would have taken some simple little water-color dabs if not for you."

Vicky glanced up at him, smiling. She stood still. "Don't look up," she said, smothering her laughter. Fritz did glance up. On the ceiling were several paintings, all in the same style of the paintings he had removed from the walls. "Will you have those repainted as well?"

"No, it is not necessary," Fritz replied, and then glanced at Vicky's face. She stood still as if frozen, staring upwards.

"What is it?" he asked gently, putting his arm around her.

Vicky shuddered, but met his eye. "I saw that painting," she whispered, pointing up to a portrait of three naked young women. "A memory flashed in my mind, from when I was first here – at the first dinner when I sat next to Prince Charles. After dinner when everyone was talking, he asked someone if he would like to see The Three Graces." She shuddered again, clinging to Fritz's arm. "He meant the little girls. I was horrified at the time at the idea of his calling his granddaughters that, but I never imagined that he would actually –" She broke off, hiding her face against Fritz's shoulder.

"We should not speak of such things here," he whispered. "Let us go to our rooms."

Fritz looked into each of the rooms of their suite to make sure no one was there, and sent Rosa away. Finally, he closed the bedroom door, and turned to Vicky. "I knew – I knew – well, I did not know that, either," he began. "When – long ago, when I was sixteen, Onkel Karl took me to a brothel.

"Many people imagine prostitutes to have chosen their way of life. They may have chosen it, but only as a last resort! I remember so well, Vicky, the look on Lina's mother's face, when she told me she had worked so hard so that neither of them would have to become 'a woman of the streets', as she said. It is often when a poor girl has suffered – as they would both have suffered if I had not intervened, as you suffered, or as Marianne's girls suffer. Or it may be that they were led to believe in a man's promise, but unmarried – and they have a child, when they are not married and not in a position which protects them, and their own family rejects them! I cannot understand such hard-heartedness!"

"I remember Mama's anguish," Vicky said, "when she told me of a visit she paid once to a prison – a prison full of poor girls who had been caught killing their own child – but killing them out of the fear of having to watch the poor child starve to death, as the poor mothers could not provide for them. They did it in the hope of being able again to obtain employment, but were caught, and nothing – *nothing* – what is to be done for them?" Vicky felt tears start to her eyes.

"They could not obtain employment, as shops and factories refuse to employ a single mother, for fear of being accused of harboring prostitutes where it is illegal. And the false moralizing which goes on is terrible! And once a poor girl suffers in this way, they are considered fair game by men, who look on it in this way: The girl is no longer innocent; she is unmarried, therefore, she must be a prostitute. They think that once a girl has given away her innocence, or had it taken from her, she has given up her right to refuse her consent! And often enough she does not know what it means, and 'consents' without realizing what she consents to. But it is the same in marriage. So many girls go into marriage knowing nothing of the – intimacies. I was so grateful that Papa and Mama didn't let that happen to any of us."

Fritz nodded, squeezing Vicky's hand. "When Onkel Karl took me to the brothel, one of the women asked if I would like someone closer to my own age." He grimaced as Vicky looked up at him. "I imagined that they only meant girls of sixteen, fifteen, perhaps fourteen or thirteen. But Onkel Karl – he gave the woman coins. Anyone who witnessed it who did not understand would simply have thought he bribed her." Fritz looked Vicky in the eye. She nodded.

"He passed through the door that the woman indicated when she mentioned 'young girls'. I know from other experiences – another time when Fritz Karl tricked me into accompanying him to a brothel – that they never allow the young, comparatively innocent boys into those rooms. They let us think they mean girls of our age. We would never think of little children. But – little girls! They have no choice! Vicky, there are girls as young as five years old in brothels!"

Vicky saw a shudder of revulsion go over Fritz's face. He dropped her arm, turning away, holding his stomach and putting his other hand over his mouth. "Fritz? Are you going to –" she began, but he breathed a long, slow breath, and turned back to her.

"Ah!" She cried out as Fritz's grasp on her hand tightened as his face hardened in a look of repulsion.

He instantly let go, and went on, "How can a man do such things to innocent children?!" He shuddered. "I cannot imagine it! Vicky, when you were ten years old, I felt very – emotionally attracted – to you, not physically in any way. That is the only way I can think to describe it. But, even considering that, I felt it was wrong to feel the wish to marry you. I knew about such things by that time. I felt it was inappropriate, and I did not wish to be anything like Onkel Karl. But my emotional attraction goes along with the feeling that I must protect the innocent. Little Lina reminded me of you as you were at the Exhibition – and I could not let anything happen to her.

"Onkel Karl is involved in this sort of thing in so many ways. Brothels with these poor young girls, his treatment of Ebi and Louischen, you, Addy, Maroussy and what he did to you two years ago. I know he has arranged such things before."

" 'Slave purchases' " Vicky said, "and 'bargaining for so many tons of flesh' – as it said in *Jane Eyre*. Bargaining in *female* flesh, it may as well have said. It was written quite plainly."

Vicky watched Fritz's face. A strange expression crossed his features, and another shudder, but he didn't speak. She felt his hand tremble. "At least Ebi and Louischen aren't really his granddaughters," Vicky said, "but I didn't know that when he called them 'The Three Graces'. And yet – it was Mariechen, Ebi and little Annchen at the time. But – thankfully – he never touches Mariechen. And she isn't – hypnotized – either, I am quite sure. It is so revolting – and so terribly sad, in a way, too. You know how the girls adore him – Louischen and Ebi, I mean. Mariechen is very cautious. But Louischen and Ebi don't confide in her, or in Marianne. It is very sad. Prince Charles plays on their wishes and spoils them – giving them '*Genußen und Leckereien*[43]' – and overruling everything Marianne does to protect them, and as they don't remember things, they won't believe anything bad about their '*lieber Großpapa*[44]'. They blame it all on Fritz Karl." Vicky shook her head. "If he didn't behave in such a revolting way, their relationship would be very touching – they really love him." Vicky felt tears come to her eyes as she looked up at Fritz.

"But why does Louischen confide in us so freely?" Fritz asked slowly. "And are you certain about her? – I mean, that she is hypnotized?"

"She wouldn't love him as she does if she wasn't," Vicky said bitterly. "She would see what is going on, as Mariechen does. I know what you are thinking. We have seen Ebi act so strangely, and I remember long ago, Marianne told me that Ebi 'tells things'. But yes, Louischen certainly is hypnotized. There must be some reason he wants her to be close to us." Vicky paused, thinking. "We have always suspected Ebi was his spy."

"Vicky," Fritz said seriously, taking her hands, "you said the girls blame everything on Fritz Karl. Surely you do not mean –" His face changed as a shudder went over him.

"Yes. I do. Marianne told me." Vicky could hardly speak above a whisper, her throat felt tight and choked, and her eyes stung with tears. "Marianne and the girls are in Italy. I saw her and the girls before they left, and she said that – Ebi – is 'sick' again. But, your question, yes, Ebi thinks Fritz Karl is Fritz Leo's father. I can't help feeling that what Prince Charles

---

[43]   Treats and treats – "Genußen means treats as in doing something to eat, "Leckereien" as in food – "Lecker" means tasty.
[44]   Dear Grandpapa

has done – with the hypnotism – is merciful to the girls in a way. At least it was before Ebi – and he had to have a scapegoat."

"And such a scapegoat!" Fritz cried. "To think he uses his own son in such a way! I can even pity Fritz Karl in a way, as if it were not for the hypnotism he certainly would never do it!" Fritz looked away, rose, and walked quickly through the room. He returned to Vicky's side, but didn't face her. Vicky saw a tear run down his cheek. "Enough of this," he said, pacing again. "I shall be sick if we go on!"

Vicky nodded. "Fritz? Why did you look through all our rooms, before you came here?" She felt the urge to change the subject. She couldn't bear the thoughts which had filled her mind. "I have noticed you doing this so often, even here."

Fritz's expression changed again, and he met her eye. "Morier told me he found his desk broken into – the one he left here, in our suite, while we were away. And it smelled of cigar smoke. Mine did too."

Vicky felt a shiver go down her spine. "Broken into – it was a spy."

Fritz shook his head. "I should have said – tampered with. The lock was not broken – it was picked. And mine was too."

Vicky shuddered. She knew Prince Charles and Fritz Karl were both trained as lock-smiths.

"So we are not even secure here, in our own suite!"

Fritz squeezed her hand. "Besides that, I have thought of Anna's appearance in my suite, on two different occasions. It is best to expose any surprises before one allows oneself to relax."

***

London, November, 1868

Vicky and Fritz sat in the carriage, on their way up the Mall to Marlborough House. As they passed the Chapel Royal at St. James's Palace, Fritz slipped his hand into Vicky's muff, squeezing her hand.

"How well I remember our first drive from here," she whispered. "You were so quiet, none of us could get a word out of you, there or at the breakfast. Here we are."

Bertie and Alix stood in the courtyard as the carriage passed the gate.

Of the children here, Vicky had only seen the two little boys. The eldest was now called Eddy, after Bertie's second name, in honor of

Mama's father. The boy's name was Albert Victor Christian Edward, and Mama always called him "Albert Victor" in her letters, but Bertie and Alix both felt he should have some other nickname.

The second, Georgie, was named for Uncle George. He also had the name Frederick, Fritz being a Godparent. Alix had written herself to Fritz – after much coaxing from Bertie and Mama – to ask him to be sponsor for the little boy, as a gesture of good-will after the Schleswig-Holstein war. Frederick and George were also the names of the elder two of Alix's brothers.

There were two girls now, too – Louise, named both for Alix's Mama and for Louise, and Victoria.

***

London, November 5, 1868

"Affie, I wish we had some time to talk," Vicky whispered, as she joined Affie and Alix in the carriage.

Affie was just leaving on a long voyage – having received a roving commission which would take him, as Captain of his own ship, to New Zealand, Australia, and the other islands of the South Pacific, as well, most likely, to India, China and Japan.

No British Prince had ever set foot in Australia or Japan – or at least they never had before Affie had gone to Australia at the beginning of the year.

His visit there had seemed a wonderful thing, but his tour turned into a disaster. There had been riots, a serious fireworks accident, and a nearly successful assassination attempt – on Affie himself.

There had been political trouble in Ireland, and Mama and the whole family had been concerned at the idea of Bertie going there last year. Alix, as she had told Vicky, had a premonition that there would be an attempt, and had insisted on accompanying Bertie, feeling her presence would prevent any disturbance. But it turned out that on the very day Alix had the dream, Affie had been shot in Australia by an Irish Nationalist. The news didn't arrive in England for a month. It came during Bertie and Alix's visit to Ireland.

Affie had been wounded, and for a few days he appeared to be paralyzed from the waist down. Somehow, a few days after the bullet was taken out, the feeling returned to his legs, and he would be able, after all, to continue his career, which he had thought was over forever.

Vicky rather wondered the fact that he was going back to the place where he had been wounded, but at the same time, smiled at his determination and bravery. He had always been so. She remembered him as the little boy who would stand on the third story window ledges, "to watch the birds more closely".

Vicky thought Affie seemed different this time than the last few times she had seen him. At the Paris Exhibition he had seemed glad to see her, but then retreated into himself, and his behavior had shown how deeply under the spell he was.

Vicky had felt very sad about this, feeling she had lost her dear little brother to whom she had always been so close before his visit in '64, while Fritz was still away in the Danish war. She was worried, too. Affie was Uncle Ernst's heir. Uncle was hypnotized, Affie was too. What would become of Coburg?

But now he did seem different. There were none of the telltale signs of the hypnotism. Mama, too, had said he behaved differently during these last months since his return. He was a little more confidential, and was kinder, too, to those lower in rank. He never tried to bring military discipline into the household now, as he had during the previous few years, which had greatly annoyed Mama.

Vicky longed to have a long talk with him, but there was no time. He was literally leaving when she arrived, and she only had time to accompany him and Alix to his ship, the *Galatea*, which waited on the Themes.

She and Alix went on board for an hour, the commander showing Vicky about. She had been impressed. She had always found the British Navy ships cleaner than other ships she had visited, but this one was in absolutely perfect condition, even the lower decks being perfectly clean.

Finally, she had gone up again, waiting to say goodbye. She returned to her carriage, thinking after all that she had been mistaken, that Affie had grown again cold to her, as he usually had after their initial meetings over the last few years.

At last Alix joined her, her face full of tears. Affie appeared on deck, looking very handsome in his Captain's uniform, tears running down his face as he waved his cap in answer to their handkerchiefs. The ship began to move, and the carriage drove away. How long would it be before he came back?

***

In England, Vicky met Mary, Mama's cousin, for the first time since Mary's marriage. In spite of being seven years Vicky's senior, she hadn't married till seven years after Vicky herself.

It was so good to see all the family again, but Vicky hadn't yet met Mama.

Arthur, Leopold and Beatrice – the little ones – she hadn't seen in three years. "Arthur?" she had cried on meeting him. The last time she had seen him, he had still been shorter than her. Now she had to look up – he was taller than Bertie.

"How strange it seems to see them all growing up," she said to Fritz, as they sat in the carriage, hand in hand. A herd of deer passed by before them, crossing the Long Walk. Vicky felt tears in her eyes at the sight of Windsor Castle – dear Windsor – the home of her childhood, and the scene of her and Fritz's first two days – and nights – alone, as husband and wife.

***

Windsor Castle

"Mama, here is my little Vicky." Vicky held the little one's hand.

Mama wore a deep purple gown, rather than her usual black. She always wore black still, for mourning, but Vicky had written warning her that little Vicky was extremely shy, frightened at every new face, and particularly scared at the sight of someone in a black gown or cloak.

Vicky sighed as the little one let go of her hand and walked towards her grandmother. "Gandma-ma?" she said, smiling. "Pa-pa come?"

The Queen lifted her up, stroking her golden curls. Vicky turned at a sound at the door. Fritz had come in, carrying Waldie.

"Pa-pa!" Little Vicky held out her arms, and Fritz lifted her up as the Queen took Waldie.

"It is so good to be home again, and to see you all," Vicky said, turning again. There was a sound of voices.

"Vicky!" Beatrice ran to her, holding her arms out. Leopold followed slowly, leaning on a walking stick, his face lighting up as he saw her.

The other children came in. Vicky rose, sitting down on the footstool by her mother's knee, where she always used to sit when they talked, watching the children gather around Mama. It was good to be home.

***

Windsor Castle, November 25, 1868

"Yer 'ighness, yer 'ighness!" Mrs. Hobbs ran into Vicky's sitting-room with a letter. "The Prince told me to bring this to you," she said.

It was a telegram from Louis. "A son," it read.

Vicky rose. "Mrs. Hobbs?" she called, hurrying to the door.

"Yes, your 'ighness?"

"Where is Fritz?"

"In 'er Majesty's rooms. 'e said they couldn't be hinter-hupted at the moment, but 'e wished you to 'ave the news."

Vicky returned to her sitting-room.

Alice had a son. It was only a seven months' child, by what Alice had said, but Alice had given her country an heir. Vicky knew from her letters that she was feeling much better; there had been no troubles. "I love my little one so much already," she had written two weeks ago. "Something makes me sure that it is a boy, just as you knew your little Vicky was a girl."

She had been right. The " 'opes of 'esse," as Mrs. Hobbs would say, were satisfied.

CHAPTER EIGHTEEN
LITTLE SOLDIERS

Berlin Schloss, January 9, 1869

"You do not know her if you think she does not have anti-German sentiments! And the way she brings up her children! One would think she had no faith of any kind! And," Bismarck went on, lowering his voice, "if I can speak in confidence..."

Vicky strained to hear the whispered words.

"She invites old gentlemen – old *generals*, I should say, to ride with her..."

Vicky couldn't hear any further. She stood perfectly still, not even breathing as Bismarck and Hinzpeter walked past the entrance to the alcove where she stood.

She had noticed Bismarck had – rather condescendingly – allowed himself to be introduced to Willy and Henry's tutor. They had been talking for some time near the alcove. Hinzpeter's gaze was directed away from Bismarck as he listened, and Bismarck was turned away from the alcove, when she slipped in. She felt she must hear what was being said.

***

The long visit in England had been very pleasant, and uneventful. It was so good to see Mama, Alix, Louise, Arthur, Leopold and Beatrice again. Vicky shook her head repeatedly at the thought of Beatrice being eleven – and by the next time she saw her, she would probably be a "young lady". It seemed impossible! Beatrice, the little baby she had cradled in her arms with such sweet hopes in her heart, a few days after her wedding.

It was pleasant also to see Christian at home in the family here, and to see Alix's and Lenchen's little ones.

But Vicky felt she didn't really know Louise. Louise had been close to her tenth birthday when Vicky married – but the family hadn't made a point of keeping her in touch with Vicky as they had with Beatrice and Leopold. On the early visits home, everything had been as before, but since Louise was grown up – there had been so few visits, and she was the only one of the siblings whom Vicky wasn't in close correspondence with.

Vicky wrote to Louise occasionally, attempting to find points of common interest – she knew Louise was being trained in art and sculpture, but even here, there was disagreement. Louise loved the stylized paintings which were not to Vicky's liking. Vicky had always been a realist in her art.

Bertie had given Fritz a set of toy soldiers as a surprise for Willy's birthday. Vicky had smiled when Fritz showed them to her, as they were a set Fritz's mother had sent Mama for Bertie's birthday when *he* was ten, a few months after the Great Exhibition.

The visit had been peaceful and uneventful, except for one thing. Mama had received strange letters from Fritz's father, complaining about their long absence from Prussia, and particularly their absence from the Christmas festivals. This absence had been agreed on in writing months before.

Mama had written pointing out that Vicky hadn't been in England for three years. He had responded with a long letter full of complaints about Vicky not observing little details of customs in Berlin, such as driving herself in a carriage with two horses and a footman on the back instead of the customary four horses with a coachman.

On the way home, Vicky and Fritz had stopped in Brussels, as they always had before. But this was so different without Uncle Leopold. Even if it hadn't been for the shock of realizing Brussels without him, the visit would have been very melancholy. Leopold the second – Mama's cousin – feared he would lose his only son, who was fearfully ill, and then there was poor cousin Charlotte.

Charlotte never mentioned Mexico or Max. Max had never returned to Europe. Shortly after the Paris Exhibition, the news of his assassination had struck the European Royals like a fierce blow.

Vicky thought Charlotte looked just as she always had, but she spoke little, and closed her eyes and hid her face when Vicky spoke to her.

Kronprinz Palais, Berlin, January 9, 1869

"I won't be content with peace before entering the capital this time," the King said, glaring across the table. "Austria's insolence is not to be born calmly."

"Austria has not been insolent, Papa," Fritz said, trying to remain calm. He handed his father a newspaper. "I hope you will read this yourself. It tells the truth." *As do the other papers if you would read them yourself*, he thought. "You can stay here and read. I have several things I would like you to see."

The King shook his head. "I have no time for such things. I must get back to the palace."

"Papa," Fritz said slowly, trying to think of something to say which would keep his father from leaving. He had been going to suggest that he read the papers aloud while the King signed papers, as he had brought some of his papers with him. But he knew Bismarck would only accuse him – Fritz – of reading the papers with his own slanted interpretation, just as he knew Bismarck did himself.

"Wilhelm longs to talk with you," he said. "He has not seen you since our return."

His father smiled. "Very well, Fritz. It has been too long since I saw the dear boy. He can come and I will read these to him."

Fritz felt a smile spread over his face as he heaved a deep sigh of relief. "*Danke*, Papa." He rose and went to the door to send for Wilhelm.

***

"Fritz?"

Fritz rose and turned to the door. He had sat in an armchair, in the next room from where his father and Wilhelm sat. He was reading to himself, but he would not leave. He wanted to know how long his father really stayed, and if he was really reading the papers. So far, everything had gone well.

"Vicky?"

Vicky yawned. "I was with your Mama at the dinner. I couldn't leave any earlier." She glanced into the next room. "I see Willy's having his lessons with his Großpapa." She turned to Fritz, a concerned look on her face. "But I thought you agreed we shouldn't let them encourage his propensity and enthusiasm for military glory."

Fritz nodded. "That is not what is going on. Just listen to what Papa is reading for a moment."

Vicky's face brightened. "I *am* glad! And it's good for both of them. Your Papa ought not to be biased towards certain newspapers as he is. *We* read them *all*, though I must say some are certainly *not* pleasant."

Fritz smiled as he looked into the next room, drawing Vicky's hand through his arm and squeezing it. "I was searching for a way to make Papa stay and read the papers himself which tell the truth of Austria's attitude towards us, instead of those who whip him up to wish again for war."

Wilhelm sat next to the King, both faces full of interest as the King read aloud. It was a treat for Wilhelm to stay up so late, as well as to have time alone with his grandfather the King.

"Fritz," Vicky whispered, "do you know if Hinzpeter has come back?"

Fritz shook his head. Vicky motioned him to sit down again, sitting in his lap and putting her arms around his neck as she went on. "Bismarck was introduced to Hinzpeter, and I heard part of their conversation. Bismarck was painting me as black as possible, saying that I have no morals, no faith, that I have nothing but anti-German feelings, and so on. It was all their usual story, except for the last thing. I couldn't make sense of it."

Vicky paused, meeting his eye. Fritz nodded. "What?"

"He said that I invite old gentlemen – he said 'old generals' as if that were particularly significant – to ride with me. What can he mean by it? I always ride with Count Seckendorff or Valerie if you can't go with me. And he said I did it to –" She paused, obviously trying to remember the exact words. "– to tire them? No –" She paused again, then nodded. "He said I did it 'to injure their health'. What can he mean?"

Vicky met Fritz's eye. Seeing his expression change, she suddenly felt her face suffused with heat, and hid her face against his neck.

"Is it – something – another implication of their vile imaginations?"

She felt Fritz sigh deeply. She glanced up at him and saw him roll his eyes. "*Ja.*" He stroked her hair. "Must I explain it or can you guess what it means?"

Vicky felt her face burn again as she thought through everything she had heard Bismarck say, his tone, his manner and gesture in speaking even when she hadn't been able to understand the words.

"No, please, don't explain it," she said, shuddering. "But what can he mean, 'to injure their health'? That's the part I still don't understand." Vicky stood again, watching Fritz's face.

Fritz shrugged. "Do not let it worry you. It is only one of their despicable slanders, as you said."

***

Berlin Schloss, January 18, 1869

"You'll come for the ice-skating race tomorrow, won't you?" Vicky whispered as she squeezed Bertie's hand.

Bertie smiled. "I wouldn't miss it. And Alix's leg is finally strong enough to participate. She would've been furious to be forced only to watch." He smiled. Alix had been seriously ill two years before, and had walked with a limp ever since. This, Vicky knew, was torture for Alix, who had always loved gymnastics, horseback riding, and other activities which had been impossible or painful for two years.

"Even though you have to get up so early?" Vicky glanced sideways at Bertie. "It's to be early in the morning. I know you usually aren't even out of bed, you lazy boy."

Bertie smiled sheepishly. "I get up far earlier than Alix does!"

"You know I don't think you're lazy," Vicky said. "I thought your work at Sandringham was wonderful, and it's a good occupation for you. Papa would be proud of you!" During her visit in England, Vicky had taken a tour of Bertie's estate, Sandringham, and was impressed and surprised by the detailed attention he took in all matters of the horse farm, orchards, and landscape gardens.

Bertie and Alix had arrived in Berlin the previous evening. At the dinner that evening, Bertie had sat next to Fritz's mother, and Alix next to the King. Alix had been very friendly. Vicky was glad.

Two years ago, Vicky and Fritz had met Bertie and Alix in Wiesbaden. Alix's parents and sister, Minny, had also been present. The King of Prussia had passed through, asking to meet Alix, who had refused, saying that she was in mourning and not receiving formal visits. At the same time, she had met several others. Bertie had been much upset about it, as he agreed with Vicky, Fritz, and the King that true peace ought to be made between Prussia and Denmark. Alix's parents – the King and Queen of Denmark – had been polite and met the King of Prussia peaceably. Alix and Minnie continued to refuse, and, at a dinner at the Embassy in Darmstadt, both wore dresses bearing the Danish colors.

At last night's dinner, Alix had been extremely polite to the King. Vicky noticed Bertie watching her closely, and several glances passing between them. She suspected Alix had received a scolding for her previous behavior, from Mama as well as from Bertie.

Alix looked lovely tonight in her lilac velvet gown with a bouquet of pink roses in her corsage. This, she had told Vicky, had been brought to her room and left on her table, with a note from the King that it was to be worn at the ball the next day.

***

January 19, 1869

"It will be a tie between the Crown Prince and the Prince of Wales, I believe!" Vicky heard a call from one of the spectators on the shore as the wind roared in her ears. She rushed forward, and saw Bertie spin around, but still keep ahead. He already took the victory for granted.

Vicky saw Fritz catch Bertie's hand and swerve to one side. She shot forward at the same moment, hearing several shouts but unable to hear what was said when cheering broke out.

"The Crown Princess wins!" Vicky struggled to stop, stopping herself at a large snow bank rather than turning the bend of the river, as had been planned. She didn't wish to go that way alone. It felt suddenly lonely, in spite of the nearby crowd, as she looked up. This end of the large pass of the river was enclosed by trees, hidden from view from the shore or the river. She turned to glance backwards. No one else was anywhere near the end.

She struggled to stand up, finally making her way back to where she found Fritz and Bertie both fallen into a deep snow bank. She couldn't hold back her laughter as one would attempt to help the other up, only to end up falling on top of the other, falling farther and farther into the deep, soft snow.

Others finally began to come up. Fritz glanced up. "No one kept on, did they?"

"No," Vicky gasped. She was still out of breath.

"Because they heard the shouts that you won," Bertie said. "Fritz, why did you pull me aside? We would have tied!"

Vicky heard others calling back and forth, some asking the same question.

"Why did the Crown Prince pull the Prince of Wales aside?"

"Why did he not let him win if he was forfeiting the chance?"

"This isn't like our Fritz! He doesn't cheat!"

Fritz struggled again to rise, finally gaining his feet, and, with Vicky's help, lifted Bertie out of the snow bank. Fritz skated forward, facing the crowd.

"Come here, but only a few of you. The ice won't hold everyone." Vicky, Bertie, and a few other participants in the race followed him as he went forward to where Vicky had stopped, then just a little farther, toward the bend hidden by trees.

The ice was broken, a deer weakly struggling in the freezing water.

Vicky saw Bertie's face change. Fritz nodded as Bertie said something she couldn't hear. The others turned back towards the crowd. When they rejoined the crowd, Fritz, Vicky and Bertie were heartily congratulated. Vicky heard several people thanking Fritz for saving their lives.

***

Berlin, January 27, 1869

"Uncle Bertie, did you say Großmama gave you these?" Willy held up one of the toy soldiers Bertie had given him.

"Yes, Willy," Bertie said, ruffling the boy's hair.

"Were you in the march-past?"

"When I was ten? No! We don't do such things in England – at least not nowadays." Bertie laughed. "My military training began when I was eighteen."

Vicky watched Willy's face as he thought over what Bertie had said. When he didn't ask another question, she rose. "Willy, it's time to prepare for the parade."

Willy jumped up and ran out of the room. Vicky turned back to Bertie. "He never did what I said so fast before," she laughed. "He's so eager about all of this. I wish – I wish," she sighed. "How should I put this? He's *too* eager, for my taste."

"Everything will go well," Bertie said. "You're over-anxious about it all."

Vicky shook her head. "You know how easily things can go wrong here. But we have discussed everything at length with Willy many times. You know what I mean," she said, meeting Bertie's eye. "And the King agrees to let Fritz do everything; he only making the speeches, as he did at your investiture."

Bertie nodded, then looked away, leaning his chin on his hand. "Affie's investiture was while Fritz was gone in the war, wasn't it?" he asked.

Vicky nodded. "Yes," she said with a deep sigh. "And Mama writes that she can't trust him, and he's rude to all her people and even to her since then."

Bertie nodded. "He certainly hasn't been himself. I think you wrote to Mama that Affie ignores you now, when he comes to Germany, too?"

Vicky nodded. "Willy will have to report himself to *all* the Generals, Colonels and *Princes*." She shook her head. "I can only pray things go well." She paused. "I do wish he took things more seriously. He hasn't been easy to manage, and he's so over-excited about all this military fuss and flair. And he doesn't take such an interest in his religious lessons as he did."

Bertie laughed. "He's only ten years old! And he's about to have a new experience which he's looked forward to – for three years! You said he's been asking when he can accompany Fritz to the riding school since he first had a military governor. It's simply his wish to imitate his father!"

"But I wish he would imitate Fritz in his modesty, not only his military prowess."

"It is a boy's excitement! Remember what I was – remember what *you* were, at his age, Vicky!"

"But he –"

"I remember," Bertie said with a smile, cutting her off as she began to speak, "I remember *your* being distracted from your lessons with Papa, and from Mama's and Miss Hildyard's readings in the Bible, when there was the prospect of guiding *someone* through Papa's great creation and the opportunity of showing off your great knowledge… Let me see, who was your special guest?" Bertie stroked his beard thoughtfully, looking at Vicky with a twinkle in his eye.

"Bertie!" Vicky slapped his hand, feeling herself blush, and they both burst out laughing. "It wasn't the prospect of guiding Fritz through the display I was so enthusiastic over. The Exhibition itself, and Vivi's company, were much more interesting to me, till we got to know each other."

"And the opportunity of showing off your knowledge," Bertie repeated.

"Yes!" Vicky felt herself blush again. "I know I wasn't a very modest child. That's part of why I'm so anxious for Willy to follow Fritz's example in that!"

"You sound like Mama about me – *you think him your caricature and wish him to follow his dear Papa's example.*"

"I know children can be easily distracted," Vicky said, "but I'm concerned – genuinely concerned – at the change in Willy's behavior, and Charlotte's, too. Neither of them are shy as they were."

"Isn't that a good thing?"

"Yes, but – not when it seems – almost unnatural or un-childlike."

"Willy certainly doesn't seem un-childlike to me."

"I only – I wish him to be like Fritz, and Papa, and as little like the rest of the Prussian family as possible – except perhaps Fritz's father. But I haven't told you about my concerns about – Charlotte."

Vicky spoke slowly, lowering her gaze. "It isn't only her health I worry over anymore, though that's as concerning as ever. She's so painfully thin, and always has a constant snuffle, but she has been so since her birth. And then there are her poor fingers. She chews her nails till they bleed, and I make her wear gloves, so as not to stain her clothes and things with blood. But *these* aren't the concerns I meant. I mean her behavior. Bertie, would you call her a little flirt, if you saw her, if you didn't know who she was?"

Bertie was silent for a moment. "Perhaps – if I dared to use such language about such a small girl. She certainly isn't the frightened, shy little thing she used to be."

Vicky nodded. "But it's worse than that. Her manner to the visiting little Princes, to the servants, even to young men – and when she's such a child! She isn't even nine years old, but she's such a little kitten – and she makes up to people in such an outrageous way. And I know *she* has taken things. She wheedles whatever she wants out of everyone." Vicky shook her head. "I can't help seeing her resemblance to – *him*, more than ever."

Bertie nodded. "I noticed her resemblance to Prince Charles at the dinner. It's quite impossible *not* to remark."

Vicky nodded, rolling her eyes. "Yes, and if you heard the current rumors going around Berlin about me, you'd see the new reason for my aversion to this resemblance."

Bertie met her eye. "I can imagine what you mean."

They were both silent. Finally, there was a sound at the door, and Vicky turned. Willy reappeared, dressed in his uniform which he had received a couple of weeks before as a birthday present from the King. He saluted and clicked his heels.

"You look very well, Willy, quite the little soldier," Bertie said. Willy beamed, and turned to leave the room. Vicky saw o'Danne waiting for him just outside the door.

"I always avoided dressing him in uniform; it's always made far too much of here," Vicky said. "You remember when we first brought him to England? Or did you see him in '61?"

Bertie smiled. "I wasn't at home, but I came for a day or two. I wouldn't have missed the first sight of my little nephew for the world."

Vicky nodded. "You remember that he wore the sailor suit then?" Bertie nodded. "Fritz is always anxious to have the boys out of petticoats as soon as possible, and I'm as determined that they will *not* go immediately into uniform. We're both so anxious that our boys should be little *gentlemen* before they are little soldiers."

Bertie laughed. "Willy is as passionate about it all as Arthur was."

Vicky shook her head. "More so, and in a way I don't like. Arthur never made a fool of himself or seemed vain about it all like Willy does." She paused, sighing. "You haven't seen little Fritz Leo, have you?"

"Fritz Karl's boy? Yes. I saw them and the boy was *on display*." He rolled his eyes. "That's the only way I can think of putting it."

Vicky looked sharply at Bertie as he said "Fritz Karl's boy". He met her eye. She continued to gaze at him as he went on. His expression did not change. He must not know the truth about Fritz Leo. She often wondered how much Mama told the others about such things.

But of course Fritz Leo wasn't their business, as her children might be considered. Papa had told Bertie and Alice about Charlotte about the time of her birth, and it was obvious there was something which wasn't as expected about little Vicky. Vicky had been surprised Beatrice and Leopold had asked no questions. Vicky had only spoken of that with Alice, though Fritz had told Mama and Bertie, leaving it to Mama to tell the others as she saw fit.

But Alice could understand these things as the others could not. Vicky's heart ached at the thought of Alice having suffered as she had, but it was – pleasant – in a strange, torturing, contorted way, to have someone so very close to her – to confide in about such things. Mama was extremely sympathetic, and Marianne had her worries over her girls, but neither of them could understand in the same way Alice could. Maroussy could, Addy could, there were many confidants who could, but they were not her sister.

"How was he dressed?"

"As a little hussar, with the fur coat, sword and all the accouterments."

Vicky nodded. "It seems he's *always* in uniform, and always has been from the time he could walk! And even before that, he always wore a little soldier's cap. Fritz Karl insisted on it being so and was – was – greatly upset–" Vicky stammered, meeting Bertie's eye and glancing away.

He moved his chair closer to her, putting his arm around her. "Vicky, you don't have to try to speak delicately of his behavior to me. I know what he is, and I know other such characters."

Vicky nodded. "He is extremely rude and – you know what I mean – if the nurses attempt to dress the boy otherwise. And Marianne has no say in the matter. But – it's time." The clock was striking, and a bugle sounded. It was time for the parade. "Bertie, it's been *so* nice to have you and Alix here for our anniversary. It is so seldom we have *any* of you for *our* events." She paused, swallowing and blinking back tears. "We'll see you at the parade, and then – goodbye." She hurried from the room.

***

Vicky saw Willy stand as tall as he could as the King's eyes passed over him. He leaned his gun against his hip, saluted, and lifted it again.

The King bowed deeply. Amidst a clatter of horses' hooves and clanking spurs, Vicky couldn't hear the beginning of his speech.

"You are still too young to fully understand the importance of the fact that you are now an officer in our glorious army… Go and learn to do your duty as faithfully as your father has…" The King's voice broke as he gestured to Fritz, and he wiped his eyes, smiling at Willy.

Willy struggled to salute without putting down his gun, and took his place. Vicky jumped slightly at the crash of the drums as the march began, and smiled.

Willy had always loved the drums from when he was a tiny baby. When he was a few months old, when he first began to move the fingers of his left arm, a drum stick was the first object which he would take hold of with real interest. He had a few drumming lessons – which resulted in more chaotic noise than actual rhythm – but it obviously gave him a great deal of pleasure.

***

Vicky's heart swelled with pride as she watched her little son step out in time with the march – but her heart twisted with pity as he fell behind, struggling to carry the gun, and, of course, unable to handle the gun and salute at the same time. Finally, he ended up running to catch up, and the man nearest to him roughly took his poor left arm. Vicky saw a look of pain cross his face. After a minute or so, he had dropped his gun, and the man quickly let go of his arm. He ran again to catch up, reaching up to take the man's left arm with his right. He stumbled, but finally caught the rhythm of the march again, his face beaming, before he stumbled again, losing his cap this time.

"Großpapa said I marched very well," Wilhelm said, beaming as he met Vicky's eye, then clicked his heels and saluted Fritz.

233

Vicky shook her head. "Our little soldier should realize he's still in the awkward squad," Fritz heard her whisper to Valerie.

Fritz knelt down, putting his hand on Wilhelm's shoulder, looking him straight in the eye. "You have done very well, Willik – Wilhelm." He felt that he should call him "Wilhelm", not "Willikens". It had been on Fritz's own tenth birthday that his parents had stopped calling him "Fritzchen".

Fritz rose, watching as Wilhelm joined Hinzpeter again. How would things go on in the school-room now, Fritz wondered. Now, when Wilhelm was afire with military affairs, and would probably attempt to spend more time with o'Danne than with Hinzpeter. Fritz shook his head. He and Vicky would continue to emphasize the boy's mental development over military matters. It would be better for him to grow a little more before his training began in greater earnest, as everything was very awkward for him.

Fritz turned, joining Vicky. "Papa says nothing of the Black Eagle for Wilhelm," he said as he closed the door to their sitting-room and sat down on the sofa. "I received *my* knighthood on my tenth birthday."

"I'm very glad to hear that," Vicky said, standing before him. "Willy is vain enough without *that*."

"Vicky," Fritz said, looking her in the eye. "Why are you so determined to crush his spirit?"

"I don't wish any such thing! I only want him to be like *you*."

"I am a military man. I am a soldier. I received my knighthood when I was ten."

"Yes, and everyone declares you a hero after each war." Vicky sat down, leaning her head on Fritz's shoulder. "But everyone praises you because you are such a *modest* hero. I don't see *any* of that modesty in Willy. I wish he would take after you more in that way." She laughed. "I never had any modesty for him to take after."

Fritz smiled and put his arm around her waist. "I understand. But it is so important –" He paused, leaning his head on his hand. "It is so important to let him feel that you believe in him. Mama did this" – Fritz's voice trembled a little as he gestured to Vicky – "what you have been doing with him – a little with me, and I felt it very deeply." He felt his face flush as he met her eye. "Tell him the truth."

"But what if the truth is – not pleasant?" She said slowly, her face flushing. "I did tell him the truth. I think him quite awkward, and I don't want to flatter him about things I don't think he has even earned honest praise for."

"Vicky, he is only *ten years old*. It is his *first* march-past. What can you expect?"

"It is just that – I did so hope his arm would be better by this time!" She burst into tears, hiding her face against Fritz's chest. "And I can't help feeling almost ashamed to see him disgrace himself so before all the army!"

"It is no shame. He is, as you said, in the 'awkward squad'," Fritz said, saying the last words in English, "but it is no shame. Many a boy has a harder time than he – simply because they are small, or they have a limp, or something of that kind."

"But –"

"The heir is a human being, too," Fritz said.

Vicky blushed at those words, but met his eye, smiling through her tears. "I remember saying that about Mama. You thought it so strange that we did things for ourselves, rather than calling the servants." She sighed, and averted her face. "I only wish it was possible for Willy to be more independent."

February 24, 1869

"Fritz? What has happened?"

Vicky lay down her brush and turned as Fritz opened the door to her art studio, a broad smile on his face. She rose, wiping the paint from her fingers and going to him. He smiled at her, bending down to kiss her.

"What is it? You never come home from the Council or from meetings with your Papa looking so elated! What happened?"

Fritz sat in a chair near the easel. He nodded as Vicky returned to her seat, taking up her painting again. "Vicky, your Mama wrote a week or two ago that 'generosity' was not in my father's or Bismarck's vocabulary."

Vicky nodded. "She wrote so to me, too. Have they agreed to return the Hanover fortune? Is that what it is?"

Fritz frowned, shaking his head. Since the war in '66, there had been a disagreement about the position and fortune of the exiled King of Hanover, who was now living outside of Vienna. "*Nein*. But – Vicky, have you heard of the floods – the inundations – in Frankfurt? You will have heard from Alice, if you have not seen it elsewhere."

"It's in the papers," Vicky said. "But what will they do? Frankfurt has to pay such an indemnity for fighting on the other side. I can't see how they can afford the repairs."

Fritz nodded. "They have petitioned for three millions of guldens, which they have a right to as they have now joined the new Confederation. Bismarck and the ministers refused more than two millions. But at today's council Papa called for me. I had been left out of all previous discussions, as usual. But Papa sent for me, putting down in writing in everyone's presence that he would give the third million – out of his own pocket if necessary – and pledging me to do so if anything prevents him! It is so noble and honorable of him! And you can imagine that Bismarck was frantic!"

"That's splendid! And I shall tell your Papa how right and generous I think it." Vicky squeezed Fritz's hand. "It's wonderful news to see that he is seeing things in a true light again."

***

Nordeney, July 25, 1869

Vicky sat on the beach, watching the children piling sand as high as they could. The setting sun cast a golden light over the shore, which at other times of day appeared ugly and desolate. A seagull screamed as it swooped low over the water.

Yesterday was Charlotte's ninth birthday. Today was Louischen's. Vicky wondered how Marianne and the girls had spent it. She turned to pack up her letters. It would soon be too dark to read any more outside.

"Oh!" Little Vicky screamed. "Papa!"

Fritz was swimming, and had come up suddenly out of the water, startling her.

"Papa, come and see," she called, pointing to the tower of sand. She ran to it, standing behind it where he couldn't see her. She always spoke in English, never in German, even with Fritz. But Fritz hadn't heard, and had disappeared again underwater.

"Don't you dare!" Willy cried, tossing a handful of pebbles – or rather bits of brick and tile from the road, as the beach was one of absolutely smooth sand. Little Vicky stumbled, and ducked away, nearly running into the tower of sand. Charlotte grabbed her wrist, pulling her away from the tower, then pushing her rather roughly away. Little Vicky stumbled over Henry's foot, falling forward, her face landing in a puddle.

"Charlotte! William! Stop this!" Vicky cried, jumping up and scooping little Vicky up in her arms, wiping wet sand out of her face.

"Mama!" Charlotte cried, her face flushing in anger as Vicky's skirt swept too close to their tower, knocking it over.

Fritz appeared again, and Vicky saw immediately from his expression that he had heard the children's cries. He began to dress immediately.

"Mrs. Hobbs – no, Hinzpeter," Vicky called to the group walking at a little distance on the beach. "Take her back to the house," Vicky said, placing little Vicky in his arms. "Come here, Charlotte. And you, Willy." She turned back. "Fritz, did you see any of what happened?"

Fritz nodded, opening his mouth to speak when Charlotte began, "We didn't do anything. Why do we always get in trouble and you favor that little nigg–"

Vicky turned on her. "Charlotte." Her voice came out much calmer sounding than she felt. "Come with me." She turned to Mrs. Hobbs and Mademoiselle d'Arcourt, Charlotte's governess. "Come. I will wish to speak to you," she said crisply.

As soon as they had reached the house where they were staying, Vicky closed the door to the first room they entered. "Charlotte. You are not to throw things at your little sister, or call her names, or push her around."

"I didn't throw anything!"

"I have seen you do so at other times," Vicky said, "and Henry too. Don't think I don't notice. Who has taught you to call her that – that word you began to say? Is it Mrs. Hobbs?"

"No." Charlotte said, putting her hands behind her back and closing her eyes.

"Look at me, Charlotte."

"But you don't want me to look at you. You don't like me to look you in the eye." Charlotte opened her eyes, staring up at her mother, looking her straight in the eye. "You don't like to look at me."

Vicky felt a little shudder go over her, but kept her gaze steady. She must not let this stop her. She took a deep breath.

"That isn't what we are talking about right now. Who is it? Who did you hear that word from?"

Charlotte shrugged, looking Vicky straight in the eye again.

"Go to your room and stay there," Vicky said. Charlotte curtseyed, and Vicky saw a smile creep across her face as she turned to leave the room.

Vicky went out, taking a long breath to steady herself. The others were nowhere to be seen.

Going to the little room next to her and Fritz's bedroom, she found Mrs. Hobbs and little Vicky. The little one's dress had been changed and her hair and face cleaned. "Charlotte push me – Willy frow stones," she cried, reaching her little arms up to her mother.

"Hush," Vicky soothed her, singing the little lullaby she had often sung in the months before little Vicky was born. There was a knock at the door, and Fritz looked in. "Fritz? Will you take her?" Vicky let him take the little one. "Mrs. Hobbs, stay here. I wish to speak to you."

"Yes, yer 'ighness."

"What have you told the children about little Vicky?"

"Oh, nothin', ma'am – yer 'ighness. Nothin you don't like. I did say some things I regret just hafter 'er birth but nothin' since. The children told me what you told 'em hafter that, but I never said nothin' wrong since. Hand certainly not the word you mean! She's my liddle darlin' too, not just yours! I couldn't himagine a sweeter liddle 'un, though I didn't expect hit hat first. I did think hit mighty hodd hat the first, but your 'usband – 'is 'ighness – hexplained it hall, and I'd never do nothin' you didn't happrove! I pity you – I must say, but heven if it 'ad been hutherwise – you bein' in the wrong, I mean – she'd still be my liddle darlin'!"

Vicky nodded, seeing the woman's honesty plainly in the tears which sprang to her cheeks. "I believe you. Do you suspect anyone of… saying things about her which the older children hear?"

"I'd say hit's Madymoysell," Mrs. Hobbs went on. "None o' the hothers would dare speak hagainst you – none that the children lis'en to."

Vicky sighed. Mademoiselle d'Arcourt was appointed by the government – officially by the King – which made it impossible for her or Fritz to dismiss her. This hadn't been the first complaint which they had against her, but nothing could be done.

"You may go now," Vicky said to Mrs. Hobbs as Fritz came in again. Little Vicky had fallen asleep in his arms.

"I spoke to Wilhelm very sternly, and I think he sees what he has done," he said, laying the little one down in her bed. "But where was Charlotte off to?"

"What do you mean? I told her to go to her room?"

"She went downstairs, not up."

Vicky rose, hurrying out and down the stairs. Vicky had done two paintings for the Exhibition which was soon to open in Berlin, keeping them in the room below the bedroom. Vicky opened the door cautiously.

"Look at this one! Mama only finished it yesterday! Isn't it –" Vicky couldn't hear anymore, as Charlotte's voice sank to a whisper. She heard another sound. It wasn't the sound of whispering.

"Charlotte!"

Charlotte started. She stood in front of one of the paintings; one of the boys who worked at the house here stood next to her, his arm around her waist. The sound Vicky had heard had been that of a kiss.

Vicky blinked, and as she did, the boy disappeared through the window, which stood wide open. Several leaves had blown in, drifting across the room.

"And you don't have your gloves on! Have you touched the paintings?"

"No, Mama," Charlotte said, in the same defiant tone she had spoken in before. She looked her straight in the eye.

"Go to your room – with Papa." Vicky said as Fritz opened the door. She must close the window and make sure nothing had happened to her paintings.

***

Vicky had looked forward to a peaceful time together with Fritz and the children at Nordeney, and until this day, everything had gone well.

They had come here to a house which had belonged to the King of Hanover until the war three years ago, when he had been sent into exile and Hanover had become a Prussian province.

Mama had written to Vicky, surprised that Fritz and she would stay at a house which belonged to those whom Prussia had "despoiled", as many considered Prussia to have done.

Formerly, until about fifty years before, Nordeney had been Prussian territory, and the people had celebrated the Prussian Kings' birthdays even under Hanoverian rule.

Fritz had been away a great deal during the spring and summer, and would be away much of the autumn, but the months had passed not unhappily. Vicky had spent much of her time in caring for the children, painting, and working with the members of her Society for the Employment of Women.

She had found great interest in a new correspondence with Miss Josephine Butler, whose writings appeared in the papers. Vicky had written to her:

"Dear Miss Butler,

"You will know that my dear father, the Prince Consort, spoke against slavery in his first English speech. He would, I know, feel proud to know that his daughter followed in his steps, and about this sort of slavery which is so rarely spoken of.

"I have read your article stating that some brothels are like palaces, and I know the truth of that statement from my dear husband as well.

"With what I have suffered and witnessed within the walls of *actual* Royal Palaces, I can feel deeply from my heart for those poor victims who have absolutely no protection.

"As I said, I know some truths of brothels from my husband, though he is an honorable man. He, however, is unfortunately possessed of relatives whose character is opposite of his own, and who seek as much to entangle and corrupt the innocence of young boys as to revel upon the innocence of young girls, thinking both a sport fit for laughter and wit to rejoice over.

"I have said that this trade is rarely spoken of – and I know that often, when ladies deign to whisper of it, they only think of 'the woman who has stolen my husband'. They think that women go into this trade only voluntarily, and that they ought to be cast out from society as 'fallen women', impossible to reform, unworthy of sympathy, worthy rather only of the worst scorn and abuse. They do not know it is only sought out as a last resort, when other sustenance is forbidden them and they must throw themselves at the world in shame and desperation.

"I seek and urge my brothers – English Princes and gentlemen – not to 'profit' by these 'houses of pleasure', as they are called, but even they do not understand the case. It has not come near to their lives as it has to mine. And, to their credit, I must say that they would never take the extremely young girls – actual children – for their own pleasures, and would be revolted at the thought that it was possible.

"I know that my sister, Princess Louise, is also in correspondence with you. She, I may admit, is the one of my sisters who is least confidential to me, but this is a matter we both take greatly to heart.

"Gratefully and respectfully, with sincere prayers that your efforts shall have some effect,

"Victoria, Princess Royal and Crown Princess of Prussia

"P.S.

"Indeed, your Biblical quotation 'But whoso shall offend one of these little ones which believe in me, it were better for him that a millstone were hanged about his neck, and that he were drowned in the depth of the sea' – cannot fit better.

"A friend of mine (and fellow Princess) who has had to suffer that cruelty which I believe to be the worst which could be afflicted upon a woman – that of being forced to watch her young children suffer this sort of abuse and to have no recourse – had written that verse in her diary, and I found it underlined in her Bible."

***

Willy's training was going well, and he had appeared in one or two parades along with Fritz and Vicky. He rode so well, even holding the reins with his left hand sometimes, so as to be able to salute.

Alice and Louis had paid a long visit to Berlin with the children in May, spending Mama's birthday together. Vicky smiled at the memory of the five little girls – Charlotte, Vicky, Victoria, Ella and Irene – at dinner with wreaths of fresh flowers the boys had picked on their heads. The little cousins got on so well together, and there was never any trouble about little Vicky when they were together.

Just at the end of the visit, Mrs. Hobbs had announced her engagement. Vicky had never suspected such a thing, but Mrs. Hobbs had met the man while they were in England six months ago.

"I'm so 'appy I can't say," she had cried.

Vicky had laughed and cried at the news. Everything would seem so strange without her. She had been in the household since the beginning, and Vicky and the children would miss her dearly.

In June, Vicky hadn't been able to restrain her tears, remembering the days of Siggy's illness and death. This time, Fritz was away on that day. The first two years, he had made a point of spending that anniversary with her.

Finally, on the 8th of July, they had left for Nordeney. Vicky and Fritz had taken many long rides along the shore. They had spent hours walking along the beach. Charlotte's birthday had passed as peacefully as every other day, which had left Vicky completely unprepared for the next evening, when Charlotte had behaved so shockingly.

***

Charlotte seemed very subdued when they all met for dinner. Fritz had kept her with him for a long time. Willy, too, was very quiet, and after dinner, he came up to Vicky.

"I'm sorry I threw things at Vicky," he said, hanging his head and shuffling his feet. "And I didn't call her names, and never have."

"I'm very glad to hear that, Willy. But be sure to apologize to your sister," Vicky said, glancing at Charlotte as she finished. "You, too, Charlotte."

***

Neues Palais, Potsdam, August 14, 1869

"Ich bin müde[45]," Fritz yawned as he lay down.

"You haven't stopped saying that since our tour. I hoped it would revive you. Such things usually do," Vicky said, laying her head on his shoulder. "It was so good to have you to myself this last month," she whispered.

Fritz smiled and put his arm around her. "But I don't mean tired as I was before. I mean – physically tired. Riding exhausts me instead of being invigorating."

---

[45]   I am tired

After they left Nordeney, they had passed through East Friesland with the younger children, having sent Willy, Charlotte and Henry home. They had ridden through fields of heather – reminding Vicky strongly of Scotland, except that the land was so flat. Fritz had picked a bunch of white heather for her – which she kept pressed in her Bible, as she had the flowers he had given her when he proposed.

"The maneuvers are coming soon," Fritz said, "and Wilhelm will get his wish this year. He will be in the parades and be with me at everything. But I wish it was over and I could rest," he sighed.

"But you've just had a long rest."

He nodded. "The more I rest, the more tired I feel. It does not seem to matter what I do. I simply feel more tired. And yet – I have not been sleeping as much. My mind – my brain – feel more active than usual. I do not understand it."

"It's been *very* nice that you haven't needed so much sleep," Vicky whispered, cuddling closer and kissing his hand. "I only hope you feel well for your trip to the East! It would be a pity if you couldn't go." Fritz's father had received an invitation to attend the opening of the Suez Canal which would take place in October. The King had declined the invitation, and Fritz was to go in his place.

He was also to go to Vienna on his way, which would be the first visit between the Prussian and Austrian Sovereign families since the war three years ago. He would also return the visit of the Sultan of Turkey, who had recently visited the King.

Visits to Greece, Palestine and Jerusalem were also decided on, and this journey must take place before the official function of the opening of the Suez Canal, which would take place on November 17, so as to give time for a tour on the Nile and a visit to Upper Egypt, and the journey home, allowing Fritz to rejoin Vicky and the children by Christmas-time.

Fritz's journey would be so interesting; he would visit so many fascinating places, and Vicky longed to be able to accompany him. But she felt she could not. Willy and Henry were to stay in the south of France for six months this autumn, winter and spring, and she would hardly see them for seven months if she left. There was a new nurse coming, too, in October, when Mrs. Hobbs would leave. Vicky must be at home when this happened.

***

Königberg, September 15, 1869

"Fritz? Won't you come to bed?" Vicky entered the library, where she found Fritz reading. "You've stayed here so many nights – I miss you!" Vicky put her arms around him from behind, as she stood behind the sofa. "I thought you would be tired after the maneuvers, particularly."

Fritz put his book down and rose, taking her hands, gazing down at her with a serious look in his eyes, but he followed her to the bedroom.

"I hope Karl and Elisabeth will be happy," Vicky said as she closed the door. "It's such a sudden thing, with his only arriving three days before, but they seem quite happy." She glanced up at Fritz. "It's funny. Only last month, Mama had written to me saying it was odd Elisabeth was still unmarried."

Karl Sigmaringen had returned to Germany for the first time since his departure to Romania. Fritz had looked forward to his visit, which had been expected for two years. Karl's engagement to Elisabeth of Wied was expected, Fritz having himself suggested her as a bride for Karl.

Fritz smiled. "You read that letter to me, and I thought of it when I spoke to him. I didn't think it likely for Alix's family to wish Thyra to go all the way to Romania, even if Queen Louise wishes all her children to be Kings and Queens. Karl's engagement with Princess Murat fell through, and that with Hilda, too. I knew he had always gotten on well with Elisabeth when they were both in Berlin, years ago."

"I would never have thought of them as a couple," Vicky laughed as she sat down on the bed. "He's so stiff and serious, and she so odd. 'am very glad that neither Bertie nor Affie took a fancy to her."

"You think him stiff and serious?" Fritz asked quietly, sitting beside her and putting his arm around her. He sounded surprised "There is something about him which reminds me of –"

"Of who?" Vicky asked, looking up. "He likes to teach, to instruct. Others think him stiff and serious. They call him 'the schoolmaster'. But it's so with many of your friends – Oscar of Sweden, and Fritz Augustenburg, for example." She glanced up at Fritz, adding hurriedly as she saw his serious expression, "Don't think I'm criticizing them. You know I much prefer the company of a scholar to that of an empty-headed man. It's only the contrast with Elisabeth which made me remark it. But who does he remind you of?"

"Your Papa," Fritz said. "He had the same manner which you refer to. Many people spoke of him that way."

"*Papa* wasn't –" Vicky began. Then she remembered hearing some of Mama's ladies talking about Papa, using the exact words she had just used. "Are you tired tonight?" she asked, wishing again she could retract her words, as Fritz still seemed uncomfortable.

Fritz shrugged and rose, glancing away out the window. Vicky followed him, throwing her arms around him. "I certainly didn't mean to criticize your friends," she whispered, holding her face up for a kiss.

"I know," he said, sighing deeply. He briefly returned her kiss, but lately, his kisses had often been brief. He turned away again as she sat down again, catching at his hand. "That is not what was troubling me." He sat down.

"What is it, then?" Vicky asked, reaching up to touch his cheek. He had often seemed uneasy when they went to bed over the last month, and often pretended to be asleep when she came to bed, or, as he had today, remained in the library until she went to sleep. His caresses had been playful rather than passionate, often seemingly designed rather to distract her from the possibility of intimacy than to encourage it.

"I suppose I am tired." He gazed at her seriously, his face reddening, and rose again.

"Then why don't you change and come to bed?"

He shook his head, then took something from his pocket, pressing it into her hand.

Vicky gazed at it, tears flooding her eyes as she tried to look up at Fritz. "Siggy would have been five years old." It was a miniature of the last photograph that had been taken of Siggy. She lay down, covering her face.

She felt Fritz's arm go around her as he kissed away her tears, his manner reminding her of the evening on board the *Victoria and Albert*, and how he had comforted her when they first left England for Germany. She wiped her eyes, throwing her arms around him. "I just remembered, I ought to have said goodnight to Valerie when we came back from the parade. I promised to go for a walk with her, but it was impossible with the maneuvers earlier."

Fritz caught her in his arms, pulling her towards him.

"I'm not going anywhere now," she whispered, laughing as he kissed her cheek, tickling her neck with his beard.

Glienicke, Potsdam, September 1869

Candlelight flickered over the glittering gold saber-hilt as Prinz Karl lifted it from its case. The light played along the length of the iron blade, nearly dazzling his eyes. The turquoises glinted as he stood it upright on the floor.

The sword was still too heavy to use in a fencing match, even though his arm was finally strong again. He lifted it up again, holding it level across his hands, watching the flitting shapes. He still felt the same satisfaction as he had when he found this sword lying on the ground after his first battle when he was a boy of thirteen. He had been so exhausted then that it had been nearly too heavy to carry, and he had sliced his hands twice on the unguarded blade. But it was such treasure as he knew he could never relinquish. That had been the beginning of his collection.

It was good to finally be able to use his arm normally again. It had taken a long time to heal properly, the doctors giving such dire warnings that he had taken things very easy, as it wouldn't do to be a cripple.

Karl lay the saber carefully back in its case, nestling the heavy length of the blade into the folds of crimson velvet, and pulling the curtains around it. He usually left it hidden when his collection was on display. It was too precious to be seen by too many people.

He walked slowly down the room, first gazing up at the small blades and pistols which hung above him, then at the floor as he stretched his arm, turning it in every direction. This was the first day in two and a half years that there was absolutely no pain.

A cripple like the Crown Prince and Princess's son, the pitiful little heir. That thought had run through his mind many times as he listened to the doctors' warnings. But it brought with it another bitter memory.

Karl had felt it deeply when Fritz Karl had spoken the words, "a one-armed man shouldn't be King." He knew his son wasn't clever enough to realize the irony of what he said, but that was a bitter point too.

Fritz Karl wasn't clever, he was not… well, he wasn't fit to be his heir. And yet – he was the firstborn of… Karl looked up, but the sight of the glittering swords was dimmed. He wiped his eyes. He was glad he was alone.

He never let anyone see him cry. He had never let anyone see him cry since Adina had married. She had always been his confidant, his friend, his support. He was so grateful when she returned to Prussia for the most part, rather than remaining in Schwerin.

He had never let anyone see him cry until the Crown Prince's speech two years ago. He had been unable to control himself then. He saw again in his mind the figure of his son lying in bed, his leg swathed in bandages. The boy had seemed well, was cheerful, and said that he had little pain, in spite of his shattered thigh. Karl had never thought that he might never see him again.

There would be another wedding in the Sigmaringen family. Karl had heard of the engagement of Karl Sigmaringen and Elisabeth of Wied. He would go to the wedding, of course, even though he didn't think this one would be in Berlin.

The last of those weddings had been very hard. He had nearly broken down, the combined physical and emotional pain being almost too much. His arm had ached so badly, and the sight of that family without one face... one face who would never appear as the groom at a wedding... it would feel more like a funeral than a wedding.

He remembered the sight of the little soldier on guard duty, always eager to please. He had been so full of promise.

But so had Fritz Karl, when he was small

Louisa. She had never betrayed him. But there had never been any promise, so there was nothing to betray. That was the secret he hadn't understood. If one was under no promise, there could be no betrayal.

Those seven years of happiness in his youth had been very sweet, but ended very bitterly. For seven years, he had been in a dream, believing that Louischen was true to him, believing that Louischen would marry him. Believing her second son was his...

He caught the little, white-handled dagger down from its perch and thrust it into the wooden table which stood nearby. It was neither part of the invaluable mahogany furniture which mostly graced this room, nor one of the sandalwood cabinets which hid the greatest treasures. It was a simple, plain table from the garden.

He brought his fist down on the table twice more. That was satisfying. He hadn't been able to express himself in so long, with his arm being so weak.

But now he had a new heir – his grandson, supposedly. That idea was absurd. Fritz Karl couldn't have a son – he couldn't have any children.

Marianne had stubbornly refused to allow him to simply switch one of her little girls for one of his sons. That would have saved her so much trouble. But she had forced him to take matters into his own hands. Her grandson, he knew, she would not abandon, either at birth or later. When she had found out her daughter's condition, she had been furious.

But not more furious than he had been when he had discovered that she had disappeared – with the girls. This was a State offence. The girls belonged to the country – they were Princesses of Prussia. And she couldn't hide. It hadn't taken long, even for Fritz Karl, to find them.

The little boy hadn't been strong – but what could be expected when the mother of a one-year-old was ten years old? Or was she eleven? Or nine? Karl had never been good at remembering people's age.

But the boy thrived. He was a tiny little fellow, but he made a fine figure in his little hussar uniform. The boy was a great amusement to Karl.

Karl turned to the other side of the room, taking down the large, heavy gold band which hung on the wall. He felt its weight, and placed it on the little table. How strong a man must be to wear such a thing on his head constantly! He had placed it on his head. It was heavier than the crowns which the European Kings wore, and this was simply a sign of marriage, a wedding-ring, so to say.

Yes. This was a token of marriage. Not a weapon or a piece of armor. This didn't fit his collection.

Prince Karl took a cloth which lay folded carefully in a hidden cabinet. The scent of sandalwood and spice wafted out. The gold of this great ring was different from most of the gold in his collection, and required frequent polishing to remain bright.

Karl had sold nine of these rings. They had brought quite a nice little fortune. Three he had sold to exhibitors for the Paris Exhibition, three to other collectors, and three he had simply sold the gold, rather than selling the item as a curiosity.

But this one he had kept. It fit the collection in the same way the elegant little white-handled dagger with the swirling V in sapphires did.

It was the mark of a conquest.

PART FOUR:
SOUTH AND EAST

CHAPTER NINETEEN
EAST AND SOUTH

Glienicke, September 1869

Karl lifted the large ring again, hanging it carefully. It glinted in the candlelight. Something about the way it reflected the light reminded him…

There had been very few people at the tavern, but Karl had felt it was important to ask for a private room for this conversation to take place in. He had turned to the door, candlelight glinting off the large gold ring as Prince kaMpande stooped, the doorway being too short for him.

Karl had met with the Bey the next day, learning that the Crown Prince and Princess would already be leaving Tunisia the next day. Then the Bey refused to have anything to do with the plans when the full idea was placed before him – even with the prospect of an enormous monetary reward. He even threatened to inform those on board the British Navy ship on which the Crown Prince and Princess traveled.

But everything had been agreed on. The situation was the only thing which would have to be orchestrated, which proved easy enough. Prince kaMpande paid a visit to the King of Italy and to the Sultan. This was enough to begin the story that he was making a tour of Europe, and had been enough to make the Crown Princess believe the story was authentic.

She had fallen for everything so easily. Her earlier visit to Glienicke during the Russian State visit had gone quite smoothly, though Karl had almost wished he hadn't left her dagger on display. Her response to it might have been enough to make her feel that it was unwise to come again.

But it hadn't. She had believed the letter commanding her presence was from the King, never suspecting it might be forged. Fritzch had been away. Abbatchen's presence had been a nuisance. It would have been more pleasant if she had brought some of her ladies with her. But it had been a simple matter to have him removed from the room once he was unconscious, so that there was no chance of his seeing anything.

In his earlier youth, Prinz Karl had always preferred to keep things to himself. It had been so difficult to have any privacy in his boyhood; as exiles and soldiers, his family had no home. Besides, his brother, Fritz, had always pried into his doings, often coming across his correspondence and telling their father of Karl's private affairs.

But as he grew older, this had changed, though he preferred situations where he was "the Master", in his own house, at his own parties.

"The Master". Yes, that was what the man had called himself. Or rather – "*il Maestro*". He remembered his face – a strange face to Karl, as the man was of mixed English, Italian and Japanese descent. Karl had never known his name – he was simply "the Master". "The island of pleasure", all the sailors called the place, and what Karl had called it when he described it to Helmkin.

Last year, Karl had spent the autumn and winter in Nice. It was good to get out of the cold weather which made his arm ache worse than ever. But he had paid a visit to the island – off the coast of Italy, an island just far enough into the sea that one could see no land.

The establishment on the island was broken up. The building was in ruins. Karl was sorry and relieved at the same time.

He remembered his first and his last visits to that island. The first had been a great adventure, during his and Helmkin's long journey in Italy. Karl had only been twenty-two when they left Germany. He felt like a schoolboy on holiday, after the restrictive life in Berlin.

But at the last party he had attended there, two years later, he had drunk so much it had ended in his passing out.

"Where am I?" had been the first thought which wandered through his mind. He had looked about through fevered eyes. He was on board a strange ship he had never seen before, not *The Royal Louisa*, which was the ship he always traveled on in his youth. Everything around him was a jabber of Italian. He had begun to learn Italian, but suddenly, it seemed as if he remembered hardly anything he had learned.

His head ached. His face became red and swollen, hardly recognizable as a face. The only thought which remained was that of his father impressing on him that it was time that he found a bride. But he was waiting, waiting for Louischen's divorce to be legalized. Her face was often before him in his fevered dreams.

When he finally was taken off the ship, a long, slow, painful journey home began. Of course, there were no trains in those days. The carriage rides were long and painful, with bumps and frequent stops.

His head never stopped aching. When he finally reached Berlin, he barely recognized his father, brothers and sisters. Nothing seemed familiar, and his mind was blank, except for a blind, fierce hunger which nothing would satisfy.

During all this time – the illness lasted two months – he hadn't been able to see the colors of people's voices, not been able to taste, smell, hear, or feel things as he usually did. Everything was strange, foreign, and flavorless. He experienced the actual smells, tastes and sensations without the extra layer where a color caused him to hear a sound, a flavor caused an inward sensation, or a voice caused a color to flood his mind's eye. This was the way, he supposed, most people perceived things, but it was very dull.

One day, he heard the voice he knew to be his father's, then the doctors. They spoke in low tones, but he could hear them. "Marriage will be impossible, if this ends as it usually does." He heard the doctor's voice go on, describing the horrors of the illness. This illness usually ended in madness, death, or a terrible deformity, or rather disfigurement, which he couldn't bear to think of.

Somehow, they had brought him through the illness. Gradually, his father's face grew familiar again, then his siblings. His head no longer ached. His own voice no longer sounded strange. One day, someone spoke and a flash of color filled his mind again.

During the illness, he had been covered in itching rashes and sores, but his head had ached so badly he was barely aware of the itching, though when he was at last recovering, his skin was torn with scratch-marks. Some of this had scarred. The most noticeable one was on his right hand – a large, red mark which people who hadn't known him previously assumed was a birthmark, as it did not really look like a scar.

The pain he experienced then was as intense as the pain in his arm. He had rarely felt such fear as that which coursed through him when Prince Ludwig had caught him. He had thought that Princess Alice was home alone, other than the household. It had been quite easy to catch her alone – even easier than it had her sister, as she was much less on her guard.

But he had never expected Princess Alice's husband to arrive just afterwards. Prince Ludwig had been kept quite busy since the war, and was often away, as Karl knew well.

The memory flashed into Karl's mind. He – Karl – had been caught in the enemy's den. He had been the one off his guard. Everything had happened so quickly he couldn't remember the sequence of events – only finding himself lying on his back, blood trickling into his eye from the gash across his face, an extreme pain in his right arm, just below the elbow. The cloud-cloak had instantly been stripped away. Prince Ludwig crouched over him, his foot planted on Karl's chest, his fury burning in his eyes, in the trembling of his hand which held the hilt of his drawn sword, in his voice as he spoke low, his voice a cloud of hot, burning burnt ocher.

If Prince Ludwig had simply met Karl's gaze, it wouldn't have been so painful. But he would look at his face, just barely not looking him in the eye. His voice was like fire as he spoke.

Karl couldn't remember the words. The pain was overwhelming without the cloud-cloak. And ever since that day until now, his arm had ached so badly. Without his cloud-cloak, which always disappeared when he needed it most – whenever he was desperately ill or in great pain – he felt everything acutely. Every emotion of his own or of others tore through him, without first being muted by the cloud-cloak.

Karl turned, taking down a little – a very little – knife with a polished black handle. It had belonged to his mother.

Queen Louise, the heroine of the war with Napoleon the first. All of Prussia idolized her.

He remembered the sight of his parents walking together, always hand-in-hand, the looks which passed between them. Everything about their relationship – as well as her sentimental idealizing of Prussian politics – was very like Fritzch and his little English wife.

The resemblance irritated Karl.

He replaced the little black knife, staring at it, but really at a memory which had appeared in his mind.

The births of his two youngest siblings, Lulu and Abbat, had brought great joy to Mama and Papa. But Karl had sensed something was different about the new little brother he was ushered in to see. This had been confirmed later. Karl could see – in the way he could tell many things – his youngest sister and brother's voices were a very different color from the rest of them, just as his own and Adina's were somewhat different than Fritz, Mouffy and Helmkin's. It had only been that he could tell the difference with his youngest brother when he was still a baby. The differences which made people's relation to each other obvious usually did not become clear until they were at least eleven or twelve.

He remembered the sight of the young Scottish nobleman – the Duke of Sutherland – with his mother. They thought no one had seen them, but he had.

But Papa, it seemed, knew nothing of this, and idolized her as he always had. He remembered the sight of Papa weeping silently after her death, and the broken atmosphere of their home.

But was she really worth such grief? Many questions had floated in his child's mind – Karl had only been eight years old when Mama died.

It was almost five years later when he and his brothers had gone to the circus where Karl had first learned about hypnosis, when he had learned the truth about himself, about his mother's betrayal, and about the ring-master, who was really Onkel Louis. That had been one of the most important days of his life.

December 14.

That had also been the date of the death of Prince Albert, the Crown Princess's darling Papa.

But his thoughts returned to Mama, and to Papa's grief over her death.

"*Ach*! Louischen, Louischen, why?" he had heard Papa cry.

Neues Palais, Potsdam, September 25, 1869

Vicky had finished packing the things she wished to pack herself when Georgiana Hobbs entered the room. She was crying, as she often had been since Emma's marriage had been announced.

"Is something wrong?"

"No," Georgiana sobbed. "Hit's just the hidea of Hemma's goin' that 'urts me so," Georgiana sobbed. "Hi'm glad for the children's sake han' for 'ers that you'll be away from home when hit comes. But hit 'll be dreadful 'ard for me."

Vicky nodded, holding out her hand. "I know how hard it is to part from one's family," she said, squeezing Georgiana's hand. "Will you please bring Charlotte here?"

Georgiana nodded and hurried away.

Vicky had returned to Potsdam to prepare for her journey to the south of France. Fritz would return for a few days before the parting. He would arrive home during the night of the twenty-eighth, to be at home on their *Verlobungstag*[46] – for the first time in five years.

While staying in Wiesbaden, Vicky had visited Alice, who, with the children, would be with her. It wasn't decided if Louis would remain with them or travel with Fritz. His uncle the Grand Duke had given permission for him to travel. Vicky had sighed when Alice told her. It was so easy for Louis to get permission for him and Alice to travel, whether for pleasure or for official duties.

Vicky smiled at the memory of her and Fritz's conversation about Karl Sigmaringen. Vicky had called him stiff and serious, but when he was with the children, he softened. His manner truly did remind her of Papa then, as Fritz had said.

But something also made Vicky uneasy. Charlotte, who had been so shy when she was very small, and had, until only a year or two ago, taken time to warm up even to family and old friends whom she hadn't seen for some time, had greeted both Karl and also members of Alice's household enthusiastically. Wally, too, whom they hadn't seen for three years, had been at Wiesbaden, and Charlotte met her as if she had seen her yesterday. Vicky wished she could be glad Charlotte was overcoming her shyness, but her manner did not seem "right". It seemed artificial, as at times she was still very shy.

"Charlotte," Vicky said, as Georgiana appeared at the door and Charlotte entered, "do you wish to bring anything particular for the stay in France?"

"No," Charlotte said. "All my books are so old, they would bore me to death. It will be a relief to leave them behind."

Vicky watched Charlotte, puzzled. When she was very small, she had been such an avid learner, eager for picture books until she could read, and then she would read the books again and again until they were practically memorized. She still would beg Fritz to read aloud from the same books. Vicky had never expected her to call these books boring. And she spoke in such a "grown-up" – though *not* mature – way about it. She acted very blasé about many things lately.

"Aunty Alice will be with us, and the cousins?" Henry asked, entering the room as well.

---

[46]   Engagement anniversary

"Yes. You will be with your cousins for nearly three months," Vicky said.

"Hurrah!" Willy cried, appearing at the door as she spoke.

Vicky smiled. Alice and the children had already visited Potsdam earlier that year. The little cousins had grown to be very good friends.

***

Neues Palais, September 29, 1869

Vicky stepped out of her dressing room. Fritz had been in his when she went in. A candle flickered on her bedside table. He lay in bed, curled up as if he was cold.

"Fritz," Vicky whispered, as she sat down. He lay on his side, turned away from her. He didn't look up. "Fritz?" she said aloud. "I know you're awake." He had been muttering to himself a few minutes before and he hadn't seemed asleep. She ran her hand down his arm and took his hand, leaning over him to kiss his cheek. His eyes were open. "Fritz," she whispered, snuggling down next to him. "Did you forget the day? You never did before. And we were together this time, but you never mentioned it."

Fritz had been at home on this day for the first time in five years. It was the fourteenth anniversary of their engagement. He had never forgotten it before. But he hadn't been himself of late. He had been so continually tired, it seemed, for the last two months.

All through the day, he had been very quiet, often looking away when Vicky tried to meet his eye. He played happily with the children, but seemed strangely uneasy whenever he and Vicky were alone together.

Vicky had given him her present that morning, after breakfast – a life-size portrait of Siggy she had begun shortly before his death and had never been able to make herself finish.

Fritz didn't turn towards her. Vicky rose, going to the other side of the bed. She sat down, stroking his hair and kissing his cheek. He turned his head, glancing up at her. She kissed his lips.

Fritz sighed, turning his face away again, barely returning her kiss, and turned over.

Vicky returned to her side of the bed, snuggling down beside him again. "Fritz?" she whispered, taking his hand and pulling his arm around her before he could turn over again. She pressed his hand to her lips, then turned his hand, covering his palm with little kisses, and pressed his hand to her heart.

Fritz moved his hand to her shoulder, but drew her closer, and she lay her head on his shoulder. Their eyes met, but he still didn't speak. She reached forward to kiss him again, but he shook his head.

"Vicky," he said, very quietly, though not in a whisper, "I don't know." He shook his head, looking away again. "I did not forget the day! I never can! But – I do not – I do not want to disappoint you."

"What do you mean?" Vicky laughed. "You can never disappoint me. Did you forget to – will my present not be here in time? Do you really think I would be seriously disappointed at such a thing? It's wonderful simply to be together on this day. I only wondered at how quiet and undemonstrative you were."

Fritz sat up and crouched beside the bed, unlocking the drawer of his bedside table. He lay back down, pressing something into Vicky's hand.

It was a locket fashioned in the shape of an actual clamshell, containing miniature hand-colored photographs of Fritz, Vicky, Waldie, and little Vicky.

"Why didn't you give it me this morning?" Vicky asked quietly as Fritz put his arm around her again.

He shrugged. "I could not find it. I thought I had kept it with our things from when we were at Nordeney." He kissed her cheek, then turned his face away again as she tried to meet his lips.

"What did you mean by you didn't want to disappoint me?"

Fritz sighed, pulling his arm away, turning away from her again.

"Fritz, please, tell me! You're making me worry about you. What happened? What's wrong?"

Fritz turned towards her again as she sat up. "*Ich bin so müde*[47]," he murmured. "If I could only rest."

"But you've been resting. You aren't ill, are you?" He shook his head. Vicky leaned over him, kissing his lips. He pulled her to him, but again, didn't return her kiss.

"I do not –" He broke off, shaking his head. "It is not true. My mind – my thoughts do not agree with it. It is simply – *ach*! How can I say such a thing to you?" His voice shook, and he didn't meet her eye.

---

[47]   I am so tired

Vicky tried to meet his eye. "What? What has happened? What have they done? Have they – are you –" She felt her face showed her alarm. "You haven't been – you don't think you've been hypnotized, do you?"

"No, no, it is nothing of that sort."

Vicky breathed a sigh of relief. "What then?"

"I –" Fritz looked down, and put his hand over his eyes. He took a long, slow breath, and drew her close to him so he could whisper very softly, "I do not feel attracted to you."

Vicky sat up, staring at him, feeling the shock of his words like a slap in the face. She had certainly *never* expected him to say that.

"What? What you mean?" she asked, with a little quiver in her voice.

"I mean what I said – and yet I do not! I said – my thoughts – my mind – do not agree with it! I love you, Vicky!" He sat up, reaching out to cradle her face in his hands, brushing his thumb over her lips. "I love you so much, and I would never say anything to wound you."

Tears had started to her eyes after his previous statement, and now they began to flow. She couldn't speak. A dull, numb ache covered her.

"*Meine* Vicky," Fritz whispered, lying down again and pulling her with him, gathering her in his arms. "I did not mean *that*! I did not know *how* to say it!"

Vicky heard his voice break, and met his eye, shaking her head. She still couldn't speak.

"It began after our trip to Nordeney – at the same time this dreadful fatigue overtook me," Fritz said. "I am as attracted to your idea as ever," he murmured against her hair. "I only mean – physically – I cannot –" He broke off again, his face flushing bright red, and he whispered in her ear.

"Oh!" Vicky met his gaze again. She threw her arms around him, kissing his cheek. "But, why did you never tell me?" Her voice broke before she could speak further, but she no longer felt the dull, numb feeling which had overwhelmed her since Fritz had said those words – "I am not attracted to you".

"I did not – how to begin such a conversation?" Fritz murmured, almost to himself. "It is so strange," he went on. "My thoughts about you are the same as ever, but – but my body will not follow suit. I wish –" He shook his head. "I simply do not *feel* anything, physically."

"Something must – have you spoken to –" Vicky paused, feeling herself blush, seeing a look of distress and embarrassment on Fritz's face. She had been going to ask if he had spoken to Wegner. But Wegner never seemed to know much of anything – his response to almost everything was "I am not a specialist". She often wondered why he had been made their personal physician.

Vicky knew how uncomfortable Fritz always was with *speaking* about such things, and how awkward he would feel about speaking of it to Wegner. Wegner was a member of their household, and not a particularly discreet one.

"You must – you must speak to someone about it. It means that something is wrong. You must –"

"I know," Fritz said, almost in a groan. He shut his eyes tight, a little shudder going over him. Vicky knew he dreaded the idea of speaking to any of the doctors of the court. That must not be done, as none were discreet about their patient's problems. But the idea of talking to a stranger about such things was just as difficult.

"Speaking to the doctors here would do no good," he went on. "I have heard them speak of such things about others and they simply say the person is experiencing stress or overwork. I have hardly been without these things during our marriage, but I have never experienced this before." He paused. Vicky watched his face, his eyes wandering as if searching for something. "I will write to Anna, to ask her if –"

"You will write to Anna about *what*?" Vicky sat straight up, again feeling the shock of his words like a slap. She shook her head, not able to believe she had understood him.

"I told you about Anna, did I not?" Fritz looked at her. She stared back, shaking her head. "But you noticed how different she was when you were with her two years ago."

"You mean – when I had the baby there? She was friendly, as she was when I first saw little Aleck. But – but she is not trustworthy! How could you even *think* of writing to *her* about something like *this*?"

"She is changed, Vicky. I thought I showed you the –"

"Changed? What do you mean? She changes all the time. I have only seen her truly friendly to us two times in all the time I have been here. All she wishes to do usually is seduce you! How can you think of talking to her about such a thing?"

"Let me explain," Fritz said softly, rising and taking his dressing-gown. He went into another room.

Vicky sat still, her head reeling. This disclosure of Fritz's had come as a great shock, though she had noticed more and more frequently in the last two months his attempting to go to bed – and to sleep – before her. He had rarely kissed her of his own initiation besides when greeting her when they had been apart for days, and all intimacy between them had been brief.

But the idea of his speaking of such an intimate matter to Anna of all people was inexplicable. Vicky shook her head again, covering her eyes. Anna! Why would he...?

Fritz reappeared at the doorway with two letters in his hands. He set them on the bed, lighted a second candle, and handed them to Vicky.

"I was at Glienicke the other day," he said. "Anna was there, but she seemed so entirely different – not a hint of her usual behavior towards me. But she was different, too, from the few times we have seen her when she is not under the spell. I heard Louischen saying something, too, about her voice being a different color than it used to be."

"So Louischen still sees those things, does she? She hasn't spoken of it to me in so long, and Marianne says she never does to her, so I thought she had outgrown it. But – what about Anna?"

Fritz met Vicky's eye. "You remember little Aleck's affliction," he began. "Blindness, malformed fingers, etc."

"Yes, of course, it is the same as Charlotte only more severe."

"Anna has suffered with other illnesses, too," Fritz said. "Far more disagreeable ones. But she has gone to a lady – a medicine lady, she calls her, in Egypt. She has cured the illness, and, Anna believes, dehypnotized her."

Vicky stared at Fritz, and then glanced over the first letter. "This – this is – unbelievable. And it gives so much hope, if it is really true, that they can be dehypnotized!"

Fritz nodded. "I have heard of these medicine ladies before – and your Mama wrote to you about the Empress of Austria going to one in Madeira. She wrote cryptically, and it was long ago, before Charlotte was born, and I was not sure if you understood it." Vicky shook her head. "In Bombay, Egypt and Madeira, I believe. And these ladies of Eastern culture understand such things as dehypnotizing, as well as curing illnesses which our medicine declares incurable."

He took something from the second letter. It was a card listing illnesses or symptoms which the lady in Egypt was able to cure.

Vicky met his eye. She nodded. She understood why Fritz wished to write to Anna.

***

Vicky lay in bed, Fritz leaning over her, cradling her face in his hands, gently kissing her, and stroking her hair. "*Sehr schön*[48]," he murmured, but the look in his eyes and the tone of his voice were gentle, affectionate, not filled with passion as they often had been in the past. She realized how that look had faded over the last two months. She had felt that something was different, but she hadn't realized what, until last night.

Their lips met, but his kisses were always very brief now. She felt her heartbeat quicken as he kissed her neck, resting his head against her chest, but she heard his breathing – calm, steady, with no change. Everything made it plain that there was no desire behind his actions, but she understood by those actions that he wished to "unsay" those words he had spoken yesterday – "I do not feel attracted to you."

He sat up, then lay down beside her, pulling her towards him, so that she rested her head where she heard his heartbeat. "Vicky," he whispered, stroking her hair, "do you remember when I first told you about them – Onkel Karl and Fritz Karl, I mean – calling me a coward?"

"Before the Danish war?" He shook his head. Vicky thought for a moment. "Do you mean – while we were engaged?" He nodded. "Yes – only you said *ein Schwachling*, not *ein Feigling*[49]. You never actually said they called you a coward until just before the war in '64. You always said a weakling."

"But do you remember the other word – the word I did not say? Can you guess what it was?"

Vicky looked at him. His expression was very serious. "*Schl… Schal… Schlapp* – yes, that was the first part of it. But there was more to it. You and Papa wouldn't tell me."

Fritz sighed deeply. "*Schlapp Schwanz*." Vicky saw a look of pain cross his face. He glanced away. "It is true, now," he said bitterly, "literally true."

***

---

[48]   Very beautiful

[49]   A weakling, not a coward.

Neues Palais, October 1, 1869

Vicky knocked on the door of Fritz's dressing-room. He had gone in over half an hour before. It didn't take him that long to dress. He hadn't seemed deeply upset about anything, which was the only other reason he sometimes stayed there.

"Vicky?" His voice was tense.

"Are you well?"

"*Nein.*"

"May I come in?"

Fritz opened the door. He stood half-dressed, surveying himself in the mirror. "It is certainly well I am going to Egypt. I shall stop to see Anna on my way, rather than writing. It is urgent."

Vicky had taken his arm. He shook her off, but a patch of hair from his arm came off in her hand, even though her touch had been very light.

"This has been happening for some time, only not so severely before today," Fritz said. "Every time I scratch an itch – and I have felt constantly tickled – and there has been much loose hair when I change my clothes."

Vicky stared at him. There were patches on his arms and chest where there was no hair. His chest and waist were covered in a dark rash. He held up his hands, then his feet. His palms and the bottoms of his feet were covered in the same, dark rash.

Their eyes met.

"I have other symptoms as well," he said quietly, his voice still tense, a look of disgust on his face. "I hope this is true." He picked up a page from Anna's letter.

"The Emperors Alexander and Franz Joseph have also gone to her – to cure intimate symptoms," Anna had written. "She says they wrote that they are completely cured."

"So what we did three years ago," Vicky said slowly, "when you insisted on our sleeping in separate beds, and not kissing. It wasn't effective?" Her mind was still taking everything in.

Fritz shrugged, and went on dressing. Finally, he turned, putting his hands on her shoulders. "I cannot say that it was not effective," he said, looking into her eyes. "If we had been intimate then, this might have been far worse. We might have suffered from multiple illnesses, as Anna says she did." Vicky nodded. "I will be out in a moment," Fritz went on, and turned away. He turned back just before Vicky closed the door. "Please, telegraph your Mama – or rather, telegraph to have Dr. Jenner meet me in München[50]. I wish him to know what is going on." Dr. Jenner was Mama's physician-in-ordinary, in whom she placed great trust.

"Vicky," Fritz said quietly when he joined her, "I said this is urgent. You know what the treatments they do for such things here are like, do you not?"

Vicky shuddered. "Mercury and the like. The treatment is equally if not twice as likely to make one insane or unable to have more children as the illness itself."

"*Oktober 5, 1869.*

"*Meine* Vicky,

"I have seen Alice and Louis, Vivi and Fritz of Baden, Anna and Fritz Hessen, and Mama and Papa. Karl Sigmaringen, too, I had an opportunity of saying goodbye to. We were very glad of this, as this brief, two-month visit of his is most likely all he will have for some years. I am only sorry to be absent when his wedding shall take place. They shall be engaged only two months as he must return to his country as soon as possible.

"Alice is preparing to join you with the children, and Louis shall join me on my journey. They, too, have suffered with strange rashes such as you had last year – and recognized them as little. I am very pleased to have his company.

"Anna has shown me everything about the medicine lady. She had, too, some of the remedy. It is a powder of black, tan and brown granules, rather hot to the taste if one takes it alone, but it is a very strong concentrate which can be mixed into anything and the taste disappears. It does not flavor other things, unless used in too great a quantity.

"But Anna explained that one must take it for a full month, and after this one is no longer a carrier of the illness, no matter what external symptoms might still remain (this is opposite to the mercury treatments, which merely mask the symptoms with no real good being done). However, after the first week of taking this remedy, one goes into a deep illness with fever, deliriousness, rashes, etc. I have taken it three days, so

---

[50]   Munich

as to put a stop to the active disease, but shall continue the treatment after my return. I have no wish to go through such an illness during my journey.

"I send you this pamphlet which I have copied from what Anna had. Read it, answer the questions for both of us. I wish to have your perspective, and there are some questions I cannot answer. You know everything necessary about me. Send it to Kassel and Anna shall send it on, so it may be prepared by the time I reach Egypt. I said that Anna had shown me the remedy, but this is a generic remedy to continue after the month's treatment. To treat the illness most effectively, it is best to answer these questions and have it made specifically for oneself."

Neues Palais, Potsdam, October 8, 1869

Vicky glanced over the pamphlet again, feeling her face burn. She could imagine Fritz's embarrassment at the idea of answering such questions.

She took it up again, beginning to fill in the answers. At the second question she paused. She had been going to answer it, but realized she didn't really know. The answer was plain enough in Fritz's case, but for her? Vicky shivered, rubbing her hands and face.

The vague memory, with no real images, which she had first experienced when she greeted Uncle Ernst before little Vicky's Christening, returned. Vicky still felt the strange rushing, swirling feeling in her head when she thought of it. She shuddered, again wiping her face.

She must speak to Marianne before she left for France, and to Abbat, too.

She laid down the pamphlet, taking up a note from Alice. "Louis starts on the 11th, still in the south of Germany. He goes to Munich and Venice, where he will join Fritz, before they start for the East. I bring no one but Orchie, Eliza, Beck and my *Haushofmeister* on our journey to the South. But you wrote, I think, that you shall bring 25 people – though many of these will be to stay with the boys after our return home. I must say I am glad you shall bring such a large nursery entourage, as I have so few for so many children."

Vicky smiled. It would be very pleasant to be with Alice again for so long. She took a pen to write a note to Marianne, stating that she wished to speak to her of what she knew of August '65. Marianne would know what she meant by that. She stepped to the door to ring the bell, calling a footman.

She handed the man the note. "To Princess Friedrich Karl. And it is to be delivered immediately."

She sat down to write to Mama, Alice, and Fritz. The time passed quickly, and she thought she heard a step outside her suite. Yes, there was a knock at the door.

"*Herein*[51]," she called.

The footman entered, clicked his heels, and announced, "The Landgräfin of Hesse-Kassel".

It was Anna.

---

[51]   Come in

CHAPTER TWENTY
CONFESSIONS AND CONFIDENCES

"*Meine* Vicky,

"**O**n the 6th, I crossed the Austrian frontier, and was greeted by several of the Emperor's aides. In Vienna, the Emperor Franz Joseph waited in Prussian uniform, and also the Empress Elisabeth, whom you thought so lovely – and whose hair is certainly a marvel – appeared. I had assumed her to be away, so her appearance would have been a surprise even without considering her shyness and reluctance to show herself in public.

"Everywhere I was well received, for they recognized the good intentions which brought about my visit. It could hardly be assumed that they felt any friendly feelings for us after their defeat at our hands three years ago. I can imagine that no other Prince of our house would be so kindly received.

"The Emperor I find changed, aged, and with a short red beard covering his face, while the Empress is very little changed. They are still quite in mourning for his brother Max and Mexico.

"The Emperor avoided political discussion, but was quite friendly. The Archdukes said that I had done my duty as a soldier and they could not hold this against me.

"Vienna itself is quite changed, its old walls being taken down and rebuilt; I did not know my way around in the least. Everything is quite planned after Parisian boulevards.

"It was quite interesting to me to see Venice as Italian territory, with the Austrian frontier at its border instead of within. To cross into the lagoons of Venice at sunrise was a lovely sight. Here, in contrast to Vienna, with its changed walls and new buildings, nothing is changed, except that two or three palaces have been cleaned on the outside.

"One thing which has changed is that poverty visibly increases. 40 thousand people do not wish to work, and find begging a more comfortable lifestyle.

"It is my fifth visit to Italy. After the dull weather in Vienna, everything was beautiful in Venice, without a cloud in the sky, moonlight and starry nights followed by the brightest sunshine. My thoughts were on the night seven years ago, as we drifted through the lagoons in the gondola to the song of the gondolieri, marveling at their talent in harmonizing with the melody of the nightingales.

"I visited the art galleries, too, and wished you were by my side. My thoughts are always with you *und die liebe Kinder.* You, too, shall make your way to the South before another letter reaches me. I send these lines to the Grand Hotel in Cannes, hoping they will find you safe and well."

Neues Palais, Potsdam, October 8, 1869

Vicky rose, watching Anna as she stepped closer.

"Your Fritz asked me to come here," Anna said softly, as she curtseyed deeply. "May I sit down?"

Vicky didn't answer, but watched Anna closely. There certainly was something different in her manner. It had none of her usual affectation, and she was dressed modestly, as she had been when Vicky saw her after the birth of little Aleck. But there was a composure in her manner which had never been there before.

"Please, I come here as a friend," Anna said, meeting Vicky's eye. "But I certainly understand if you do not feel comfortable welcoming me. How could you, when I have done – done such dreadful things!"

Vicky still couldn't speak. She hadn't realized before, just how much Fritz's sudden correspondence with Anna about intimate matters had rankled in her mind. It had irritated her, sitting in the back of her mind and stinging every little thought the last few days.

What if Fritz was wrong, and Anna had tricked him into confiding intimate secrets to her, under the guise of being "de-hypnotized"? She remembered the day all too well when Fritz Karl had read aloud her note which Anna had stolen, twisting the meaning as he always did. If he got a hold of these matters – how he would gloat over the fact of the old name he used to call Fritz being "the truth", as Fritz had said.

"My Papa," Anna said, then covered her face with both hands. "Oh! I loved him so, when I was a small child!" Her face changed, flushing bright red as tears came to her eyes. "I called him my 'golden-Papa' – I don't remember why, but it was such a dear little name. But – I am so ashamed to think of my love for him, now, when I know things."

Anna hung her head, and Vicky saw she couldn't meet her eye this time.

"Please, may I sit?" Anna asked again.

Vicky nodded this time. She still couldn't speak, but Anna's tone sounded very humble. They each took a seat.

"I know what you think of me, and how you despise me, and how I deserve it!" Anna cried. She looked up, shaking her head. "I know your Fritz is my brother, and I have always known it, when I am – *myself*, since I was eleven. But –" She broke off, a shudder passing over her.

"Is it – is it really true?" Vicky asked. Her throat felt choked, and she couldn't speak above a whisper. "Is it really true you don't remember meeting me the first five years I was here?"

Anna nodded vigorously. "After Aleck's birth is the first I remember you, even though I know I was at your wedding festivities, and your brother's. I vaguely remember arriving in England, but nothing else."

She shuddered. Vicky saw a strange, blank look pass over her face; her eyes seemed glazed as she gazed at the chandelier. "That year – after Aleck's birth, I did something – something which displeased my Papa. He – he – he –" Anna began to shudder, her hands clutching the ruffles of her dress, then going to cover her eyes, as if they moved involuntarily.

Vicky reached out, gently putting her hand on her shoulder. "Anna?" she said softly.

"He made it so I had to remember – *everything*," Anna went on, her hands still clenching and unclenching mechanically. "And – and that Aleck is his child, and –" She took a deep breath. Vicky thought she looked as if she might be sick any moment. "And what I did – what I did to you!" She squeezed her eyes shut, shaking her head. "I remember how furious I was with your Fritz for fighting 'against my country', as I said, though I know it was my Papa I should blame. And I remember your Fritz locking me in the bedroom in Paris. I don't remember – *anything* like that, before that. How many times did I behave so shamefully?"

"At least three times that I know of," Vicky said.

"I feel so ashamed," Anna said. "Everything I have done makes me feel as if I have betrayed all my loves – for I felt forced to betray my Papa, in spite of my childhood love for him; I betrayed your Fritz, whom I really loved as a cousin and brother; and in what I did, I betrayed my love, for I would have been unfaithful to him, if your Fritz had –" She didn't finish her sentence.

"But you are de-hypnotized? Are you quite certain?" Vicky asked.

"Oh, yes. I do not remember the process; it was very strange, but I have done many things and said things which I know used to put me into that state, and nothing changes. And I know now, since he made me remember things."

Vicky nodded, leaning forward and holding out her hand. "I was so angry at Fritz for saying he would write to you about – our troubles just now," she said slowly. "I couldn't imagine why he would dream of such a thing! And I'd never actually been angry at him before!"

"I can imagine how you feel! I must confess something," Anna said. "You know how your Fritz always checks the rooms before you settle into your suite?"

Vicky nodded, wondering what was coming.

"I hid once, when I was – you know – but I hid once, and watched you. I watched you and him –" She shut her eyes, shuddering again. "I wish I could wipe the memory from my mind, but how I was seething with jealousy at the time. I was so completely under the impression that *I* was his love, and you had taken him from me! I had to confess it! I know this isn't something which is easy to hear, and I would understand if you could never forgive me!"

Vicky shook her head. "I know you wouldn't have done it if you weren't under the spell. But what should I do now, since you're here? Fritz told me to send the pamphlet on to you, and that you would send it to Egypt."

"I will take it with me. And you can trust me. I won't read it or pass it on to Fritz Karl." She blushed, but met Vicky's eye. "I am so sorry," she sobbed.

Vicky nodded. "I must speak to Marianne and to Abbat before I finish filling it out. But I shall have it ready tomorrow, as I must leave the next day for Cannes."

Anna left the room, and Vicky turned back to her letters. She looked up when the door opened again. Anna reappeared with a little boy in her arms.

"I have brought my little one," she said, "my little Fritz." She came forward, placing him in Vicky's arms. "would it be possible for him to stay with you while I am here? I do not like leaving him at Marmor or Glienicke."

Vicky looked up at her thoughtfully, and then down at the dark, curly hair which covered the little boy's head. He looked down shyly, but then reached up, playing with the locket which hung round her neck.

"I said I'm leaving for Cannes in a couple of days," Vicky said, "but he may certainly stay while I'm here. But I'm taking my nursery with me."

Anna nodded. "I am leaving, too, in two days." She smiled, taking the little one from Vicky again. "The other children call him Fischy. I called him Fritz, but he calls himself Fischy, now he is beginning to speak more."

***

Another hour had passed. Vicky had gone on writing after Anna had left, occasionally pausing to watch the little boy. Vicky began to grow impatient, when finally, there was a knock at the door, and the footman who had taken her note reappeared.

"Where is Princess Friedrich Karl's answer?" Vicky asked, when he simply clicked his heels and stood still.

He shook his head.

"Is Prince Friedrich Karl at home?"

He nodded.

"Did you deliver my letter? Please tell me."

"He took it." The man spoke briefly, glancing about the room nervously, but didn't say any more.

"You may go." Vicky nodded, rising and going with Fischy into the nursery rooms. Since Siggy's birth, she had no longer had the younger children far away in the upstairs nursery. Little Vicky and Waldie's rooms were within her and Fritz's suite.

She put him into Mrs. Hobbs' arms. "This is Princess Anna's little boy," she said hurriedly. "He will be your charge for two days. But I must go. Nastya," she called to the young woman who sat nearby.

"Your Highness?" Nastya spoke English and German with a strong Russian accent. She rose, and Vicky looked up at her. Nastya was quite young, only sixteen, and hadn't finished growing when she joined Vicky's household three years ago. But she had already been over six feet tall, and extremely strong, two years ago, when Vicky had first told Alice about her new bodyguards.

"I wish you to come with me to the Marmor Palais."

"But Alga is – am I not to remain with the children?"

"I wish for you to come, because you are taller. I want you to make as much of an impression as possible."

Nastya grinned. Vicky studied her face. She and her sister were very different from anyone she had encountered before. With their enormous size and strength, one would hardly fancy them to be young girls, and yet, if one looked at a photograph of them with no size reference, they appeared very elegant young ladies, dressed to perfection. Neither was particularly clever – they were, as Fritz and the Weimar family would say, not of great mental development – but they were very loyal

***

Guards saluted but didn't move as Vicky and Nastya passed through the courtyard of the Marmor Palais. Vicky was glad to see that Fritz Karl's carriage wasn't there. *He must have gone away after taking my note.*

Vicky never liked to bring her other ladies to Marmor, or to Glienicke when she had gone there, but with Nastya, she felt comfortable. There was no one about as they went in.

"Stay in the room you come to when we come to the top of the staircase. The center door is to the dining-room, and where they most likely are. If you hear raised voices, come and help me, or whoever is in trouble." Nastya nodded, smiled, and stood quietly in a corner, out of the way and mostly out of view.

Vicky went forward and opened the door to the dining room, quickly shutting it behind her without turning toward it.

"Oh! You shouldn't have come!" Vicky heard Marianne's voice as she closed the door. She glanced around. Marianne sat in a large dark green armchair at the opposite end of the room; the girls huddled behind her in the corner.

"Why not, if you are alone?" Vicky glanced around the room, saw no one else, and hurried forward. "Did you know I sent a note? I did hope you would come to the Neues Palais, as I don't wish to speak of it here."

Marianne started up, and there was a cry from one of the girls. Vicky heard a slight sound behind her, and felt a hand on her shoulder. She felt the grip just in the place where Prince Charles had grasped her shoulder at the laundry. She felt a shudder of revulsion go over her such as she hadn't felt for six years.

She tried to turn, but both his hands gripped her shoulders painfully, pushing her forward. She tried to cry out, to do something to alert Nastya, but her voice was gone.

Finally, she stood against the wall, still feeling a hand on her shoulder.

"Sit." She tried to sit, but found herself pressed roughly against the wall. "Not you." The voice was a loud, harsh whisper.

She glanced sideways, seeing Marianne return to her chair. Tears were in her eyes, but Vicky couldn't read her expression; there were too many emotions. The girls' eyes were wide with alarm.

The hand left her shoulder, but she felt frozen. There was a jerk on her arm, forcing her to turn around.

Fritz Karl stood in front of her, leaning forward so his bloodshot eyes met hers. He pushed her again, making her lean against the wall. "You wish to know about what happened in August three years ago?" His voice made her shiver, but she still felt as if she couldn't speak. "I can tell you what happened – or better, show you!" He pressed his face into hers.

Vicky threw up her hands, pushing him away as she felt the rough stubble of his beard touch her face. She tried to step aside. He caught at her arm again, and she stumbled. He had stepped on the bottom of her crinoline, making it impossible for her to get away.

She wasn't sure what happened next. She fell heavily on the marble floor, but was careful not to let her head hit. She held her arms over her face and chest, feeling his hand grip her shoulder again.

Her eyes must have closed for a moment. She heard a scream, "No! Papa, *nein, nein*! You shall not!" Vicky opened her eyes to see Fritz Karl kneeling down on the floor at her side, but his head was jerked backwards, a hand gripping his hair, another arm around his throat.

Vicky struggled to sit up. Finally, her voice returned to her. "Mariechen!" she screamed. She saw Fritz Karl shake Mariechen off, throwing her to the floor.

But then, Fritz Karl wasn't there. Mariechen lay on the floor, a bruise rapidly forming on her forehead, but she smiled at Vicky. "I wouldn't let him – he – he must not!" she sobbed, reaching her arms out to Vicky.

Vicky looked up. Nastya stood there. Fritz Karl's legs kicked, but he didn't have his boots on. That was why Vicky hadn't heard him enter the room. His arms were held to his sides, and Nastya's hand was over his mouth.

"Marianne," Vicky called, and Marianne and the other girls came to her side. They helped her up, and Marianne lifted up Mariechen.

Vicky still felt stunned, and could hardly speak above a whisper. "Come, Marianne," she murmured, "you must not stay here." She turned to Nastya. "Can you keep him from following us, but join us in the carriage?"

"Oh, he won't be following me," Nastya said with her usual smile. She turned. "Will you open this door, so I don't have to uncover his mouth?"

Vicky opened the door, and then joined Marianne and the girls, who were already nearly at the bottom of the grand staircase. Soon, they were in the carriage.

"Oh, what shall I do?" Marianne murmured. "I could never forgive myself if –" She broke off, shuddering. "But – oh, he will harm the girls – even more so, if I 'interfere'. He does something worse each time I try to resist him."

"You must not put yourself or the girls in more danger," Vicky said, putting her arm around her. "I only wish I could have cried out, but my voice was gone! I wish one of you would have screamed sooner. I told Nastya to come in if she heard raised voices. But he didn't raise his voice. That was what I was expecting."

Marianne shuddered. "When he is nearly silent is always the worst," she whispered.

Vicky nodded. "His bite is worse than his bark, which is certainly bad enough."

"It is terrible!" Marianne cried. "I have told you how – how I feel when he speaks so in front of the girls. And it is not just the girls," she sobbed. "He is beginning to encourage Fritzi to speak so!"

Nastya appeared. She only smiled when Vicky tried to ask her about Fritz Karl.

It was cold now that the sun was going down, and they had no warm wraps with them. Vicky saw the girls huddle closer together. "We will be there soon," she whispered.

When they reached the Neues Palais, Vicky put her arm around Mariechen as they went in. The girl shivered, not meeting her eyes, but following where she led. Marianne already seemed much calmer.

"Come, now, Mariechen," she whispered as they entered Vicky's sitting-room. Vicky let Mariechen sit on the sofa, and she sat next to her.

Valerie had met them at the door to Vicky's suite. "Bring me blankets for the – the girls," Vicky said. She had been going to say "little girls".

Mariechen was taller than Vicky; she was fourteen now. She was a young lady, no longer a little girl. But Vicky still always thought of her as a little girl.

Finally, her eye met Vicky's when she leaned over her to kiss her forehead.

"Aunty," she murmured. "I couldn't let Papa –" Her voice broke, and she began to cry. "I told you, Aunty, before the war – six years ago, nearly – I didn't want him to die. But – oh!" She broke into sobs. "I don't want to wish anyone's death, but – he must not!" A strange look came over her face, and her teeth began to chatter.

"Mariechen," Vicky whispered soothingly, stroking her hair. "It is *not* wrong to wish oneself and one's loved ones out of harm's way. That's all you really mean, isn't it?"

Mariechen nodded, smiling slightly. Vicky took a handkerchief, dampened it from a glass of water, and bathed her forehead. Her sobs became quieter, and she soon drifted off to sleep.

Vicky glanced around. The other girls were asleep too. Neither of them had spoken the whole time.

Marianne rose, going to the sofa farthest from the girls. Vicky followed her. "You wished to ask me about –" She met Vicky's eye, not finishing her sentence.

"Yes. But I must explain the situation. I told you about the rash I had last year?"

Marianne nodded.

Vicky whispered in her ear. "And Fritz has – well, Anna – do you know about Anna?"

"That she is dehypnotized? Yes."

"Do you believe it? That it's permanent, I mean?"

"I do. I mean, she could be re-hypnotized, I suppose, but she is cautious, as we are. I heard Louischen talking about her and from what she says – she doesn't talk about it to me, but I have heard her speak – I am quite certain."

Vicky nodded. "It still feels so strange to think of Fritz writing to *her* about such things."

Marianne nodded. "I can imagine so. But what does she have to do with the matter?"

"She had gone to a medicine lady in Egypt. She knows how to cure this illness, and many such illnesses. I'll show you the pamphlet."

She rose, leading Marianne to the table where her writing desk was. She unlocked it, taking out the pamphlet and Fritz's letters about the matter, as well as a couple of Anna's which Fritz had left with her.

Marianne quickly read through them, nodding. Vicky pointed to the pamphlet. "Three years ago, after little Vicky's birth, you told me that Fritz Karl told you everything. You said you thought it was important I know that." She paused. "I was answering the questions, when I realized I didn't know this one." She pointed to the pamphlet.

Marianne's face flushed. She rose, pacing through the room, pausing next to the girls, bending over them. She nodded, and returned to Vicky's side. She wrung her hands, her face reddening, then turning pale.

"Vicky," she began, in a low, intense whisper, "it wasn't only the Zulu Prince; it wasn't only him and my father-in-law." She shuddered. "Fritz Karl – he – he –" A look of revulsion passed over Marianne's face, and she looked away.

"It was him, too?" Vicky felt her throat go dry as Marianne nodded. "He did say – when I came to you – he would *show* me what had happened."

"Oh, but it wasn't even only him! The – what do they call them? The pygmy – he was not only the poisoner. He was 'rewarded'. And – the Duke of Brunswick." Marianne spoke the last words in a rush, hanging her head.

Vicky nodded slowly. Her thoughts went back to the story Papa had told her when he first told her about Prince Charles.

The Duke of Brunswick was extremely friendly and a supporter of Fritz's politically when he wasn't hypnotized. But when he was, he was extremely dangerous. But it wasn't really *him* who was dangerous. Vicky knew that. It was similar to the situation with Fritz's parents, only they hadn't been made into murderers.

"I had dreams," Vicky began, "after little Vicky's birth – or rather, it was after I saw Uncle Ernst for the Christening. After I was at Glienicke, when I went to Coburg, I tried to kiss him. It did awaken some memory, and I had dreams, but they were strange, confused dreams, only about Fritz, but it was as if he had *eight hands*."

Marianne shuddered again. "Must we speak of this anymore?"

Vicky shook her head. "You have given me the information I needed. I shall speak with Abbat, too, to be sure if our memories match."

Marianne rose, returning to the part of the room where the girls still slept. She bent over Mariechen, lightly kissing her forehead.

"She is growing up; she is no longer a child. And I believe she has feelings for the young Altenburg Prince – Prince Albert – but I don't see how that can be. He is in the army here, and has no place, so it would not take her away." She covered her eyes. "Oh, my poor girls! My poor girls!" Marianne rose, pacing the room again. "If they fall in love with anyone here, it is only a further heartbreak, as they must not marry so that they remain in Berlin!"

Neues Palais, Darmstadt, October 10, 1869
"Darling sister,

"My dear, tender-hearted Louis and I had our parting this morning, and my tears are not yet stopped. He does not like to leave his home and family, and seemed quite as moved and upset as he did at our parting after our engagement.

"I know it is not any easier for you and your dear Fritz to be separated for so long a time, but you are more accustomed to it than Louis and I are. We are both so blessed in our husbands, and I am more grateful than ever for his tender, patient, caring nature as the years go on.

"I only feel it so hard that they who are so true and faithful should suffer from this dreadful malady through the sins which have been afflicted upon us.

"We shall soon be together, and I long for the long talks I know we shall have. Though it has been so pleasant to be more together these last two years, I could not confide in you, and I felt the strange distance. But you know so well what it is to not be ready to speak about certain things, even to one's nearest and dearest. This was so for me, but now, I long for you, and am so pleased we shall have two and a half months of each other's company.

"The sea-side will be pleasant, and hopefully help me to regain my strength, which has never happened really since Irene's birth, and even less so these last three years. The quiet company of your own dear self is as good as the interest and activity in Berlin, and your conversation as good a mental stimulant.

"The children are so excited at the prospect of being again with the dear 'cuddles' – as Ella still always says instead of cousins – for so long a time.

"Ella is so funny with her constant wish to be 'pretty'. I would not call her vain, but she is certainly more occupied with the matter than we ever were. But with it all, she is a kind, caring little person.

"They are all such different characters and such interesting little people to puzzle out and encourage the growth of, in mind, body and spirit.

"Victoria is becoming quite a little companion for me; she is quite as ready for any fun as ever, and certainly does not share Ella's ambition.

"Irene, too, is a dear little thing, but I can't make out her fancies well so far. Baby is beginning to talk, and is very dear.

"I look forward to having such a long time for studying your little people. Willy is such a nice boy; I only wish he knew his Aunty better than he does. Give them all a kiss from me, particularly Waldie,

"Your loving sister,

"Alice."

Cannes, October 18, 1869

The hours passed quickly in Alice's company, and were spent pleasantly in long walks on the beach, long drives into the surrounding neighborhood, or sitting on the beach watching the children play. Vicky usually brought her painting, Alice a book they were reading together. Sometimes they were alone, sometimes the in company of Count Seckendorff and Valerie Hohenthal.

When Fritz's and Louis' letters came, they read them aloud, often laughing over the differences in each account of the same event, which brought out so plainly the personalities of each. But no letters had come for a few days.

Vicky had been relieved to receive a letter from Marianne, addressed from Anhalt. "The girls are delighted to be here, and to see their cousins. It is very pleasant here, though I cannot help feeling bitter that my father and brother maintain that there is nothing to be done about our situation. How I wish we could always stay here, but I cannot abandon the boy, and they will never let me take him. The girls feel this as deeply as I do." Fritz Leo had been left behind in Berlin.

Vicky and Alice often stayed up talking long into the night. They could talk about everything again.

Over the last few years, Vicky had felt that she and Alice had grown closer and further apart at the same time. They had experienced so many of the same things, but these were often such painful things that Vicky could not bring herself to mar their pleasant time together.

Last year, when they were together in Gotha, and a few months ago in Potsdam, Vicky could tell by the look in Alice's eyes when she touched on the matter that she wasn't ready to speak more of Prince Charles, just as Vicky had barely told Alice anything when she had asked about little Vicky.

Now, there were no barriers again. Vicky often felt that Alice was the only one of her siblings whom she could talk to about many subjects, both on these matters and on German politics and on almost every other topic. Bertie was certainly much more mature than he had been, but Vicky often felt it impossible to make him a confidant about the real state of things in Berlin.

The others were all so young still, and their lives had, for the most part, not been intimately touched by the matters which Vicky felt most deeply.

Today, it was Fritz's birthday. It was Mrs. Hobbs' wedding day.

It was also ten years now since Prince Charles had trapped Vicky in the laundry.

CHAPTER TWENTY-ONE
SOUTH AND EAST

"Oktober 16, 1869

"Meine Vicky,

"Tomorrow we shall embark, and head first for Corfu, where our Corvette, the *Hertha*, is to meet us on the 19th. I find that she travels very slowly, and I often wonder whether our intended time can be kept. It may be that my official visit to Constantinople shall coincide with that of the Emperor of Austria.

"I am glad Anna told you all – from the hints you give in your letter, I understood she told you all she has told me. I certainly understand that you did not wish to write more in a letter, even by messenger.

"I, too, saw her little boy, who is a charming, serious little fellow, though I must say I do not think the name Fischy fits him. I wish Alice could see Aleck, as he is so wonderfully talented in musical matters, already playing the piano, violin and accordion when he is not seven. Anna means to send him to a school of music for the blind when he is old enough.

"I am so very, very thankful that the scene with Fritz Karl went no further, and also that Marianne and the girls are safe in Anhalt while we are away. I only wish we could obtain Papa's allowance for them to have their own home, and have Fritz Leo with them! I am very pleased that Nastya has proved herself so valuable."

Oktober 19

"We left Brindisi on an Italian passenger-steamer, reaching the Isle of Corfu the morning of my birthday. Jasmund and Schleiniz have suffered on board as you often do, but the rocking of the vessel was indeed horrible.

"The rain prevented me from obtaining an idea of the charms of Corfu until evening. The place is surrounded by high rocky mountains, the valleys filled with olive-woods.

"Your presents have safely arrived on time, and the cake was very welcome. My thoughts were with you, and I knew before I received your letter that you would think of the fact that it has been ten years since that dreadful day, which, as you say, robbed you of your innocence.

"We were hardly two hours underway and in sight of the Albanian coast when Louis caught sight of the North German flag; it was the *Hertha,* who arrived on time after all. The little Austrian steamer we were on carried no signaling flags, so we had to steer straight for the Hertha and make ourselves known by waving handkerchiefs and other such arm-telegraphy.

"Finally, though there was still quite a roll, no one was sick, and we enjoyed the panorama spread before us, first under the light of the setting sun, then in the silvery light of the full moon. How my thoughts went to you, and of what you could make of such beauties!

"Everything stirs memories of my early studies of ancient Greece with Curtius, the son of my old nurse."

Cannes, October 20, 1869

Vicky met Alice's eye, trying to hide a smile. She turned back to look at Count Seckendorff and Valerie. They sat close together, whispering and laughing together as they often did. "I think I know someone's secret," she whispered to Alice.

"I think I know a secret," Alice said, meeting Vicky's eye, then sharply turning her face away, watching as the children ran up the beach.

"But why will you not call me Vicky?" Vicky asked Count Seckendorff. "Count Perponcher did. Baron Stockmar does. I so much prefer it if my friends will. And you do consider yourself my friend, don't you?

"Of course, your Highness," he said.

"And don't think rank matters in this way to me," Vicky said. "I call my friends by name, no matter what their rank, unless they have told me they prefer me not to like Mrs. Hobbs. Would you mind it if – *we* – called you Gottfried?"

She paused, watching his face and Valerie's. She had been going to say "I", not "we".

Valerie said nothing. Some change passed over Seckendorff's face, but Vicky wasn't sure what he was thinking.

Vicky smiled to herself again. He seemed so different of late, and Valerie did too. Seckendorff was animated and full of jokes, as she had never seen him before. Usually, he seemed rather quiet and shy, reminding Vicky very much of Fritz's manner at the Exhibition.

Valerie, though never so fun-loving as Wally was, had grown to be a pleasant companion, full of comical stories and jokes. Now, she often sat quiet and brooding, only seeming to "wake up" at the times when they were all together.

Vicky heard him whisper something again. "If you can call Valerie by her name, why is it so awkward to call me by mine? Surely it's easier to call a friend by name than the one whom one –" She broke off, hiding her face in her hands, wishing she hadn't spoken. She hadn't meant to say anything which told so plainly that she thought that he and Valerie were on intimate terms, when she had no more proof of this than her suspicions.

She glanced up at the sound of a loud laugh from Valerie. Vicky was surprised. She hadn't expected this response from her. She didn't think Valerie was in love with Seckendorff, as he obviously was with her, though she seemed very fond of him.

Vicky could hardly make herself look at Seckendorff, who sat silently, his face deeply flushed, his eyes on the sand. Oh, how could she have said such a thing? How could she have exposed him to this embarrassment, and to the horrible humiliation of having Valerie laugh at the idea of his being in love with her?

Vicky turned back to her painting, half hiding herself behind the easel. A gull swooped low over her, screaming as it passed. She closed her eyes, turning away, tears blinding her eyes. She felt as if she couldn't go back and talk with the others, but now, she couldn't go on painting. The gull had made a mess of her easel. At least she hadn't made much progress, so it wasn't a great loss. But she almost wished it had been a nearly finished picture. She deserved that humiliation.

"Mama, your face is all red," a little voice said.

Vicky looked down. It was little Vicky. Vicky turned her around, not wanting her to see the ruined painting. "Come, Vicky," she whispered, lifting her little daughter in her arms and walking towards the shore.

Little Vicky squirmed. "But – my dress!"

Vicky looked down. There were red stains on the little white dress. Vicky set her down, looking at her hands. She realized little Vicky hadn't meant that she was blushing or crying, when she said her face was red. Vicky had been in the middle of painting the red roses Willy had brought her that morning, when she paused to talk to Seckendorff. She hadn't wiped her hands before she covered her face.

***

"Yes, Hedwig, I'll have to burn this, too. There's no way I can save it." Vicky had removed the painting from the easel. But the easel itself was spoiled.

"*Ja*, there is a way to save it. And – I do not blame you, your – Vicky."

Vicky turned quickly at the sound of the voice behind her. Seckendorff had spoken in German, which always startled her when she knew Fritz was away. His voice and German accent sounded so exactly like Fritz's.

"I'm so very sorry," Vicky said, turning and looking up at him. She was glad it was Hedwig and not Valerie with her this time, but he probably wouldn't have spoken if it had been. "But I must say, all my friends and family – and my enemies – know me for saying whatever I think."

Seckendorff nodded. He seemed about to speak, but a blush spread over his face, and he turned away. He turned back, seeming to remember something, again opening his mouth, but he only clicked his heels and turned away again.

"And you certainly don't have to do *that*." Vicky laughed. "I much prefer not to have military discipline in my household." She paused, watching his face. "But you – you did call me Vicky. Would you prefer it if I called you Gottfried, or Count Seckendorff?"

A look of confusion crossed his face again, and he said, barely above a whisper, "Count Seckendorff."

"And do you object to calling me Vicky, or do you not mind it?"

He shook his head. "No, your – Vicky. I don't object. But I think it better I don't, your Highness."

Vicky felt herself blush as she listened to his stammering. Why was he being so polite, and trying so hard to please her, when she had done such a thing to him? "I must apologize again. I certainly didn't mean to embarrass you or humiliate you in any way. I only wish for your happiness." She held out her hand.

He nodded, a blush passing over his cheeks again as he knelt and kissed her hand. He rose, swallowed, and nodded. "As I do for yours, your – Vicky," he murmured, and hurried from the room.

***

"Alice," Vicky whispered, sitting down and helping Alice take her hair down. "Do you think Count Seckendorff is in love?"

Alice was silent for several minutes. Finally, she turned towards Vicky, meeting her eye. "No." She held her gaze for a minute, then looked away, taking the brush and beginning to brush her hair. "But I do think he is –" She didn't finish her sentence.

"Valerie certainly doesn't care for him," Vicky went on, "at least, not in the same way."

"She certainly does not care for him as more than a friend, but – he does not –"

"But she might have learned to," Vicky interrupted her. "She might have learned to, if I hadn't let my stupid tongue get in the way and spoil things! Now she knows how he feels, and he knows she scorns the idea!"

Alice laughed. "She does know how he feels, just as I do," she said quietly, meeting Vicky's eye again. She paused, looking uncomfortable. "Never mind. It is probably only a fancy of mine." She let Vicky take the brush from her, turning away. "Willy was so sweet, bringing you flowers this morning. My children love the wild-flowers around Darmstadt. I have books about them, and even Baby always wants to bring me flowers."

"I meant to paint the flowers, and have my painting as a present when Fritz came home," Vicky said. She turned to face Alice. "Alice," she began, "I only wish I felt more confident about when Fritz comes home."

"What do you mean? Have you – but you and Fritz never quarrel."

Vicky shook her head. "You are right, Alice, we haven't quarreled . But, I haven't told you about what he said. I can't help thinking about it, even though I know it's – it's only because of the illness." She said the last words more confidently than she felt.

"What was it?" Alice squeezed Vicky's hand.

"He said he wasn't attracted to me anymore." Vicky struggled to keep back tears as she met Alice's eye.

Alice shook her head. "I do not believe that! But tell me all about it! Just what did he say?"

Vicky let her thoughts go back to the evening of their *Verlobungstag*[52]. She told Alice everything.

"Just so!" Alice said, making Vicky look her in the eye. "He didn't say he wasn't attracted to you *anymore!* He said he didn't feel attracted to you – and he should have said 'at the moment'. It is all because of the illness!"

"I know," Vicky said, hiding her face. "But I can't help letting it prey upon my mind. He hasn't wanted to kiss me in so long, and I didn't know what to think."

"But you said he said he didn't want to disappoint you."

"Yes." Vicky rose, walking through the room as she went on. "He 'doesn't want to disappoint me', and therefore he does *everything* he can to disappoint me in those matters. He would hardly kiss me, less and less over two months. He would go to bed early, before I could, and pretend to be asleep, even though he said he was needing less sleep than usual. Or he'd stay up reading when I was ready to go to bed. I can't help it if it makes me feel I unattractive."

Alice sat up, shaking her head. "He will never find you unattractive."

Vicky paused, meeting her sister's eye. "Many thoughts pass through my mind – things he said long ago, which were so caring and thoughtful, but now they turn around to bite me! In '59, when he came home after" – she paused, returning to the bed and snuggling down by Alice's side – "after – *Prince Charles*. I said I could never be intimate again, and Fritz said that *that* wasn't what he cared about – he cared about *me*. That meant *so much* then, but now! My mind plays with his words, and it's come up with the idea that he doesn't care about intimacy with me, and that now that it's gone, he doesn't wish for it back!"

"That is absurd, Vicky! You know it! You said he was eager to find something to do about – about his symptoms, even before the others came out and you knew what it was."

"I know. I know all of my thoughts are absurd, but – what I said before, about his not kissing, and his avoiding going to bed at the same time. You know he was always uneasy in speaking of intimate matters,

---

[52]   Engagement anniversary

about – physicalities. And so, once he finally did tell me, he was already in the hurry of preparing for his journey, and his words were such a shock, we never had an opportunity for discussing how I *felt* about it all."

Alice nodded sympathetically, kissing Vicky's cheek. "He was probably feeling just as insecure as you are now. As you said, he said he did not want to disappoint you."

"Yes, but – his reaction doesn't make sense. If he *didn't* want to disappoint me, why would he withdraw any and *all* kisses and caresses? Either that or make it so obvious he felt uncomfortable, as he did the day after he told me."

"From what you say, it sounds like he *cannot* do anything else. You said he said he *feels nothing physically.*"

"Yes," Vicky sighed heavily. "But – I only want to feel – oh, we've had enough times of abstinence!"

Alice nodded again. "But with this illness, it is fortunate you have not been – intimate – so much, during this time when he is having active symptoms. But I am sure you have nothing to worry about, really, about his saying he did not feel attracted to you. As I said, he ought to have said 'at the moment', or something of the sort."

"Alice," Vicky whispered, taking her sister's hand, "how would you have felt, if Louis had said such a thing to you, with no warning, and then said that he should have written to Maroussy about it?"

"I would have had far more reason to resent it than you have," Alice cried, blushing, "as there is no resemblance between Louis' relationship to Maroussy and Fritz's to Anna. Louis was in love with her – he was intimate with her – while you know Fritz knows Anna is his sister, and would never –"

"I know, but it is the closest example I could give," Vicky said, struggling to keep her voice calm. "Alice, you know I never mean to hurt you, but – it is that very fact, which would make you feel it even more strongly than I felt what happened. You can understand, can't you, looking at it this way? How *would* you feel?"

Alice stared – almost glared – at her for a moment, then tears flooded her eyes, and she threw her arms around her. "I understand how you felt, Vicky," she whispered. She hid her face against Vicky's shoulder, and then met Vicky's eye again. "Fritz and Louis will have the remedy when they come home. We will all get well again."

"Oktober 22, 1869

"Meine Vicky,

"The lovely moonlight, which I spoke of in my last letter, lent to the Acropolis the aspect of a perfect structure from ancient Greece. Only climbing the hill led to the sight of the actual ruins.

"The sight of the many ruins is magnificent, especially when one lets one's mind wonder over what they must have been. The ground is covered with an incredible amount of mosaic and other beauties.

"Only in some places I have been disappointed. These are where the archeologists of England, France and Bavaria have carried things away to museums, filling their places with glaringly new facsimiles, without taking care to age them, or even in some cases to make them of the same material.

"The young King is as pleasant as ever, and his mannerisms remind me much of Alix and Minnie. His position is not always an easy one, though the boy King is quite popular. He is an excellent husband and father.

" 'Little Olga', whom I think you did not meet when the Russian Imperial family were in Potsdam nine years ago, is already a mother, and on her way to being so twice over, though she is so young. I had never yet met a Royal bride younger than you were.

"Tino, as they call their little boy, is a charming little fellow, quite obviously as to features a mixture of his parents. Greece shall again someday be ruled by a King Constantine. The fact that they have named him this is extremely popular in Greece."

Constantinople, Ottoman Empire, Oktober 25, 1869

"I find it impossible to describe the Bosphorus and the Golden Horn. Making a journey in an Imperial caique – a great row-boat manned by twelve rowers, a small pavilion at one end – in the radiant sunshine or silver moonlight is an indescribable delight. One's expectation is gratified in the first moment as one gazes along the lines of towns and estates along both shores of the sea, one side full of European character and the other distinctly Asiatic. The Beylerbey Palace in which Louis and I reside lies on the Asian side.

"On arrival we passed the Serai point, the magnificent view unrolling before us with every splash of the waves. We passed the Sultan's residence, the Dolmabagdsche – which in German means something like Cabbage Leaf – to be received by the Grand-Vizier, the Ambassador, and conducted by gilded caique to the steps of the palace.

"Here stood the Sultan in his gorgeously embroidered uniform adorned by the star of the Black Eagle, surrounded by the colorfully dressed officers of his guard. The Sultan gave me his hand, and we passed silently through rows of bowing officials making the salaam.

"Beylerbey's interior overflows with a profusion of color and costly ornament, only it is far too large to use 'overflowing' as a true descriptor. The eye does not know where to settle, dazzled as it is by the many-colored splendor. In front of an enormous vase with Papa's portrait – a gift from the King to the Sultan two years ago – our interview took place. The conversation moved on in the usual Eastern story-telling fashion."

Cannes, October 27, 1869

"Vicky, I must go to Berlin for a few days. I wish to collect some of my things."

Vicky looked up from her paintings of the different shells and flowers the children had gathered. Waldie clutched at a card, but Vicky took it from him, lifting him up in her arms.

"Of course, Valerie. Hedwig is here with me. I'll have no trouble, only I'll miss you."

Valerie nodded quickly, a strange look coming over her face as she hurried from the room. Vicky sat down and began to show Waldie the pictures again, but her thoughts were far away.

Valerie didn't seem well. Vicky had thought she was brooding over an attachment, until it seemed so obvious that she did not care for Count Seckendorff. Now, remembering the look of discomfort on her face, and certain other things about her behavior of late, Vicky thought she had realized what was really going on.

Valerie was in the same condition Vicky had just realized she was in herself.

She was expecting a baby.

***

Cannes, November 2, 1869

Vicky gathered her painting materials, wishing Valerie was with her to help her carry her things. Just as she reached the last door, she heard a step behind her.

"Would you like me to carry these for you, your Highness?" Count Seckendorff asked in German. Vicky felt the strange sensation go over her which she always felt when she heard him speak German. He sounded so much like Fritz.

"Yes. Alice went with some of the children to visit the Duke de Vallombrosa, but I was tired. I was wishing there was someone to help me, but the solitude was pleasant. I didn't wish to call the servants. But you have yours to carry as well," she added, seeing that he was already carrying an easel.

"I'll carry the easels; you can carry the small things," he said, taking hers.

"You're going to paint too?" Vicky asked, following him out onto the beach.

He nodded. "It's a splendid day for it."

Vicky followed his gaze. The long stretch of smooth, sandy beach was completely empty. The sun shone on the water, and there were three sailing-boats at varying distances towards the horizon, their white sails flashing in the sunlight. The palms swayed gently in the breeze, the sanderlings piping and the gulls calling as they ran about the shore or wheeled overhead.

"But," he went on, "as you found the solitude so enchanting, I shall go on for a distance."

"Oh, no, I should like someone to talk to now. I simply didn't wish to call for anyone." Vicky paused, looking at him. He glanced away towards the beach.

"It's such a temptation, being so near Italy," Vicky said in German, as she readied her easel and paints. "Fritz writes that he's been there five times now! I've only been once! There's so much beauty there, and so much to learn. I feel I know so little still, and there's so much to learn of the history of art. It's one of my favorite studies."

"What isn't?" Seckendorff asked, laughing as he met her eye. "I saw you practicing your target shooting the other day. I saw you giving your boys lessons in chemistry. I heard you naming every flower in that wonderful field we passed through by their English, German, French and Latin names. What do you not know?"

"So very much," Vicky said, looking down, feeling herself blush at his praise.

"Do you know the names of the flowers in Italian?"

"No."

"Do you know any Italian?"

Vicky thought for a moment. "*Un po*[53]."

"Would you like to learn? It wouldn't be difficult for you, with so many languages already, and Latin and French particularly."

"Oh, yes, *ja, oui,* – I mean, *si!*" Vicky smiled as she looked up, going on in mixed German and English, as they often spoke together. "I *beginnt Italianisch zu lernen* when we went on our tour of the Mediterranean, and again after the last war when we visited the wounded prisoners, but I've never found much time for studying it."

Seckendorff nodded but turned his head, gazing out to sea again.

"*Ich helfe dir beim Lernen,*" he said. "*Es ist ein Wunder, dass ich Du etwas beibringen kann.*[54]"

"I would prefer it if you spoke English more," Vicky said in English. "It makes me feel strange when you speak German, you sound so like Fritz."

She glanced up when he didn't say anything, to find him watching her intently.

"Very well," he said slowly in English.

"But I should like you to help me learn. And my painting is almost ready for you to finish." They were each painting a scene, which they would then paint each other into.

"What's that in Italian?" she asked, pointing out to a sailboat just disappearing at the horizon.

***

---

[53]   A little
[54]   I'll help you to learn. It is a wonder, that I can teach you anything.

"*E come sta la mia cara sorella oggi?*" Vicky called to Alice as she, Willy, Henry, Charlotte, Victoria and Ella came into view, the girls' arms full of flowers and the boys carrying large baskets of fruit.

"What?" Alice called back.

"How is my dear sister today? *E come sta la mia cara sorella oggi?*" Vicky repeated. "Count Seckendorff is kindly teaching me Italian."

"*Oh.*" Alice looked at her for a moment, and then came closer. "Willy and Henry helped me pick these beautiful oranges. I thought you would like some. We went to the Duke of Vallombrosa's *Jardin de Hesperides*. It is so beautiful there, Vicky, you ought to go and paint it!"

"I shall! And Count Seckendorff can paint me into the picture," Vicky said, smiling at him.

"Mama! Have you ever had a banana?" Willy called, running to Vicky with his basket of fruit. He hurriedly set it down, shuffling through it to uncover the long yellow bananas. "We picked these outside in the gardens! Can you fancy these growing everywhere? I couldn't believe it!"

"You have had a banana before, but I suppose you don't remember," Vicky said. "In the hothouse at Sans-Souci."

Vicky carefully broke the peel open, holding it out.

He shook his head violently. "No, Mama, this is for you. We've eaten all we can."

"Aunty," Ella cried, pulling at Vicky's skirt, "Victoria tried to put a crab on my head!"

"But it wasn't even alive!" Victoria called. "You were so taken up with the butterflies, and didn't mind them in your hair, I thought you would look very nice with that crab's pretty shell."

Vicky covered her mouth, glancing at Alice, who was also concealing her laughter.

"Mr. Washfield gave us these," Henry said, holding up a little case full of pins. "He said we can use them for mounting our collections." Vicky smiled. Mr. Washfield was an English gentleman who lived just outside of the town of Cowes, who had been a friend of Leopold's when he had stayed in Cannes when he was about Henry's age, just before Papa's death. He had proved a very kind friend to her children as well.

"And he said the eucalyptus branches were excellent for drying seaweed and other things on," Charlotte added, setting down her basket of pink anemone blossoms. "Can you believe we can pick all of these at this time of year?"

***

Cannes, November 5, 1869

"Valerie is here, but she says she is here to say good-bye," Hedwig said, as she handed Vicky a packet of letters.

"Good-bye? But I thought she already did. Has she not gone to Berlin? Where's she been?"

"She has gone to Berlin, to collect her things. She says she is leaving the court."

"*Leaving* the court? Tell her to come and see me. I'll be in my sitting-room."

Vicky went to her sitting-room, her thoughts running over possibilities of the reason for Valerie's wishing to leave the court.

Her thoughts were still busy when the door opened and Valerie appeared. Vicky looked at her, shocked. Valerie's face was growing thin – she seemed greatly changed in the last few days.

"Valerie, what is it? I can see you're unwell, but why do you wish to leave?"

"I cannot stay here any longer!" Valerie's eyes were full of tears. "I don't mean here, but – in the court! You see my condition, don't you?"

Vicky nodded. "How long have you known?"

"Known that I was expecting? Only the last week." Valerie's voice was thin and tense.

"I could see it before you left for Berlin," Vicky said. "I wondered. Who...?" She wasn't sure what to say.

"Oh, must *you* ask me *that*?" Valerie stared at her, a wild look in her eyes. "You know, don't you? You don't think I was – that I would – when I'm not married! You understand, don't you? I don't have to – say it!"

Vicky met her eye for a moment, and then looked away. The look in Valerie's eyes was all too familiar. "Prince Charles?" Vicky asked, her voice a soft whisper. Valerie burst into tears, throwing her arms around her. "When was it?" was all she could think of to say.

"When I went for the walk at Königsberg – you remember?" Vicky shook her head. "You told me you would come with me, but you never did." Valerie whispered. "The fifteenth of September."

"Oh! I'm expecting a baby, too, and that day –" Vicky met Valerie's eye.

"It is Fritz's? You haven't been – again –" Valerie's voice was tense and anxious.

"It *is* Fritz's." The fifteenth of September – what would have been Siggy's fifth birthday – was the last evening that Fritz hadn't been either away, asleep or pretending to be asleep before their *Verlobungstag*[55].

Earlier that day, she had promised to go for a walk with Valerie, but she had been unable to go before or after the parade at Königsberg.

"Gottfried," Valerie suddenly said. "Count Seckendorff – he isn't in love with me. You know that, don't you?" she said, looking Vicky in the eye.

Are you so certain of that? Vicky thought. She didn't say anything. She wasn't sure what to say, but she wouldn't return to the previous subject if Valerie didn't wish to speak more of it.

"I know he isn't. He told me so, after he was so embarrassed by what you said. He was simply – well –" Valerie paused, looking down. "He was thinking of someone – someone he cares for, and has cared for, for many years. I don't say 'in love', because – he says he cares too much for her to allow himself to be 'in love' with her. But one can't help a natural attraction, can one? You don't think it is wrong, do you? He asked me to ask you."

Vicky shook her head. "My Papa spoke of such things. He said when someone acts so, *that* is very loving. So many 'love affairs', as society terms them, are nothing but selfish lust which fades and does nothing but harm everyone involved. But to care for someone *un*selfishly is no sin. But – poor boy, I wish he could be happy."

"He says he is not unhappy." Valerie looked down. "Count Üxkull loves me, I believe, but – oh, I don't love him and I can't marry him! But I have nowhere else to go. Wally can't take me in, and I have nowhere to go! I wish I didn't have to leave you, but –" She turned and looked around. "I will go and see the children now," she whispered with tears in her eyes. "Good-bye." She paused, turning back again. "I shall live in Count Üxkull's house. Everyone will say it is 'a sin', as you said, to live in a

---

[55]   Engagement anniversary

man's house unmarried, but I knew *you* would understand. I hope you will explain it all to Wally some day. I simply cannot speak of it to anyone else."

Vicky rose, walking through the room as Valerie closed the door. This new revelation staggered her. She had imagined Valerie to be involved in some sort of love affair. She simply hadn't imagined the truth.

Why had she left the poor girl alone? Tears flooded to Vicky's eyes as her thoughts went to her conversation with Wally a few years ago – that day when Wally had seen Siggy and Mrs. Adams had declared that he had water on the brain – and when they had discussed Prince Charles. They had discussed the fact that they and Marie Lynar should have told each other what happened and protected each other. Now, this had happened to Valerie, too.

She ought to mention Valerie's leaving to Fritz, but she felt uneasy to speak of such things in a letter which would go so far. She also hated the idea of spoiling Fritz's holiday with matters of this kind, as she would have to give some explanation for Valerie's departure. It was so pleasant, in spite of the fact that they were traveling separately, to be out of the Berlin atmosphere for so long, and for Fritz, away from military duties as well.

She must decide what she would write to Fritz, as she would have to mention Valerie's departure. But first, she must read Fritz's letters which Hedwig had brought.

"Oktober 29, 1869

"Meine Vicky,

"I have explored Constantinople on every side, on horseback, on foot, and more regularly in the twelve-oared gilded caique. My constant companion is a man from our embassy who is quite a master of both the Turkish language and the curiosities of the town.

"But for all the splendor displayed for the Sultan, one looks for corresponding wealth in the town, and there is as much difference as there is in Russia. All the magic is lost far too quickly when one enters the dirty streets of the city, which can only be compared to dried-up riverbeds.

"The Emperor of Austria has arrived, and the *Hertha* was the first ship to salute him – the first such greeting since the war.

"The Sultan has appointed him the state-rooms in the Dolmabagdsche, and has withdrawn himself into the Sereglio. Here, accordingly, I was received for my farewell. And so, I have been within the Harem, though without more of a glance of its usual residents than a shimmer of their silk and embroidery through an iron latticed window.

"I have found – from report – that most of the women are of the Near East – European – often Slavic or Circassian, not Turkish or Asiatic – and the eunuchs who guard them are from the Nile regions. This, they say, is a result of one occasion when a eunuch was not a eunuch, and the Sultan's son was not the Sultan's son. This would be far too obvious in the circumstances which exist now.

"Yesterday we visited the barracks at Scutari, and were served a kind of cherry soup, strong with sugar and onions, and a very pleasant rice pillaw, the second of which I required no time to grow accustomed to. At court, too, this has been served, thoroughly mixed with extremely sweet French cuisine. These are also joined by meat served on a spit, which they call a 'kebab', and Turkish coffee, which tastes similar to that which we had in Tunisia.

"One cannot pay a visit or enter a barracks without being invited to drink coffee and to smoke. The servants are always ready with the required paraphernalia for smoking, which, as you can imagine, is an annoyance to Louis and to myself. It is difficult to know what to do, as it is considered offensive to refuse.

"This and one other custom were displeasing, as you can imagine. This second is one which is considered part of the outfit of a visiting Prince's sleeping apartments – the appearance of a young girl, her figure barely concealed by thin, lacy garments, far less opaque than your nightgowns. This choice gift one finds lying in one's bed – or rather divan – on entering the apartment, and everyone thinks one extremely strange for wishing to abstain from such pleasures."

"Jerusalem, November 9, 1869

"Meine Vicky,

"How deeply moved I am at being in Jerusalem is too much to describe in writing. How I wish you could have come, but one must experience for oneself the deep peace and contemplation of life which I have obtained.

"It will be a happiness for my entire life to have walked in the places where Jesus Christ lived, the places where his foot trod, to have seen the mountains and waters which His gaze knew so intimately. Above all, the Mount of Olives, Gethsemane with the Kedron, as well as the wild rock shores of the Dead Sea, the Valley of the Jordan and the country around Bethlehem.

"The richest reward of all was the evening ascent of the Mount of Olives. I reached the summit shortly before sunset, and took my seat so that the whole of the city of Jerusalem unrolled before me, while on the opposite side the singularly beautiful formation of the rocky walls bordering the Dead Sea were to be seen.

"I often thought what you could do here with your artist's eye, even though everything here is in tones of grey, with little green or other color to comfort the eye. But at the golden hour of sunset all was lit up golden-red, warmth and life apparently flooding the landscape. The walls of the Dead Sea, which reminds me vividly of Lock Muick at Balmoral, took on the red glow of the evening sun, and the waves shimmered brighter and brighter.

"My thoughts were now on those scenes we have read so many times since childhood, but for the first time I was truly able to picture our Savior as he tarried here.

"All I had brought with me was a Bible, whose lines my eyes followed as long as there was light, when they were not on the magnificent scenery. The ancient olive trees of Gethsemane, which are quite probably contemporaries of our Lord, are indescribable. How I wish you could have painted the scene.

"Finally, nature fell into that great silence which has always something solemn about it. Here, one could detach one's soul from all one's earthly worries, considering the great work and sacrifice of salvation.

"So far I have pursued my feelings, giving free rein to my fancy. How I wish I had more time for writing, that my descriptions should not be so poor!

"We had a favorable passage of five days, moving on to Palestine and landing in Jaffa, where I felt, indeed, as we did when we landed in Tunis in '62, that we were truly in the East, with everything so entirely different than it is in Europe.

"We passed on, as the next night was to be spent in a tent camp at Bel-el-Wad, surrounded by camels.

"We heard jackels howling quite near us. I slept very lightly, while Louis, who shared my tent, slept so soundly that he was not aware that he sneezed loudly several times, waking several of the more timid of our party just as they had drifted off when the jackels grew quiet.

"Several of our party occupied themselves throughout the night with the topic of scorpions and other such pleasant desert visitors."

"*Damascus, November 12, 1869*

"With a three days' ride through the desert and three nights spent in tents, I think it justifiable to say that we Europeans crave repose, as well as longing for the daily conveniences we are accustomed to. Several of our party had to return after the first day of desert, the long ride in the heat not suiting their constitutions.

"Our first excursion here was into a bazaar. European clothing is hardly to be seen, not even modern Turkish uniforms, so we feel ourselves indeed in the East!

"My first sight of Damascus from a distance, with its white houses, mosques and minarets, surrounded by a mile-wide ring of orange and lemon groves, brought distinctly to my mind the idea of a pearl surrounded by emeralds.

"In the evening, when we returned to our quarters, I was suddenly asked to stand as best man in the wedding of the fifteen-year-old daughter of the house, Sophia Chami. Her bridegroom, Selim Chalhaub, is secretary to the man appointed as my attendant here. This family is of the Greek Orthodox faith, and so I was to witness such a wedding for the second time in my life, though on a very different scale of course, the first being Sasha and Minnie's.

"I had, of course, to hold the crown over the bridegroom's head. Before the ceremony, the bride went to change, which was done with the door wide open! Diamond flowers hung over her forehead, as well as that of the bridegroom's mother. The bridal gown – or dress, I ought to say, as I do not know if it would be considered a gown without a crinoline – was pale pink with threads of gold silk woven through it. The priests wore rose-colored silk stitched with gold flowers, very like that of the Russian priests."

"*November 19, 1869*

"We spent a night floating outside of Port Sa'id, an unpleasant night disturbed by waves ten and twenty feet high.

"The Empress Eugenie has appeared aboard the *Delphin*, which, along with the Grille – on which Louis and I shall pass through the canal, the *Hertha* being large after all – and the *Elisabeth* and many others, shall pass through the canal.

"In the morning an imposing array of ships were packed into the small harbor. Before all the visitors, the blessing was pronounced according to Protestant, Catholic and Arabic rites. The cheers broke out in mixed German, Italian, French and other languages I could not identify.

"On the 17th, the Canal's inauguration took place – an event which shall be a wonder for trade, shortening the journey to India incredibly. If only we could make that journey some day! But I do not see it as possible, in spite of this shortening.

"The procession began at half past ten. We were prepared to follow the Emperor of Austria's ship, but the officers of one of their steamers shouted that their second ship must go too. After this, the English mail steamer pushed forwards. We, therefore, were nearly at the end of the procession, as the Dutch and American ships also took advantage of our delay.

"Throughout the passage, there was nothing to see but the straight walls of the canal. The *Elisabeth*, who led the parade, stuck three times in the sand, but otherwise the seven-hour passage was peaceful enough."

"*November 20, 1869*

"Thirty ships lay in the basin near Ismalia.

"The pink sand reflects the moonlight beautifully, and curiosity soon took Louis and myself ashore, to the sound of trumpets and tambourines. We soon found ourselves in the midst of a tent-encampment of over thirty thousand Arabs, headed by their Sheikhs.

"At noon we reached the town of Suez, set at the foot of a mountain and bathed by the blue waves of the Red Sea. To think that within three months I have swum in the North Sea, sailed on the Red Sea, and cast my eye on the Black Sea, though I barely entered it.

"There was little time to ponder, as I was to take the private train belonging to the Viceroy of Egypt, and this evening again to be aboard a vessel, though this time on the Nile.

"The passage of the Canal has no charm in itself. I can only say that the sight of so much sand of this rosy color brings a feeling of home, and its glittering and glistening a fascination which it never holds in Berlin. I found a welcome opportunity of writing while on board.

"I should only have liked to see more of the Arab encampment, with its tambourines and strange songs. The fairy tales of one's childhood find realization here, without any stretch of the imagination."

"*November 21, 1869*

"*Meine lieber, geliebtet* Vicky,

"My first thoughts on waking today were with you, as I have never spent it away from you since the first after our engagement. Fourteen happy birthdays! How my thoughts go back to the first we spent together, nor can I deny that they wander four days farther!

"How I long to be situated as we were then! I kiss you and kiss you in thought. We little thought then that I would one day spend the evening hours of that day floating on the Nile instead of in your arms.

"To think that we have been apart for seven weeks, and must be for nearly five more is very hard, but it is always a pleasant thought that you have so long a time with Alice. How are *die liebe Kinder*[56]? What lessons do the boys have? Have they begun their Natural History Museum?

"I have heard myself from the medicine lady, and I shall meet her in Cairo. She has quite a scientific mind, it appears, and her correspondence would greatly interest you, though it is such that I do not like to send by our messengers. I shall keep it for when I return.

"I have, however, been given a diagram and explanation of the chemical compounds of the remedies she makes, and this I do send after making a careful copy. Show the children this, and give them their next chemistry lesson on the difference between this and mercury, and ask them which they think safer to administrate.

"I sit writing this floating under a grove of palms, watching the circling pelicans and eagles, and wonder how you are occupied."

Cannes, November 25, 1869

Vicky pressed Fritz's letter from her birthday to her lips. Reading over his lines, she felt her face glow. And yet, the memory of the day after their *Verlobungstag*[57] rankled in her mind. Why did he write this way, if he

---

[56] the dear children
[57] Engagement anniversary

didn't feel so? And yet – she remembered, he said that his thoughts of her were the same as ever. But this felt so strange, to think of him having an imaginary relationship with her, and yet, in person, he had largely avoided any caresses.

It still did not make sense. His words, "I do not want to disappoint you", did not seem to fit his behavior.

Her thoughts wandered to the morning after their *Verlobungstag*. She knew that he was trying to comfort her, to console her for the fact that he had said he did not feel attracted to her, but… She shook her head. All her thoughts about the matter contradicted each other. She certainly felt *that* was disappointing. They could have returned to the physical relationship they had after she had recovered from Willy's birth and before Prince Charles had trapped her – when she wished to have a full year to recover from the birth. And if not that, surely Fritz could have simply kissed her as he usually did.

"*December 1, 1869*

"*Meine* Vicky,

"Four days we spent steaming up the Nile, without any alteration of the scenery. The temperature grows from day to day, though after sunset it is quite cold.

"All is very comfortable here, and I may say we live rather too well in these days of no exertion, after being accustomed to six-hour rides through the desert. Our life is quite reminiscent of the journeys on the Rhine, only marked by the absence of the many castles.

"Last night, I lay out on deck, studying the stars. It is Jupiter who illuminates the night here, and is reflected in the water before the rise of the moon. Our great Bear, whom everyone knows so well in Germany, is quite beyond the horizon, which makes me feel how very far indeed I have traveled from you.

"You would find great pleasure in the company of Professors Lepsius and Dümichen, who kindly accompany us on this stretch of our voyage.

"On the evening of the 24th, at the North German Confederation's Consulate, we were to be treated to the dance often shown to guests.

Everyone took seats in a semicircle, when the women appeared, dressed in brightly colored folds of half-transparent cloth hanging mostly from their shoulders, with little underneath. Gold coins were braided into their black hair. More coins woven into more half-transparent cloth formed the only covering for the intimate regions of the body.

"All made a round to kiss our hands. Finally, the dance began – a skillful bending and twisting of all parts of the body which I never thought possible. For a time I expected a resemblance to the native dances which occur in our provinces, but there was only the repetition of what I mentioned before – and added to this, a shaking of certain regions which became quite indecent. I am afraid I must admit that I took my leave – to the astonishment of my hosts and most of the other guests. I must have appeared very strange to them!

"I cannot write much more. All correspondence must be ready by the third of December, to catch the last post at Alexandria before our own departure. I will therefore let my description of the pyramids remain to be told in person, which shall be easier to speak of than to write.

"The people one sees in the fields – if one can call the sandy expanses by this name – go quite nearly naked. The color of their skin so nearly matches the color of the soil here, and they wear so little clothing that they can move about quite freely while hardly being seen. What little they do wear if it happened to catch one's eye would simply give an impression of a small animal moving strangely slowly – for in this desert heat all little creatures move quickly on the hot sand. The first time this happened it is truly what I thought I saw – and then I blushed to realize what I had actually been looking at.

"The women, on the other hand, are clothed in long folds of light material which fall gracefully from their shoulders. They walk with a straight and proud carriage which comes from their bearing heavy clay vessels on their heads for so many hours a day. Such a sight reminds me of certain paintings we saw at the galleries in Florence, and thence arouses my admiration.

"We often heard tell of the Nubian costume of women, which is nothing but a belt from which hangs many tassels, sometimes adorned with cowrie shells. I – thankfully – have only seen a few young girls in this costume."

CHAPTER TWENTY-TWO
RESULTS AND CONSEQUENCES

"*Cannes, December 12, 1869*

"Dearest Mama,

It has been so pleasant, in spite of the long separation, to be away from Berlin for two months now. Alice's company, too, is one of the great charms, in addition to the splendid sea-shore, the gorgeous flowers and fruit, and all the time I could wish for painting, learning, and working as Papa would have wished me to.

"My thoughts and Alice's – and I know Fritz's and Louis' – are with you in the approaching days. It seems impossible to think that it has been eight years since dear Papa left this world, and I can never deplore my children's loss more than now, when the eldest are certainly old enough to understand and absorb his wise teachings. I do all I can to bring them up as he would have wished!

"The children are in excellent health, and the winter in this mild climate, with plenty of fresh air and exercise, will do the boys a world of good.

"It is good, too, to have such a long time of leisure to study the characters of each other's children as well as our own. The little cousins agree as well as ever, and enjoy each other's company as Alice and I do. To see how she has developed, and all the work she does for Darmstadt, is wonderful, but I think at times she craves a broader sphere, as there is so very little intellectual society there.

"I hear from Fritz as regularly as can be expected during such a journey as his, and I know now that they are on the last voyage before reaching home. His letters are great treasures, as it is probably the closest I shall ever come to being in such places, and I shall ask Count Seckendorff to make copies of them for you to read. I believe Fritz's ship is to pass

Crete today or tomorrow. We are to return to Berlin, Alice traveling with me as far as the Rhine, and to be home and together again by Christmas.

"Fritz has heard from the medicine lady I mentioned to you before, but I shall write more of this by messenger.

"As to what you say about Abbat, I am quite satisfied. I must say I neither wish him to leave Berlin nor Louise to come here, and I have certainly never painted Berlin as an attractive home, so I am glad there is an end of the matter, and that I was away so that there was no question of my being the person to tell my Papa-in-law that you would refuse his gracious offer."

Vicky lay down her pen, wiping her fingers before she leaned her head on her hand. If there had been no objections, if the Berlin court had been a safer and more pleasant place, it would have been pleasant to have a sister in Berlin. But Vicky would have preferred it to have been Lenchen rather than Louise. But Lenchen had wished to remain in England, and now, it turned out that Louise did too.

There had been a prospect of Louise's marrying Abbat, and the King had been so kind as to give permission for him to have a residence in England if he wished. This, however, would rob Vicky of her companion at Court events when Fritz wasn't present – an old arrangement made before the King's coronation so that it would no longer be necessary for Vicky to walk and sit with Prince Charles.

As to Abbat himself, Vicky knew he would certainly not be heartbroken if this marriage did not come to pass. He had, in fact, also been suggested by some as a husband for Lenchen. Vicky knew him to be in love with a lady who wasn't a Princess, but that he wished to marry officially and to have a family. She felt sure he would be a kind, loving friend to whoever he married.

Now, also, as the boys grew older, they wished more than ever to have a trustworthy friend in the family. Willy and Henry were to remain in the south of France for several more months, under Hinzpeter's care. They were to move to the Villa Gabrielle, which was smaller and less expensive than the *Grand Hotel de la Mediterranee* where they had been staying.

Abbat had come to Cannes at the beginning of December, living at a nearby villa, and came to visit regularly. Vicky was glad he would remain for the duration of the boys' stay.

Also in Cannes were Prince and Princess Frederick of the Netherlands and the Dowager Duchess of Mecklenburg Schwerin.

Aunt Lulu and her husband, and Aunt Adina.

In the company of Aunt Lulu, as Fritz called Princess Frederick, Vicky felt there could be no harm. She, the youngest sister of Fritz's father, was a gentle, mild-mannered woman, rather frail, and had never been caught up in the web of the Kreuzzeitung party. Her husband, too, was kind, but Vicky had never gotten to know him very well.

Aunt Adina, on the other hand, was one of those whom Vicky least wished her children to be more closely acquainted with.

They had met in one of the gardens nearby. The Grand Duchess's behavior was the same as ever.

"So, *you* are here," were the words she had greeted Vicky and Willy with, casting a scornful glance at Willy, slightly curling her lip as if her gaze rested on something distasteful.

As if you didn't know that, Vicky thought. She felt sure the Grand Duchess was perfectly aware of her residence in Cannes, and had come as a spy. She bent down to whisper in Willy's ear, "Please do not say anything, no matter what she says." He nodded, squeezing her hand.

"I wonder at you staying in such a shabby town," the Grand Duchess went on, "when Nice is so nearby. It is far more desirable."

"Alice and I prefer the quiet life here," Vicky said calmly. She would not add her real thoughts, that Nice was only a rendezvous for gamblers and bad society. She must not let the Grand Duchess provoke her.

"I shall soon take myself there," the Grand Duchess said. "I will leave you to your solitude. I hear your Fritz will not be home for some months yet, as he is too busy enjoying the pleasures of the Turkish and Egyptian courts." She paused, a knowing smile crossing her face as she looked past Vicky. "I don't suppose you miss him much; you have plenty of company."

"Fritz will be home before Christmas," Vicky said calmly, turning to see who the Grand Duchess had meant by "plenty of company". Count Seckendorff stood a few steps behind her, carrying her folded parasol and a basket of things she had bought in the town for the children's collections. She had no lady accompanying her. Abbat and Hinzpeter stood further away, holding Charlotte and Henry's hands. Vicky was grateful they hadn't allowed the children to come closer during the conversation.

***

Cannes, December 13, 1869

"I will join the children, if you do not mind," Alice said. She and Vicky were just returning from a long walk, accompanied by Count Seckendorff and Hedwig.

Vicky nodded. "I don't feel inclined to join them at the moment." She went on, walking slowly, gazing out to sea.

"Fritz will return in about ten days," she murmured to herself. She longed for his return, but at the same time, she still felt uncertain. The idea of returning to Berlin and possibly arriving before Fritz also made her uncomfortable. "He'll have the remedy, and we'll all get well again," she said, repeating the words Alice said every time she brought up the matter.

Vicky longed to have a long talk with Mama, but her current troubles were ones she did not feel comfortable writing in a letter which would pass through several countries. Besides her own troubles, Vicky's thoughts went, as they always did at this time of year, to Mama and the *Geschwister*[58]. Vicky longed for Papa's advice intensely. She had always been able to tell him everything.

She had told Mama about many of Fritz's symptoms and about the medicine lady, but she could not write more. She had only written of the symptoms which had come out on October first, not of the original reason for Fritz's wishing to go to the medicine lady. Besides, she felt he wouldn't like it if she did, even though he had asked her to send for Sir William Jenner before his departure. She remembered in the early years of their marriage how astonished Fritz had been at how openly she wrote to her mother.

She and Alice had talked it over several times, and each time, Vicky felt a little more confident. Letting her thoughts have free rein in these conversations had soothed her feelings, yet every time she began to feel better, doubts soon surged again in her mind. Fritz's letters also encouraged her. He wrote as he always did, in his affectionate, unassuming, modest – what some would call prudish – way, which was so dear to her, with little hints of precious memories they shared which made her cheeks burn when she read his letters in front of the children, with his earnestly expressed desire that she could always be at his side.

Of course he wished to get well, too. She wondered why she could not shake the idea of Fritz's condition being ongoing. Her face burned as she remembered her words to Alice, mentioning his saying that intimacy –

---

[58]   siblings

physical intimacy – wasn't what he cared most about. She had let her mind twist his meaning so much that she could interpret the memory of those words as a selfish whim! She shook her head as she sat down beneath a little cluster of palms, covering her face.

His words had meant so much to her at the time when they were spoken, when he came home the morning after his birthday ten years ago. Those words had clung in her mind when all the rest had been a blur of pain and shame.

"Don't you know, that that is not what I care most about? I care about YOU, and want you to be as happy, as comfortable as you can be."

When she had difficulties, he was ready to give up the prospect of intimacy at a moment's notice, even when she said "she never wished to be intimate again". Why could she not do the same when he had a problem?

"Oh, why am I so selfish?" she cried aloud.

She had almost resented his effort to comfort and caress her, his simply going through the motions with no passion behind it, when he must be suffering deep insecurity and a sense of loss. But hadn't she done so for him, when they had re-begun their married life on his birthday after Charlotte's birth?

She recalled that time, and the great effort it was, and the words she had spoken. "Pleasure is no pleasure, and it must be so for a time… I felt as if my body betrayed me – and you." It was all in such a very different way than how she had meant it, but these words probably fitted Fritz's current feelings precisely.

She hadn't told him yet that she was expecting another little one. It was three months now. She had felt surprised when she realized she was expecting. It must have been September 15, as she had mentioned to Valerie. That was the last day that Fritz hadn't pretended to be asleep, though she hadn't expected any result.

She smiled, but she felt somewhat anxious, too. She had been reading over more papers about the medicine lady which Anna had given her while they were in Potsdam. They mentioned the remedies being perfectly safe for children to take, as well as adults. This was very good to hear.

But it did not mention whether it was safe for the unborn.

She jumped at the sound of Fritz's voice nearby, and looked up, realizing it was Count Seckendorff. He and Hedwig had come close to where she sat, and were talking together in German. Hedwig nodded, and headed towards the spot where Alice and the children sat.

"Your Highness?" Count Seckendorff's voice again interrupted her thoughts. "I wished to ask –"

Vicky turned to look up at him. "Oh, you are not looking well!" She was startled to see his face. He looked pale, and his face struck her as looking rather thin. The contrast startled her. He had looked so well and handsome last month. *Is it really true he does not care for Valerie?* she thought. He hadn't looked so unwell, before her departure.

"I wish to ask for leave before – before the Crown Prince arrives."

"You do not wish to be here to welcome him home?" Vicky asked.

Count Seckendorff met her eye for a moment, and then glanced away. "I should like to go to my family for the holidays. My mother is unwell, and I should like to be with her."

"Oh, yes, certainly, you may certainly go. Only, I'll miss you." She smiled up at him, holding out her hand.

He didn't meet her eye. His gaze was on the sand, and he didn't take her hand.

"I should have liked you to be here when Fritz comes home," she went on. "He'll be as grateful as I am for everything you've done for us."

Count Seckendorff turned away, his gaze following a gull gliding out to sea. "I do not wish to be – I only wish to be reunited with my family. You will have that happiness."

"Of course, of course, I understand," Vicky said. "But of course you'll say goodbye?"

He nodded, taking her hand, bowing slightly. "I should like to go as soon as possible," he said. His gaze wandered again, and he went on a little awkwardly, "Someone… I simply feel I should go right now."

Vicky nodded, giving his hand a sympathetic squeeze. "Valerie," she began, taking out her handkerchief and playing with it. "I thought you cared for Valerie. But – it's not true."

He laughed briefly, and Vicky was glad to see a small smile cross his face. "No. Valerie is a dear girl. She has been one of my best friends since I joined the court, and I shall miss her very much. But I never thought anyone might suppose we cared for each other in any other way until you said it." He laughed again, but then his expression grew melancholy once more, and he turned away, his face reddening. "No. I foolishly care for someone who will never care for me – in that way, and it is right that she shouldn't," he said, a little sharply. "It's nothing I deserve sympathy for."

"But it isn't wrong to *care*. Valerie spoke of that. She said you wished her to." He nodded and Vicky went on. "It isn't wrong to care for someone. Love – love is such a beautiful thing. I don't mean to say anything which might wound you, but as Valerie said, you said you wouldn't allow yourself to be 'in love' with the woman you care for. I believe you are showing *true* love –true, unselfish, patient love, as you seem – as I believe you feel.

"Love is patient, love is kind. Love does not demand its own wishes." She paused, realizing she was telling herself this as much as she was speaking to him, though it applied in a different way. "And it is not envious; it does not boil over with jealousy. I suppose that is the most difficult lesson to learn, in some situations." She looked up with a sad smile, but he had turned away. "I'm sorry if I've said too much!" she cried. "But I told you before, everyone knows me for saying whatever I think."

"No," he said, his voice barely above a whisper. "It is just what I need to hear."

"And –" Vicky began again, "I don't know if it is kind to say this just now, but you will understand my real meaning. I only wish your happiness."

"As I do yours." He paused. "I shall not say goodbye again," he said. "Good day, your Highness." He knelt, kissing her hand, rose, went through the motion of clicking his heels, though no sound was produced on the soft sand, and swiftly strode away towards the hotel.

"Poor boy, I know what Valerie said about his not being unhappy is not true," Vicky said quietly to herself. "How I wish he and Valerie had cared for each other, and that they might have been happy together. It would have been better for them both than what has happened."

***

"Alice?" Vicky whispered, searching for Alice's hand. "Are you awake?"

"Yes."

"I've been so selfish and wrapped up in my own problems, I never asked you –"

"You have not been selfish, Vicky."

"Yes. I have. But I have never asked you what symptoms you and Louis had." Vicky turned, struggling to see Alice's face in the dark. There appeared to be no moonlight tonight. "You said that it was your idea that Louis travel with Fritz."

Before Fritz's departure, Louis had permission to travel, but it hadn't been decided whether he would remain in the South of France with Vicky and Alice and the children or accompany Fritz. The later had been decided very quickly, and he traveled unofficially as part of Fritz's entourage.

Vicky could vaguely see Alice nod. "We – had the strange rash like you had," Alice said, "at least I did. Such swelling and itching, I couldn't recognize myself." Vicky squeezed her hand, wincing at the painful memory. "For Louis – it didn't swell so, but it was all over. He was simply covered in it. It lasted about two weeks for each of us, as you said it did for you. Did Fritz have this?"

"No. We didn't realize what the rash meant, just as you didn't, and so we thought we had been blessed with no consequences of Prince Charles's scheme – unless you call little Vicky a 'consequence'." Vicky laughed, and then smiled. "I wouldn't have her otherwise to what she is. She's my little darling. But no, Fritz didn't have a rash until two days after he told me about – the other – when *all* the symptoms came out."

Alice nodded. "I have been thinking of the journey home. I have so few people, I should like to travel part of the way with you. It will make it easier for my nursery."

Alice had traveled with an entourage of four – two nurses, a gentleman and a lady, while Vicky's consisted of twenty-five at the beginning of their stay in the South of France. Six of these – Hinzpeter and o'Danne, Dr. Schrader, Lieutenant Dresky – who still helped Willy with his daily exercises – a valet and a housekeeper, formed a separate group, who would remain with Willy and Henry during their extended residence.

Another six formed the nursery staff – the new nurse, Mrs. Wakelin, Lina and her mother, as well as a housekeeper, maid, and cook.

Then there were Mademoiselle d'Arcourt and her maid, Valerie – before her departure – her cousin Hedwig, and another of Vicky's ladies, Fanny Rentvelow. Count Seckendorff and Count Reisach were the gentlemen, and Rosa – Vicky's maid – Georgiana Hobbs as housekeeper, the ladies' maids, and a cook who would also remain with the boys later, completed the party.

"You're certainly very welcome," Vicky said, squeezing Alice's hand again.

"Uncle Alex offered to take the children home – he'll be here soon anyway – but I declined, though I trust him absolutely."

"Fritz never seemed to think so much of him," Vicky said. "I remember his speaking of the story of Prince Alexander of Hesse's flirtations in Russia. When Fritz and Louis were at the Tsar's coronation, Fritz seemed to think Prince Alexander wasn't a good companion for his nephew."

Alice laughed. "That is all a ruse, a show he puts on," she said. "Before he was married, he never supposed he would be allowed to marry the woman he loved, as she was a lady-in-waiting of his sister and a ward of her Imperial father-in-law. He proposed to the Grand Duchess Olga, proposing that he marry her, but that they would raise his children with Aunt Julia – Miss Hauke, as she was then. But the Grand Duchess refused, and so he eloped. He knew the Tsar would never consent. And he has kept up that reputation in the eyes of the world, though his family honor his true one."

"I'm glad to hear he's not such a reprobate as I heard," Vicky said. She laughed. "Mama was quite taken with him when he was in England after Bertie's wedding. She said he reminded her of Papa. In what way, I couldn't say."

"I do see that," Alice said, "and he is a very clever diplomat and statesman. But above all, he is a very dear, kind, faithful husband and loving father – and uncle. He is always so kind to us and our children, and I trust him absolutely as I said. His children are so nice – his Marie was a great comfort to my dear Mama-in-law when Annchen died. And his boys are so nice, though Sandro is a little rough. Ludwig is such a little gentleman, and I was so pleased that Mama and Affie were able to get him into our Navy in spite of his being beyond the age."

"You say *our* Navy," Vicky said. "Do your children ever get confused by you saying 'our' and 'we' about England, rather than about Hesse?"

Alice was silent for a moment. "They have never seemed so. But I remember you said Willy was confused in that way."

Vicky nodded. "I can never stop thinking of England in that way. I'm more proud of being Mama's daughter and an English Princess than of any so-called honor the Prussians can give me, though I wish so much for Prussia's good. Being Fritz's wife is the highest honor I can have there." She sighed, her thoughts returning to their previous theme.

"Our Grand Duke is always so kind," Alice said. "I am so glad he gave Aunt Julia and the children the titles of Prince of Battenberg. It would have been such a shame if they were hidden away and unacknowledged. They deserve the title of Prince, in a way which so many who have it do not.

"Louis Battenberg was so pleased at Bertie and Alix asking him to be in the crew on their Nile cruise," Alice went on. "I hear Alix's leg is much better since they went. I believe some of our family already knew of this medicine lady before Fritz learned of her."

Alix had been severely ill two years ago, and had suffered severe hearing loss and a limp ever since. This was a great trial, Vicky knew, to someone as active and agile as Alix was.

"Liko is a funny little boy," Alice said.

"How did they come to call him Liko when his name is Henry?" Vicky asked.

"Their nurse called him *Enrico*." Alice laughed. "Sandro turned it into Liko. Little Franzjos is a scholar, and so is the eldest – Ludwig, we call him, to distinguish him from my Louis. You should have seen his paintings from when he was only five years old! They are quite wonderful."

There was a knock at the door. Vicky rose. "Rosa?" she called.

"Ma'am," Mrs. Wakelin's voice came in reply. "Your Highness," she went on, as Vicky opened the door, "I think you should come. The little one is ill."

Alice hurried to follow Vicky. "Which little one?"

"Waldemar," Mrs. Wakelin said.

***

"*Mein Schatz*[59],

"I hope this will reach you in time. I write in great anxiety as Waldie is very ill. Alice and I have spent a sleepless night, and my heart aches in memory of three years ago.

"However, everyone says it is very different from darling Siggy's illness; there are none of the horrible convulsions which tore my heart to pieces. This was my first fear, though I don't know why. He is feverish and sweating, his throat swollen, and with a dreadfully hoarse cough which hardly sounds like so young a child.

---

[59]   My darling

311

"At a time like this in the year, you will feel as deeply as I do how my heart aches.

"We all hope this reaches you in time that you should direct your voyage here instead of the original plan of going home. I think it a very pleasant idea to spend Christmas all together, and I know the children will be delighted at it too. If only our little darling is spared!

"How I long for your return I cannot say. I kiss you and love you,

"*Deine Frauchen*, who loves you,

"Till death do us part."

***

Half past ten in the evening, Cannes, December 14, 1869

Vicky knelt by the cradle, clasping Alice's hand. The doctors had done all they could for Waldie, they said. They must wait and see if the fever would break.

Vicky felt as if she couldn't breathe as she watched Waldie's struggles to do so. She must not close her eyes, as the image of Siggy's last moments flooded her mind every time she did. Waldie's deep, hoarse cries, with a strange voice which hardly sounded like a small child, were so different from the horrible, shrill, high cry Siggy had given as he reached out his little arms to her.

"Mama!" Waldie cried. His breaths came far too fast, the perspiration visible on his crimson cheeks.

As the minutes crept by, Alice's hand clutched hers more firmly. Vicky felt the pain Alice must be feeling at this moment, and tears finally crept into her eyes. She had been unable to cry all day.

At about ten minutes before eleven, something changed. Waldie's breathing suddenly grew very slow, and his hand grew cold instead of hot.

"Oh, are we going to lose him just at the time we did Papa?" Alice cried.

Vicky felt as if something was strangling her. She knew Papa had died at eleven o'clock, exactly eight years ago. Alice had been at his bedside, holding his hand, while Vicky hadn't known until the next morning.

Waldie gave a strange cry. Vicky felt a hand on her shoulder.

"Is the little one any better?" a voice asked in a low murmur.

312

"Oh, Abbat, I don't think he'll make it!" Vicky turned and flung her arms around Abbat's neck.

Alice squeezed her eyes shut at the sound of Vicky's words as Vicky let go of her hand. Waldie cried out "Mama!" again.

The pain struck at her heart. Here was her little boy, who called Vicky "Mama". She lifted him out of his cradle, pressing her lips against his damp forehead.

"Vicky," she cried, but her voice wouldn't come out above a whisper. "I believe the fever has broken. He will make it. God will not take him at this hour."

"Oh, thank God!" Vicky cried, her tears flowing afresh.

Alice turned to look up at Abbat and started.

It was not Abbat. It was Count Seckendorff.

Alice stared for a moment, remarking the stricken look on his face. His face flushed even deeper as he met her eye. She had never seen a man blush so deeply.

"Go to your sister; the little one is getting better," he said in a low murmur. Vicky turned, not looking up at him, almost snatching Waldie from Alice's arms. Count Seckendorff turned to leave the room very quickly.

"I will return in just a moment. I wish to speak to Dr. Schrader," Alice said, rising and hurrying after Count Seckendorff, closing the door after her.

"Count Seckendorff?" she called.

He started, turning around. "Your Highness," he said, bowing slightly. "You sound so like your sister," he said. He shook his head. "I never meant anything. You won't give me away, will you?"

"Certainly not," Alice said. "I respect you for your restraint. But I thought you had gone. We both did."

"I simply couldn't go without saying goodbye again," he said, his voice faltering. "And when I heard the little one was unwell – I couldn't go without expressing my sympathy." His voice broke.

Alice nodded. "I know. I will let Vicky believe it was Abbat, as she does."

Count Seckendorff swallowed, blinking. "*Danke,*" he whispered. "I must go now. My things are all ready and I must catch the train."

"And I must go back to my sister and Baby," Alice said. She held out her hand. "I respect you for your restraint," she repeated, turning to go.

"Baby's so much better," Vicky said, looking up as Alice opened the door. "Why did Abbat go so suddenly? And what did Dr. Schrader say?"

Alice shrugged. "Abbat will be back soon," she said. She had sent a note to Abbat, asking him to come immediately, but informing him that Baby was better. "Dr. Schrader said that Baby should recover now that the fever has broken. But we must not travel into the cold German winter until he is completely recovered."

Vicky nodded. "I only hope Fritz and Louis receive our letters in time to come here."

CHAPTER TWENTY-THREE
MY DEAREST MAMA

Cannes, December 17, 1869

"I didn't show you Bertie's letter because it made me feel – it brought up all my doubts again," Vicky said, taking a letter from the drawer and not meeting Alice's eye. They had been discussing things in the letters Vicky had received for her birthday a month before.

"What did he say? You said it helped you to talk it out before."

Vicky glanced down at the letter, and finally placed it in Alice's hand. "I write to send my love and Alix's for your birthday, your last before you are thirty," Bertie had written.

Vicky sighed. "It makes me feel old," she whispered, leaning her head on her hand.

Alice laughed. "Old?" she exclaimed. "Louis turned thirty two years ago. Is he old? Bertie will be thirty in two years himself."

"But it's different for a man than for a woman," Vicky said. "I must be old. That is why –"

Alice shook her head. "Have you not stopped brooding about that? I thought you said you were feeling better."

"I keep thinking I am, and then it all comes again. I was reading Mama's letter about Beatrice and Leopold. That makes me feel old, too. To think that Beatrice will be grown up the next time I see her! Already, seeing her so big last year made me feel very strange. And Arthur! I had to look up to him! To think of those babies as men and women is impossible."

"Your children are only a little younger," Alice said. "Does that make you feel old?"

Vicky met her eye, thinking. "N-no," she said slowly. "Somehow, it doesn't. I suppose – Beatrice was, in a way, a symbol of my hopes and dreams. To see Mama have a baby just then, before my marriage, when my heart was so full of girlhood's innocent dreams of love– I suppose it is just that! Seeing her so grown up shows me how far away I am from that, and how long it's been since I was a girl. A girl who knew *nothing*, really, of the troubles I've known and seen. And Arthur!" Vicky paused. "Arthur – 'the baby of the Exhibition', Fritz always calls him. To see him – a man – seems so unbelievable!"

"But you were only ten years old then," Alice said. "You are not old."

Vicky sighed, hugging her sister. "It's odd," she said after a few minutes of silence. "I never thought of thirty as old. I always called Mama and Papa my children's 'young grandparents', and they were nearly forty when Willy was born. Mama was thirty-two at the Exhibition, and she was – she *is* – certainly not old. I hardly believe she ever can be," Vicky laughed.

"Mama called herself old after Papa died," Alice said softly. "And it was hard for her to see us so young and happy."

Vicky nodded, trying not to cry as she kissed Alice's cheek. "Goodnight," she whispered.

A few minutes of silence had passed, and she had begun to fall asleep, when Alice whispered, "Vicky?"

"Alice?"

"I was thinking of what you said before – about your thinking of the things Fritz had said, and your mind changing it to mean he does not wish for –"

"Oh! I've convinced myself *that* isn't true!" Vicky said. "I can even laugh at it a little. I know Fritz wants to get well. I'll feel better when he returns. I *can* say *that* now. You remember – it was his return I was anxious about."

Alice squeezed her hand. "But I was remembering something you told me the first time – the first time we talked after I was married."

"What?"

"Your saying that Fritz had believed you didn't like – kissing."

"Oh, but that was only while we were engaged. After – but no," Vicky said, her thoughts going back to a certain night almost twelve years ago.

***

316

Windsor Castle, ten in the evening, January 26, the day after the wedding, 1858

Vicky sat on the sofa in the sitting-room, finishing her note to Mama. She had been away from Mama and Papa for more than a whole day. What felt even stranger was that she had been away from her siblings for more than a day, and she had slept in her husband's arms for the first time.

And yet she was still an innocent girl. Nothing had changed since they had gone away yesterday after the wedding, besides the fact that she and Fritz had been completely alone together for the first time, and she had slept in a man's arms.

What should she write to Mama? Mama wrote so tenderly, so full of care for Vicky's happiness and comfort. And Papa – Papa didn't write, but Vicky knew he felt her absence deeply. Dear Papa, how could she leave him?

But she was leaving him – leaving her home – to make Fritz happy. She would live surrounded by his care, love and tenderness instead of her parents'. She would be his wife.

"Fritz and I are very happy," she wrote truthfully, thinking of their conversation last night. "I feel so honored to be your and Papa's daughter and Fritz's wife." She paused, now thinking of Fritz's disconcertedness the night before, and started a little when the door opened and closed.

Vicky put her desk and letter aside, rising and running into Fritz's embrace. But she stopped short before she reached him. She had suddenly become aware that she hadn't tied her nightgown, so that the neck was far more open than usual.

But more than this – Fritz stood before her without his coat or shirt. She stared, unable to move. Yesterday, she had been so eager, so eager to be – his wife. Now, he had given her time to grow nervous. She tried to look up, but couldn't make herself meet his eye. She felt still more embarrassed just standing there staring at his bare chest.

"*Meine* Vicky – *meine Frau!*" Fritz's voice was an intense whisper as he stepped forward and caught her in his arms, holding her closer to him than he ever had before.

Vicky felt her heart race as she found herself clasped tight in his arms, her face tickled by the golden curls which covered his chest. When he relaxed his embrace for a moment, she turned her head slightly, pressing her lips to his chest.

Fritz lifted her gently in his arms, going into the bedroom, laying her down on the lounge at the foot of the bed, kneeling by her side. He pressed her in his arms, beginning to caress her as he had on that evening when Papa had fallen asleep, though without once kissing her lips. She was about to speak, but caught her breath as she felt Fritz's lips touch her neck, then slightly lower than they had on that same evening. His hand rested in the opening of her nightgown, and she felt her heart race again at his touch on her bare skin.

"Fritz!" she gasped, reaching up to touch his chest with one hand, his cheek with the other. It was the first time she had spoken since his sudden appearance. She sat up, rising, putting her arm around him, and lay down on the bed. He, too, lay down, drawing her close to him so her head rested on his shoulder.

"*Meine Frau*?" He stroked her cheek, his thumb brushing her lips, as he had before the first time he ever kissed her. She opened her lips to speak, but his fingers traced a path down her neck to her collar-bone.

"Oh!" she gasped, catching at his hand. It was difficult to think of her question with him touching her so. "Fritz, why don't you kiss me? I mean – my lips." She hid her face against his chest, suddenly overcome with shyness.

"I thought you did not care for it," he said softly. "I thought you did not care for it, but only did it to please *me*. And now, I want to please *you*." Their eyes met, his face reddening, but he didn't look away.

"How could you think that?" She still looked him in the eye, feeling herself blush as well.

He gently kissed her lips. "Until last night, you only ever began or returned my kisses when we first were engaged, when we first met during each visit, and when we said good-bye," he said, "never during my visits. And never when it was more – more –" He trailed off.

"More passionate?" Vicky asked. "That was only because I felt Mama wouldn't approve. She still thinks me so young. And when Papa fell asleep – I felt so shy and strange – but no! I love you. I want to be your wife. I love to –" She didn't finish her sentence, but pressed her lips to his, wrapping her arms round his neck as he turned to lie on his back, returning her kiss warmly.

∗∗∗

Cannes, December 17, 1869

"I was only thinking – perhaps Fritz thought you did not find him attractive, sometimes, when you were engaged," Alice said.

"Oh, no! He can't have thought that!" Vicky said hurriedly.

"But – he did! I remember things you told me. I didn't understand it then; I was only a little girl, but – he did! I know it!"

"But I always found him attractive."

"Did you tell him so? Did you show it?"

"N-no," Vicky admitted.

"No," Alice said, "and he was always the less – well, self-assured of the two of you."

"But I only didn't show my feelings when we were engaged because of Mama. I told him so."

Alice nodded. "I know. But I am sure he has felt what you have been feeling."

Vicky shook her head. "Not since we were married. I never made any secret of my feelings."

"What about these last two months before we came here?"

"He didn't want such attention. He made that very clear."

"Are you sure? Or did you begin to ignore him when he began to ignore you? Or rather avoid, as he was not ignoring you."

Vicky put her hand over her eyes. "I think I *did* begin to ignore him when he began to avoid me. It is not true if you reverse those words, though. He certainly did *not* ignore me, he always seemed overly aware of my presence, when normally we would each be reading our own letters and things, before we shared them. And I never avoided him."

Alice yawned. "Good-night, Vicky," she whispered. "I can't stay awake anymore." She kissed Vicky's cheek, and then whispered, "They will be home in a few days."

***

Villafranca, December 21, 1869

"Mama! Mama! There's Papa!" Charlotte almost screamed.

Vicky and Alice clasped each other's hands. "There's Louis!" Alice whispered. She waved her handkerchief. Her face was beaming as Louis waved back.

"Where's Papa?" Vicky asked Willy, who stood on her other side.

"There!"

"Fritz!" Vicky called, even though she knew he was still too far away to hear.

They had driven to the harbor of Villafranca, and now, the *Hertha*, the *Elisabeth* and the *Grille* were well in sight. The *Hertha*, which Fritz and Louis were on board, was in the lead.

Finally, the *Hertha* had come to shore, and Vicky could see the entourage joining Fritz and Louis on deck.

But more than anything else, she saw Fritz as he walked down the gangplank. He was next to her in a moment.

"Fritz!" she cried, as he caught her in his arms and kissed her with nearly all his old enthusiasm. But that wasn't true, she realized. All his old enthusiasm *was* there. It was simply something which he couldn't control which was missing.

She turned to greet Louis, who had caught Victoria up in his arms, as Fritz turned to the children, and then to kiss Alice's cheek. Irene, little Vicky, and the babies were in the carriage.

"Come on board for a moment," Fritz said. Vicky saw Willy and Henry's faces beam, and Willy leapt in the air.

***

Grand Hotel, Villafrance, December 21, 1869

"Your letter found us in Naples, and we were able to take the train a great distance. We only had to steam along the coast from La Spezzia. Louis and the others had gone on to Rome before me, as I wished to see more of Naples, and they had not gone to Rome before."

Fritz and Louis each sat at the ends of the sofa, Willy, Charlotte and Henry between them. Louis held both Ernie and Waldie in his arms, and the little girls sat on the floor at each end of the sofa. Vicky and Alice each sat in an armchair across from them. They had stopped at the Grand Hotel in Villafranca, where they would spend the night, returning to Cannes in the morning, as it was already too late for the hour-long carriage drive.

"Is it true you really rode a camel, Papa?" Willy asked. "Like the camels we see at the Tiergarten?"

"Well," Fritz said, "these were Dromedaries, not Bactrians. Do any of you know what this means?" he asked, looking about at the children.

"They only have one hump," Charlotte said before any of the others could answer.

Fritz smiled and nodded. "One feels almost sea-sick atop the camel's hump until one gets used to the motion, but it soon becomes quite comfortable. The camel knelt down, and I felt as if I would be thrown off as it lunged up, bellowing like a stag."

"You said you had photographs taken, didn't you?" Vicky asked.

"Oh, yes! We have hundreds of photographs," Louis said. "I only wish they could have already been developed, so you could have seen them all together."

"Have you ever had a banana, Papa?" Henry asked. "Or an orange?"

Fritz sighed and closed his eyes. "To eat the ripe oranges straight off the tree, out of doors, in the winter months!" He sighed, a look of pleasure on his face.

"We did so too!" Willy and Charlotte cried. "But have you had a banana?"

"Not outside of a hothouse," Fritz answered. "Have you had a Mandarin orange?"

The children nodded. "We went with Aunty to the *Jardin de Hesperides*," Charlotte said eagerly. "It's so beautiful there! And everywhere here! I have such quantities of flowers in my rooms. I only wish they could grow at home!"

"Papa," Victoria said, taking Louis' hand, "what were the dancers like?"

"Yes," Willy said, "what were they like?"

"Mama stopped reading to us when she reached that part of your letter," Charlotte said to Fritz.

Fritz turned his face away; Vicky saw him and Louis glance at each other.

"Were they like the dancers we saw in Potsdam?" Victoria asked. "The funny women who hopped about on stage with short skirts?" Victoria and Ella had seen a ballet for the first time a few months earlier.

Fritz leaned forward, his head resting on his hand with his eyes covered – his usual posture when he had to speak of something which embarrassed him.

"But those weren't dancers – they were giant – giant – what are they? – puppies!" Ella cried. "They can't have been real people – people don't act so."

"Giant puppies!" Charlotte laughed. She looked at Ella for a moment, and then went on, "Puppets, you mean! Oh, *you* are the funny little puppet!" she said, rather condescendingly patting Ella's head. "But she's right, isn't she, Papa? Puppets and puppies both come from *Poupet*, in the French, do they not?"

"Yes, Charlotte," Vicky said, "but don't poke fun at your little cousin."

"And that performance was during the Khedive of Egypt's visit," Charlotte went on. "When his dear little boy sat between us," she said, smiling at Victoria, "and we kissed him so much, as he could not speak to us." She giggled, and then glanced up at Fritz. "He saw our dancers, and now you have seen theirs."

"But what were the dancers like?" Victoria asked again.

"I do not know," Fritz muttered, more to himself than to the children. "I did not stay to see the performance."

"Well, they were nothing like those dancers we saw a few months ago." Louis laughed, shaking his head. "They were dressed with scarves of pink and gold and sky-blue, with gold coins woven into their black hair."

"They sound pretty," Ella said, looking up at him.

"They – *were* – pretty," Louis said slowly. "And they danced like this." He rose, doing a comical dance which Vicky knew had no similarity to the Egyptian women's dance, except perhaps in the arm movements and hand gestures.

All the children laughed, and Fritz smiled, glancing at Vicky and shaking his head. Vicky glanced at Alice. She didn't smile, and her face was deeply flushed.

"They certainly did dance in a way I *never* saw before," Louis said as he sat down again, his face reddening as he met Alice's eye. Vicky remembered the lines of Louis' letter which Alice had shown her. His description of the women's dress had been very similar to Fritz's, but he had continued:

"As the dance went on, the women appeared to pretend as if bees or ants or some stinging creature had gotten into their clothing, gradually stripping off their scarves until they stood quite nearly unclothed, all the while starting at the apparent stings, flinging out each body part in a manner quite unimaginable, and increasing their gyrations all the more. By this point I shared Fritz's feelings, and wished to leave, but felt that we ought not to give the offence of both of us leaving the performance which was considered an honor."

There was silence for a minute, and Vicky saw Louis' face grow even redder as everyone's gaze was on him. She was about to break the awkward silence when Victoria asked, "What about the pyramids? Mama said you climbed them."

Fritz sighed. "I still feel tired when I think of that," he said, leaning back and closing his eyes. "It is only to be done so that one can say one has done it. Our guides practically had to pull us up the second half of the height; the steps are so high one's knees feel as if they have lost their use."

"But the view from the top is worth the effort," Louis said. "And the view, also, of the pyramids from the base, when the sun is just behind the top, is wonderful."

Fritz sighed and shook his head, putting his hand to his head, leaning toward Vicky. "I did not feel well, and it was not worth it to me. On the descent I felt dizzy on top of everything," he murmured. "But to go inside was fascinating," he continued more loudly. "I wonder if crawling through a mine-shaft is any easier. One had to pull oneself along, two or three of our guides pushing or dragging us as well, up and down, on all fours, or on one's back."

"And when we finally we reached the path to the burial chamber," Louis said, laughing, "we all slid down on top of each other."

He and Fritz both laughed. "No one could stop laughing," Fritz said.

"Papa! Papa! I'm a camel!" Little Vicky ran by, trotting about the room as the children often did when they played horses. Vicky had noticed her taking one of the small melons from the basket of fruit sitting nearby, laboriously tying it into a blanket. Now, she held the blanket wrapped round her, the melon on her back as a hump.

Everyone laughed – everyone but Charlotte. "That is my melon!" she cried, rising suddenly from her seat.

Little Vicky started, dropping the blanket. The melon landed with a loud *splat* as it split open, the juice quickly soaking through the blanket.

"And now you have ruined it!" Charlotte almost screamed as she snatched up one of the oranges, raising her arm to throw it. "How dare you, you little n–" She broke off as Fritz caught her arm before she could throw the orange. She glanced at Vicky, her eyes wide. "I didn't say it," she said, sitting down again, her face crimson.

Alice and Louis had both risen, Louis still holding Ernie and Waldie, Victoria and Irene both clinging to his coat. Vicky saw Alice whisper something to Willy and Henry. Ella followed her mother, taking her hand as they left the room.

"I know you didn't, Charlotte," Vicky said, "but you still ought to apologize for frightening your little sister. She probably didn't know it was *your* melon."

"*Kommst du[60],*" Fritz said, lifting little Vicky onto his knee and putting his arm around Charlotte. Vicky couldn't hear what was said, but Charlotte leaned forward, kissing little Vicky on the forehead, and then turned to leave the room with Willy and Henry.

"How has Charlotte been with the little ones?" Fritz asked as Vicky came to sit by his side. "And with you?"

"She's behaved quite well. There were no scenes before today. I think Alice is a good influence on her."

Fritz nodded, kissing little Vicky on the forehead and setting her down as Mrs. Wakelin came in. "How do you like the new nurse?" he asked after the door closed.

"Very well. The children are all already fond of her, and Mrs. Hobbs writes so often they don't feel abandoned. The change of scene at the same time was very good."

Fritz put his arm around Vicky. "I have the remedy for us. I will show it to you tomorrow, when we are back at Cannes and my things are unpacked. I shall begin to take it when we begin our journey home. I wrote to you that a deep illness will take place, a week into taking it. This must not be until after our reception back in Berlin."

Vicky nodded. "And I shall begin to take it when you've been ill a week. Anna suggested that, as she said the illness can last two weeks."

Fritz looked at her. "Separate beds were suggested during the illness."

Vicky sighed, but nodded. "Fritz?" She leaned her head on his shoulder. "How long did Louis remain – at the performance? After you left, how long did it go on?"

---

[60]   Come here

"About a quarter of an hour, and Louis rejoined me immediately afterwards. He said they invited him to stay to the meal which took place afterwards, but he declined." Fritz met Vicky's eye. "You know what this means?" She nodded. "He said he did not wish me to think ill of him, and he wished to be able to tell Alice about it honestly."

"I'm glad to hear that. I wish Victoria hadn't asked about it, or at least not until he could have spoken of it privately with Alice. And he should *not* have mentioned that the women were pretty. Poor Alice, did you see her face?" Fritz nodded. "Did you read his description?" Vicky asked.

Fritz nodded again, his face flushing. "He told me more, too, than he wrote. He said that at the meal afterwards the men were surrounded by the women, still attired as they were after they had removed their scarves." Fritz shuddered, a disgusted look crossing his face. "I could not sit there and watch even the early part of the performance, because" – his face grew very red – "I felt as if it would be a betrayal to you, and not only in the obvious way." He whispered in her ear, then shook his head, covering his eyes with his hand.

"Oh, Fritz, I understand!" Vicky cried, kissing his cheek. "It's just how I felt about – about what happened at the laundry." She met his eye, forcing herself not to look away. "You remember the things I said. I was thinking over my words, and they seemed to fit your situation so well, even before you told me this. 'Pleasure is no pleasure… I felt as if my body betrayed me… and you'."

Fritz nodded. "I had remembered your words as well. It is exactly what I have been feeling." His face flushed bright red. "It is so shameful," he murmured to himself.

She put her arms around him, kissing his cheek. "Come, lie down," she said. He lay with his head in her lap. "I was shamefully selfish, while you were away. I let my thoughts run wild to the extent that at one time I was trying to believe that you didn't wish to recover our relationship. But then I thought of how unselfish *you* always were when *I* had difficulties, and that brought me to my senses."

He didn't meet her eye, but muttered something to himself again, his face flushing.

She bent over him, kissing his brow, stroking his hair. "Fritz, I care about YOU, and want you to be as happy, as comfortable as you can be." She kissed his forehead again. "Do those words sound familiar?"

He smiled. "*Ja*. But *you* cannot say *truthfully* the words I said before those[61]."

"Oh, Fritz, but I *do* care about you!" Vicky cried, kissing his forehead, the tears rushing to her eyes. "I do care about YOU, more than about – but I haven't been living those words in my thoughts of late, certainly."

She met his eye, then looked away, feeling her face flush with shame. "It's always been about *me*, hasn't it?" she said slowly. "You always gave things up for *me*. When *I* had difficulties, and when we were being cautious – after Willy's birth and before little Vicky's – *you* were always ready to sacrifice *your* own desires. But I never questioned whether you did or didn't wish for intimacy, until now. It was always what *I* wanted, what *I* was able to do. And – how I said, when we *had* to – before and after Charlotte's birth, when *that* part of our marriage was stripped away. *I* learned to love *you* more – to *respect* you. But I! I've always been *so* selfish!"

She saw a tear run from his eye, and tears flooded her eyes again as he reached up to touch her cheek. He sat up, taking her in his arms. He gently kissed her forehead, and then looked her in the eye. "You are not selfish," he said. "I would not have wanted anything else."

"But I haven't told you everything!" she cried. "And I won't say the things I would have said to you several times during your absence. At least – I won't say it as cruelly as I would have. But you have a right to know how I was feeling." She paused, meeting his questioning gaze. "If we had met a few weeks ago, I would have asked you – 'do you still find me unattractive?' "

Fritz's hand trembled in hers. "Vicky," he whispered. "Did I really leave you to think that, for *three months*?" He rose, pacing through the room. "I never meant *anything* like *that*!" His voice was choked with emotion. "I did not know how to say – how I wish I could simply speak of physical details, without saying something so *cruel*! It is I who was cruel, not you!" He turned back to her, cradling her face in his hands. "How can you ever forgive me?"

Vicky put her hands over his. "I already have."

"But did you *really* think that I was no *longer* attracted to you?" Fritz's voice was still more agitated.

---

[61]   Fritz said he cared more about her well-being than about their physical relationship.

Vicky hung her head, feeling her face flush. "I did and I didn't. It was what I said to Alice the first time we spoke of all of this – but I really didn't believe it, but my thoughts did run wild. Alice would talk me back to sense each time, and I would see things clearly, but then something would start my thoughts running on again. But her books have been a comfort."

"What do you mean?" Fritz sat down again, intently watching her face.

"You know the things which Alice studies – the medical books, etc. I've been reading one of them these last few days, and I never thought such a thing could be such a comfort. I'd read a great deal about the human body, but not on *this* subject particularly, and, oh! How I wish I had! I wish I had ten years ago. It would have helped me so much to understand *my* feelings. I wouldn't have blamed myself so much!

"It makes me understand what you said about yourself – at the performance." She paused, trying to meet his eye, but he looked away. "And about myself – my memories after – Prince Charles." Fritz's gaze wandered back to her face. "Our bodies are only doing what God made them to do. It is our minds – our thoughts – which make it feel shameful. But one's body does not recognize that something of that kind is wrong. It simply acts as it is told to – by physical stimulus."

"But why, then, could I not – but of course it is the illness," he said.

Vicky nodded. "And perhaps – perhaps – if it's not actually *only* caused by the illness – perhaps – the absence during this journey was what was needed. It says when a man suffers in the way you are, it's sometimes from too great familiarity. That makes sense, doesn't it, with what you said about the dancers?"

Fritz blushed again, but he finally nodded.

"Knowing and understanding this," Vicky said, "was what finally let me see things in the light of reality, and know that there was *no* truth in the idea that you might be no longer attracted to me."

***

Cannes, December 26, 1869

"Fritz," Vicky whispered as she saw him open his eyes, "I didn't like to wake you before, but you must hurry now. It's only an hour till the train."

The Christmas festivities had passed pleasantly. She was glad to have spent the time out of Berlin. Abbat had also come to their dinner.

Vicky had smiled as the little cousins exchanged presents. Willy had given Victoria a new butterfly net, and Ella the largest fan shell he had found. Willy had been delighted at the storybooks Louis had given him, which he promised he would read all of during his stay in Cannes.

The day after Fritz and Louis' arrival, Vicky and Alice had gone for a long walk together. "Louis told me everything about the dancers," Alice had said, "and Fritz spoke to me about it too – about Louis. I am so glad Louis left before the meal." She squeezed Vicky's hand. "You know what a meal like that means, don't you?"

Vicky nodded. "But I'm sure Louis would never dream of partaking in such things. Aren't you secure in his love and his character? Just think of what you wrote to me in your letter before we came here. You said he's 'so true and faithful'."

Alice blushed. "Yes, he is, but – it is not that I don't trust him, but – how naïve he is about some things. Even more so than you or I. And he doesn't have Fritz's aversion to drink, so – I am only thankful he came away."

Vicky squeezed her hand. "I understand. Fritz told me about it, and said Louis came away just after the beginning of the meal, as he wished to be able to tell you honestly about it, and he wished Fritz not to think ill of him." She paused, smiling. "I'm always so glad he and our brothers look up to Fritz so much. He's such a good example and a sort of conscience for them. They want to be able to speak honestly to him of their travels, etc. I always know when Bertie has been –"

***

Vicky stepped into the train, turning back again to look at Willy and Henry, but her eyes were blurred with tears. As she wiped them, she saw Willy jumping about, while Henry stood crying aloud. Hinzpeter stood by his side, his hand on his shoulder.

Her heart ached. Could she really bear to leave her boys behind for so long? It would be four long months before she saw them again.

Willy continued to jump about as the train whistled and pulled away.

She sat down by Fritz's side, tears pouring down her cheeks. He took her hand, gently squeezing it. "It is for their good," he murmured. "And to keep them away from Berlin is particularly satisfactory."

"But we won't see them till May!" Vicky sobbed, leaning over and hiding her face against Fritz's chest.

***

December 28, 1869

"My dear boy,

"We are well on our way home, but half my heart is left behind with you and Henry. I feel quite lost when I turn to say something and find you – nowhere to be found.

"Papa and *die Geschwister*[62] all send their love and we hope you find the Villa Gabrielle as comfortable as the Grand Hotel. We hope you will spend a pleasant winter (if one can call it so with that splendid climate) and come home safe and well. I trust you will give Hinzpeter no trouble.

"Write as often as you can. I long for news, and shall send all I can in return,

"Your loving Mama.

"P.S. I must admit that Henry's tears were more in sympathy with my feelings on saying goodbye – what were you thinking, jumping about like a mad monkey? You almost seemed glad to see us go."

***

Vicky watched as Fritz took the little tin from a box, opening it to reveal the black, tan and grey granules which he had described. He took a pinch, sprinkling it into his mouth.

She watched him close his eyes tight – she remembered his saying it was quite hot to the taste – and swallow. He nodded, meeting her eye.

"And *this* shall make everything right?" she said, taking it and looking at it.

Fritz shrugged. "Anna and the Emperors Alexander and Franz Joseph attest that it will. She is quite famous in Egypt for her medicines."

"Fritz," Vicky said, clutching anxiously at his arm. "There's something I haven't told you – and it's something which wasn't touched on in the papers you sent or what Anna brought. And I haven't told you."

---

[62]   siblings

"What?"

"That I – that *we* have hopes again," she said with a little smile, trying not to show the fear she felt. "But this little one – must have been – it was while you were suffering from the active disease, though we didn't know it yet, and – is the remedy safe?"

"She said it was safe for children to take it, even babies," Fritz said, putting his arm around her and kissing her. "Why did you not tell me before?" he murmured, kissing her hair.

She looked down. "I don't know. I felt so uncertain about everything. I know she said it was safe for children, but – is it safe for the unborn? That's often a different question. If I take the remedy, and my body is trying to purge the illness, what will happen to the baby?"

Her voice quivered and she felt tears come to her eyes. Fritz embraced her, stroking her hair. "Which risk would you rather take? To have a baby which may be deformed, or suffer in some other way from the illness, and also to – we must not risk re-infection," he said. "I am taking the remedy now. What shall we do, if you do not take it, too?" He put a finger under her chin, raising her head so she looked him in the eye. "I do not wish you to –"

She shuddered at his touch on her chin, snatching herself away. "Don't do that!" she cried, but she wasn't sure why.

Fritz looked at her questioningly. "What?"

"Lift my chin with your finger like that. I don't know." She shuddered again. "There's some memory which I don't remember clearly." She met Fritz's eye. "And it's sad, as you did that when you proposed, and I thought it so sweet. But – I think it was Prince kaMpande."

Fritz nodded, gently embracing her again and kissing her forehead. "I was only going to say, I do not wish you to go for several more months without taking the remedy, and let this illness ravage your body. Women often do not show it as much as men, but that does not mean they do not have even more damage to their interior."

She nodded. "I'd decided that in my own mind, but I wished to know what you thought. I didn't wish to do anything which might possibly harm *your* child without your knowledge."

Cannes, January 4, 1870

"My dearest Mama,

"I was only jumping about because I was cold. That day was cold, compared to other days here. We have not had another cold day since you left.

"Hinzpeter took us to see a glass factory like the one we saw in Gotha. I blew another bottle and shook hands with the foreman, and everything looked very clean. We went without anyone expecting us. Hinzpeter says this is important in Royal visits.

"I have written both to Großpapa and to Grandmama in England, but not yet to Großmama. I hope she will not mind this, but I did not know what to write.

"I hope Papa and *Geschwister*[63] and Uncle and Aunty and Cousins are well. Are you still together?

"Great-Aunt Alexis came here yesterday, and Aunt Sanny from Russia and Uncle Friedrich of the Netherlands have also come. Uncle Abbat was here during our Greek lessons, as he says he wishes to refresh his memory."

Kronprinz Palais, Berlin, January 4, 1870

Fritz raised his head. It was the first time in two days he had been able to sit up and look about the room without feeling like it and his head were spinning in opposite directions.

Vicky sat by his side, holding a warm drink to his lips. His hands trembled, and he was too weak to hold the cup himself. He took a sip, and put his hand to his throat.

"Oh! I – my throat!" He could hardly get the words out, his voice was so hoarse.

"Is it so very bad?" Vicky asked, stroking his hair. He nodded.

---

[63]   siblings

"I must speak to Papa," he murmured, but he could not remember what he wished to speak about. The memory of the last two days was so vague.

Their arrival at Berlin had been greeted with great warmth by the crowds and the authorities. Papa had been kind, though little attention had been shown them in the midst of the rush of New Year's ceremonies and speeches.

Vicky had been very sick on the journey, and had gone immediately to bed on arrival home.

"It is not Papa I – *ach!*" Fritz struggled to sit up straighter, but his head swam and the pain in his throat overwhelmed him. He lay down again, closing his eyes, and then motioned to a stack of paper on the table. Vicky fetched his desk.

"It was not Papa I needed to speak to, at least I do not remember if I did," he wrote. "It is my throat. I was thinking of when my throat was so severely sore before our visit to the Paris Exhibition." His sore throat had been so severe then that their visit was officially delayed, only to be reinstated when he suddenly felt better.

"My throat – it is sore in just the same place as it was then," he wrote, glancing up at Vicky. "It is only one certain spot. But I was remembering how it was so swollen, and only during the day, for several days, and then went away, as suddenly as it had come. It was like the rash you had."

"My dear Mama,

"We saw Mr. Washfield, and ate breakfast at his place with nine English boys and girls – six boys. After breakfast we played musical chairs, croquet, chess, and other games. I liked it – the games and the girls and the boys.

"Hinzpeter has shown us a lithograph of the idea of the tunnel from Calais to Dover. I send you a copy I made as carefully as I could, showing you the pillars and things.

"We have collected smoky topaz when we are walking, and porphyrite in red, green and other colors. I bought my own specimen box today, and have some wonderful urchins and other sea creatures. Next month we are to go to the *Jardin de Hesperides* again, and I am looking forward to it more than I will say."

Vicky read Willy's letters eagerly as they arrived. He wrote in German mostly, and wrote quite well. His handwriting was messier than the other children's, but that could be expected.

Vicky picked up the soft, fluffy acacia blossom Willy had sent her. It had such a sweet smell.

But she couldn't enjoy it fully. Something worried her, and she couldn't discuss it with Fritz while he was so ill.

"Great Aunt Alexis". Willy had written mentioning this person. There was only one person it could be.

"Why do you write calling the Grand Duchess of Meckenburg-Schwerin 'Great Aunt Alexis'? Alex is the correct abbreviation, as we do not wish you to be so familiar as to call her Aunt Adina."

Vicky had thought that the Grand Duchess had gone on to Nice, as she said she would. But now she knew she was still in Cannes. Vicky shivered. She didn't want the boys to be in the Grand Duchess's company, particularly when they were so nearly alone. She hoped Hinzpeter wouldn't accept the invitations she knew would be sent. He was usually quite independent, and wouldn't be concerned about offending a Princess when he knew that Vicky and Fritz did not wish her company for his charges.

***

Kronprinz Palais, January 14, 1870

"Fritz?" Vicky looked up at him, trying to focus her eyes, but her head spun. She shook her head, but finally closed her eyes.

Fritz sat on the bedside, holding a letter in his hand. She had seen that he looked serious.

"What is it?" Vicky was very glad Fritz was better now, now that she was beginning to feel very ill.

"I have a letter from Mama – my Mama," he said. "She says that you are to install a Grand Maitresse and another older lady instantly."

"But I haven't had a Grand Maitresse these nine years," Vicky said. "I find someone when I need one for the grand events, but I don't need one *always*. Besides, it lowers our expenses not to have one."

Fritz sighed. "I saw her yesterday and she said you were to fill these vacancies immediately. She said she had written to you at Cannes about it, and had given you three weeks' time, and that it was extremely disobedient to have ignored it. Papa, too, has written about it, in just the same tone. You know he is usually sensible about such things."

Vicky opened her eyes and nodded. "Bring me my desk. I wish to write to some letters, and I'd better do it now, before I'm ill."

Fritz brought her desk, and handed her the letter he held. Vicky glanced it over.

"This sounds like Prince Charles's tone," she said, "and that last letter from your Papa did too. Are you certain they're really from them?"

"I saw her write this," Fritz said. "And Papa has written so at times, too."

Vicky sighed, and rolled her eyes. "You ought to have brought one of the overseers of the harem at Constantinople home with you, as they think management and order so wanting." Vicky laughed, looking up at Fritz. "Such a person could look after all the *females in the establishment* very well. Don't you think this would be a much more agreeable situation?"

CHAPTER TWENTY-FOUR
FIRE!

Cannes, January 19, 1870

"My dearest Mama,

"We walked to the hills above Cannes, and saw the great chain of the Alpes Maritimes. Vallauris lay in the valley to our left, and to the right the dark sea of the Gulf of Antibes, and Nice straight before us in the distance, at the foot of mountains which look nearly black, and appear to fall down into the sea.

"Henry and I saw the old ship the *Provence,* and saw the rooms where they used to keep the galley-slaves. I thought it quite horrible as I sat on the bench.

"We saw some Arabs like Papa described walking on the beach, standing still and watching the sun set. They gave us some dates, which I thought very tasty.

"You will like to hear we saw some pretty English steam-yachts. They were much cleaner than the other ships, as you always say. The exterior, too, seemed brand new.

"I hope Papa is well again, and you and *Geschwister*[64] too. Hinzpeter gave us something which he said you wished us to eat each day, and seemed to expect us to be ill, but we were not.

"Tell Papa I think of how I behaved each day when I go to bed, and thank God for what he has done, and try to be a better boy.

"P.S.

"I am reading *Bruin or the Great Bear Hunt,* which Uncle Louis gave me. I can find all the countries on the map, and I wish I could see all the

---

[64]   siblings

bears in the book – not to shoot them, as the boy in the book does, but to see all the different kinds. I did not know there were so many."

Bornstedt, January 25, 1870

Vicky sighed as the pine glade around the farmhouse came into view, and she listened intently for the few calls of the winter birds. It was the first sunny day since she'd been ill, and she had not been outside for ten days.

Fritz stepped down from the carriage, coming to help her. She walked unsteadily, and was glad when she reached the invalid's chair which waited outside the farmhouse. The snow had been cleared, and it was quite pleasant in the sun.

Fritz sat beside her in another chair, and took something from his pocket. He took her hand, and Vicky felt him slip a ring onto her finger. She held it up in the sunlight, the ring sparkling with a pearl surrounded by lapis lazuli.

"It's so beautiful, Fritz." She looked up at him, smiling. "And so like the bracelet."

Fritz nodded, smiling, and leaned over to kiss her forehead. The ring was very similar to the bracelet he had given her when they became engaged. Today was the twelfth anniversary of their marriage.

***

Kronprinz Palais

Vicky walked carefully up the staircase with Fritz's arm around her. Another invalid's chair awaited her at the entrance.

As Fritz pushed her through the rooms, she heard him say something to himself. "What?" She turned to look up at him.

Fritz shrugged. "I said nothing."

Vicky looked at him questioningly. "But I heard you – oh, Count Seckendorff," she said, seeing Count Seckendorff and Hedwig coming towards them. "Welcome back." She held out her hand, smiling.

Count Seckendorff returned her smile, bowing and kissing her hand. "I hope you are well, your – *Ihre Hoheit*[65]," he said, beginning in English and finishing in German, glancing at Fritz as he changed languages.

Vicky sighed. "I'm much better than I was. And this illness is expected. We were taking a remedy for – *something*," she said, glancing up at Fritz. He shook his head very slightly, and she nodded.

"Where are the letters you wished me to copy before my holiday?" Count Seckendorff asked. "I'll finish them, if you haven't already had someone do so."

Vicky nodded. "I had Hedwig begin…" Vicky paused, looking about. Hedwig had left the room. "Hedwig began, but she's not so swift as you and Valerie are. And you can do translations, too. Hedwig only speaks German. You do it all so splendidly, I must thank you again."

Count Seckendorff bowed deeply, turning away and coughing. Finally, he turned back.

Fritz held out his hand. "I must thank you as well. I certainly wish my mother-in-law to read my account of my journey, and it is not everyone whom one could trust to copy one's intimate letters. We do not have very many friends whom we can trust so implicitly."

Count Seckendorff shook Fritz's hand as soon as it was offered. When Fritz finished speaking, Count Seckendorff bowed once more, and again turned away, coughing more violently than before.

"I hope *you* are well," Vicky said. "I must say you look much better than you did when you left. But I suppose it's not uncommon for everyone to have a cold here this time of year."

Count Seckendorff nodded quickly and left the room. Vicky looked up at Fritz. "Count Seckendorff is an excellent translator. Did I tell you he was helping me to learn Italian while we were at Cannes?"

Fritz nodded, smiling. "I am very pleased. But how I wish you could have come with me. You have still only been to Italy once."

"Hinzpeter wrote that he'd taken the boys to Italy, to a splendid villa called Zirio, in San Remo. I wished I could've accompanied them."

"You have wished to learn since our tour, haven't you, and when we were in the Giant Mountains?" Vicky nodded. "Perhaps you may teach me, now," Fritz went on. "I am shamefully ignorant, as usual, although I have been there five times."

---

[65]   Your Highness

"One can't travel there that many times without picking up *some* of the language," Vicky laughed. "You probably understand all that I can. I didn't learn so very much." She sighed, looking out the window as Fritz closed the door to their bedroom. "We went out just in time. Look."

Fritz followed her gaze. It was beginning to snow, the first large flakes settling on the window sill.

"I hope Count Seckendorff is well," she said. "He was suffering from unrequited love of some lady, when we were in Cannes, and seemed quite miserable when he went away. Poor boy, I pitied him." She rose, throwing her arms around Fritz.

"That is not something we can sympathize in from shared experience," Fritz murmured, leaning down as if to kiss her. Their lips barely met, when he stood straight again, shaking his head. They must not be intimate in any way until it had been a month since she began to take the remedy.

Vicky sat down again, still looking up at Fritz. "Oh, but that reminds me – of something I *can* certainly sympathize with because of shared experience. I never told you in my letters, as I didn't wish to spoil your holiday with such things. It's Valerie. She left the court, because –"

"Because of Onkel Karl. I know." Fritz looked down at her, his expression hardening. "Mama told me."

Vicky nodded. She covered her eyes with her hands. Her head was beginning to ache again. "I'm not well enough to speak of it more," she said, her voice shaking.

***

Kronprinz Palais, February 2, 1870

Vicky's heart ached at Willy's absence on his birthday, but she spent much of the day in writing to him and to Mama. She'd already written a letter which she hoped would arrive soon after his birthday. She wished she'd written it before her illness, so that it could have been sent to arrive on the day.

The children were now also being given the remedy. Charlotte was extremely ill. She had always, since birth, had strange patches of orange, wrinkled skin on her temples. During the illness, this spread to cover her whole face. Vicky's heart ached at the sight of her.

"Poor Charlotte looks like a wrinkled old woman," she wrote to Mama. "Willy and Henry write that they haven't been ill in the least. My little Vicky was so, and Waldie too.

"Alice writes that Louis and she were both very ill, and Victoria, Ella and Irene, too. Ernie is perfectly well. It's such a relief that our boys, excepting Waldie, have no ill effects.

"Victoria, Ella and Charlotte were all ill in the same way, with frequent fainting, numbness in the legs and hands, and a strange interior sensation which Charlotte describes as her stomach being strangled, though without any sickness. Alice writes that the doctors were convinced Victoria had scarlet fever at first, but then the symptoms changed. They all cough up what looks like very perfect, white lace flecked with blood. Alice writes very alarmed at this, as Ella has always choked extremely easily, but perhaps this shall be better after she is well.

"Fritz and I, Waldie, and little Vicky all have the dreadful, swelling rash – poor Fritz has it in his throat and could barely speak for the week – with headache, fever and delirious spells. Poor Louis has both sets of symptoms; Irene was ill in a different way – Alice has not written details."

Vicky sat thinking as she finished her letter. She ought to tell Maroussy about the medicine lady. She knew Maroussy was a carrier of the same illness which affected Charlotte, and Louis had also become a carrier, though his and Alice's children had never exhibited symptoms until now.

*****

February 6, 1870

"Marianne, you're looking so well; I've never seen you so," Vicky cried, kissing her friend's cheek. "And the girls too," she said, embracing each of them in turn. "How's Fritzi? I'm delighted you were able to bring him," Vicky said, lifting the little boy in her arms and kissing him. "He's certainly gaining weight."

Marianne nodded, smiling. "Fritz Karl was away when we came home, and hadn't taken the boy with him, so I was able to bring him," she said. "He certainly is gaining weight. I am so pleased; he has always been so frail."

"How are your father and brother?" Vicky asked.

Marianne's face changed. "My Papa is not well, but he is not an invalid. I only hope I have an opportunity to see him again, and I wish my girls could have known him more." Tears hung in her eyes, but she wiped them away.

"Mia," Fritz Leo said as Vicky set him down. He turned to Mariechen, pulling at her hand and holding his arms up to be carried.

"He calls Mariechen Mia," Marianne whispered to Vicky, "and Louischen has taken to calling her so as well. She seems to like it, but Ebi and I don't seem to be able to break our old habit. She has always been my little Mariechen, *meine kleines Marichen*." Marianne turned, kissing her daughter's cheek. "It is strange to see her so big."

Mariechen had more color in her cheeks, and didn't look so thin as she usually did. Vicky looked up at her. She had grown even more since Vicky had seen her, and was quite a young lady now.

"I'm so glad to have you," Vicky said, embracing Marianne again. "How long is Fritz Karl to be away?"

"At least a week," Marianne replied. "I should like to remain here, if you are fine with that. I have no wish to return to the Schloss any earlier than I have too."

Vicky nodded. "Of course. Prince Charles *is* in residence there."

"And it is always so cold at the Marmor Palais in the winter," Marianne said. "It isn't built to be a winter home."

Louischen looked up at her mother, and at Vicky. "It's always summer here – and wherever you are, Aunty," she said.

***

Kronprinz Palais, half past twelve in the morning, February 8, 1870
Vicky lay in bed, humming softly to herself the old lullaby Papa used to sing. She smiled to herself. During the illness, she had felt the baby move very little, and she had felt very anxious on this account. Today, Baby had been very lively. Vicky was thankful. She had hoped that the remedy would have no ill effects.

She shivered, and rose to take her dressing-gown. As she did, she was startled by a touch on her shoulder, but it was Fritz.

"I thought you were asleep," she said, slipping on her dressing-gown.

Fritz shook his head, watching her. "Are you cold?" he asked, motioning to the dressing-gown.

Vicky nodded as she lay back down, her thoughts going back to a conversation four years ago.

Vicky had always worn her dressing-gown as well as her nightgown during the whole time she was expecting Charlotte, and afterwards, she had always worn it when she struggled with memories of Prince Charles. Fritz had taken this as a signal that she was 'inaccessible', as he had said.

Vicky smiled. Four years ago, they were sleeping in separate beds. She had been humming the lullaby, thinking about Baby and feeling her movements – little Vicky in those days – and she had worn her dressing-gown because she was cold.

"It has been a month," Fritz said, as he lit a candle and placed it on the table. He turned to face Vicky, his gaze running over her. There was something in his expression which she hadn't seen for months – indeed, for half a year.

"Yes, it *has* been a month – since I began to take the remedy," she whispered. "Do you feel well?" She glanced up, tried to meet his eye, then fixed hers on the pattern on the carpet. She felt herself blush intensely under the fire of his gaze, and felt overwhelmed with a shyness she hadn't felt in years.

He stepped forward, catching her in his arms and holding her close to him, in the same manner he had so long ago, on the second night of their marriage. Vicky felt her heart race as wildly as it had then.

"Are you still cold?" he murmured in her ear, his words punctuated by little kisses along her cheek and neck.

"No, how could I be?" Vicky laughed, as he unfastened her dressing-gown.

***

One in the morning

"Fritz," Vicky whispered, leaning over him to kiss him, her hair tumbling down over his face, "did you hear something?"

"I see and hear nothing but you," was his reply, as he reached up to touch her cheek. She lay down, laying her head on his shoulder. They lay looking into each other's eyes, he stroking her hair.

A smile passed over his face, and then his expression became very serious.

"What is it?" Vicky asked, unable to control a smile. "You look so solemn. What *can* it be, at a time like this?"

Fritz pursed his lips, glancing away for a moment. "Are you still afraid – afraid that I no longer find you attractive?" He spoke seriously, but his suppressed laughter showed in his eyes and heightened his voice.

"Fritz!" Vicky playfully slapped his hand. "Don't be a tease!" she laughed.

"Are you still cold?" Fritz murmured against her hair, drawing her to him. His voice was still full of laughter. "Perhaps you would like to put your dressing-gown back on."

Vicky shook her head, still laughing, but then she froze. There was the sound again.

"Did you really not hear it?" she asked.

Fritz shook his head. "It can be nothing but the pounding of our hearts, which have not been so fast nor so loud in months," he said, with another mischievous smile, kissing her passionately before he drew her again into his embrace.

***

Half past one in the morning

"There was the sound again."

Fritz sat up. "I did hear something, but – never mind," he said, drawing Vicky closer to him again. She had sat up, listening. "Come, it is nothing. There is probably a carriage passing by."

"But the sound came from inside – or above us, not from the street," Vicky said, closing her eyes and relaxing under his caresses.

She started up. There were definitely hurried footsteps outside their room. Now came a cry, a cry which was repeated and echoed farther away.

"Fire!" a man's voice screamed outside the bedroom door.

"Fire!" Vicky screamed, jumping up and running to the door.

"Vicky!" Fritz cried, starting up and catching her hand as she fumbled with the lock. "Come back here!"

"But there's a fire! We must get out! I knew something wasn't right!"

Fritz pulled her back toward the bed. "Get dressed!"

Vicky looked down, obviously realizing her situation for the first time since the scream at the door. She ran to the foot of the bed.

"My nightgown isn't here! Where did you put my nightgown?"

Fritz blew the flickering candle back into life. He had hurriedly put on his dressing-gown.

"Find one in your dressing-room," he said. "We must get out!" There were more cries and screams from outside their suite.

Vicky ran to the door again instead of to her dressing-room, but Fritz caught her. "Here it is!" He snatched her nightgown from the bed where it lay half covered by the blankets.

She slipped it on. "It's torn!" she cried. Fritz met her eye. There was a look of panic on her face. "You never tear my clothes!"

There was a large tear from the throat of the nightgown, but the top could still be tied. "It is well enough," Fritz said, going to the door. "There is no time for a dressing-gown as well. It may well be too late to go through the halls!"

"But I can't go out in a torn nightgown and nothing else!" Her voice sounded as if she was about to burst into tears. She sat down, hugging herself, rocking back and forth.

Fritz turned back to the bed, then ran to her dressing-room rather than attempting to search. He grabbed one of her dressing-gowns which he knew hung near the door. When he came back, she still sat, rocking and hugging herself. Her face still wore a look of panic and terror which did not seem unusual considering the situation, but something about it seemed familiar. He shook his head. There was no time to think about it.

"Put this on." He lifted her up, helping her to put on the dressing-gown. She clutched at his arm as he unlocked the door.

The roar of fire grew louder at first as they hurried through the halls. Many members of the household were also making their way through. In one passageway, volumes of smoke poured out towards them, and they had to turn and go a different way. The door of one of the staircases was locked, at which many cries echoed through the passageways.

Screams echoed through the building.

"We're trapped!"

"Help!"

"The door is locked!"

Finally, everyone began to gather in the courtyard. Fritz felt Vicky shiver. It was extremely cold out, and there was deep snow on the ground. Many others besides themselves had bare feet, but there was nothing to be done about it.

Fritz could see the firemen working. He looked at Vicky's face. She stared upwards at the roof of the palace, where flames roared and smoke billowed.

"Marianne!" Vicky called, as Marianne and the girls joined them, Mariechen carrying Fritz Leo. Mrs. Wakelin, the new nurse, appeared, leading little Vicky and carrying Waldie in her arms. The little ones were screaming.

"My feet! Why is the snow so hot?" Little Vicky cried. Fritz lifted her up in his arms, and she soon grew quiet.

"We're safe," Mrs. Wakelin called, "but I don't know where Charlotte is. She wasn't in her room."

"Charlotte! Where's Charlotte!" Vicky cried, the tone of panic returning to her voice.

"Charlotte? Where's Charlotte?" Louischen's voice echoed her words.

Fritz clutched Vicky's hand as she broke away from him, trying to run back to the Schloss.

"I'm here!" Charlotte's voice called from the last group who straggled into the courtyard.

"Oh, thank *Gott*!" Fritz cried. He handed little Vicky to Marianne and ran to Charlotte, catching her up in his arms. "Is everyone out?" he called as he returned to Vicky's side, setting Charlotte down and smiling as they threw their arms around each other.

The firemen had already been at work for some time. Soon, there was a sizzle and a hiss, and a great cloud of smoke, but the fire appeared finally to be nearly extinguished.

"Fritzi is finally getting rather heavy," Fritz heard Mariechen whisper to Vicky. "He never was before, but he is growing well this year." She gently set the little boy down.

As his bare feet touched the snow, he cried, "*Scheiße!*", holding up his arms to be picked up again.

Mariechen covered his mouth, leading him a little away from Louischen, kneeling down and speaking to him in a whisper with a very serious look on her face.

Fritz glanced at Marianne. Her eyes followed Mariechen and Fritz Leo, while she held Ebi and Louischen's hands. From her expression, it was obvious she had heard the boy's exclamation.

***

"Everyone must get their feet out of this snow," Vicky heard Fritz call. Many carriages had been drawn up in the courtyard, being pulled by people rather than horses. Fritz, Count Seckendorff, and several of the firemen stood in a row, arms interlinked, letting people through who wore no shoes, and holding back the rest. The crowd still milled about, but no one cried or screamed anymore. Finally, Fritz joined Vicky, Waldie, and little Vicky, as well as Marianne, Fritz Leo and the girls in a carriage. They sat rubbing warmth back into each other's feet.

"My feet hurt!" little Vicky cried as Mrs. Wakelin rubbed them.

***

Kronprinz Palais, Berlin, February 9, 1870

Vicky wore her dressing-gown in spite of being nestled in Fritz's arms, and she felt him shiver as well, in spite of the extra blanket spread on the bed. All the windows had to be open because of the strong odor of smoke.

"I'm so thankful it isn't worse." Nothing had been lost except for old furniture which resided in the attics, most of which was so old it broke if one attempted to sit in it. Much of the roof and loft were gone, but only a few rooms of the interior were touched.

"But it makes me shiver to think of *that*," Vicky whispered, pointing upwards. The floor of the room above them had nearly burnt through.

She felt Fritz shudder. "It would have to have been much worse to convince me to move back into the Groß Schloss," he whispered. "I would not have you live there again for the world."

Vicky blushed again. "Only think if we *had* been there, and I had run out as I tried to," she laughed. "In front of *everyone* – not only our suite."

"It's so funny now." Vicky looked down, not meeting Fritz's gaze "But my fear was so real, and there were other fears on top of it."

"What do you mean, other fears?"

"The memory of when my arm caught on fire. And – and – my nightgown. I couldn't wear a torn nightgown and nothing else to go out. It – it – the laundry!" Her voice broke and she hid her face against his chest.

Fritz nodded, remembering the look of panic and terror on her face, and the way she covered her chest with her arms when she put on the torn nightgown.

"I remember," he said softly, stroking her hair, "when I came home, the day after my birthday, you were clutching your torn chemise to you. You would not let me see what it was at first, until I tried to kiss you, and I took it from you. That is when I knew – I *knew* –"

Vicky nodded, the old look of fear creeping into her eyes again. "I didn't even know I brought it with me till you tried to take it. And I couldn't speak of it! But – Fritz," she whispered, leaning her head on his shoulder, "these old fears haven't come to haunt me in so long," she said with a little shiver.

He kissed her forehead, stroking her hair.

"I said you never tear my clothes, and that *is* true. You've always been so – *polite*. Why, this is only the *second* time – and in *twelve* years" – yesterday had been the twelfth anniversary of her first arrival in Berlin – "that you didn't lay my nightgown out neatly at the foot of the bed, where I always leave it during the day. The sight of that tear brought back – that situation – and – I could see – him – tearing – and feel him – touch me – oh!"Vicky's voice was broken by gasps and sobs, and she hid her face against Fritz's chest again.

Cannes, February 1870

"My dearest Mama,

"I was very frightened when Uncle Abbat read Papa's letter about the fire in Berlin, I hope all of you are safe and we did not lose our things.

"I have begun to write a fairy tale, the first I ever have. I hope you and Papa would like me to read it to you and *Geschwister*[66] when we are home. I have read part of it to Hinzpeter and to Henry, and they laughed a lot. It is about a knight who encounters a witch who traps him in a burning house, and I do not know what will happen yet."

____

[66]   siblings

PART FIVE:
THE THIRD WAR

CHAPTER TWENTY-FIVE
HIS LITTLE DAUGHTER

Kronprinz Palais, March 12, 1870

"Vicky, I wish we could live here always," Marianne sighed, looking up from the picture she was painting. "That week last month was so pleasant, in spite of the fire and the cold." She sighed again.

The Kronprinz Palais was nearly back to normal, and was no longer full of workmen, nor freezing cold inside because of the windows thrown open to the wind.

"Would you not rather live in Anhalt, with your own family?" Vicky asked, putting her letter down.

Marianne shrugged. "Not if it means leaving Fritzi behind. But –" Marianne's face changed, her cheeks growing crimson. "I don't think I told you Hubert was in Anhalt while we were." She looked down, looking away, but not hiding the smile and blush which made her face glow.

"I thought you were looking *very* well when you came back," Vicky said, smiling. "And the girls were too."

Marianne nodded. "Albert of Altenburg and August of Oldenberg were there. Mariechen and Ebi are very fond of them. But – I think I told you – Mariechen feels it impossible to let herself care for Albert, as he is in the army here, and you know she can't help wishing to leave Berlin."

"It must be hard for her," Vicky said, squeezing Marianne's hand. She took up her letter again. "Have you heard from Leopold Sigmaringen? I think you're very good friends."

Marianne blushed slightly as she nodded. "He is always very kind and charming, but he is so with everyone. Is he to go to Spain? I couldn't make out what he meant in his letter."

"I don't know. I hope not. Spain is such an unruly throne, I don't suppose anyone is envious for the position. I heard other Princes have been suggested, and all have refused. I believe Leopold has refused. His life in Sigmaringen is so pleasant, I can't imagine him wishing another. He has no adventurous spirit like his brother Karl, and seemed quite puzzled by Karl's wish to go to Rumania."

Marianne nodded. "I suppose his letter could be interpreted to say that he has refused. His father certainly wishes him to go."

"I believe my Papa-in-law has refused the proposition altogether," Vicky said, "and Prince Hohenzollern will certainly obey his King. I don't even believe it would do any good if he were Minister-President, as he was before my Papa's death, except that it would mean Bismarck wasn't."

Vicky glanced over her letter again. "That reminds me, I must write to Mama on the matter. Fritz wished me to, but I wish he would do so himself. I don't like to be mixed up in a matter of this sort."

"Why? I thought you – like your Papa – liked playing the diplomat," Marianne said, smiling.

"Papa didn't '*play* the diplomat'. England didn't wish him to be involved in her politics, and he had to have *something* to do. Mama was glad not to have to deal with Foreign Affairs so much." Vicky rose to look out of the window. "Fritz is coming home; I didn't expect him till evening. But as to your question, it's a difficult situation which I don't wish to be involved with. You know they wouldn't hesitate to blame my 'meddling' if anything went wrong.

"France doesn't wish for a Prussian Prince to be King of Spain, as they would think they would have to keep up their border there, as well as their border to Germany, and they think we're attempting to encircle them.

"Affairs have been tense between the French Government and ours since the Luxembourg crisis three years ago, though the Emperor and Empress are as kind as ever personally."

Vicky and Fritz, with Alice and Louis, had stopped to visit the Emperor Napoleon and Empress Eugenie on their way home from France.

Marianne closed her eyes. "I am very grateful for your explanation, but I still can never comprehend the political intricacies like you can," she said.

Vicky shook her head. "You understand things quite well. I know you do! I've heard you speak of them. But I'm glad you're so modest about it; I only wish you realized you understood."

Babelsberg, Potsdam, April 18, 1870

Fritz sat at the Council table across from his father. Also at the table were Prince Hohenzollern and his sons, Leopold and Fritz; Treschkow, the head of the King's military household; Roon, the Minister of War and Fritz Karl's former Governor; Wrangel; General Prim, the Spanish emissary; and Onkel Karl.

Fritz had been astonished at receiving his father's invitation to the Council. This had happened so infrequently in the last years, he no longer expected it at all.

"I am very thankful Bismarck is away," Fritz had told Vicky before he left Berlin. Bismarck was ill and had retreated to his family estate, far from Berlin. "Perhaps Papa will be sensible. And Onkel Karl is always more careful where the Sigmaringen family is concerned."

Vicky had nodded. "They are some of the few people he seems really to care about – and even more so since Anton's death. He doesn't want another of them to die."

"One certainly can't rely on protection from an army which has made many revolutions in the last forty years," the King was saying to Prince Hohenzollern. "But I know you wish your son to be the King of Spain, just as you wished one to be the King of Rumania. I would not wish such an unstable throne for my son."

"But," General Prim began in heavily accented Spanish-German, "Your Majesty, I speak with respect of your opinions, but I received a letter saying that you would raise no opposition if a Prince of your House showed an inclination to our throne."

Fritz saw his father's expression turn to a glare, as he turned to each in turn, studying the others' reactions to the emissary's statement. Finally, he spoke. "Have you said such a thing?" he asked Prince Hohenzollern.

Prince Hohenzollern shook his head. "And neither of my sons show any inclination," he said, nodding to Leopold and Fritz. "Leopold is satisfied to remain my heir, and Fritz is happy in his military life." Both of his sons nodded, but didn't speak.

"But France suspects us," Wrangel cried. "Suspects us of encircling them! We must not let them believe ill of us unfounded!"

"If we make a plain declaration that we are not interested," the King said, looking at the Sigmaringens, father and sons, "then there is nothing for France to suspect."

"Very well," Prince Hohenzollern agreed. "To keep peace with France, it would be worthwhile. You shall write the letters," he said, nodding to Leopold and General Prim.

"All of Germany would most likely rise up if France did strike," Onkel Karl said slowly. He seemed about to say more, but remained silent.

"But we shall have no war," Fritz said, "if the Sigmaringens refuse Spain. They can have no reason for striking." He paused, looking towards Onkel Karl, but looking up, not meeting his eye. "And we must have no war."

Neues Palais, Potsdam, June 12, 1870

"Vicky is very well – incredibly so. We just returned from a two hour walk, and she said she was not in the least exhausted, and this in her condition."

Vicky smiled as she heard Fritz greet Abbat, who came with him to the little table she and Fritz usually sat at when dining alone. She did feel very well and agile, considering that she was expecting the baby to come at any time.

Abbat bent to kiss her cheek. "I am thankful you are both so well again, and that you shall have no lasting effects from –" He trailed off, blushing as he met Vicky's eye. "Fritz told me everything," he whispered. "But I do wish I could have done something to protect you." He looked down, not meeting her eye, and squeezed her hand.

Vicky shrugged and smiled at him as he took his seat. "It was God's Will that we should have our little *Möhrchen*. I wouldn't have her be anything she isn't."

Fritz nodded and smiled at her when Abbat glanced at him.

"You'll have received Mama's letter," Vicky said. "We would have liked very much to have you as a brother, but you won't blame me for saying I don't wish any of my sisters to live here, nor do we wish to lose the boys' guardian – the only possible one."

Abbat nodded, and a strange look passed over his face. He was silent, gazing out the window and not eating for several minutes. Finally, he sighed, and glanced at Fritz and then Vicky. "Will you have the children come here? The little ones particularly – you understand, don't you?" He looked at Fritz as he finished speaking.

Fritz nodded, and Vicky took his hand. "You long for a family of your own?" she asked softly. He nodded. "We're so grateful for you staying with the boys for so long."

"It was no trouble remaining so long in the South of France – what a paradise it is there!" He laughed, and Vicky was glad to see a more cheerful expression on his face.

***

Neues Palais, Noon, June 14, 1870

The sword slashed rapidly through the leafy foliage of the bushes, the blade glittering in the sunlight as it shaved off the small, lower branches of a tree. Vicky blinked, and the sword seemed to have disappeared. But there it was, standing erect on its point, the tip stuck in an enormous old tree stump. She watched it, wondering what would come next, and jumped as a small knife whizzed through the air to stick in another tree a couple of yards from her.

Vicky clapped. "Very good! *Sehr gut!*"

Willy jumped up and down. "When can I try?" he asked, running to Fritz, scooping up a handful of the loose leaves and throwing them up so they fell in a shower at Fritz's feet. The boys had returned home at the beginning of May.

Fritz shook his head, laughing. He looked down into his son's eyes, putting his hands on the boy's shoulders. Vicky couldn't hear what was said, but Willy's face became serious. "I don't want you to go away again, Papa!" he cried, as Fritz threw his arms around him. "But you must, if Großpapa orders it."

Fritz turned towards Vicky, and crouched down by the side of her chair, still breathing heavily. He took the satchel down, which hung evenly across his back. "Sword-fighting is no more work with this on than it is unloaded," he said as Vicky attempted to lift it. It was extremely heavy. "It distributes the weight perfectly, and does not make one's arms feel as if they would fall off, either." He wore, also, his new cuirass, a conjoined breast-plate and back plate of armor.

Vicky nodded as she rose, walking slowly across the field. "It's what you wished your men had in the last war, when you said they had to leave their provisions behind," she said, closing her eyes tight at a sudden jolt of pain in her back. She breathed slowly, and kept walking.

"*Ja*. But, Vicky, are you well?" Fritz asked, rising and hurrying to her side. He put his arm around her supportively. "Lean on me," he said.

"Oh!" she groaned. "It's nothing serious yet – but the time's come."

Fritz watched as Vicky paced slowly back and forth, groaning softly. She had been present at luncheon with Fritz and Willy, but had not eaten. At five o'clock, Fritz had sent for the doctors, the midwife, the British Ambassador and the head of the King's household, whom they wished to be present in the next room as witnesses of the birth. Another hour had passed, and Fritz could hear the carriages arriving.

Vicky sat by Fritz's side on the sofa in her sitting-room, leaning her head on his arm. Now she rose, but didn't go into the bedroom. Fritz followed her.

"Where are you going?" he called.

"I want to be on the garden side," she called back. "I had a bed set up there the other day. I don't want to be stuck in bed with no view, as I was after Willy's birth."

Fritz caught up with her, gently putting his arm around her. "Why do you say such a thing? You have never been laid up for so long again. Is – is something wrong? Tell me." Fritz tried to keep the fear out of his voice, but he knew his face and eyes would show his feelings.

Vicky looked up at him as he cradled her face in his hands. "I don't know. Something – oh!" Her face turned pale, and she leaned more heavily against him.

Fritz followed her closely, but she insisted she could walk alone. She went to the closet, spreading the extra sheets on the bed herself. Finally, however, as she knelt down, Fritz saw her face turn very pale again as she tried to rise, and she sank down, not moving.

Ach! Gott! Do not let it be like Wilhelm's birth! Fritz prayed silently. "Vicky?" He knelt down at her side, breathing a sigh of relief when he saw that her eyes were open.

***

Half past eight in the evening

"Oh! Help me!" Vicky cried, looking up at Fritz as she clutched at his hands. His heart ached at the look in her eyes, which were glazed over in pain. He crouched on the bed, pillows piled around them, supporting her as best he could. His hands ached from her grip, as they had during Wilhelm's birth.

One of the doctors came to Fritz's side, his face very grave. "This must not go on," he said. "The labor is not progressing properly, and she must not grow exhausted."

Fritz nodded. "What do you think necessary? Have you discussed it with Fraulein Stahl?"

The doctor nodded, and whispered in his ear, but Fritz couldn't hear him over Vicky's sudden scream.

"All will be well soon, *meine* Vicky," he murmured, kissing her damp forehead and stroking her hair. He leaned close to the doctor again, and then nodded. "Let me do it."

The doctor looked at him, surprised, but returned to a table, taking several things and bringing them to the bed.

Vicky watched through half-open eyes as Fritz took a cloth and a bottle from the doctor's hands. He opened the bottle carefully, pouring a couple of drops onto the cloth.

Another overwhelming pain wrenched through her as she realized what was happening. She couldn't restrain another scream. Birth shouldn't be like this! But at least help was here; they weren't surrounded by three panicking doctors who were incompetent in such a situation, as they had been at Willy's birth.

The pain eased, and Vicky met Fritz's eye. A look of inexpressible pain sat there, and brought fresh tears to Vicky's eyes.

"I don't want to see you suffer," he murmured, kissing her forehead.

Vicky nodded, reaching up to touch his cheek, murmuring "I trust you". She could feel another wave of pain beginning as he put the cloth over her nose and mouth, but she no longer felt the urge to scream. Soon, everything went black.

Five minutes past nine in the evening, June 14, 1870

"Wah! Wah!"

Fritz held the little girl in his arms as the doctors worked over Vicky. He couldn't take his eyes off the small, pale face, the little hairless head, and the little hand which reached up towards him. The little eyes blinked, and he saw they were just the same shade of blue as Vicky's.

"Fritz?" he heard Vicky's weak voice call. He turned towards her, sitting by her side and placing the baby in her arms.

"Oh, my baby," she said weakly, pressing the little one to her heart and looking up at Fritz, the color returning rapidly to her face. "*Our* little daughter," she murmured, leaning against Fritz as he took her in his arms, the words half a whisper and half a sigh.

June 19, 1870

Fritz sat on the bed, his arm around Vicky, watching the sleeping infant in her arms. "*Meine kleine Tochter*[67]," he whispered.

"Mama? Why doesn't Baby have any hair?" little Vicky asked. She lay on Vicky's other side, and Fritz had thought her asleep.

"Charlotte didn't have so very much when she was born," Vicky said. "Siggy didn't either," she whispered, looking up to meet Fritz's eye.

---

[67]   My little daughter

Yesterday had been the fourth anniversary of Siggy's death; it had also been the day of the Thanksgiving service after the birth of another Princess.

"Why didn't I know Siggy?" little Vicky asked. She still almost always spoke in English. For the first three years, she never spoke a German word, although she obviously understood German as thoroughly as the others.

"You were only nine weeks old when – he died," Vicky said, turning to put her arm around little Vicky. "Come, here is your little sister. Siggy loved to watch you and help take care of you when you were born," Vicky went on, trying to keep the tears out of her voice.

Vicky had been greatly astonished when Willy hardly seemed interested in his new little sister. He always had before, and all the others had been, little Vicky hardly wishing to leave the room.

"It's almost bedtime," Vicky whispered, but little Vicky clung to her.

"I want to watch Baby sleep."

Before Vicky could answer, there was a knock at the door. "Rosa?" Vicky called. "*Herein*[68]."

Rosa entered, handing a telegram to Fritz. Vicky watched his face as he read the message.

"It cannot be true!" Fritz rose, taking little Vicky in his arms and carrying her to the room where she slept. He quickly returned. "Papa says that he received a letter stating that Leopold has accepted the throne of Spain!" Fritz walked through the room, returning to the bedside. "Papa only left for Ems in the confidence that there should be no political worries. But – how? Prince Hohenzollern has written to me quite frequently, and never mentioned it again since the Council."

"Perhaps it isn't true," Vicky said. "Perhaps someone misunderstood it?"

"No," Fritz said, shaking his head, his face very grave. "Papa says the letter is from Prince Hohenzollern himself. He says that General Prim had written stating that they had received indications that we were still open to the possibility, and he encouraged his son to accept. Leopold did so this time, believing that Papa would not oppose it."

Vicky met Fritz's eye. "What will the Emperor Napoleon say, after being assured that nothing of the kind would happen?"

---

[68]   Come in

"Has he received that assurance?" Fritz asked, still pacing. "I hope he has not. If he has, his government may consider this as an occasion for war."

***

Neues Palais, July 1, 1870

"My dearest Mama," Vicky wrote, "Leopold Sigmaringen *has* accepted the throne after all. Everyone is in a tumult about it, and the papers in France and Germany show inclination to war on both sides.

"Baby is a darling, and Fritz was delighted as you can imagine with *his* little girl. But in these circumstances, her Mama's heart can't be so light as it ought to be. I am well, and strong considering what the birth was, which Fritz wrote about to you.

"Now we can only pray that Leopold will again withdraw, making it plain that his refusal is for now and forever, and that France will see things sensibly.

"I have heard that the King, you, Cousin Leopold and the Emperor Napoleon himself have all written to Leopold and Prince Hohenzollern begging them to do so, but peace is not confirmed. France is indignant at what they perceive as a challenge, and you can imagine that all of Germany feels a challenge from France – from a Bonaparte – very heavily, with the Great Napoleon's tyranny over Germany being so fresh a memory for the older generations."

Neues Palais, July 4, 1870

"Fritz calls her the prettiest of our children as a newborn," Fritz heard Vicky say as she took Baby back from Marianne, who sat at her bedside. "But – oh, she's *his* little girl, at last," Vicky murmured, pressing her lips to the baby's forehead.

"She is lovely," Marianne murmured. "And you say she has no ill effects from the illness, or the remedy?" Vicky shook her head. "Or from the birth? It was not like Wilhelm's?"

Vicky shook her head. "She didn't have her arms twisted up behind her head like he did, poor boy. And everything was so much shorter. And we didn't have to wait for the arrival of the specialist this time."

"Fritz," Marianne said, turning as he came in, "I must speak with you." Her voice was constrained.

"Are you strong enough to hear her?" Fritz whispered in Vicky's ear. Vicky nodded.

"I cannot – I cannot stay with him any longer!" Marianne stammered at first, and the words seemed to burst from her lips. "You know that our house laws allow separation without divorce," she began.

"*Ja,*" Fritz said, "but one must have the King's permission for such a thing."

"You can help me, can't you?" Marianne cried, wringing her hands. She rose, and began to pace through the room. "I cannot – cannot stay any longer! I told you before – or I told Vicky – they have begun to take the boy to their vile parties, and to teach him to drink, and to say such things – oh! To hear it from a child's lips is terrible!"

Fritz reached out to take her hand as she passed him, but she shook off his hand, continuing to pace.

"And my – my poor girls! It is bad enough to have to bear the whims of Fritz Karl, and how he twists my words, forbids the simplest requests I make – and, oh, that is enough!" Marianne sobbed, hiding her face in her hands.

"At least we know *they* aren't his. I mean, I always felt – at least Prince Charles is not so vile as to do *that,*" Vicky said, speaking slowly and hiding her face.

"Oh, yes, Mariechen is as safe as Charlotte is," Marianne said bitterly, "but if only the others *were his* little girls. Either granddaughters or even his own daughters! I would willingly sacrifice myself!" Marianne turned, meeting Vicky's eye, then Fritz's.

Fritz looked down, and saw Vicky, too, had dropped her gaze. He felt sick at the thought Marianne's words brought to his mind. "I would have willingly given up myself if I had known it would mean I did not have to watch my children's innocence torn apart!" Marianne went on, pacing back and forth again. "But, you know, when I was engaged to Fritz Karl, my – mother – made my father-in-law promise –"

"Your mother?" Vicky began, and then nodded, obviously remembering what Marianne had told her shortly after her arrival in Berlin.

"You remember – I told you, didn't I? That my Mama-in-Law is really my mother?" Marianne whispered. Vicky nodded. "She made my father-in-law promise never to touch her daughters. He made that promise, and he has kept it – to the letter. He would never touch her *daughters*. But she never said anything about her granddaughters.

"If only I had never fallen in love with *him* – you know who my love is! And who he looks like! If only I had never had children besides Mariechen, or others with her father! Oh! But I long for love," she turned, gazing at Vicky and Fritz.

Fritz watched her, feeling that it was impossible to speak. He had never seen such terrible pain in anyone's face as he saw in Marianne's. "I long for a love, such as I have seen in your house," she said, the tears flooding to her eyes again. "And I have never, *never* had that. My love – of course, he is so much older than I, and we are apart so much, he has never been absolutely faithful to me." She shook her head. "But that matters little, in comparison to my poor girls – my poor Ebi! Three times, now, three times!" She wrung her hands.

"Ebi is –" Vicky trailed off, unable to meet Marianne's eye. "Again?" Marianne nodded, her lips trembling as Vicky took her hands.

Neues Palais, July 15, 1870

"How I wish there was something to do for Marianne," Vicky said, looking up from a letter as Fritz came in. "This is from your Aunt Marie. It makes my heart ache! Marianne told her she *wished* this war would take place – but then she said she didn't mean *that*. It's just that it would be such a relief to her and the girls for Fritz Karl and Prince Charles both to be gone, and Fritz Leo left at home." She looked down, taking Fritz's hand. "It's very hard –"

Vicky broke off as the door opened and a footman came in, clicked his heels, and announced, "Prinz Friedrich Karl."

The footman withdrew, and Vicky stared, clutching at Fritz's hand nervously as Fritz Karl appeared.

He came toward them, taking a seat at the table and leaning his head down. There was none of his usual brusque, swaggering manner, none of his usual hostility. There was simply a puzzled, troubled look on his face as he slowly raised his head again.

"Fritz," he said abruptly, "Marianne is insane – literally *insane*. There's no other explanation for it."

CHAPTER TWENTY-SIX
"I MIGHT NEVER SEE HIM AGAIN!"

"**M**arianne is *not* insane," Vicky burst out, but Fritz squeezed her hand harder than usual, and he shook his head very slightly when she looked up.

"What makes you think she is insane?" Fritz asked calmly, following Fritz Karl's movements without meeting his eye.

"Everything! She says I've beaten her, and that I have done – done *unspeakable* things, to the little girls." Fritz Karl spoke in a soft voice, in a higher tone than Vicky had ever heard from him. As he spoke the last words, disgust became obvious in his voice. "Unspeakable things such as what Papa does," Fritz Karl went on, the disgust showing all the more obviously on his face. He shuddered. "I would *never* do such things with *a girl*."

Vicky glanced at Fritz and opened her mouth to speak, but he shook his head again.

"I would gladly live in a different residence than her – such a woman is impossible to live with!" Fritz Karl went on, "But I don't see why she torments *me* so about it. I'm away so much, I can't possibly be a nuisance to her. And there are plenty of unclaimed rooms in the Schloss, where she lives in the winter."

Fritz was still silent, and still pressed Vicky's hand in a way she knew meant he wished her not to speak. He simply nodded.

"You will speak to your father – the King – won't you, Fritz?" Fritz Karl said. "I can't speak to him without Papa finding out, and you do not know what my life is with his constant bullying." Fritz Karl leaned forward, covering his eyes. "It makes my head ache. My nerves can't bear such shouting and going on, and now with Marianne's constant ill-treatment and violent temper, I don't know how I can live at home!"

"We will –" Vicky began again, but Fritz silenced her again.

"She never used to be so," Fritz Karl said. "She has such an unreasonable temper, it makes me long to be away! But military life is no pleasure to me, you know. And Papa shall go to the war as well. Sometimes I wish we could change places, he be in command of the Second Army, and I have my leisure at the Royal Headquarters, and be allowed to live a pleasant life for a change!"

He shook his head, covering his eyes and sighing as if exhausted. "Sometimes I wish he would go away and I might never see him again," Fritz Karl murmured. He rose suddenly, and he looked at Fritz. "I have something to say I would rather not in front of her," he said awkwardly, looking at Vicky.

Fritz did not meet his gaze. "If it is something you cannot say in front of her, then I have no wish to hear it."

Fritz Karl shook his head. "I must say it! I really must believe Marianne has gone insane! There's no other explanation for the things she says I've done! I said before – I would *never* do such things with – *a girl.*"

Vicky watched him as he turned away, pacing the room. She had rarely seen him blush before, but during this conversation he was often blushing from embarrassment, and he was without the usual flushed look he had when he had been drinking. Fritz rose, following him toward the door.

Fritz Karl lowered his voice, stepping closer to Fritz. "You – I can tell *you* the truth. You know I've always been *immune to feminine* beauty," he said. He spoke very softly, but he was near enough that Vicky could hear every word.

Fritz stepped backwards several paces, continuing to back away until Vicky took his hand. He had been about to run into the little table.

"I will speak to Papa," Fritz said hurriedly, offering his hand to Fritz Karl. They shook hands, and Fritz Karl turned to leave.

Fritz turned to Vicky. "I must see that he really leaves," he whispered, and left the room.

***

Vicky sat at the table, waiting for Fritz to return. She thought of ringing for Mrs. Wakelin to bring Baby, but finally, the door opened. Fritz's face looked very serious as he entered, holding a packet of letters or telegrams.

"Benedetti has gone to see Papa," he said. Benedetti was the French Ambassador to Prussia. "Papa has written to Bismarck, and to me, and ordered his telegram to Bismarck to be made public. But I cannot believe Papa would write or speak so roughly, particularly when he has not been in the company of either Bismarck or Onkel Karl of late." Fritz sat down, glancing over the letters again.

"What is it?" Vicky asked. "What has happened?"

"Benedetti came to ask that Papa authorize him to telegraph to the Emperor that Papa bound himself never to consent for any of the Hohenzollern-Sigmaringen family to become the King of Spain." Fritz glanced at Vicky before he continued.

"He – Papa – wrote me that he refused rather sternly to do this, and that he could not do so without hearing whether Leopold had actually withdrawn, and had not already been declared King. You know," Fritz continued, looking at Vicky, "that the Spanish Parliament must approve a candidate's Kingship." Vicky nodded.

"Papa told Bernedetti that he refused to see him again, and would send the message by an adjutant when he received it, and he had nothing more to say to the Ambassador."

"But that sounds reasonable," Vicky said. "Of course one can't give such a promise if one doesn't know if such a promise is too late!"

"Exactly!" Fritz said. "But the French press has whipped itself up into a war rage, and this is like a red cape to a bull." He paused, looking at the letters, but not reading. "But I do not consider this a cause for war. It is absurd to put two countries' armies at risk for such a thing! Peace must be preservable!"

Neues Palais, July 19, 1870

Fritz stood outside the open schoolroom door, listening to the children's conversation. Wilhelm, Charlotte and Heinrich were just sitting down to dinner with Hinzpeter, o'Danne and Mademoiselle d'Arcourt. "Papa says war is likely," came in Wilhelm's voice.

"*Oui*, and it's all my poor stupid Emperor can do," Mademoiselle d'Arcourt said.

"You call your Sovereign stupid!" Wilhelm looked up at her, his astonishment showing plainly on his face. "Anyone who said such a thing of Großpapa here would be arrested, wouldn't they, Ditta?" Wilhelm looked at Charlotte.

Charlotte opened her mouth to speak when Fritz entered. "Oh, Papa, what is it?" Charlotte cried, jumping up and throwing her arms around him.

"Mademoiselle," Fritz cried, going on in French, "your countrymen have lost their heads! They want war!" He knelt down to be at eye-level with the children, looking Heinrich in the eye as the others crowded around.

"Papa, I wish I was old enough to go with you," Wilhelm cried, meeting his father's eye.

"Thank *Gott* you are not!" Fritz gathered the children in his arms, kissing them on the tops of their heads. He felt a great lump in his throat. "*Ach! Meine Kinder,*" he cried, his voice breaking, "what a disaster, what a tragedy this is!"

July 21, 1870

Vicky lay in bed, her pillow wet with tears, clutching her baby to her heart. France had declared war two days ago, and French mobilization had already begun before that.

Fritz must leave within a few days. Little Sophie's Christening would be on the 24th – Charlotte's tenth birthday – and Fritz would most likely leave the day after.

"France will likely have already occupied the Rhineland before we can reach it!" Vicky had cried when Fritz told her the news. "What will happen to Alice, and to Vivi! Where – how will they live?"

"Papa has offered for Alice to come here," Fritz had said, taking Vicky in his arms and soothing her like a child.

"But how can the Emperor justify this? It was a provocation, but not so serious as this! It's an insult to demand a promise one can't give!"

Fritz Karl and Abbat were already prepared to go to the war, but no one was to leave until after the Christening. Abbat was to be one of the sponsors, or Godparents, as was Marianne's sister, the Duchess of Altenburg.

Vicky had seen her father-in-law a few days ago, and thought he looked ten years older. He had always appeared much more youthful than he was, in spite of his white hair.

Uncle Ernst had arrived in Berlin, and he, too, had broken down during a conversation with Vicky and Fritz about the war. Vicky was glad he was to be in Fritz's army.

There were to be three parts of the army:

The First Army would be accompanied by the King himself, but under the command of General Karl Friedrich Steinmetz. This would be the Grand, or Royal, Headquarters, where Vicky knew Prince Charles would also be.

The Second Army would be under Fritz Karl's command, and – as Fritz had said – that of all the best officers, whose assistance Fritz Karl, no doubt, would be in need of.

The Third Army was to be Fritz's. This reverse in Fritz's and Fritz Karl's military rank rankled in Vicky's mind the first day she was aware of it, until Fritz explained the reason.

The South Germans, consisting of the armies of Wurttemberg, Bavaria, and Baden – many of whom were extremely anti-Prussian — would be under Fritz's command. All of Germany would fight against France, but the King had felt it impossible to place these men under Fritz Karl's command.

Vicky was well aware that the South Germans would revolt under Fritz Karl, and that they would follow Fritz with no question.

***

July 22, 1870

Vicky sat on the edge of the bed, her head in her hands. She still felt so weak. With all the emotion and turmoil, she wasn't recovering properly from the birth, which had already been so difficult. Her head ached at the constant clank of spurs and swords, and the raucous singing in the streets. She could hardly bear to have the windows open, it was so loud even in Potsdam, though she longed for fresh air, and to enjoy the summer as she had expected.

Baby was thriving, and tomorrow Fritz would be able to spend the day at home. Vicky clung to this idea, hoping and praying that a last, precious day together would not be taken from them.

Today, Sir William Russell, who was to be the British Foreign Correspondent during the war, was coming to see her. She had asked Count Seckendorff to bring him to the garden outside her sitting-room.

She rose, slowly walking to her dressing room. She was still in her nightgown, though it was the middle of the day. She must at least wear her dressing-gown to receive such guests.

As she stepped outside, she glanced backwards. All the blinds were closed. This would be a gloomy welcome for her guests.

Soon, she heard voices – Count Seckendorff, Augustus Loftus – the British Ambassador – and a stranger's voice, who must be Russell.

"Yes, everything is ready, as we may start at any time," Count Seckendorff was saying. Fritz had wished Count Seckendorff to remain at home with her, as he had during the Danish war, but he had refused, insisting that he wished for the experience of the war.

"I'm very glad to see another English face," she said, shaking hands with Russell and nodding to the others. "What a dreadful time this is! And how will it end? How many will come back?" Vicky couldn't keep these words back; the thoughts had haunted her mind for days. "It's our harvest time, besides, and the French will ravage the Rhineland before we can reach it!"

***

Neues Palais, ten in the evening, July 23, 1870

"I shall not have one of the Sigmaringens as my Aide-de-camp in this war," Fritz said, putting his arm around Vicky. "They are far too mixed up in the business."

"Who shall be with you?" Vicky asked. "You said that Mischke shall go with you, and I know Count Seckendorff goes – he told me – and I know who your staff shall be, but who will be your Royal Aide-de-camp? Or shall you have one?"

"I have thought of Bernhard," Fritz said, a slow smile crossing his face. "I should like to have Lotte's son with me. I have long wished to get to know him better, and he is old enough for such a position now."

Vicky nodded. "You'll not be lonely with his company; he talks enough for three." She laughed.

"Yes, but his talk is well-informed and interesting, you must admit that," Fritz said, meeting her eye.

Vicky nodded. "I'm fond of the boy, I didn't mean to criticize him." She paused as Fritz's face became very grave, and finally, he sat up. Vicky felt a tear drop on her face. "Fritz, I didn't mean to say anything –"

"It is not that," Fritz whispered, his voice trembling. "You said I would not be lonely, but I shall be," he murmured, lying down again, muffling his face in the pillow. "And that it should be just now, when everything is – is right again," he said, glancing at Vicky and then at Baby, who lay in her cradle a few feet from the bed. "And what a birthday it shall be for Charlotte! And Louischen!"

"Marianne shall be glad to see certain people go, and the girls will too – at least Fritz Karl. His absence will be a most wished-for birthday present for Louischen."

***

Neues Palais Chapel, July 24, 1870
Vicky walked slowly between Fritz and Hedwig, leaning against Fritz as they entered the Chapel. The lights glittered on the men's medals and the women's jewels, the crowd crowned with plumed helmets.

Vicky saw Wrangel, Moltke, Roon and Blucher standing together – the first of whom had fought against the first Napoleon. Bismarck wore his uniform and breast-plate – one did not often see him in uniform.

Around the font stood Fritz's parents, Aunt Elisa, Princess Leignitz, Vivi and Fritz of Baden, Abbat, the Duke and Duchess of Altenburg – the Duchess being Marianne's older sister, the Kings of Württemberg and Bavaria – all the Godparents except for Leopold, who Mama had asked the King to represent.

Vicky watched as Fritz walked through the crowd. She saw the look of sadness on his face as he greeted the guests with his usual kindness. "Which of us will come back?" She knew the thought was in everyone's mind.

Vicky took her seat, Count Seckendorff standing nearby. She glanced around, smiling as she met the eyes of many friends, but searching for other faces.

She smiled again as she saw Hinzpeter and Mrs. Wakelin usher in the children. Willy and Henry soon stood on either side of her, Charlotte and little Vicky seated in front. Hinzpeter carried Waldie in his arms, placing him gently on Charlotte's lap. Vicky glanced around. There was Marianne, with the girls and little Fritz Leo.

Finally she heard Baby's cry rise above the hum of conversation and the *clink, clink* of spurs and swords. Everyone stood still as Mrs. Wakelin walked through the crowd again, placing the little one in her grandmother's arms.

Heym, the Court Chaplain who had performed all the Prussian Royal Christenings in the last two decades, began the ceremony. Vicky watched little Sophie as well as she could, but her attention was soon distracted.

"Don't let the man hurt Baby!" little Vicky's voice rose over Heym's voice and Baby's cry. "Oh, don't let the man hurt Baby!"

Vicky caught her hand, and Waldie's, as they both jumped from their seats, Waldie crying nearly as loudly as little Vicky. "Ssh," Vicky whispered, pulling them to her. "He's not hurting her. Nothing bad will happen to Baby," she murmured, but little Vicky's sobs did not stop until Baby was in the Queen's arms again.

Soon, everything was over, and the room began to clear, everyone filing into the Marble Hall for a dinner. Fritz returned to Vicky's side as the children were gathered and taken out again.

"Do you wish to go to dinner?" he asked.

Vicky shook her head. "I don't have the strength for it. But I don't wish to leave yet. I wish to say goodbye." She nodded to a group of young soldiers, young men who were good friends of theirs, who would leave for the front tonight.

Fritz nodded. "Let me know when you wish to go," he said, and strode away to speak to the British Ambassador.

"The last Christening here," Vicky heard someone say, "was the day before the Crown Prince left for the war with Austria." Vicky turned, seeing it was one of the older officers whose name she could not remember, speaking to William Russell.

Her heart ached at the thoughts his words brought to her mind. *God, protect my little ones*, she prayed. Thoughts of Siggy flooded her mind, and she couldn't keep the tears from her eyes as more young men – some of whom she remembered had been wounded in that war – came to say goodbye before passing into the hall for the dinner.

The room was nearly empty now. Vicky could see across the room, and saw, standing in the window recess, Fritz Karl. She had wondered if he was present, but hadn't been able to find him in the crowd. There had been present many of his regiment of Hussars, who wore scarlet uniforms and bright, shining black boots, so he didn't stand out as he often did.

Heym walked through the room, approaching Fritz Karl, and reached out a hand, touching his shoulder. Fritz Karl remained as he stood, leaning against the wall, his arms folded.

Vicky saw Heym rest his hand on Fritz Karl's shoulder, and his lips move, murmuring, Vicky supposed, "*Gott* bless you", as he had to everyone else. Vicky flinched as Fritz Karl's hand flew out, nearly catching a blow on Heym's face. She was glad she was too far away to understand his exclamation, but she could hear – almost feel – the intensity of his voice. She saw the color drain from Heym's face as he turned and walked rapidly away.

Vicky looked up at a touch on her shoulder; it was Fritz. "Fritz?" she whispered, and went on when Fritz bent down to listen, "does Fritz Karl not like Heym? He always seems such an amiable man."

Fritz straightened up; he didn't speak. Vicky glanced up at him. There was a strange look on his face. "You saw what just happened, didn't you?" Vicky asked again.

Fritz nodded stiffly, not looking down. "He was Fritz Karl's tutor when we were boys," he whispered in her ear after a couple of minutes had passed. "But they have not been friends for many years." He paused, maintaining his silence again for a couple of minutes, and then looked down at Vicky. "Do you wish to go?" he asked, as she lay back on the sofa, half covering her eyes.

"Yes, I don't feel strong."

Fritz helped her up, putting his arm around her supportively. Count Seckendorff appeared with Hedwig, and Vicky took their arms. "Help her back to her rooms, or if there is an invalid chair, fetch it. She is not strong."

***

"I go tomorrow morning," Count Seckendorff said as they reached the door of Vicky's sitting-room.

Vicky nodded, trying to smile as she looked up at him, but her eyes filled with tears. "I know," she said, struggling to keep her voice steady. Hedwig went on into Vicky's suite.

"I'm sorry you are going," Vicky sobbed. "Your company would've been very pleasant." She swallowed, holding out her hand. "Goodbye."

He looked down at her, and she saw a look in his eyes which seemed familiar, but she wasn't sure why. He nodded several times, and knelt, taking her hand in both of his.

"I will write to you, whenever the Crown Prince has not much time for writing," he said. "We have agreed on that." He kissed her hand, rose, and turned to leave the room.

Neues Palais, July 26, 1870

Fritz opened the door to Vicky's sitting-room and glanced around the room. "Vicky?" He expected her to be there to see him off. He didn't see her anywhere.

Yesterday, he and Vicky had gone to pay a quiet visit to Siggy's grave, accompanied by the older children. Marianne and the girls had come to the Neues Palais, Fritz Karl having left that morning.

Louischen had been sobbing when they arrived at the Neues Palais.

"What is it, Louischen?" Vicky had asked, taking the girl in her arms. "Uncle is still here for your birthday, and you always said you were happy when your Papa was away."

"Oh, y-yes," Louischen sobbed, "but – but – Großpapa! *Mein lieber*[69] *Großpapa!*" She tried to swallow several sobs, and went on, "He – he said he would give me something special this year, on my birthday, and now he is gone away! Without saying goodbye! And – I might never see him again!"

"And what a blessing that would be," Fritz saw Marianne mouth. Vicky looked at Fritz, too, as he took Louischen in his arms while Marianne drew Vicky aside. They both knew that Prince Charles did not leave till tomorrow. Fritz listened carefully to their whispers in spite of Louischen's sobbing.

---

[69]   my dear

"Don't let her – or the others – know that he is not gone yet," Marianne said in an urgent whisper. "Louischen will never forgive me if she knows."

"She still thinks he's blameless?" Vicky whispered back. Marianne nodded.

In the afternoon, Fritz had received a notice that he must leave just after dawn, if he was to pay a visit to Munich, Stuttgart and Karlsruhe before the Sovereigns of Bavaria, Württemberg and Baden were to depart for the front.

He went on, toward Vicky's boudoir. He opened the door softly, glancing in.

Vicky sat on the sofa with Baby in her arms, her head leaning down. The baby's face was nestled against her breast, lightly covered by a white lace shawl. Both slept peacefully.

Fritz stood, gazing at Vicky's face. How could he wake her to the misery of saying goodbye? And to say goodbye for how long? This war might be a terribly long one. And if he didn't wake her, and… He turned, swallowing a lump in his throat, and went upstairs to the boys' room.

Wilhelm and Heinrich were both asleep, their faces peaceful, though Heinrich's hand twitched frequently. Fritz bent down and kissed them, and then went to Charlotte's room. She, too, slept. Two days ago had been her 10th birthday; today… He bent down and kissed her gently on the forehead. *Meine kleines Mädchen,*" he murmured, and turned to go downstairs again. He slipped quietly into his and Vicky's suite again, but went directly to the nursery rooms.

He opened the door softly. Mrs. Wakelin sat in the corner, fast asleep, holding Waldie in her arms. The little boy whimpered in his sleep. Fritz sighed. Waldie was having nightmares frequently since the beginning of the war scare.

Fritz turned, bending over one of the little beds. Little Vicky's eyes flew open as his beard tickled her face. "Papa!" She stretched her hands up to him and threw her little arms round his neck. He lifted her up.

"Möhrchen, you must be good and quiet; Papa must go," he said gently. She looked up at him, tears appearing on her cheeks.

"Papa – Papa go – go to war?" He nodded, laying her back down in her bed. "No, no, Papa," she sobbed, clinging to him.

He sat down on the bed, taking her hand and patting it against his cheek. "Hush," he murmured, stroking her hair out of her face. She looked up at him, swallowing her sobs. "Will Möhrchen be a good girl and be quiet and not wake Mama?" he asked. Her eyes grew wide, but she nodded silently. He rose, looked about, and took a piece of paper from a little table, wiping a tear away as he wrote. He lifted little Vicky up again, controlling a sob he felt rising as he felt her little arms go around his neck again.

He opened the door of Vicky's boudoir very softly, closing it behind him. He set little Vicky down on the sofa next to her mother, holding a finger to his lips, and placing the note in her hand. "Give it to Mama when she wakes," he whispered. She nodded.

He turned toward the door, but stopped, looking back, unable to go. He stepped forward, going to the sofa again, knelt, and gently kissed Baby's forehead, and then, very softly, touched Vicky's lips with his.

"Fritz?" she murmured, smiling a little and turning her head. "Fritz." She sighed and settled down, holding Baby closer to her.

Fritz stood, and went to the door. He couldn't wake her. He would take that final picture with him in his mind, not that of her tearstained face, as he had in the previous wars. But he stood still for a long time, before he finally turned and closed the door behind him.

CHAPTER TWENTY-SEVEN
VICTORY, REVOLUTION AND EMPIRE

Neues Palais, July 26, 1870

"Fritz?" Vicky woke, vaguely aware of Fritz's kiss on her lips. She looked about. Fritz was nowhere to be seen.

She shook her head, and looked about the room again. She sat on the sofa in her boudoir, with Baby in her arms. She had fallen asleep nursing Baby, waiting for Fritz to come home. He had told her he must leave early that morning.

The sun was peering in through the windows. She lay Baby down in the cradle which stood at the end of the sofa. She would wait for him.

She turned to settle down again, but saw that little Vicky sat by her side, her mouth open, snoring softly. In her hands was clutched a small piece of paper.

Vicky took it gently from her hands, unfolding it to read:

"*Meine* Vicky,

"The order came to depart even earlier than expected. I came for a goodbye, and you and all the children slept, except for our little Vicky. You looked so peaceful, I could not bear the thought of waking you to the misery of parting. I wished to spare you that pang. May *Gott* keep us both, *auf wiedersehen*[70]."

"Oh, I might never see him again!" Vicky sobbed, clutching little Vicky in her arms.

"Mama! Mama, Papa gone!" little Vicky sobbed as she woke.

"Yes, Vicky, I read his note – but – oh, Fritz, how could you do this?" She sobbed the last words to herself, soothing little Vicky in her arms at

---

[70]   Till we meet again

the same time. The thought of sparing her the misery of saying goodbye was so kind, but he was gone – gone without a kiss – and…

She mustn't say "I might never see him again" in front of the children. "May God watch over Papa's precious life, and bring him home safe," she murmured, trying to comfort herself as well as little Vicky.

July 26, 1870

"*Meine* Vicky,

"My heart is with you as we march, and my thoughts upbraid me for not waking you. Such homesickness as comes when one leaves for a war is so deep, so incomparable even with other, longer absences, but somehow, it is not memorable. With each war it has come upon me unexpectedly, but never more seriously than now."

August 1

"The King of Bavaria greeted me kindly on my arrival in Nuremberg; he seems grown up at last, and no more such a simple school-boy.

"All the rest of the Bavarian Royal family, as well as a great guard of the army, received me in Munich – Dowager Queen Merrichen, my old playmate, was as kind as ever, and is still just as much 'the Queen' as always, in spite of her son's increased maturity. How well I remember her wedding – the first occasion I ever saw a Royal couple[71] walk together and hand-in-hand!

"I was taken by surprise and delight at meeting here Fritz Augustenburg, who has joined the Bavarian army, determined to serve in the war under my command, but equally determined *not* to don a Prussian uniform. To have this dear old friend with me shall be a great comfort.

"The dinner together with Queen Merrichen and her son was very pleasant, and would have been more so had it not been for the young King's off-color jokes. At one time he asked me if it was still the custom in the Prussian Army for every soldier to bring his doxy with him on campaign! 'I wouldn't know,' I answered, and in my thoughts went on, 'Ask my cousin, not me.'

---

[71]   Merrichen's older sister Elisabeth and her husband – Louis' parents

"The Bavarian soldier is so entirely different from the Prussian, the men's physical build in general being much more inclined to corpulence, and to a Prussian mind, he is very clumsily trained. But they, as all I have met, greet me as their leader with great enthusiasm, though on my train's first arrival, before my appearance, all was cold silence, as they were expecting Fritz Karl.

"At Stuttgart King Karl of Württemburg received me with his family. He met me with his usual stiff, formal politeness, but I remember you have not made his acquaintance. His wife, my cousin Queen Olga, whom you have had the pleasure of meeting, was much more gracious than she was to you twelve years ago.

"King Karl speaks much of his 'Kingly duties' as if he has been King far longer than anyone (he only took the throne six years ago). He speaks of the duties, too, of a 'brave soldier', and in the same exaggerated tone as both the King of Italy and Fritz Karl.

"In personal appearance, I am struck more than ever by his resemblance to Louis, and also by his eyes – eyes which you would not like to meet, and whose expression as well as shape bear resemblance to a certain person of whom neither of us is fond. The color, too, is the same grey-green.

"I have spent two pleasant days with Vivi and Fritz of Baden, also Maroussy and her husband. Maroussy's little girl, I am sorry to say, bears resemblance to our Charlotte, even down to the red hair and green eyes (you will understand what I mean). The little boy, Max, is altogether different.

"I must close here. Tonight I was joined by Bernhard and Onkel Ernst, and so with Fritz Augustenburg as well, I am in pleasant company.

"In spite of this, or rather because of it, my heart yearns all the more for you *und die lieber Kinder*. I long to introduce you and the children to some of my friends, with whom you have not the pleasure of acquaintance, and more than anything, I long for you – for you and Baby, *meine kleine Tochter*[72], whose precious early days I am forced not to witness."

---

[72]   My little daughter

Neues Palais, August 1, 1870

"Louis and I parted late in the evening," Vicky read, "outside the village where he was quartered for the night. We watched each other until there was no more to be seen. May the Almighty watch over his life, and bring him safe home to me!"

Vicky felt her eyes brim with tears as she read Alice's letter. She longed to have had such a parting with Fritz. Vicky sighed heavily. The thought had been very kind, and she knew he had taken a kiss with him – and the sight of her with Baby in her arms – instead of the image of her tearful face which she knew had haunted his mind through the previous two wars.

Alice had written nearly the exact words that Vicky had written to Mama – "May God watch over his precious life!"

"I shall not leave here unless our troops should retreat and the French come," Alice had written. It had become quite clear already that the Rhineland would not be occupied by the French, as Vicky had feared. Everyone had expected that Darmstadt and Baden would be overrun, and Fritz would hardly be able to gather his army.

"I should be better off personally with you," Alice's letter went on, "but I feel I should remain here, in Louis' home, nearer to him. His dear parents would feel my absence very much, with all three of their sons in the war, as our Willy[73] serves as a Johanniter."

August 4, 1870

"*Meine* Vicky,

"What has not happened since I wrote my last long letter? To witness such a fight is indescribable. For the first time in sixty-five years France has been beaten in a battle of this importance. All has ended in many, many prisoners (French) as well as their retreat.

"A triumph of this kind raises the Bavarians in their own eyes as well as ours, and does much good to work unity between my mixed armies, and hopefully, in the future of our great country.

---

73   Louis' younger brother

"During the hours of conflict the suspense, need I say, was intense. I had a good view of the field and was thus enabled to give the necessary orders.

"It seems strange that yesterday I was peacefully swimming in the Rhine, and today in the midst of battle."

Neues Palais, August 5, 1870

"Mama's position, I can imagine, is difficult," Vicky wrote to Alice. England was neutral, but France had bought ammunition from English trade. There was much resentment in Prussia about this fact. "A wounded man ceases to be an enemy," Vicky went on. "He is only a suffering human being.

"I have had letters from Fritz from Stuttgart and Karlsruhe, and he is quite startled by the cordiality with which he is received. Dear Fritz, he certainly deserves it!

"I hope to come to Homburg, as you do not come here. I shall work to get up a small hospital at my own expense. I know much more about nursing, etc., too, since reading your books last year, than I did in the other two wars."

"Mama," Willy called, and Vicky laid down her pen. "Why does Papa mention green eyes, when he says Aunt Maroussy's little girl resembles Charlotte? Ditta doesn't have green eyes."

"Willy," Vicky said, a little sternly, "you aren't supposed to be reading my letters." She had left one of Fritz's letters sitting on another table, and Willy had come into the room while she was occupied with Alice's letters. "I told you I would read them to you."

Willy hung his head. "But why does he say green eyes?"

"Willy, come here." Vicky put her arm around her son as he sat by her side. "You remember what I told you, after little Vicky's birth, don't you?" Willy looked puzzled. "About Charlotte. When you and she were asking about little Vicky looking so different?"

Willy nodded. He said nothing for a while, and then his face reddened as he looked up. "Is Aunt Maroussy's little girl – Ditta's sister?" Vicky nodded. "Why doesn't Papa say so?"

"Willy," Vicky said seriously, "we can't speak of such things openly in letters which go to another country."

"Even by messenger?" Willy asked. "You always mention writing things by messenger being different."

"But it's different again during a war. There's always a risk of Fritz – Papa's letters getting taken and released into the press." Willy looked indignant, but he didn't say anything. "Are you satisfied? And will you go and read something *else* while I finish writing to Aunt Alice?" Willy nodded, and left the room.

"I shall not come to Homburg," Vicky wrote, "until I get my Papa-in-law's permission, and until Marianne leaves. She and the children are with me, and I must arrange things for the children before we both go.

"How pleasant it is, that you and I can be together this time. We aren't forced apart as in the last war. I shall be delighted to introduce my darling Sophie to you, *his* little daughter at last! She is my comfort and pleasure, as you can imagine my sleep and appetite are not the best."

Sulz, August 5, 1870

"*Meine* Vicky,

"A warm wind blew through in the evening, and soon we were cooled by a thunderstorm, as today I set out on the march to France. The landscape of the foot-hills is lovely; the villages look prosperous, but are all abandoned, due to the silly rumors that we Germans – particularly Prussians – are cannibals.

"All this loveliness was a great refreshment, especially after being forced to ride over part of yesterday's battle-field, the description of which I shall not give in detail. Every time I behold such things, the revulsion grows stronger.

"Everywhere, we came upon discarded weapons and knapsacks from the French soldiers, and have come into possession of some wonderfully fresh French breads and other rations, of much more delicate taste than ours."

Sulz, August 5, 1870

"Your Highness will be pleased to hear more from this field of misery and pain – those afflictions which we, thank *Gott*, do not suffer, except in the suffering of looking on.

"What emotions overtook the Crown Prince were obvious, as he saw dying and severely wounded men spring up by sheer force of will to show him what joy they have to be led by him. From the windows and from the ambulances, even the most severe cases wave or make some demonstration as he passes by – a perfect burst of enthusiasm overwhelms the well and hearty.

"We all hope and pray that your Highness and the little Princes and Princesses are well and hearty, that your recovery goes well, and that the littlest Princess thrives in spite of her father's absence.

"G. von Seckendorff."

Worth, August 6, 1870

"*Meine* Vicky,

"I have little time to write today, but I must send you my love. The long battle has brought a fatigue as you can imagine, and there is much to do.

"The Bavarians, whose conduct I watch with interest, made little progress in today's battle, and I was finally at the end of my patience. Calling to Major von Freyburg, our Bavarian representative, I said, 'Ride to your countrymen, at Fröschweiler, and tell them that the Crown Prince of Prussia orders them in the name of their King now to engage the enemy properly; say to them, "You alone come to a standstill where everywhere we advance victoriously!" '

"This was strong language to the men who have had so little battle training or even experience with maneuvers; one sees the Bavarians are a peaceful people, but these words served the purpose I intended, and they helped us to win the battle as they did two days before.

"Slowly, the thunder of guns retreated, and we truly had the French on the run, led by Marshal MacMahon. Again and again burst out the sound of another shower of shots, and we thought the fighting went on, that the Bavarians had taken my word so seriously as to pursue the French singlehandedly. This turned out rather to be the Bavarians' way of celebrating the victory, by firing repeatedly into the air!

"Bernhard has seen his first action, and was in the shock of the battle still when everyone retired early. To see the tears in his eyes, so like Lotte's, made my heart ache.

"I am determined that our prisoners shall be treated in a gentleman-like manner, and when I came to visit the wounded French, one of their Colonels recognized me by my decorations. He greeted me with the words, 'Ah, *monseigneur,* what a defeat, what a disaster; I shall be disgraced, a prisoner; we have lost everything!'

"I answered him, 'You have fought gallantly, and in doing so, you have not lost your honor.'

"The man gave me such a grateful look and smile, and I told him I would send news of him to his family if he would let me know his name. Another man, too, bemoaned his prisoner-ship, and was very indignant when I told him we meant to treat the prisoners honorably. 'Huh!' he snorted, 'they snatched my gun from me!' I told him how everything should be done, if he would behave peaceably.

"All the French speak in quite an embittered manner, some quite disrespectfully, of their Emperor, and it is clear he is in no way popular.

"This short letter has grown quite long, and I must close, and sleep, and I know I shall dream I am in your arms."

August 6, 1870

"We are, thank *Gott,* well, and none of our Princes are wounded. The sight of the battlefield, nevertheless, is one of horror and pain unimaginable. The Crown Prince says he is well-rested, but his face in the morning shows how he struggles in the night with grief, which he, I believe, feels more deeply than any other I have seen.

"I often wonder what your Highness would think if you could see the Crown Prince as he is in the midst of a battle – he is no more the mild-mannered man we are accustomed to, though he always keeps his humane gentlemanliness – but his face flushes, not from diffidence, but from the excitement of the scene. There is a spark in his eye I had never seen before, and he speaks but to command.

"When he must chide or scold, no one who is the subject forgets that scolding soon, though I admit I laughed at what his idea of 'strong language' was. Such things as he said would not be called that by any other soldier on the field.

"The brave soldier indeed comes out in him, but in such a way as is certainly not seen in those who boast of being 'brave soldiers' – one never hears a boast from his lips; one only sees true courage melded with thoughtful care, the daring leader who, minutes after the battle, lifts the head of the dying man with the tenderest hand imaginable.

"How proud you must be to have such a husband, and I shall repeat the words I have heard many men – French and German – speak: That to attempt to be like the Crown Prince, in modesty, bravery, courage, gentleness, and true in loving-kindness to friend and to enemy – to attempt to be like him is to attempt to be the best of men, and I think one can hardly have a higher ambition.

"Your husband has received the photographs of his little daughter with great delight, and shared them among his headquarters, quite beaming with pride.

"G. von Seckendorff."

Sarburg, August 13

"*Meine* Vicky,

"Every time I go to visit the wounded or the prisoners, if I forget and leave my visor down, everyone is silent and fearful. Several times I have been asked, 'Are you Prince Charles?' I answer that my uncle is with the

King, and then they answer that they meant the *Prince Rouge*[74], as they call Fritz Karl. All is joy and relief when they know I am me.

"At Obermodern, the church clock rang just as the one in the Great Quadrangle at Windsor, giving me a pleasant feeling as if I were at home. But this feeling made me long for home all the more, as you can imagine.

"Tomorrow is our dear Heinrich's birthday – may it be a pleasant day for you all and may Gott's blessing rest upon the dear boy. To think he has completed eight years of life! May he and his brothers one day help to complete Germany's task in peacetime, as it is my duty to do so in this time of war."

Nancy, August 19, 1870

"*Meine* Vicky,

"Last night I was relieved by the arrival of my messenger, a young Count Hanstein – a second cousin, I believe, of your step-grandfather – who has brought several letters from you, Alice, Marianne, and the children. A few days ago I received five letters from you at once – how enriched I felt!

"I grieve often to think that Papa, at seventy-four years, must be in bivouac. It is useless pity, I know, as he thrives on such a life, and always has.

"I hear that Louis and his division have been in a battle, and he is decorated as a hero. Alice writes so proudly, as, no doubt, she does as well to you. What a misfortune that he should be in Fritz Karl's army, and not my own.

"I spent much of last evening in company of Onkel Ernst, whose conversation is a pleasant pastime. In imagination, I am speaking with your Papa; I search for the resemblances in their voices – which you know are not hard to find – and it is very soothing."

Ligny, August 24, 1870

"*Meine* Vicky,

"To think that you go to Homburg and to Alice pleases me much, and your intention of establishing a model hospital there is very good. All is sure to go well under your joint instruction. The hospitals I have visited are in a disgusting condition.

"I hear of the Emperor Napoleon following his army about, although he is no longer in the position of *Generalissimo*. I hear, too, that he is in

---

[74] The Red Prince

pain and not well, that Paris is becoming very unsettled, and that he dreads to return to it. Such a position in one's own country brings pity for him, in spite of his treachery in declaring such a war."

Neues Palais, August 26, 1870

"I know how pleased you will be," Vicky wrote to Alice, "to see how the English papers do Fritz the justice he deserves, and do not only mention Fritz Karl, as ours do. How proud you, too, must be, to see Louis decorated for bravery. My heart is fit to burst at the thought of it all, and yet – how we only long for them home. Military glory is well enough, but family love is worth it all many times over!

"To think all of these news come just on this day, when our dear Papa would have been fifty-one! How often my thoughts go to our girlhood, when we were ignorant of the strife and wickedness in the world, and yet – how easily I can trace the threads of present evils far back. Many of Papa's teachings and warnings come home to me, and I see how true what he said was.

"What would he say to the happenings of today? German unity grows nearer, but not, I fear, by the means which he strove so faithfully for.

"How I wish more than ever that our children could have known him, and that he could have helped us to watch over their precious education and development. You say Victoria asks many questions on the day's politics – my own little Vicky and Willy each in their own way take an interest in the war."

*****

Neues Palais, Potsdam, August 1870

"I shall be sorry to leave you; it has been so pleasant to be together," Marianne said to Vicky as she sat down beside her.

"Yes, but you go to beautiful Italy. I go to be with my dear sister, so we shall both be pleasantly occupied."

"Yes," Marianne sighed, blushing, "and Hubert will be there. To see him twice within a year!" Her face flushed even more deeply. "I told you he was in Anhalt when we were. And to know that I leave the children home safe!" Marianne breathed an enormous sigh. "To know that means everything to me!" There were tears in her eyes, but Vicky wondered if she had ever seen tears of joy in Marianne's eyes before.

"I can imagine so," Vicky said, squeezing her hand. She glanced across the room, where Ebi lay on the sofa, her figure showing her condition more obviously than it ever had before. She was a young lady now, no more a child, and things were very different for her this time.

"I am glad my children have the company of yours," Marianne said, glancing around the room. Charlotte and Louischen sat on the floor, playing a game of chess. Mariechen, Willy and Henry sat together near Ebi, with Willy and Mariechen taking turns reading aloud. Little Vicky and Waldie lay on the floor with little Sophie between them, watching with fascinated eyes as their newest little sister crawled across the floor.

"Where is Fritzi?" Vicky asked.

Marianne's face grew serious. "He was very naughty this afternoon," she whispered, her face flushing again. "I mean – he has said things –" Marianne's voice trembled.

"I want champagne!" Vicky heard a scream in Fritz Leo's voice. "I want champagne!"

The little boy ran into the room, followed by a flustered Frau Kampmann, from whom he had obviously escaped.

"You aren't to have champagne," Marianne said, rising quickly and crossing the room. She whispered something in Frau Kampmann's ear, and the nurse left the room, closing the door after her.

"I want champagne!" Fritz Leo roared again, stamping his foot and bringing his fist down on the little children's table he stood next to. "Papa always lets me!" Marianne caught his hand before he could bang the table again. "I want wine, then, Mama," he said, staring up at her defiantly. "And I'll have it, too, whatever you –"

Vicky winced as a torrent of epithets streamed from the little boy's lips. Willy and Charlotte both looked up with a look of startled horror in their eyes. Vicky saw a look of shame on Ebi and Mariechen's faces, while Louischen, abandoning her game with Charlotte, retreated to the sofa, burying her face in the cushions.

Fritz Leo snatched his hand away from Marianne's grasp, rushing across the room, and would have trampled over Baby Sophie if Willy hadn't pushed him away.

"Stop it!" Willy cried, but Fritz Leo grabbed at his left arm, jerking it, and Willy gave a cry of pain. Fritz Leo turned, running across the chessboard and scattering the pieces.

Waldie and little Vicky had both begun to cry aloud. Fritz Leo ran past them, slapping little Vicky's face.

Vicky, who had felt stunned by the little boy's outburst, finally regained her senses. She crossed the room, taking him up in her arms. He flailed about, more violently than Charlotte had ever done, a stream of curses flowing again from his mouth.

Vicky covered his mouth, but felt small teeth bite into her hand. She swiftly carried him from the room, hurrying through the corridors, his screams echoing through the palace.

Vicky looked back, and was glad to see Marianne following her. Finally, they reached a little medicine closet. Vicky handed the boy to Marianne, and took two bottles from the closet, one large and one small.

"Why are you giving him wine? It will spoil him all the more." Marianne watched her, a shocked look on her face.

Vicky opened the small bottle, mixing a miniscule amount of something white into the glass of wine. "I can't speak of it in front of him," she whispered. Fritz Leo still roared at the top of his voice, and had taken no notice of what she was doing. "I'll explain all about it. I did this with my boys, and they've never wished to taste wine or any liquor." She turned to Fritz Leo. "Here, Fritzi, drink this."

Fritz Leo's face brightened, and his tears immediately ceased. He took the glass, drinking about half of it. "Drink it all," Vicky encouraged.

"Papa never gave *that* much," he said, his eyes sparkling as he finished the glass. Vicky nodded to Marianne, who still looked extremely puzzled.

"Come back," Vicky said, and hurried back to the room where the children were, sitting again by Marianne's side.

She saw that Marianne, Mariechen and Ebi all watched Fritz Leo intently. The boy lay on the floor, a dejected look on his face. He held his stomach, making a face when he met anyone's eye. He was very subdued.

"Marianne," Vicky whispered, "you mentioned that Count Wangenheim was in Italy. You still haven't ever told me why your father-in-law hates him. Do you know what happened between Prince Charles and my grandmother?"

Marianne blushed. "Yes, but I can't speak of it in front of the children."

Vicky nodded, rising and going towards the door. "I wish to explain about the wine, as well." She felt something under her foot as she crossed the room, and nearly stumbled. She wore only her slippers. She looked down. It was a chess-piece which Charlotte and Louischen hadn't cleared away.

"Charlotte, clean up your things." Vicky spoke a little sharply. "Don't leave such a mess, please."

"Why are you always so angry with Charlotte?"

The words were very softly spoken, almost a whisper, but Vicky whirled around, startled. It was Louischen who had spoken. Her eyes were wide with alarm, as if she was afraid she would be in trouble. Vicky stepped towards her, and knelt down by the sofa, taking her hand. "What do you mean?"

"I didn't mean to say that," Louischen muttered, looking around and seeming to shrink into herself.

"You didn't do anything wrong," Vicky said gently, embracing her. "Tell me what you mean," she encouraged.

"I don't wish to speak of it – to explain it – before the others," Louischen whispered. Vicky nodded, glancing at Marianne, who had obviously heard the conversation. She nodded to Vicky, and turned back to the other children. Louischen stood, and she and Vicky went into the next room.

Vicky turned to her, kneeling down as Louischen sat down in a big armchair. "Tell me what you mean," Vicky said again.

"I see the colors of your voice," Louischen began slowly. "I told you, years ago, about different words having colors."

Vicky nodded. "I remember what you told me." It had been about five years since Louischen had spoken of these things to her.

"People's voices have colors, too. Women are usually purple, men green. But I see feelings – emotions – your voice is usually pink when you are alone with your family, or with us, or your other close friends. But when you speak to Charlotte, a streak of blood enters your voice. That is anger, you remember."

Vicky nodded, smiling at the memory of Louischen speaking of when Fritz Karl was "so bloody angry". Then she sighed, wondering how much to tell Louischen. Marianne was quite certain Prince Charles behaved in the same shameful way to Louischen as he did to Ebi – and yet they had no proof. Louischen had always seemed ignorant of anything unusual when Marianne questioned her.

"Louischen," Vicky said slowly, "Charlotte has done nothing wrong – I mean, it isn't *her* fault that I'm angry. Are you satisfied, knowing that?"

Louischen looked at her. "You are angry at someone – as Ebi and I are?"

Vicky nodded slowly, pausing to think. Louischen looked uncomfortable, but didn't seem to wish to speak further.

"You know about your little brother – you know he is not – exactly your –" She trailed off. She wasn't sure how much Louischen knew about that, either.

"That he is Ebi's child? Yes." Louischen spoke of it so plainly, Vicky felt much less awkward. "But what does that have to do with Charlotte?" Louischen paused, and then her eyes filled with tears. "I know what you mean," she cried, and threw her arms around Vicky's neck.

"Louischen, you may go," Marianne said, as she entered the room. The girl nodded, curtseyed to her mother, and left the room.

"Why did you give Fritzi the wine?" Marianne cried. "Why encourage such behavior? I never thought you would do so!" Tears flooded her eyes again, as she stared at Vicky.

"I told you I did it with my boys, and they never wished to taste alcohol." Vicky went to the door, calling to a footman passing by. "Fetch me the book, *The Tenant of Wildfell Hall*, from my library, as quick as you can!" she called. She turned back to Marianne. "You may read it, or I will read it to you, only it must be after I return from being with Alice. It is not published in German, so I do not suppose it would be easy for you. But I can show you the passage."

"I had much trouble at first in breaking him of those evil habits his father had taught him to acquire, but already that difficulty is nearly vanquished now: bad language seldom defiles his mouth, and I have succeeded in giving him an absolute disgust for all intoxicating liquors, which I hope not even his father or his father's friends will be able to overcome. He was inordinately fond of them for so young a creature, and, remembering my unfortunate father as well as his, I dreaded the consequences of such a taste. But if I had stinted him, in his usual quantity of wine, or forbidden him to taste it altogether, that would only have increased his

partiality for it, and made him regard it as a greater treat than ever. I therefore gave him quite as much as his father was accustomed to allow him; as much, indeed, as he desired to have —but into every glass I surreptitiously introduced a small quantity of tartar-emetic, just enough to produce inevitable nausea and depression without positive sickness. Finding such disagreeable consequences invariably to result from this indulgence, he soon grew weary of it, but the more he shrank from the daily treat the more I pressed it upon him, till his reluctance was strengthened to perfect abhorrence. When he was thoroughly disgusted with every kind of wine, I allowed him, at his own request, to try brandy-and-water, and then gin-and-water, for the little toper was familiar with them all, and I was determined that all should be equally hateful to him. This I have now effected; and since he declares that the taste, the smell, the sight of any one of them is sufficient to make him sick, I have given up teasing him about them, except now and then as objects of terror in cases of misbehaviour. 'Arthur, if you're not a good boy I shall give you a glass of wine,' or 'Now, Arthur, if you say that again you shall have some brandy-and-water,' is as good as any other threat."

"It pertains so precisely." Marianne's face brightened as Vicky translated for her. "I understand now, and thank you," she whispered, squeezing Vicky's hand. She took the book, glancing through it. "And this is just how I feel," she said, pointing to another passage.

"So the little fellow came down every evening in spite of his cross mamma, and learned to tipple wine like papa, to swear like Mr. Hattersley, and to have his own way like a man, and sent mamma to the devil when she tried to prevent him. To see such things done with the roguish naïveté of that pretty little child, and hear such things spoken by that small infantile voice, was as peculiarly piquant and irresistibly droll to them as it was inexpressibly distressing and painful to me; and when he had set the table in a roar he would look round delightedly upon them all, and add his shrill laugh to theirs. But if that beaming blue eye rested on me, its light would vanish for a moment, and he would say, in some concern, 'Mamma, why don't you laugh? Make her laugh, Papa— she never will.'"

Marianne read aloud, and finished, saying, "You see I can read it quite well now. May I take the book with me?"

Vicky nodded. "I shall ask Mrs. Wakelin to continue to give Fritzi this," she said. "I think it better Frau Kampmann not know."

"Yes, certainly," Marianne nodded. "And – about your Grandmama," she whispered, but there was a knock at the door.

"Mama, Aunty," Mariechen cried as Vicky opened the door, "Fritzi was sick all over Baby Sophie, and I don't know what to do!"

Senue, August 29, 1870

"*Meine* Vicky,

"The house where I stayed here gave me an extremely friendly welcome, without their knowing my true identity. German population is still quite thick here. The old mother of the house was laid up with a broken leg, but I spent some time in conversation with her. She took notice of my star and other decorations, and I spoke a great deal of my farm at Bornstedt, of my wife and six living children. At parting, she begged me to send her regards to you, my wife, whom she admires as an excellent mother, housekeeper and farmer's wife."

Sedan, September 1, 1870

"*Meine* Vicky,

"I certainly think I can say we have fought the decisive battle when we come out with the Emperor and fifty generals as prisoners! What happenings these are, and all goes so fast my head spins in disbelief.

"On the height from which I watched the battle, I could see Papa and his army waiting in the distance, Count Seckendorff having met him and told him of our condition, and they stood by in case of a need for reinforcement.

"The old fortress of Sedan, the Emperor's headquarters, is indeed something to have captured, and without too bloody a fight. I cannot say that there were not many wounded, but it is not so much as other battles have been.

"There was a rumor that Napoleon was in occupancy, but we did not believe it. After a time, the French soldiers began to run about unarmed; to a soldier's eye the whole scene was a demoralizing one.

"Papa gave orders to bombard the fortress, but it had little effect, as it is almost entirely of thick stone which would not budge.

"During an interval in the battle, Papa, Bismarck, Roon and I discussed, hardly more than as a joke, the possibility of having Napoleon himself in our hands.

"The bombardment had gone on for some time, when a messenger was sent off, for what reason I was unsure. Soon, the Bavarian officers pointed out that white flags were floating over the fortress, and the French declared themselves surrendered.

"A message was brought from the fortress to Papa, which read in French, 'My dear brother, not having been able to die a soldier's death, I must surrender my sword into your Majesty's hands. Napoleon, Sedan, September 1, 1870'.

"The astonishment was very great, as you can imagine. Papa wished to write to the Emperor, giving conditions of surrender, but of course we had no table to write on in the middle of a battlefield. There were, however, two chairs to be found outside a burnt farmhouse, and laid cross-ways on the arms of these, Gustedt lent his sabertasche as a table-top, I gave my writing paper and eagle signet, and Onkel Karl of Weimar supplied the pen and ink."

Sedan, September 2, 1870

"*Meine* Vicky,

"Surely now the war is nearly over, as the Empress Eugenie as Regent will not prolong the war. I cannot help my thoughts from wandering to when we were their guests, and they hosted us so kindly only a few months ago. How little we thought how the situation would have changed so quickly!

"I arranged for a private interview between Papa and the Emperor. Napoleon expressed his belief that he had been set against Fritz Karl's army, when Papa answered that it was I and the Crown Prince of Saxony who besieged Sedan. Napoleon asked where Fritz Karl was. Papa's answer: in Metz.

"The Emperor was obviously taken aback; his face quivered painfully. He had been in full belief that our whole army had been in the field.

"When he saw me, he held out his hand to me, the tears running down his cheeks, and he wiped them away with his hand, being without even a handkerchief. The French armies are in a despicable state of disorderly disdain towards their Emperor. Many regiments have mutinied, and there is fear of revolution in Paris. His fear for the Empress and his boy keeps him awake at night, as he has had no news of them for a week.

"He asked Papa for permission to telegraph the Empress, and he is to go to Wilhelmshohe in Kassel, to be in comfortable imprisonment, with the company of many of his generals."

Corbeil, September 20, 1870

"*Meine* Vicky,

"The war goes on with the new government in Paris, and we march on to Paris, just as Fritz Karl marches from battle to battle since Metz's surrender.

"The high-road to Versailles, though paved, is made quite impassable by the French cutting down trees and leaving them in the street, digging trenches and tearing up stones, but late this afternoon I have reached Versailles.

"The commander of the National Guard, Monsieur de Franchet d'Esperay, met me – I cannot say welcomed me, but did not receive his enemy with hostility. We had played together as children in Berlin and not seen each other since those days, therefore it was strange to meet again under such circumstances.

"We hurried quickly to the Palace and watched a magnificent sunset from the terrace. My heart went out to you, searching for you, wishing you were by my side in very different circumstances. To one who has been treading through the horrors of a battlefield, this place seems incredibly beautiful. I thought of the fine, warm Sunday evening three years ago, when the fountains played in honor of my father and the Tsar, and you were by my side, with a host of Princely guests – guests of Napoleon and Eugenie!"

Homburg, September 24, 1870

"Mein Schatz, mein lieber, lieber[75] Fritz,

"I have been here with Alice for nearly a month, and now your Papa writes to me that I must return to Berlin. He says I left without permission (which is entirely untrue) and that 'the female portion of the family ought to remain together'. This is so absurd it makes my blood boil, as I did not leave Berlin until your Mama, Aunt Marie and Marianne all did so as well. I shall certainly not go until Alice's Baby has safely arrived and a wet-nurse has been settled for it."

Versailles, September 24, 1870

"Meine Vicky,

"I went to the Royal headquarters in the Chateau of Ferrieres. This place was suggested by Onkel Karl, he having interrupted Papa's interview with Bismarck and myself to suggest such a place. It is a giant cabinet of curiosities in Renaissance style, and so to Onkel Karl's taste, but Papa finds it very dull.

"Abbat has paid a visit to me; he is very lame after being knocked senseless and thrown ten feet across rocky ground by the explosion of a shell, but he says he has no serious injuries, only bruises."

Versailles, September 28, 1870

"Last night, accompanied by a patrol who were quite ignorant of my identity, only thinking I was 'a high-ranking officer', I took the men on outpost duty into the palace. Creeping through the shelter of laurel and orange trees, we gained entry to the chateau without anyone's having an inkling.

"We passed through the noble gallery, and the men were examining the great oil painting which hangs from the wall and represents the arrival of you and your family in '55. I pointed out who the chief persons were, and pointed to your figure, announcing, 'my wife'. Two of the men started, but still seemed unable to make out who I was, but the third suddenly knelt down, kissing my hand, and the others soon caught on.

---

[75]   My darling, my dear, dear

"To think that tomorrow is again our *Verlobungstag*[76], fifteen years since then, and since that visit of yours to Paris.

"I took them next to see Napoleon's apartments, and we saw the Council table on which the declaration of war was written. All the living-rooms were obviously suddenly abandoned, the Empress's work-basket and invitation cards lying about."

Neues Palais, Hesse-Darmstadt, October 8, 1870

"My little Fritz," Alice murmured, her eyes locked on her baby's face.

Vicky sat by her side, stroking the little one's head. "I've only seen *my* little Fritz once since his birth." Vicky's baby born close to when Waldie was born had been named Fritz, in spite of his being raised in England. Vicky and Fritz were, officially, his Godparents.

"If only Louis could see his little son," Alice said, smiling as she looked up at Vicky. "To think he spent three weeks without being under a roof!" She shook her head. "*We* have such comforts, and yet we take them for granted."

"I'm glad you have such comforts as you do," Vicky said. "And I'm very thankful I could be here. I didn't like the thought of your having a doctor who has been about the wounded at such a time. It isn't good, especially as you said his sister just died of childbed fever."

Alice shuddered. "I was afraid," she whispered, squeezing Vicky's hand. "And I wondered what I would feed my little one, too. We have no goats or cows just now, and you know I have not been able to nurse since Ella."

Vicky smiled. She had written to Fritz that she would act as wet-nurse to Alice's baby. "Fritz will be delighted at your naming your little one for him."

There was a knock at the door, and a footman opened it, setting a packet of letters on the table and retreating. Vicky rushed to take the letters.

---

[76]   Engagement anniversary

"From Mama and *die Geschwister*[77]," she cried. She took Mama's letter first, glancing over it hurriedly before settling down to read it thoroughly. "Louise is engaged!"

"To Lord Lorne or one of the others?" Alice asked. Mama had written that she had invited several young men of the English nobility to Windsor of late, as it was settled Louise would not marry a Prince.

"Yes. To Lord Lorne. How pleased Papa would be to have the Duke of Argyll's son as his son-in-law." The Duke of Argyll was one of Papa's old friends, one of the scientific circle who had been somewhat involved in the organization of the Great Exhibition. He was married to Elisabeth Leveson-Gower, the eldest daughter of Harriet, the Duchess of Sutherland, Mama's first *Mistress of the Robes*, or *Grand Maitress*, as the position was called on the continent.

Versailles, October 18, 1870

"On this, the Crown Prince's birthday, his breakfast table is spread with plates of bonbons and the remnants of your Highness's excellent cake, which he – with just pride – shared about as the production of 'my wife'. His gentle pride in your Highness's accomplishments shines always in his eyes at every word he speaks of you.

"He spoke to me last night, his thoughts going back over the past year of his life, which opened in Corfu in the course of his Eastern travels. He praises *Gott* that you and the children are safe at home, though his homesickness is all too obvious.

"His grief, too, at the death of his friend von Jasmund shows in his face. He had believed him for some weeks only to be badly wounded, and just on his arrival at the place where he thought to meet his friend, he heard the news of his immediate death after the battle.

"The other day, as he made his rounds with visor down and no other identification, we happened upon a small campfire surrounded with a crowd of Bavarian and Württemburger soldiers. They were discussing the Crown Prince of Prussia, and we heard the words, 'if he had been our leader in the last war, we would have beaten the Prussians!'

---

[77]　The siblings

"Your husband came away laughing, but his face soon grew serious. He is pleased they do not consider him as 'one of the Prussians', but rather as '*Unser* Fritz', but he does not wish such sayings to reach the ears of Bismarck and Prince Karl.

"The Crown Prince's modest objection to showing claim to this place where he lives in Headquarters touches the French who are his hosts. He is the conqueror, and yet he asks in the humblest manner for permission, and always makes every attempt to avoid inconveniencing the family who lives here.

"G. von Seckendorff."

Versailles, Oktober 18, 1870

"*Meine* Vicky,

"This day comes again, and we are apart as last year – and yet not as last year. The events of that day, gliding peacefully down the Nile – were very different indeed from these great happenings going on around me now.

"My thirty-ninth birthday – 'the last before forty' – as Bertie would say. Twenty years ago I was in France, on a holiday excursion from Bonn. Ten years ago was that day when *Gott* gave you back to me in a way you had feared would be impossible. On my birthday was Papa's coronation – on my birthday was the Christening of our little Sigismund.

"You see how my thoughts jump from year to year – but particularly to that first birthday after our marriage – my first *happy* birthday – when you showed such splendid faith in me – the first that I felt strength and belief in myself. The first with peace, hope, love; the first without doubt, fear, loneliness and longing. *Gott* had given you to me – and he had given me life – and never again have I felt the wish to leave this life, which had often haunted me before.

"*Meine Frauchen,* you have given me hope – you have shown me what courage means – and faith – and what it is to face the greatest trials and deepest fears.

"To think that in my fortieth year we shall surely see – for the signs are growing all round me – Germany a united Empire. But by what different means than those your dear, ever-to-be-remembered father wished, hoped, strove – and taught you – for.

"My thoughts are often on him, as well as with you and *die liebe Kinder*[78], especially as Onkel Ernst is often my companion. Our conversations often turn to conversations of old – those at the Great Exhibition, in Babelsberg in '58, and in Coburg in '60, particularly, as we were all – he, we, and your dear parents – together on those occasions.

"My greatest joy is to receive your letters and those of the children. I see by the photographs that Baby is growing in beauty and strength. You must be well satisfied in your wish for 'as many children as possible' with Alice's little one dependent on you as well.

"I have received the letters you forwarded from your dear Mama and *die Geschwister*[79]. That of Arthur shows him a sensible boy, and he takes as great an interest as ever in every detail of his career. To think of him – the baby of the Great Exhibition – twenty years old!

"By what different means, as I said, Germany's unification is being brought about. But – may *Gott's* blessing rest upon it – and may it bring Peace to our nation!"

"*Mit viele Liebe und Küssen, ewig*

"*Dein treuester Freund,*[80]

"*Fritz.*"

----

[78]   The dear children
[79]   The siblings
[80]   "With much love and kisses, ever Your truest friend

Dear Reader,

I hope you enjoyed *Under the Sword*, the third installment in *The Rival Courts*. This story is incredibly close to my heart, and I'm so grateful you've taken this journey with Fritz, Vicky, and the other characters who have become so dear to me—I hope they have to you as well.

While this chapter of their story has come to a close, there is still so much more to uncover. If you're eager to find out what happens next, be sure to check out book 4, *Under His Heel*, which continues the saga of Vicky, Fritz, and the dangerous intrigues of the Prussian court.

I would love to hear your thoughts! What resonated with you? What moments did you love or find the most challenging? Who's your favorite character and why? Your feedback means the world to me and inspires me to keep exploring the hidden stories of the Victorian and Prussian courts. Feel free to reach out to me by email at **Luv.Lubker@gmail.com** or find me on Facebook at **TheRivalCourts**—I'd be delighted to hear from you.

If you have a moment, I would be incredibly grateful if you could leave a review. Loved it, hated it—I welcome all your feedback, as your words have the power to shape the future of my stories. You can find all of my books and leave a review on my Amazon page:

https://www.amazon.com/stores/Luv-Lubker/author/B0C5TRY327

Thank you once again for reading *Under the Sword* and spending time in this world I've created. Your support truly makes a difference.

In gratitude, *Luv Lubker*

P.S. Be sure to continue reading for a sneak peek at book 4, *Under His Heel*!

UNDER HIS HEEL
PROLOGUE

Königsberg, 1808

"Karly, what are you doing? Mama told us to stay with her and be quiet."

Karl turned to look at his brother, snatching his arm away from his grasp. He looked back at the little caravan of carriages he had been watching. "Oh, Helmkin, she'll look at *you*, but she won't take a moment's notice of me," he said disgustedly. "That's not fair! You weren't even paying attention to her."

"Paying attention to who? You're supposed to stay in the tall plants, where we can't be seen."

"That beautiful girl in the carriage, of course. There." He pointed and looked up. "Oh, well, she's just gone out of sight behind the trees." He shrugged. "That's your loss." Karl turned, standing upright, and following his brother as he crawled back towards their mother and siblings.

"Get down, Karl," Fritz hissed. Karl crossed his eyes and stuck out his tongue, but sat down as he drew nearer to his mother. He gazed at his brothers, who were wearing wreaths of flowers their mother was making. He attempted to make the contempt plain in his eyes.

He caught up a stick nearby, jumped up, and imitated the manner of one of the officers he admired, holding the stick as if it were a swagger-stick. He jumped forward, swiping several flowers away; his stick was now a sword. "Why do you sit here allowing Mama to make such babies of you when there is an enemy to fight, one's glory to be won, and best of all, young ladies to win the attention of!"

"One's country's honor to defend, family to protect, and the honor of one's people to guard," Mama was murmuring. The others looked up at her, smiles on their faces, as they nodded and nestled to her.

"Karl." He dropped the stick, jumping at the urgency in his mother's voice.

"Karl, come here. The French troops are here." Queen Louise crawled forward, taking Karl's arm and dragging him back with her.

"*Ach!* Ow! You're hurting me!" he squealed.

She clapped her hand over his mouth. "Be quiet, Karl. You must not draw attention to us," she commanded. Karl's eyes grew wide. She let go of him, and he remained on the ground, looking up at her with a strange, un-childlike look in his eyes.

She sighed, turning back to the other children. Karl was a strange boy. She was often very proud of him, and he was always so full of fun and pranks. Everyone called him the most beautiful of her children, but they made that opinion too plain to him. The others were all so good and obedient.

Karl had such strange thoughts for a seven-year-old. His constant desire for the attention of young ladies was absurd at his age. She sat up a little further, watching as Napoleon himself rode by on his horse, several soldiers following him.

The children were all spread on the ground, except for Karl. He stretched up, the same way she did, watching the troops eagerly.

"There are no ladies among them," Karl whispered. "Napoleon is such a small fellow. He rides the biggest horse, but he isn't much taller than we are, I think." He paused, looking at his brothers. "Even old Wrangel could conquer him single-handedly."

"Be respectful of your officers," Fritz whispered.

Mama nodded to him, smiling. "Wrangel is a young man, and a very brave officer. I hope you will all follow his example, and fight for your country's honor as bravely as he does, when the time comes."

"Oh, yes!" Karl jumped up again, but Mama pulled him down. "I shall take his place as soon as possible. Everyone will think me a hero!" He smiled up at his mother, but she didn't return his smile as she did with the others.

"Don't be vain, Karly," Mouffy whispered.

"I wish to be the savior of our country, as Papa said about Wrangel, in his speech. We will defeat the French. We must!"

Queen Louise looked down at her little sons and daughters, meeting Helmkin's gaze. "Mama, I wish to guard the country's honor, as you and Papa do," he whispered. She smiled, reaching out and putting another chain of cornflowers around his neck.

"Let this be your highest decoration," she said. "Keep this before you, whenever you go to serve your country." She placed another around Fritz's neck. "I invest you with the Order of the Cornflower." She paused, smiling and laughing, but her laughter turned quickly to tears. Her country was in grave danger, and she felt it deeply. So, she hoped, did her children. At least some of them did.

She embraced Fritz. "Let it be a symbol of purity, childlike innocence, protection of family, love of beauty and of your country." She laid a third chain of flowers around Mouffy's neck. "The cornflower shall be our symbol of freedom from Napoleon's yoke. But don't let hatred of the enemy overtake you." She held up two more, but Karl had wandered off again, and little Adina crawled after him. She sighed, and placed them on her own head – the chain for Adina being almost as small as the wreaths – and around her own neck. "We are all human beings, all equal in God's sight. Love your enemy, and serve those who hate you. When the worst comes, turn the other cheek. Don't let selfish ambition and glory and vanity overtake you."

Louischen's synesthesia.
Other characters are different.

Personality:

Green = masculine. Purple = feminine. Yellow = child.

Tree = usually man or powerful woman. Flower = usually a woman.

Personality when activated in the hypnotism:

Greyish shade of other color = not deeply hypnotized. Grey = "do what your told".

Colorless (with strong emotions) = out-of-control hypnotized (or drunk).

General emotions/feelings:

Green = happy. Blue = sad. Red blood = anger. Red spikes = mischief.

"Rainbow" of reds and blues = fear. Pink = love.

Orange = physical attraction. Brown = insincerity.

Amusement = shimmering/shiny.

HISTORIUM PRESS

www.historiumpress.com

Visit Luv Lubker's Historium Press Page

www.thehistoricalfictioncompany.com/luv-lubker

www.therivalcourts.com